"Once again, Lynette Eason delivers a suspense-filled romance in *Life Flight*. Prepare to stay up all night as this book grips you from page one and won't release you until the satisfying conclusion. The twists and turns had me holding my breath. Highly recommend!"

Robin Caroll, bestselling author of the Darkwater Inn series

"When you pick up Lynette Eason's *Life Flight*, buckle up and brace for a wild ride! The story dips, twists, and spins with danger and deception on every page, all leading to the breath-stealing conclusion."

Lynn H. Blackburn, award-winning author of the Defend and Protect series

LIFE
FLIGHT

Books by Lynette Eason

EXTREME MEASURES #1

LIFE FLIGHT

LYNETTE EASON

Revell

a division of Baker Publishing Group
Grand Rapids, Michigan

Published by Revell
a division of Baker Publishing Group
PO Box 6287, Grand Rapids, MI 49516-6287
www.revellbooks.com

Library of Congress Cataloging-in-Publication Data
Names: Eason, Lynette, author.
Title: Life flight / Lynette Eason.
Description: Grand Rapids, MI : Revell, a division of Baker Publishing Group,
    [2022] | Series: Extreme measures
Identifiers: LCCN 2021018698 | ISBN 9780800737337 (paperback) | ISBN
    9780800741068 (casebound) | ISBN 9781493434169 (ebook)
Subjects: LCSH: Serial murder investigation—Fiction. | GSAFD: Romantic suspense
    fiction.
Classification: LCC PS3605.A79 L54 2022 | DDC 813/.6—dc23
LC record available at https://lccn.loc.gov/2021018698

Baker Publishing Group publications use paper produced from sustainable forestry practices and post-consumer waste whenever possible.

21 22 23 24 25 26 27   7 6 5 4 3 2 1

To my incredible family,
many of whom are in the medical field.
Thank you for your dedication and commitment
to helping the sick.

But those who hope in the LORD will renew their strength. They will soar on wings like eagles; they will run and not grow weary, they will walk and not be faint.

—Isaiah 40:31

CHAPTER
ONE

Today was not going to be the day they died—not if she had anything to say about it. EMS helicopter pilot Penny Carlton tightened her grip on the throttle of the MBB Bo 105 chopper and prayed the wind would calm down long enough to get their patient to Mercy Mission Hospital on the other side of the mountain.

Flying in bad weather was nothing new, and Penny often did it without hesitation, knowing it was a life-or-death situation. But today was exceptionally bad, with rain and ice slashing the windshield, requiring all of her concentration to keep them on course. Not to mention in the air as the potential of icing increased.

"Come on, Betty Sue, you can do this. We've come this far, we're gonna make it, right?" Penny talked to the chopper on occasion—mostly when she was worried.

She'd protested the flight to her supervisor, and he ordered her to do it or find another job. With only a brief thought that she should walk away, her mind went to the person in jeopardy. At the time, the weather hadn't been nearly as violent as it was now, so she'd ignored the weather warnings and agreed, praying they could beat the storm long enough to get in, get the patient, and get out.

Unfortunately, things hadn't worked out that way, and now she battled the weather while fifteen-year-old Claire Gentry fought to live.

Claire had been hiking with friends along one of Mount Mitchell's most rugged trails when a gust of harsh wind had blown her off balance and over the side of the mountain onto a ledge below. Once the rescue team had gotten her back up, it was Penny's turn to make sure Claire lived to see sixteen. "How's she doing back there?"

"Not good," Holly Cooper said into her mic. A nurse practitioner, Holly could handle just about any medical emergency that came up. However, controlling the weather was out of their hands. "Raina, hand me that morphine," she said. "She's hurting. And get pressure back on her side. She's bleeding again."

Raina Price, the critical care transport paramedic, moved to obey. The three of them had been saving lives together for the past twenty months.

Thunder boomed and lightning lit up the sky way too close for comfort. Penny tuned out the familiar beep and whine of the machines behind her, knowing the best way she could help Claire was to get her to the hospital.

A hard slam against the left side of the chopper knocked the cyclic control stick from her grip, sending them sideways. Yells from Raina and Holly echoed in her ears. "Hold on!" Penny grabbed the stick, righted the chopper, and pushed the left antitorque pedal, the helicopter sluggish in response to her attempts to turn it into the wind.

"Penny! What's happening?"

"We got hit with something! I think it damaged the tail rotor. I'm going to have to land it."

"You can't." Holly's calm words helped settle her racing pulse. A fraction. "Claire's most likely going to die if we don't get her to the hospital."

The wind threw them into a rapid descent, sending Penny's stomach with it. The chopper wasn't spinning, so the tail rotor wasn't completely damaged, but something was definitely—desperately—wrong. "I don't have a choice!" They would *all* die if she didn't do something now. She keyed her microphone and advised air traffic control of the emergency and their approximate location.

". . . breaking up . . . please repeat."

Penny did and got silence for her efforts. "Mayday! Mayday. Anyone there?"

Nothing. She was out of time.

The instrument panel flashed and went dark. "No, don't do that! You're not supposed to do that."

"Do what?" Holly yelled.

Penny ignored her and got a grip on her fear while she tried to make out the fast-approaching ground amid flashes of lightning. The last one allowed her to spot a small neighborhood with a row of houses farther down the side of the mountain—at least she thought that's what she saw. The storm was now raging, visibility practically nil.

She would have to go by the memory of the brief glances. The top of the mountain had looked flat with a bare area where she thought she could safely land. Or at least not crash into trees—or homes.

The throttle was set, controlled by the governor. Now all she had to do was point the nose of the chopper downward to keep them from entering an out-of-control spin. "Come on, girl, you can do this," she muttered. "We can do this. Just a little farther." The trees were somewhere straight ahead. The loose watch on her left wrist bounced against her skin in time with the movement of the chopper.

"Penny!" Holly's tightly held fear bled through her voice. "Tell me what we're doing."

"Just focus on your patient and I'll get us on the ground. We're going to be fine." *Please, God, let us be okay. Please.* She'd trained for this. Over and over, she'd practiced what to do if she lost a tail rotor or had engine issues or whatever. The engine was still good, and a Messerschmitt-Bölkow-Blohm could perform amazing aerobatic maneuvers when called on. For a brief moment, her panel flickered to life and she quickly checked her altitude and airspeed. So far, so good. For now.

"I can do this," she whispered. "Come on, Betty Sue, please don't quit on me now."

They'd *all* trained for situations like this. Mostly, focusing on how to keep the patient stable in the midst of an emergency landing. *Landing, please. Not a crash.*

When her panel fluttered, then went dark once more, she groaned and squinted through the glass. More thunder shook the air around them, but the nonstop lightning was going to be what saved them.

The landing spot she'd picked out wasn't perfect, but it would have to do. At least it was mostly flat—and big. "Brace yourselves," she said. "It's going to be a rough landing, but we *are* going to walk away from this. *All* of us."

The tops of the trees were closer than she'd like, but the small opening just beyond them was within reach. "Almost there!" A gust of wind whipped hard against her and debris crashed into the windshield, spreading the cracks. Penny let out a screech but kept her grip steady. "Come on, come on." She maneuvered the controls, keeping an eye on the trees through the cracked windshield. Okay, the tail rotor was responding somewhat. That would help. "We're going to have a hard bounce! Be ready."

She whooshed past the trees, their tips scraping the underbelly of the chopper, but she cleared them. Her heart pounded in her ears. Down, down . . .

The helicopter tilted, the right landing skid hitting first and sliding across the rocky ground. A scream came from the back and supplies flew through the cabin. Something slammed into the side of Penny's helmet, and she flinched and pushed hard on the collective, angling the rotors, desperate to get both skids on the ground. They bounced, rocked, then settled on the skids. Upright and still breathing.

She'd done it. She was alive. *They* were alive. With shaking hands, she shut down the engine and took off her helmet. *Thank you, Jesus.*

She turned to see Raina and Holly unbuckling their safety harnesses. Holly dropped to her knees next to the patient while Raina dabbed at a cut on her forehead.

"You okay?" she asked Raina.

"Yeah. This is minor compared to what it could have been."

"How's Claire?" Penny asked.

"Hanging in there," Holly said. She pulled the stethoscope from her ears. "Where are we?"

"I don't know, but there's a rescue team on the way. I hope." If they could get through. Even now, the rain and wind whipped at the chopper body. "We just need to stay put until someone comes."

Raina met her eyes. "You did good, Pen. I don't know how you did it, but you did."

Penny wasn't sure either. "God did it. I was praying the whole time, so that's the only explanation I've got."

"Yeah."

She needed to check the chopper and see what the damage was. Not that she could fix it, but . . .

She glanced upward. "Thank you," she whispered.

Holly shot her a quick look. "What?"

"Nothing." Penny eyed Claire and didn't like what she was seeing. She snagged the radio again. "Mayday, Mayday, Mayday. This is Medevac 2646 advising of an emergency landing somewhere on top of Mount Mitchell. Requesting immediate extraction. Four passengers. One critical. Over." Then waited. No reply.

With another glance at her passengers, she tried one more time, all the while knowing it was useless. "Mayday, Mayday!"

No response.

"Okay, that's not good," she muttered. She snagged her cell phone from her pocket. One bar. She dialed 911 and waited. The call dropped. She tried again with the same result. If she had a sat phone, she could use that, but she didn't have one, and she didn't have time to be angry over the reason why.

Think, Penny, think. She turned back to the others, who were monitoring Claire. "Holly, I can't get a signal and nothing's happening with the radio. I'm going to have to try and walk until I get something."

Raina scowled. "Stupid mountains."

"All right, here's the deal," Penny said. "I have no idea if anyone heard my Mayday—or anything else. You guys keep Claire stable. I'll be back as soon as I can get word to someone where to find us. I saw a few houses scattered in the area. I just need to find a road and follow it. Hopefully the closer I get to a neighborhood or house, I'll pick up a cell phone signal."

"Can't they track the ELT?" Holly asked.

The emergency locator transmitter. "They should be able to, but I don't want to take a chance on it malfunctioning. Something's going on with the electrical. The instrument panel keeps flickering and the radio's not working."

"You can't go out in this," Raina said. "This weather is too dangerous."

"If Claire wasn't in such bad shape, I'd sit it out with you guys, but I've got to try—and when we get back, we're having a fundraiser for a satellite phone." She was going to have it out with her supervisor as soon as she saw him face-to-face. Thanks to his budget cutting, they could very well die out here. If she had a sat phone, she could—

Nope. Not going to think about that.

Penny grabbed the poncho from the bin next to the stretcher. "If I'm not back and help arrives, you get Claire to the hospital. I can wait for the next ride."

"But, Pen—" Holly started to protest, but Penny was already shaking her head.

"I mean it," she said. "You know you can't wait on me to get back."

"Fine," Raina said. "But if you're not back in an hour, I'm coming looking for you."

"Don't you dare. Holly needs your help with Claire. I'll be fine. If I can survive juvie, this little storm is child's play."

"Juvie?" Holly asked. "Why is this the first I've heard of that?"

"Long, boring story. I was a bad girl, they sent me to juvie, and I got my head on straight. End of story."

"Right."

Penny pulled four protein bars and two bottles of water from the small pack she carried on every flight. "Just in case you guys get hungry." She slid the pack with the remaining protein bars and bottles of water over her shoulder and grabbed the emergency flashlight from the box, then opened the door. The rain had slacked off slightly—at least she thought so. She pulled the poncho over her and the pack and hopped to the ground. "Keep her alive! I'll be back!"

Penny shut the door behind her and turned. With her cell phone clutched in her left hand, she darted into the woods.

■ ■ ■ ■

FBI Special Agent Holton Satterfield jerked his feet from the desktop and slammed them to the floor even while he pressed the phone to his ear. He hadn't thought the day could get any worse. First, his conversation with his sister Rachel about their older sibling, Zoe, had gone so far south, it was probably north at this point. And now this. "I know you didn't just tell me that."

"Unfortunately, I did," Gerald Long said. The Special Supervisory Agent didn't sound any happier than Holt. "But Rabor is armed and on the run."

"How?"

"He had help. His loyal girlfriend, Shondra Miller, disguised herself as a nurse and walked right in with a key to the cuffs." Gerald's disgust echoed through the line.

Holt didn't bother asking how she managed to bypass all the security and ID checks to get to the patient. That was someone else's responsibility to investigate, but it had happened and now he needed to deal with the fallout.

"When?" After Darius Rabor had killed a federal judge, the FBI had joined the hunt for him. Holt had been lead on the task force that put Rabor away a year and a half ago. He'd been on death row, his execution date coming up next month.

"Two hours ago," Gerald said. "Rabor was in the hospital for emergency gall bladder surgery. Killed a nurse and the two transport officers. One of the hospital security guards is in surgery. I'm reconvening the original task force, as everyone is already familiar with this guy. I need you and Sands in Asheville, North Carolina, yesterday."

"Asheville. Of course he'd go back there," Holt muttered. Rabor knew the mountains well and had family there. Holt was in the Columbia, South Carolina, field office, and Rabor had been incarcerated at the Broad River Correctional Institution just a few miles away. Where Holt's sister was also an inmate. He grimaced at the unwanted thought. But there was nothing he could do about Zoe. He had a killer to capture again before anyone else died by his hand.

"He had surgery yesterday," Gerald said. "This afternoon, he was in his room, cuffed to the bed. The next time someone checked on him, he was coming out of the bathroom, dressed in street clothes. Before the guard had a chance to pull his weapon, Rabor used a knife to stab the guy three times."

"That's his weapon of choice. A knife slipped to him by his girlfriend, along with the key?"

"No doubt. And the clothes to allow him to blend in. After he killed the guard, he took the man's weapon and, in the ensuing

16

chaos, shot his way out. The two then stole a car from the valet parking attendant and headed out of town with police after them. They made it to Asheville, then crashed at the bottom of Mount Mitchell. He and Shondra took off on foot, going up. I'm sending you the coordinates. Police chased them up the mountain and put out an alert for residents to lock their homes and report anything suspicious. Asheville's RA is expecting you and will be offering support." He paused. "On the ground anyway. Air support is iffy at this point, with the storms getting ready to unleash their worst on the area. But you're going to have to take a chopper to get there. It's standing by. When you land, the RA has a car waiting for you."

Great. "We're on the way." He hung up, took a moment to gather his thoughts and emotions, then shot to his feet.

His partner, Martin Sands, looked up. "What now? More stuff with Zoe? Her kids okay?"

Marty was the one person Holt felt comfortable venting to about his sister and her confession to killing her husband two years ago—and the fact that he'd finally conceded that she did it. He ignored the shame that tried to creep in every time he thought about her. He should be turning over every rock to find evidence to the contrary, but the truth was, his sister was guilty of murder. Why work to prove her innocence when all the evidence and her own words said the effort would be a waste of time?

"No, she's on the back burner for now. Her kids are fine." They lived with his parents for the moment. Twelve-year-old Ellie and eight-year-old Krissy. His precious nieces that he never got to see enough of. "Rabor and his girlfriend are on the loose. You and I are now officially back on the task force to recapture him."

"What? You're kidding me. How?"

"I'll explain on the way."

Martin followed him out the door, muttering his displeasure. Holt let him vent while he concentrated on how best to catch the man. Again. It hadn't been easy the first time.

It would be even harder now, as Rabor wouldn't make the same mistakes twice—and he had his girlfriend helping him this time. However, he was one day out of surgery. How far could he get? Then again, the fact that he'd managed to kill three people in spite of being on drugs and, most likely, in pain, sent dread coursing through him. Holt knew better than anyone just how resourceful the killer was, and he had the scar to prove it. His hand went to the area just below his vest on his left side, but he didn't need to touch the place to know what was there. The nightmares reminded him most nights.

They headed for the chopper while thunder boomed in the distance. It wasn't raining yet, but it was about to start at any moment. The pilot nodded to them and soon they were in the air, headed toward the mountain. Thirty minutes later, Holt slid into the driver's seat of the Bureau's waiting sedan and checked the weather app on his phone. "This is going to be a fun drive. It's cold and icy, and storm warnings are everywhere."

"We've driven through worse. Right?"

True, but he didn't like it any more than Marty did—and Marty *really* hated bad weather. Holt's phone dinged again. "Command center is on the way too. We'll meet them there."

They drove through the blowing wind and rain with Holt fighting to keep the vehicle on the road. Across the street from the base of the mountain, the mobile command center had already been set up in the elementary school parking lot. Holt ducked into the customized motor home and shook the water out of his hair. Marty entered behind him. Seated in front of the first computer to Holt's left was Julianna Jameson. "Jules? What brings you here? He hasn't taken any hostages, has he?"

"Not yet."

Julianna was one of the Bureau's most skilled negotiators with the Crisis Negotiation Unit. She was also one of his favorite people, with her quick wit and dry humor. However, she usually didn't go into the field unless the situation called for it.

"I was in the area doing some training. When I got word about the situation, I hightailed it over here. I'm here as a precaution," she said. "Local cops are swarming the area in spite of the weather. There are six small neighborhoods spaced out along the road that leads to the top of the mountain. Two cop cars are assigned to each one. One at the entrance and one that's driving a constant loop."

"What about the houses that don't have neighborhoods or fences or alarm systems?"

"We've activated the Reverse 911 and officers are going door-to-door and asking residents to phone everyone they can think of to warn them, but it's definitely possible someone will be missed."

"Yeah."

"That's not all. We've gotten word that a medevac chopper made an emergency landing about an hour ago in a clearing on top of the mountain, and Gerald asked me to be on-site just in case Darius manages to get there first."

"Oh no." He took a seat opposite her.

She studied him. "It's Penny and her crew, Holt. They've got a fifteen-year-old patient in pretty serious shape."

Holt raked a hand through his hair. Penny, Holly, and Raina had been the ones to save his life eighteen months ago. He and Penny had hit it off and gone out a few times after he'd recovered. While their relationship was only at a friendship-but-could-possibly-be-more stage—and had been for longer than he liked as he was ready for the "more" part—their schedules hadn't allowed more than brief dinners and short conversations on the phone. But he cared about Penny. A lot.

She and Julianna were tight friends, sharing a past that he still didn't know all the details of. "All right, then we need to head that way and get them down off that mountain. If Rabor or Shondra run into them . . ."

"Yeah. And unfortunately, they're not answering the attempts to contact them. The emergency locator beacon is the only thing they have to go on right now."

"That doesn't sound good."

"This storm is only going to get worse in the next little while," Julianna said. "Hopefully, we can get to them before too much longer."

"We?" Julianna wouldn't normally do something like that, but since it was Penny—

"I'm going with you." She narrowed her eyes. "There's a killer up there. And so are Penny and the others. If he manages to grab one of them, it's not going to be good."

"Yeah."

"I need to be there."

"I agree," Holt said. "Rabor knows we're on his tail and is going to be looking for someone he can use as leverage. I don't want to give him that opportunity."

She nodded. "Exactly."

With practiced movements, they gathered their gear, satellite phones, and rain ponchos and headed back out into the storm.

CHAPTER
TWO

If Penny hadn't had her watch and cell phone to tell her what time it was, she'd have thought a week had passed by the time she located one of the houses she'd seen from the sky.

In reality, it had been forty-seven minutes. Her first dash from the chopper had taken her to a steep drop-off, and she'd had to backtrack until she could find a way through the thick under-growth that actually led down. Thankfully, she stumbled onto a neighborhood about two miles from where she'd landed. At least she thought it was two miles. She was having to go by memory of her numerous flights over the mountain and her judgment. Which might be flawed.

She approached the fourth house on the street, praying some-one would answer the door. The first three she'd tried, no one was home and all the doors were locked. Unfortunately, no lights shone through the windows of this house, but there was an old truck parked in the single driveway. So, either no one was home or the power was out. She was banking on the latter.

Pushing against the whipping winds and the lashing rain, she gripped the strap of the backpack and trudged up the drive. She finally made it up the porch steps of the small home. With a freezing fist, she pounded on the oak front door. The structure might be little, but even she could see it was well made. Hopefully, sturdy enough to withstand tornado-force winds.

No one answered and Penny beat against the wood again. "Hello! Is anyone there?" She banged a few more times. "Hello?"

Again, no response. She tried the knob. Locked. "Of course," she muttered. A gust of wind sent a branch at her head and she ducked just in time. It clattered against the door and fell to the welcome mat. Her wisdom of trekking about in the storm might be questionable, but Claire was at the forefront of her thoughts. The girl needed to get to a hospital. ASAP. And Penny would give just about anything to be warm again.

She shivered and glanced at her phone. No bars. Typically, the higher one went, the better the service, but she'd been as high as she could get on top of the mountain and had nothing. So she'd have to go lower and pray she stumbled on a tower—or someone with service. Most of the homes this high up had satellite phones or landlines. If she could get inside, she could make the call. She circled around the side of the house, following the stone path. The wind knocked her off balance and against the siding. The slam jarred her shoulder and she winced but pushed on to the back door. Penny twisted the knob, and wonder of wonders, it opened.

She practically fell inside and shoved the door shut. Finally. She dragged in a ragged breath while the freezing rain sloughed from her poncho to create a large puddle on the carpet. She'd owe the homeowner a roll of paper towels and an apology, but she'd be happy to pay up as long as Claire lived.

Penny's mother would have a fit if she came home to the mess she was making in the stranger's home. She groaned at the thought of her mom. The woman suffered severe anxiety despite the calm, cool exterior she presented to the world, and Penny's job often sent her into a tizzy. If Penny didn't check in soon, it would be months before she'd hear the end of it.

But, again, Claire trumped her mother.

Penny glanced around, surprised at the size of the home. The outside appearance was definitely deceptive. The lower level boasted a pool table, air hockey table, and a six-seater media area.

But no landline phone in sight.

Penny hurried to the stairs. "Hello? Anyone up there? I got caught in the storm. I'm harmless. Please don't shoot me or anything. Hello?"

She flipped the stairwell light on—so much for her theory that the power was out—and started climbing. At the top, she came to a closed door. She knocked, called out one more time, then turned the knob.

The door creaked open and she stepped into a lovely, updated kitchen. Through the bay window behind the dining area, Penny had a good view of the outdoors. The wind still blew, but she thought it might have lessened a bit and the rain might have slowed. Then a hard gust of wind rattled the window and lightning flashed way too close and she shut off the wishful thinking.

Okay. Phone. Please have a landline.

She wanted to just hurry and search the place but was afraid of getting shot by a terrified homeowner. "Hello? I'm just looking for a phone. Anyone here?"

When she still didn't get an answer, she decided it was better to move quickly. Claire needed her to.

No phone in the kitchen.

She slipped into the adjacent den area and scanned the end tables, the walls . . . and still nothing.

Finally, she was convinced the house was empty of people and searched faster. In the master bedroom, she finally found the landline. With a relieved cry, Penny grabbed the handset and dialed her boss's number.

He answered on the first ring. "Life Flight, this is Mike Bishop, program director." His gravelly voice grated across her nerves. She simply didn't like the man and only tolerated him because she loved her job.

"It's Penny."

"Penny! Where are you?"

His shout made her wonder if he'd been worried. "I had to emergency land on the mountain." *Because you made me fly in weather that should have grounded us.* She bit her tongue so the words wouldn't escape her lips. She could have refused, but like always, she put the victim first. She gave him the location.

"That's where the ELT put you." His voice dropped. "Her parents are here. Don't let that girl die, Carlton."

Since when did he express such concern for the welfare of the patient? He was a numbers and appearance guy. "Who are they?"

"Senator Randall Gentry and his wife. They're also big supporters of this hospital."

Well, that explained Mike's concern. "Claire's in the best hands she could be in at the moment," she said, "but she's bad, Mike. There's no way an ambulance can get up here. It's rugged. I had to hike down some rough terrain and break into a house to find a landline."

"Break into—I don't want to know. Are you sure an ambulance can't get to her?"

Penny closed her eyes and sighed. "Positive. There's no road that goes to that little bit of open space where I landed."

"Is there room for another chopper to land?"

She wanted to say no. "Yes. Barely, but yeah. A skilled pilot *might* be able to do it. Don't send a newbie."

"I'll have another chopper on the way within minutes."

"It's bad out there. I'm serious, Mike. Don't play around with this."

"Byron can handle it."

Byron Hamilton was a great pilot, but even he couldn't control the weather—or a damaged chopper. She didn't bother to protest anymore. Mike would do what Mike would do. "I'm heading back to the chopper. We'll all be there when Byron gets there." If he managed. He could refuse to fly. Of course if he did, he'd be looking for another job, but he might decide it was worth it this time.

A door slammed and Penny jerked. "Someone just came home. Now I have to go explain to a stranger why I'm in their bedroom."

"Please don't get killed. I don't want to have to explain that to the press."

"Wow. Thanks." She hung up and hurried out of the bedroom. "Hello?" A scream erupted from the kitchen and Penny hurried down the hall and into the foyer. "I'm harmless, I promise." She rounded the corner and pulled up short.

A woman in her early thirties stood at the kitchen island. In her shaking hands, she held a gun that she pointed right at Penny. "Get out of my house," the woman said.

"I'm sorry," Penny said, raising her hands to shoulder level. "I'm a pilot for Life Flight and the storm knocked something into the chopper and I had to put her down and then the radio was busted and my patient is going to *die* if I don't get her some help, so—" She broke off, wondering if she was making any sense at all. With the exception of when she was in the pilot's seat, she always talked too much—okay, *rambled*—when she was nervous or afraid. Both emotions applied at the moment.

But at least the woman hadn't shot her. Yet.

"Truly, I'm sorry"—how many times had she said that?—"so sorry to scare you. My cell phone wouldn't work and I had to find a phone. Your basement door was open. I was hoping I could get in and out before anyone came home. To, you know, avoid . . . this." She gestured to the gun. "Look at the logo on the poncho. See? I've also got a uniform on under this with the same logo." With one hand, she lifted the front of her poncho. "And here's my ID." She moved so very slowly, not wanting to make the woman any more nervous than she already was.

Penny unclipped the ID badge from under her poncho and held it out. The woman examined it, blew out a low sigh, and lowered her weapon. Penny's knees chose that moment to go weak and she had to lean against the wall or she'd end up on the floor. "I'm Penny, by the way."

A laugh, bordering on hysteria, slipped from the woman. "I'm Kacey. I was on the way home from work and was listening to the radio. There's a serial killer roaming this area, and when I heard you in my house . . ."

"A serial killer?" Penny's brows shot up. "Where?"

"On the mountain somewhere. We have orders to stay in our locked homes and report anything suspicious. Cops are all over the place."

Great. Just great. She swallowed hard. She didn't relish going back out in the weather, but adding a killer into the mix really kind of bothered her.

But Claire . . .

She had to get back and let the others know help was on the way. "You don't have a satellite phone, do you?"

"No, sorry. I just have the landline for up here and a cell phone for when I go into town."

Penny nodded. "It was worth a shot. All right, thank you so much for not shooting me"—Mike would be happy about that at least—"but I've got to get back to the chopper." She bit her lip. "I don't suppose you'd let me take one of your cars."

"Take it where? There's only one place to land on this mountain, and cars can't get up there."

"Yeah, I noticed, but . . ." She'd walked at least two miles and the last mile had been paved road. "There's an old truck in the drive. Could I take it partway?"

Kacey hesitated, then rubbed her eyes. "The last and highest house on the road belongs to the Bensons." She gave her the address. "Leave it on their curb and I'll get my husband to go with me to pick it up tomorrow. He's a fireman in the middle of a twenty-

26

four-hour shift, but the truck will be fine until we can get it later."
She took the keys from a hook on the wall and handed them to
Penny.

"Thank you," Penny said. "I can't tell you how much that's
going to help."

Kacey frowned. "Be careful."

"You too. Lock up. And I'm sorry about the puddle in the basement. Lock that door too!"

Penny slipped out of the house and ran to the pickup, battling
the whipping wind and rain. She cranked the engine and headed
up the mountain road as fast as she dared. If there was a serial
killer on the loose, she had to warn the others.

■ ■ ■ ■

In contrast to his urge to hurry, Holt drove the Bucar at a snail's
pace up the winding road, fighting the wind that threatened to
overturn them or send them off the road and over the side.

Martin white-knuckled the door grip and kept his eyes closed.
"This time we're going to die, aren't we?" he asked.

"How did a wimp like you ever work up the gumption to apply
to the Bureau, much less actually qualify to become an agent?"
Holt asked, his tone mild.

"Bad guys scare me. Storms terrify me. I can work with fear.
Terror is another matter."

Holt chuckled. In the rearview mirror, he spotted Julianna's
grin. They both knew Marty was one of the finest agents in the
organization and he'd trust the man with his life—had done so on
many occasions. But Marty's fear of storms was legendary stuff
and he took a lot of ribbing because of it.

"How far do you think that drop-off is?" Julianna asked.

Holt shot Marty a sideways glance. "Not more than a hundred
feet or so."

"I'm so going to get you for this."

Marty's muttered threat pulled a tight smile from Holt. A gust of wind rocked them and he clutched the wheel, keeping them on the road, while Marty sucked in an audible breath.

The radio crackled. "This is Dunn and Gresham. We're at the location of the last reported sighting of Rabor. Nothing so far."

"We're almost there," Holt said. He gave their location, then turned to his partner. "All right, dude, I need you to open your eyes and see if you spot anything. We're getting close. Look to the right. We know what's on the left." Twenty minutes ago, a homeowner had called in a possible intruder hiding in their toolshed. Their dog had gone crazy, darting out the doggy door before the owner could grab him, barking and snarling at the building. Someone had run from it, disappearing into the storm.

But maybe he hadn't gone far.

Marty scowled and opened his eyes, a visible shudder running through him.

"I actually think the wind is lessening," Holt said.

Marty snorted. "Right. That's why you almost went off the road back there."

"I thought you weren't watching."

"Didn't have to watch to know what was happening." He scanned the area. "Is that the house?"

"121?" Julianna asked. "It's hard to see through the rain, but according to the GPS, we've arrived."

"And in one piece, no less." Marty's relief was palpable. "Amazing."

"Shut up," Holt said.

His partner laughed. It sounded a bit strained, but at least it was a laugh. Holt parked on the curb and prepared himself to get saturated, in spite of the rain slicker and gloves. He hated the cold about as much as Marty hated storms.

"So," Julianna said without looking up from the iPad in her lap, "if I'm reading this right, Rabor started killing because his wife dumped a pot of hot tea on his head?"

"Yeah. They had an argument about her role in the marriage.

She took exception to his interpretation of what the Bible means about wives submitting to their husbands."

"And what was his interpretation?" Julianna asked.

"That they're basically slaves. He expected his wife to cater to his every demand, desire, whim, et cetera, and one day, she got tired of it. Told him off and dumped the pot of tea on his head."

"I would have done the same thing."

"Well, Rabor decided she should be punished. Said she just needed the proper training. When she didn't go for it and tried to leave him, he killed her with an overdose of Oxy, sat her at their table, fixed a new pot of tea, and had a tea party with her every day until she started to decay. Wrapped her in plastic and buried her in the backyard."

"Then went to find another victim," Marty said, "because he said his eyes were opened to his true purpose. He was to train single women before they were married."

"But he killed them, so what was the training for exactly?"

"He never could answer that question," Holt said. "What really got to me was that he buried his wife with the teapot and said it was so she could learn to serve tea for all eternity."

Julianna shuddered. "Did no one explain to him how eternity works?"

"I sent the prison chaplain to talk to him," Holt said.

"Even after he tried to kill you?" Julianna's eyes went wide. "You're much more forgiving than I."

"At the time, forgiveness didn't have anything to do with it. The man's eternal destination did. The chaplain said the man wasn't open to hearing anything."

"That's tragic."

"Yeah." Holt squinted through the blinding mess. "So, where are Dunn and Gresham? I thought they would have been in touch by now."

"Maybe they're chasing the guy and we can just wait here where it's warm and dry?" Marty's hopeful tone drew a chuckle from Julianna.

"They haven't called for backup, so I doubt it," she said. "Come on, you two babies, let's find this guy before anyone else gets hurt."

Holt stepped out of the car and icy rain slashed him in the face. He raised a gloved hand to swipe it away, and his gaze landed on a body on the ground near the tree line. "Jules! Marty!"

Forgetting about the weather, Holt dashed toward the fallen agent. His feet splashed in the ankle-deep water, and the cold bit his exposed skin, but all of that was in the background while his focus stayed on the man on the ground and the surrounding area. Knowing he could feel the bite of a bullet at any moment, he rushed on and dropped to his knees next to the agent. "Gus!" He shoved the Maglite between his teeth so he could work. He pressed his fingers to the man's neck, searching for a pulse, and came across a bullet hole. It didn't gush, so maybe it had missed the jugular. Otherwise . . .

"Come on," he whispered. "Don't do this. Please, Gus." Not again. He couldn't lose another friend.

Jules stopped. "I'll look for Gresham."

"Jules, that's not what you do. You can't—"

"I'm looking for Gresham. You guys keep Gus safe."

She rushed past him into the woods and Marty leaned over Gus. "Is he alive?"

A faint beat finally fluttered against Holt's fingers. "Yeah, but his radio and gun are gone. Get me the first aid kit from the trunk and call for an ambulance. And let them know Rabor most likely has our radio and is listening in." Holt pressed on the agent's wound with one hand. "Jules! Where are you?"

She stepped out of the woods and hurried back toward them, tears swimming in her eyes. "I found Gresham. He's dead."

Holt ignored the punch of her words. He would grieve later.

Marty appeared next to him and lowered himself to his knees with the first aid kit. Holt grabbed it while Marty held an oversized tarp over Gus's upper torso and head. "I'm going to have to hold this or it's going to fly away," Marty said. "Can you work on him without my help?"

"I'll manage."

Now that the rain wasn't hitting his face, he could finally get a better look at the wound. A former paramedic, he had some medical training he could only pray would be enough to save Gus's life.

CHAPTER
THREE

Penny parked the truck on the curb of the Bensons' home as she'd been instructed and turned off the wipers. The heater stopped, too, and she grimaced. For the past mile, she'd managed to thaw out slightly and didn't look forward to getting out of the cab, but the others were waiting for her to get back to them.

An older gentleman stepped out of the house and waited on the porch. She ran to him and ducked under the roof. Rain sluiced off her poncho and a crack of thunder boomed around them. "Thank you," she said, passing the keys to him.

"It's not a problem. Kacey explained everything." He handed her a Styrofoam cup with a black lid. "Thought you could use some coffee. It's black, but if you need some cream and sugar, I can get it."

Coffee. "God bless you, sir. Black is just fine." She normally liked a good bit of sugar in hers, but for now, this was perfect— and warm. She sipped the hot brew and grimaced when it burned going down. But it was wonderful. "Thank you."

"You be careful. There's a serial killer somewhere around here." His green gaze narrowed on the wooded area behind her.

"Yes, sir, I know."

"You got a satellite phone?"

"No." At his raised brow, she shook her head. "It's a long story."

"Take mine. You need it more than I do. I have a landline and my wife has the backup sat phone." He handed her the device. "I'd appreciate getting it back, though."

His generosity touched her. She slipped the phone into her pocket, shivered, and took another sip of the coffee. "Thank you again. I'll see that the phone gets returned to you."

He nodded. "Now, when you get over to the woods, look for the trail. It leads up to a viewing area I built last year. I even put a little bathroom in it. Got a couch and a satellite television, too, though I doubt you'll have time to enjoy those features." A glimmer of amusement shone through the concern in his eyes. "A little man cave, you might call it. Anyway, once you pass that, the terrain gets a lot rougher, but you came down the mountain, so guess you know that."

"I came down a different route and made my way around to the houses I spotted from the air. You think I can get back to the chopper if I go up this way?"

"The whole mountain is shaped like a tepee with a flat top. As long as you're going up, you'll get there."

Pretty much what she'd thought, but his confirmation was a relief. "Okay, thank you so much."

"Be careful, little lady. This is a dangerous place to be right now."

Penny gave him a forced smile, handed him the half-empty coffee cup, and waved goodbye. When she hit the edge of the woods, she stopped to pull out her emergency flashlight and dial Mike's number on the satellite phone. While it rang, she found the trail and headed up.

"Life Flight. This is Mike Bishop."

"You and I are going to have a serious chat when I next see you," Penny said, "but I need to know if you have another chopper on the way."

"Where'd you get the phone?"

"Long story, but at least I have one now. The other chopper?"

"Yeah, Byron should be in the air in five. He said he was on the way shortly after I hung up with you."

That had been a good twenty minutes ago. "The hospital is just ten minutes away from where I landed," she said. Penny honestly didn't see how Byron would manage to get through this mess. She was one of the best pilots in the program and even she would balk at flying right now. Then again, there was Claire. "It's bad out here, Mike. I've never seen it like this before."

The wind whipped her around and into a tree. She grunted and pain raced along her already sore shoulder.

"How's Claire?"

She shoved the pack higher on her back and focused the light on the muddy path. "How am I supposed to know? It's not like I can call and ask because there's not a satellite phone on the chopper!" She knew she was yelling, partly because she needed him to hear her over the sound of the storm, partly out of sheer fear for those she'd left at the site, and partly out of frustration with the man.

"Let me make something clear to you, Penny. She'd better not die, or this program is finished. You, and everyone else, will be out of a job—and no one will need a blasted sat phone!"

"Well, there's not much I can do about that at the moment. I've got to go before I lose my footing and break my neck." A gust of wind swept icy water into her face and she sputtered and spit. And pushed on. "I'll call when I know more."

■ ■ ■ ■

When the ambulance finally arrived, Gus was still clinging to life. Holt had notified Gerald of Gresham's death. The ME was on the way and local officers were protecting the scene. As much as he hated to leave Gus, their buddy was in capable hands. The best thing he and the others could do would be to find Gresham's killer. He slipped back inside the Bucar, ignored the fact that he was cold and wet, and focused on the fury that burned in his chest.

Julianna slammed the back door. "I want this guy," she said, her voice soft, low. Tense.

"Yeah. And the girlfriend." Assuming it had been Rabor or Shondra, there was no sign of them now. "Let's keep going up. I have a bad feeling things are going to get worse before they get better."

"You think they're going to go for the chopper?" Julianna asked.

So, it had crossed her mind too, and Marty was nodding.

"Well, they're not here and this place *is* on the way to the top of the mountain. He's a former Air Force pilot, and if he has access to a radio or a phone, he has access to the news and knows the chopper is there. What would you do if you were in his shoes?"

"Yeah, I agree. No more stopping until we're there," Marty said.

Saving Gus's life was worth the delay, but it had given Rabor that much more time to put distance between them. *Please, God, don't let Gus die.* At least Holt had been there to help this time. He put the sedan in gear. "Hope you brought your hiking shoes. We're about to run out of road."

Five minutes later, they were parked at the spot where the road ended, dressed in their slickers with FBI logos prominently displayed, gear on their backs, and pushing upward through the slashing rain. Other teams just like theirs were searching all around the mountain, and as soon as one of them spotted Rabor, he'd hear about it.

Using his satellite phone, he called the command center. "We're heading up the mountain. Expect to arrive at the chopper in about fifteen minutes. Any word from Penny or the crew?"

"Just spoke to her supervisor, Mike Bishop. He said Penny had managed to land the bird with few injuries—really none. Just some bumps and bruises. The radio was damaged and she had to go out and find a phone to call him. She just checked in and is in possession of a satellite phone and was heading back to the chopper to let the others know help was on the way." He gave the number to Holt, who tapped it into his phone.

"And the patient?"

"Penny didn't have an update on her at the moment, but she was critical at the time they landed. Call Penny and find out how far she is from the chopper. We had another reported sighting of Rabor. Held up a delivery driver and stole the food."

"Who in their right mind is out in this mess delivering food?"

"Hey, I'm just reporting what's coming in."

The rage burned hotter. "Did he hurt the driver?" Holt was proud of the calm in his voice.

"Knocked him out cold, but at least he's alive. Driver said he never saw it coming. Kid is seventeen years old with a concussion. Do *not* let Rabor get away."

"That's the plan. Any sign of the girlfriend?"

"Negative. If they're smart, they split up." He paused. "Or she's served her purpose and he killed her."

"Yeah. I'll call Penny." Holt hung up and dialed the sat phone's number.

"Hello?"

Just in that one word, he could hear her exhaustion. Her voice triggered memories of a day not unlike this one when Penny had braved the odds and saved his life. "Penny, it's Holt. I'm out here on the mountain looking for you and your chopper. Mike Bishop said you were on the way back to it."

"Boy, am I glad to hear your voice. Are you looking for that serial killer too?"

"I am. Well, a lot of us are. But I want to find you before—"

"Before he finds me or I find him? Seems like we've done this dance before. Serial killer on the loose, you chasing him, me in the picture. Not sure I want to be in close proximity to you anymore."

She'd just almost crash-landed a helicopter, marched partway down the side of a mountain in one of the worst storms in the state's history, found help, and was heading back to the landing site—and she was cracking jokes. He'd liked her before, had been incredibly grateful for her brave and skilled actions that had saved his life, but now he might just have tumbled into love. "Yeah, I can understand that. We can discuss that later over pizza. Where are you?"

"Almost to the chopper, I think. I hope. It was a bit easier coming down the mountain, but it's impossible to just go straight up. I'm having to walk sideways a lot before finding a way up. And even then, I'm slipping and sliding everywhere. Where are you?"

"Closing in on you. We're having to do the same thing."

A grunt slipped from her. Then a gasp.

"Penny?"

Silence.

"Penny? You there?"

"I see him," she whispered.

Holt stopped walking and held up a hand. Rain pounded him. "Can you hide?"

Julianna and Marty pulled up, their eyes on his.

"Not really." Her hushed voice vibrated with fear. "He's going for the chopper, isn't he?"

"We think so."

"He'll kill them all if he reaches it."

"We're not going to let that happen. We're on the way." He motioned to the others and they started moving again, faster, a new desperation pushing them.

"I have to get there, Holt. To warn them. They don't know he's out there, that they're in any danger other than from the storm." She paused. "If I can get there, I can lock us in the chopper and buy enough time for you to do your thing."

"Penny, don't risk it."

"I have to," she whispered. "Hurry."

CHAPTER
FOUR

Pressing the phone to her ear, Penny huddled against the tree for a brief moment before she dared a glance around the trunk.

He was gone.

No, no, no. Where'd he go? Fear pounded through her veins. She looked left, right. Nothing.

Great. Just great.

She'd lost sight of him, but he was out there. Penny could almost feel his presence and the desperation that drove him.

Heart in her throat, she pushed away from the tree, noting the rain seemed to have slacked a little in the last minute. The lightning flashes came much farther apart and the darkness had lessened. *Please, God, make it stop.*

"Penny? You see him?"

"No," she said, keeping her voice low. "Not anymore. I don't know where he went, but I'm almost back to the chopper."

She'd finally arrived on flat land and, through the trees, could see the chopper in the small clearing.

Still no Byron in sight. He should have been there by now. The rain had slowed some, allowing for more visibility with each flash of lightning. She'd turned the flashlight off at the first sight of the man near the tree line. Had he seen her? Heard her phone vibrate? She didn't think so but couldn't be sure.

But with that flash of lightning, he was gone. Had he even been there or was she just seeing a serial killer everywhere she looked?

From her hiding spot, she continued to watch, praying Holt and the others would get there soon. They couldn't be that far away. The chopper was just ahead. Flickers of light came from the cabin, which meant the flashlights were still working, but no signs of distress to indicate danger had invaded. *Please, please, let Claire still be alive.*

With another look around and no sign of the man she thought she'd seen by the tree line, she started forward, noting the wind was even less, the rain not as hard.

"Thank you, God," she whispered.

The sound of blades beating the air reached her and relief hit, making her knees weak. But if she could hear it, no doubt everyone else could too. Including a serial killer on the mountain.

Three people dressed in FBI uniforms broke the tree line just ahead. Holt, Julianna, and Marty. Hope sprouted that the end of this was in sight. Just a little longer and everyone would be safe.

A chopper, twin to her own, appeared and drew closer, hovered, then lowered into the space near her downed aircraft.

Byron.

Holt, Marty, and Julianna ducked against the wind stirred by the blades and aimed themselves toward her chopper.

Penny did the same, running flat out until she reached the cabin door. Marty and Julianna positioned themselves on either side of the chopper, weapons drawn, faces tight. "Thank you, guys, for showing up!"

"Couldn't let you be the only hero in the bunch." Julianna shot her an encouraging smile and Penny pounded on the door.

Holt stepped up beside her. "Can I do anything to help?" he shouted.

"You can help us get this patient transferred to the other chopper."

"I can do that."

"It's really good to see you, Holt. Thanks for coming to the rescue."

"You did just fine all by yourself. Local cops, state police, and more FBI are combing this mountain for Rabor, but we need to get you all out of here."

"I really like that plan."

The door opened and Holly stood there, the strain of the last couple of hours stamped on her pretty features. Her face morphed into an expression of relief. "Thank goodness you're okay," she blurted. "I was so worried."

"I survived. How's Claire?"

"Hanging in there, but she needs surgery."

"Let's get her transferred to the other chopper and on the way. I can stay here and go down the mountain with the agents and someone can pick me up."

"I can make sure you get home," Holt said.

Penny nodded.

A hand on her arm stopped her. She looked up to find Holt's green eyes on her. "I need to know where you saw Rabor," he said.

"In the woods." She pointed. "That way."

"Did he see you?"

"I have no idea. I'm honestly not sure he was even there. Between the lightning, my stress level, worry for Claire and the others"—she shrugged—"maybe I dreamed it."

"Or maybe not."

"Yeah. Or that."

For the next few minutes, she, Holt, Raina, and Holly worked to transfer Claire to the other chopper while Marty and Julianna kept an eye on the tree line and the surrounding areas.

The storm was finally passing. The wind still blew, but the rain had slacked to a misty drizzle. She was cold, wet, and hungry, but as long as Claire made it, Penny would be okay.

A crack echoed around them. Marty cried out and went down. Penny froze for a split second before the ground spat up dirt onto her pants leg.

"Get down! Everyone down! Penny, get down!" Holt's sharp cry sent her to the ground.

But she couldn't just leave Marty out in the open, a vulnerable target. She pushed to her feet to charge toward him. Holt was racing for the man as well. Raina and Holly had paused their monitoring of Claire to watch in frozen horror.

Julianna beat Penny and Holt to Marty and pulled him to his feet. "Cover me!"

Holt paused, then whipped his weapon toward the tree line where the bullets had come from.

Blood streamed from Marty's left thigh. Penny darted toward the two of them and a bullet whipped past her cheek.

Screams from the chopper, the blades beating the air, her own heart pounding in her ears—all combined to roar like white noise in her head. Penny focused on helping Marty. She joined Julianna and slid a shoulder under his other arm while Holt scanned the woods.

"I don't see him, but hurry!" he said.

"Get him to the chopper," Julianna yelled.

The helicopter lifted, shifted, then settled again, and she realized Byron was trying to use the craft to shield them. Holt drew closer, backing toward them, allowing them time to get Marty on the aircraft.

The agent panted, his pain almost tangible.

"Hang on, Marty," Penny said, "we'll get you fixed up in just a minute!"

Julianna scrambled into the helicopter, turned, and shoved her hands under Marty's armpits. She tugged and Penny pushed until he was inside, lying on the floor. "Get in, Penny!"

Julianna screeched and fell back, clutching her left arm. Blood flowed between her fingers, but her eyes were focused over Penny's shoulder. "Holt!"

Penny turned to see Holt racing into the woods. "Holt! Come back!" Cold dread centered itself in her midsection. He was going after a killer all by himself. Where were the other teams of agents? On the way to help, no doubt, but would they arrive in time?

A gust of wind rocked the chopper and Byron turned in his seat. "Get in!"

Raina had already started pressure on Julianna's arm, and Holly was focused on Marty's leg.

"I can't just leave him there." She stepped back. "Go!"

"No!" Julianna cried. "I'll go!" She scrambled for the door and Holly yanked her back.

Penny ducked and ran from the chopper.

"Penny!"

Holly's yell floated after her as Penny headed toward where she'd seen Holt disappear. The helicopter lifted and roared away. For a moment, there was silence until her ears readjusted to the sounds of nature.

And a gunshot.

■ ■ ■ ■

Holt ducked, but the bullet was wide and it slammed into the tree beside him. He continued to chase the man, barking his location into his radio, demanding to know where his backup was. Static answered him. He gave up for the moment as he pushed through the bushes, dodged tree limbs, and kicked at the underbrush, desperate to keep Rabor in sight.

He burst through into an open area and skidded to a stop. Ten yards ahead, the earth came to an end. He had no idea how steep the drop-off was, but he had no desire to find out.

Heart pounding, sweat beading on his forehead, he whirled to see Rabor step out from behind a tree. He held what was probably Gus's stolen weapon on Holt and wore a smirk Holt still saw in his dreams. And yet . . . there was something . . . off.

"Well, well," the killer drawled, "Special Agent Holton Satterfield. I'd recognize you anywhere."

Holt's stomach twisted and he could see his death staring back at him through the drizzling rain. "Rabor. Why don't you put that gun down and come on in nice and easy? Save us both some trouble. I don't know about you, but I'm really tired of being cold and wet."

The man laughed. A chilling sound that scraped along Holt's nerve endings. This wasn't going to end the way he wanted it to. "Where's Shondra?"

Holt caught a brief flash of movement to his left before Penny launched herself onto Rabor's back and sent his weapon flying. A scream of rage ripped from Rabor's throat as he went to his knees, and Holt bolted for the man. The killer rolled for the gun, grabbing it inches from Holt's foot, and shot to his feet. Rabor whipped around and snagged a handful of Penny's strawberry-blond hair.

Her high-pitched cry echoed and Holt's heart shuddered.

"Stay right there!" Rabor pressed the gun against her temple, and Holt stopped so fast, he almost lost his footing on the slick ground.

"Let her go!" He lifted his own weapon and aimed it at Rabor's left eye.

"Not until you drop your weapon."

"I'm not dropping my gun."

"Then she's dead." Rabor drew the gun down her cheek and whispered something that Holt missed. Penny never reacted to whatever it was he said, keeping her eyes locked on Holt. He had to ignore the pleading on her face and concentrate on Rabor, who'd finally stopped muttering and met Holt's gaze. "Say goodbye to the pretty lady."

Think, think!

Penny's arm shot up in a smooth self-defense move, knocking into Rabor's forearm. Once again, he lost his grip on the gun. She stomped on the inside of his right knee, scraping her heavy boot down onto his foot. Then jabbed a hard punch back with her elbow.

The man howled, then punched her in the side of the head just as Penny jerked away and fell on her rear. But she was loose and Holt was moving. Penny used the momentum to roll away from Rabor's reaching hands, and Holt threw a hard punch to the man's gut. The breath whooshed from his lungs and he bent double. And stayed there, gasping, his hand gripping his middle. But at least he wasn't anywhere near the weapon.

"Get back, Penny!"

She scrambled backward, out of the way.

"Drop the knife, Rabor!"

The man jerked up, a knife flashing in his left hand.

"You think I'd fall for that one again?" Holt asked.

"Doesn't matter. I'm going to finish what I started the first time we met."

A brief flash of the struggle, the surprise of finding a knife in his side, a pain like he'd never experienced before—the long road to recovery. All of that surged to the surface in warp speed. Holt shoved all that aside and focused on the man who wanted to kill him.

From the corner of his eye, he could see Penny rubbing her head and watching. She rolled to her knees, then staggered to her feet. Worry shafted him. If he failed, Penny would die too.

Rabor charged him. Holt braced himself, but at the last minute the man changed direction and went after Penny.

"No!" Holt shot forward and threw himself in between them, taking a hard hit that sent him to the ground. Rabor let out a low grunt, gave a yell, and hoisted himself over Holt. Pinned to the ground, Holt stared up.

The knife flashed.

Started toward Holt's throat.

A hard thud echoed around him and Rabor and the knife were gone. He was free. Holt rolled to see Penny hit the ground, tangled with Rabor. The killer roared his fury and flung himself to his feet, swinging the blade dangerously close to her face.

"You're going to die for that, little girl." He stepped toward her.

Before Holt could move, Penny swung a leg out and connected with Rabor's ankle. The man stumbled, tripped over an exposed root, and crashed to the ground with a harsh cry.

Then was still.

Holt raced to snag the gun before Rabor could move again. He shoved it into his waistband and aimed his own weapon at the still form. "Put your hands behind your back, Rabor." Into his radio, he shouted, "Need backup ASAP. Track my sat phone."

"Holt!" Julianna's voice came through, sending relief into his shaking limbs. "Help's on the way. Do you need medical assistance?"

"Yeah, get them here one way or another." Rabor still hadn't moved, but Holt knew his pattern well. Pretend to be unconscious while hiding the knife, then attack when approached. "Hands, Rabor! Show me your hands! You know how this works." He glanced at Penny. "Watch the area for his girlfriend. She's just as dangerous as he is." Back to Rabor. "Hands behind your back! Do it! Now!"

No movement.

"I don't think he can," Penny said and started toward the man.

"Penny, don't!"

She met his gaze and frowned but continued her cautious approach.

"Penny?" Holt's fingers flexed around the butt of his weapon, ready to put a bullet in the man's head. Why wouldn't she listen?

She finally touched Rabor's shoulder and Holt prepared himself to fire. But again, the killer didn't move.

"Get away from him, Penny!"

She placed two fingers on the side of the man's neck, then lifted her gaze to Holt's. "He's dead."

CHAPTER
FIVE

Penny stood frozen, head aching from Rabor's punch. She clasped her arms around her middle, shaking and slightly nauseous, while the coroner rolled Rabor to his side. The knife he'd almost used on her and Holt was embedded in the left side of his chest. Straight through his heart, if she were to make an educated guess.

A shudder rippled through her. Holt finished his conversation and walked over to her. "There's no sign of the girlfriend. The search will continue until she's found."

She nodded and he placed his hands on her shoulders. His gaze met hers, and she finally was able to move.

Straight into his arms to bury her face against his hard, soggy shoulder. She clasped the material at his waist, felt the vest under his shirt, and sucked in a ragged breath. "I was so scared," she whispered.

"Of course you were," he said, his lips moving against her hair. "I was too."

Another shiver shook her. The blanket someone had tossed around her was saturated and did nothing to keep her warm. "I killed him," she mumbled.

"He killed himself." He placed a finger under her chin and tilted her head upward. She let her eyes meet his. "You understand that, right? Rabor's dead because he made a lot of bad choices. In the end, one of those killed him. He stumbled because you were defending yourself. His death was pure accident brought on by his own evil intent."

"Yeah. Right. I mean, I know that. Mentally. It's just . . . weird. I fought back and a man is dead."

He squeezed her closer and she was content to huddle against him, desperate to convince herself she'd gotten a happy ending.

"Don't mourn too much for him, Penny," he said. "Don't let him stay in your head."

"I won't." She hoped. "And I really do realize that if things hadn't played out the way they did, one—or both—of us would be dead. I've just got to work on wrapping my mind around that."

"You'll be all right, Penny. I'll help you get through this."

"Have you . . . you know?"

"Killed someone before?"

"Yeah," she whispered.

He sighed. "Yeah." He cleared his throat. "You know, I've only ever pulled my gun four times with the intention of using it if I had to. One of those times, I did."

"I'm sorry."

"I was too. Still am. But I don't let it eat at me. I did what I was trained to do, and I saved a victim's life. The person I shot made his choices. I made mine." He paused. "What did he say to you?"

"What?"

"Rabor. When he was holding the gun against you, he whispered something to you. What did he say?"

Penny blanked. "I don't know."

"Did you not hear him?"

"I guess not. I was so focused on mentally walking myself through the self-defense move that I must have missed it."

He frowned. "Well, the man's dead now. Maybe it doesn't matter. That was a great move, by the way."

"Thanks."

He looked up, touched the side of her head. "Doesn't look too bad."

"It's not. It was more of a glancing blow. It stunned me for a second, but it's fine."

"Good." Relief shone in his eyes and he shot a look at the sky. "It's stopped raining."

"Of course it has." She laughed without humor and pulled the satellite phone from her pocket. "I need to return this to Mr. Benson after I call Mike and fill him in on everything. Although I imagine Raina or Holly have already given him some of the scoop."

"I'll make sure he gets it back. Probably tomorrow."

"Will you be staying in town for the night?"

"Yeah. I'll be here working the case until we find Rabor's girlfriend. For now, I need to get an update on Gus, as well as Marty and Julianna. So I'm heading to the hospital as soon as I drop you at your house."

"Why don't I just go to the hospital with you? I want to check in on Claire anyway."

"The patient that was on your bird?"

"Yes."

Blades thumped the air and he looked up. "There's our ride."

"I'll call Mike from the air."

He grasped her hand and together they darted for the chopper. Once on board and buckled in, she pulled the headset over her ears. Exhaustion swept over her and she closed her eyes for a moment, relishing the heat blasting from the vents. As soon as she quit shivering, she plugged her phone into the headset and called her boss to fill him in on everything. He was nicer than usual—downright solicitous—and she frowned. "What's going on with you, Mike? You haven't bitten my head off once."

"Your mother called."

Penny froze. "What?"

"She was checking up on her little girl who was flying in dangerous storms."

"I see." Penny wanted to crawl into a hole.

"See you when you get here, Penny."

She hung up and groaned.

"What's wrong?" Holt asked.

"I don't think I want to talk about it, okay?"

"Sure."

"Sorry, it's just work. My boss is a jerk."

"Thought you didn't want to talk about it."

She laughed and immediately her mood lightened in spite of everything. "I appreciate you, Holt," she said, her voice soft.

He squeezed her shoulder and she shut her eyes, focusing on the moment she could step into a hot shower.

When the chopper landed on the hospital helipad, Penny jerked, realizing she'd dozed off in spite of her saturated attire and absolute fury with her mother.

Fortunately, she lived at the base in one of the wings of the hospital when she was on duty and could grab a change of clothes. She'd already done her twelve-hour shift—and then some—and would be off for the next twelve.

Once again, Holt grabbed her hand and led her out of the chopper and toward the hospital. Bulbs flashed and voices yelled questions at her. "What was it like crash-landing the helicopter with a patient, then finding yourself trapped on a mountain with a serial killer?"

Holt's harshly expelled breath puffed across the nape of her neck. "You've got to be kidding me." He practically growled the words. "Who let them up here?"

"Penny, have you been in touch with your mother?"

Flash, flash.

"Penny, how does it feel to survive something that would have killed most people?"

"Penny, you're being hailed as a hero. How does that feel?"

"Penny, word is that the serial killer is dead because of you. Can you tell us that story?"

Flash, flash.

"Penny, you've come a long way from your days in juvie. Do you have any words of wisdom for parents struggling with their rebellious children?"

For a moment, she couldn't move. Couldn't breathe. It was her nightmare come true. She'd been successfully hiding away in her beloved mountain town, working a job she was born to do, and had made friends with genuine people she adored. With each shouted question, she could feel that slipping away.

Only Holt's comforting hand on the small of her back, guiding her through the throng of reporters, kept her from shattering apart.

But an anger was building. A familiar fury that she was worried she wouldn't be able to leash and return to the mental compartment she'd learned to keep locked up tight.

She continued her forward momentum, ignoring the fact that the media rotated like a pack of wild dogs to follow her and Holt into the hospital.

There was only one way they could know about her part in the rescue, then crash—okay, rough landing—and how Darius Rabor died.

Mike Bishop.

Without a word, she followed the maze of the hospital halls to Mike's office. She threw the door open and stepped inside, mentally ordering herself to control her words. The effort vibrated through her.

Mike sat at his desk to the right of the door. The television mounted on the wall to her left played on silent, the closed captions flashing at the bottom. He looked up, met her gaze . . . and swallowed. Then gathered his features into a hard mask. "Penny?"

"You called them."

"Now, Penny . . ." The mask slipped and he held out a hand in supplication.

Penny stayed still, feeling Holt at her back. "Don't you even deny it," she said. "You called them and now my life is going to be turned upside down."

"It'll die down in the next couple of weeks. As soon as a more interesting topic comes along."

"But . . . why? Why would you do this?"

Mike glanced behind her. "Who's that?"

"A friend." She didn't bother turning. "Well? Why?"

"If your friend wants to wait outside, we can have a private conversation."

"He can stay."

"Then we'll talk later."

"Mike!"

"This is business, Penny!" His shout echoed off the walls.

"Argh!" Penny whirled and eyed Holt, who looked like he'd already bitten his tongue in half with the effort not to intervene. "Will you please wait outside? I won't be long." She was actually proud of the control in her voice.

"Are you sure?"

"Oh, for crying out loud," Mike said, "I'm not going to hurt her."

Holt met the man's gaze. "I wasn't worried about *her*."

At the look on Mike's face, a bubble of mirth formed at the back of Penny's throat, and that was all it took for her to grab a deep breath. Her pulse slowed a fraction and the boiling in her bloodstream settled to a low simmer.

Holt eyed her, then Mike. "Sure, I'll wait outside."

He left and Penny turned back to Mike. Before she could open her mouth again, her phone buzzed. She resisted the urge to groan but wiggled the device from her wet pocket. She really wanted to change clothes. "It's my mother."

"Guess you'd better not keep her waiting."

Penny hit the green button on the screen. "Hi."

"Have you seen the news?"

"I haven't, but I take it you have."

"You could have died! Are you crazy? You want me to lose another child? This is payback for all those times I wasn't there for you, isn't it? I've tried, Penelope, I've tried, and you know I have, but you just continue to . . ."

Penny tuned out her mother's rant, closed her eyes, and pulled in a steadying breath. If she didn't manage to escape and have a really good, really long cry, she was going to explode.

"Mom, I'll have to call you back." She hung up. She'd pay for that, but—

"Did you just hang up on Geneva Queen?" Mike looked like he might be in danger of exploding, himself.

"She's not Geneva to me. She's Mom. Forget about her. This is about us and this program and the fact that you called the newshounds out here—"

The door opened and she turned.

"What's going on in here?" Larry Kirkpatrick, Life Flight's medical director—and Mike's boss—stepped into the room.

"Nothing," Mike said. "I've got this."

Penny gave a harsh laugh that drew a raised brow from the doctor and a glare from Mike. "No, Dr. Kirkpatrick, he doesn't *have this*." She was so going to lose her job. "He's been here six months and has made radical changes that risk our lives and the lives of our patients every day."

"Penny!" Mike's face flushed a deep red and his eyes leaked his anger. "Shut up while you still have a job."

"I'm just glad I still have my *life*! It's only by the grace of God that Holly and Raina and Claire are still alive. You're so worried about appearances and making sure we 'look good'"—she wiggled air quotes around the last two words—"that you've cut safety areas."

He placed his fists on his desk and leaned forward. "You need to stop these baseless accusations, Penny."

"No," Dr. Kirkpatrick said, "she needs to keep talking. I've always encouraged my staff to let me know if there's a problem. Sounds like there's a problem."

Finally. Penny turned to him. "Do you know that two months ago Mike discontinued our satellite phone service?"

The man blinked. "What?"

"Serial killer notwithstanding, we were on that mountain with no way to communicate. No cell phone signal, no radio, nothing. With a seriously injured patient who I still don't know if she's alive or not. But this is the last straw. Telling reporters what went on up there and then inviting them to meet me on the tarmac? That's just wrong. And it could have, once again, put someone's life in danger. What if we'd had a patient on board?"

Mike's face was beyond red. Penny almost expected to see smoke curling from his ears at any moment.

Dr. Kirkpatrick studied her. "Are you finished?"

"Yes." Probably in more ways than one. Sick at the thought of losing the job she loved, Penny could only hope it wouldn't be in vain. Maybe her sacrifice would save lives. If so, it would be worth it.

"Yes," Mike growled, "she is. Penny, you're fired."

She jutted her jaw and glared at him. "Fine. I'll go pack up my locker." She turned to Dr. Kirkpatrick. "But if you don't do something about this, someone's going to die and that's going to be on you." She started to sweep past him.

His hand on her arm stopped her. "Why didn't you come to me?"

She raised a brow. "I tried. I sent you emails and an interoffice memo. I even stopped by your office and asked your assistant to put me on the calendar to meet with you."

He frowned. "I never saw an email, a memo, or an appointment."

"Then talk to your assistant, because I did all of the above. Sir. I'm sorry, I'm not trying to be disrespectful, but when lives are at risk because safety measures are discarded . . . well, it fires me up."

"I can tell." Something flickered in his eyes, but Penny couldn't put her finger on what it meant. "Would you mind stepping outside and waiting?" he asked, his tone mild. "I'd like to speak to Mike alone for a moment. Things are becoming more and more clear."

Things? What things? She bit her lip on the questions. "Sure."

Penny pulled the already cracked door open and walked out into the hall. She shut the door with more force than necessary, but it felt so good, she almost opened it to do it again.

"You okay?"

Penny jumped. "Oh, Holt. You're still here." He was definitely still here and the desire to sink into his arms was . . . overwhelming. But the look in his eyes was odd. Like he'd just put ten feet worth of distance between them.

"Of course I am. I wasn't leaving you until I knew you were going to be okay—or at the very least keep you from committing murder."

The words belonged to Holt, but that look . . .

"He's still alive and I'm jobless, but I'll survive."

"I heard."

"You did?"

"Dr. Kirkpatrick left the door open. It was kind of hard not to hear."

"Right." She raked a hand over her drying hair and realized they were alone in the hallway. "Where's the media?" she asked. "I didn't figure they'd give up that easily."

"Security ushered them out."

"Oh. Good."

"Speaking of security . . ." He nodded to two of the armed officers that worked hard to keep the hospital safe. Clark Haverty and Greg Lehman approached.

Penny frowned. "Hey, guys, what's going on?"

"Dr. Kirkpatrick called and asked us to come up here and escort a terminated employee from the premises," Clark said.

She gaped. "Me?"

"No, not you." Greg motioned at her with a sweeping hand. "Step back from the door, will you?"

Confused, Penny locked eyes on Holt, who shrugged. They moved aside just as the door opened and Mike stormed out.

When he spotted Penny, he pointed at her. "This isn't over. You're going to pay for this."

■   ■   ■   ■

Holt started to go after the guy, but Penny laid a hand on his arm. "Don't." She stood still while she watched Clark and Greg walk a now-silent Mike Bishop down the hallway. "Okay," she said. "What do you suppose that means?"

"It means," Dr. Kirkpatrick said from the open door, "that Mr. Bishop is no longer in charge here."

"I was kind of getting that feeling."

Holt had taken note of the fury in Bishop's gaze. "He's just made a veiled threat against Penny."

"I'm sorry about that. He won't be around much longer. He'll get over it."

"You fired him?" Penny's disbelief echoed around them. "But . . . I didn't mean to get him fired, just some training or . . . something."

Dr. Kirkpatrick pulled the stethoscope from around his neck and shoved it into his lab coat pocket. "I didn't fire him solely based on what you said. I'm not completely in the dark about what's going on in my department. At least, I didn't think I was. But all the training in the world isn't going to help that man if his integrity has already slipped down the drain."

Holt agreed.

"I have a question for you," Dr. Kirkpatrick said to Penny.

"Sure."

"You said you sent me a memo detailing what you were observing in the program. Specifically, Mr. Bishop's lack of leadership and poor funds management."

"I did."

"And that went to my email?"

"It did."

He nodded. "Did Mr. Bishop know you were going to send it?"

"No. I never mentioned it to him, so I don't see how he could have. After a confrontation I had with him when he'd decided to cancel the satellite phone contract, I simply went to my computer and typed the email to you."

"And when I didn't respond, you figured I gave him the green light?"

Penny ducked her head. "Something like that. I did think it was out of character for you, but . . ." She shrugged.

The doctor scowled. "I've been doing some investigation into the man and I haven't been pleased with what I've dug up." He paused and studied her. "Normally, I wouldn't say anything, but in light of your involvement, I think you're owed an explanation. Could you step back inside the office so we have some privacy?"

"Sure."

"I'd like to hear this," Holt said. He showed the doctor his badge. "Bishop made a threat and I may need to follow up on it."

"Of course."

They followed him inside and he shut the door. "It seems Mr. Bishop and Ms. Long, my assistant, are in a relationship. I've noticed him in the area a lot more often than is necessary. At first, I just chalked it up to being extra busy or something. But this morning, I caught him and Ms. Long in a rather compromising situation in the very clichéd supply closet. They quickly gathered their composure and went their separate ways, but in light of this new knowledge, I suspect she's been protecting him by deleting your emails and shredding anything you may have sent through hospital mail."

"And not telling you I wanted to make an appointment with you."

"And that."

Penny sighed. "Well, that would explain a lot."

"Both Ms. Long and Mr. Bishop are fired and will have to find employment elsewhere. You, however, are an excellent pilot and I don't want to lose you."

Penny nodded. "Well, thank you."

"Now, why don't you and your friend go get into some dry clothes, get some rest. Take the next couple of days off. We'll see you back on Monday."

"Oh, but I was supposed to work—"

"Byron can handle it. Or one of the other pilots. You just did some pretty miraculous flying, had a showdown with a serial killer, and learned one of your coworkers betrayed your trust and the trust of your team. In fact, I'm not sure what he did wasn't illegal and will be consulting with hospital lawyers about that. Regardless, you need some downtime. Take it." He cleared his throat. "And it will give me some time to deal with the media. Mr. Bishop's actions have stirred up quite the storm here."

"I know. I'm sorry."

He quirked a half smile at her. "I had no idea your mother was Geneva Queen."

"Well, I don't advertise it. I don't necessarily hide it, but I—" She paused and Holt wondered at the conflict in her features. "Actually," she said, "yes, I do, but she has her life and I have mine." A sigh escaped from her. "Or had. I'll . . . resign . . . if that will make things easier for you. If you think it's necessary—after trying to quiet the storm, so to speak."

"I just said I didn't want to lose you. I meant that."

Penny bit her lip and nodded. "Thank you."

"Good." Dr. Kirkpatrick brushed past them, and a shiver rippled through Holt. He just realized he was freezing and really wanted to get out of his sodden clothing and then check on his friends. Gerald would call Nick Gresham's family and let them know about the man's death. Hopefully before the media found out.

And he needed to reevaluate his relationship with Penny. A cold, hard knot had settled in his chest as soon as he realized Penny had lied to him. She'd never mentioned her mother or her fame or the fact that she'd spent time in juvie. Okay, not outright lied, but a lie of omission was still a lie.

But that could wait for a better time.

"You okay?" he asked her.

"Yes. I'm . . . more than okay, actually." She shook herself and focused on him. "Are you okay?"

"I have some questions for you, but let's address that later."

"Questions?"

"Later, okay?"

She frowned. "Yeah, sure. Can you tell me how Julianna and the others are?"

"I texted Julianna while doing my best not to interrupt your conversation with a punch to Bishop's face. She said she was fine. Her wound was merely a graze. Marty's is a bit more serious and he's still in surgery. Gus too."

Penny eyed him, her brows drawn tight. "Then let's change and warm up. You can use the men's locker and I'll find you some scrubs for now. Once we're human again, we can head down to the waiting room."

"Thanks." He followed her down the hall. "That worked out well."

"What? Oh, with Dr. Kirkpatrick? Yes. For now. As soon as I step outside the hospital, I'm sure the media will be waiting to pounce once again."

"Can you slip out the back way?"

"I can try."

He fell silent a moment, then decided to ask the question burning a hole in his brain. "Your mom is Geneva Queen?"

She raised a brow at him. "You didn't know?"

"No."

"How did you not know? I figured you'd done a full background check on me."

LYNETTE EASON

He wasn't sure if she was kidding or not.

"Dumb joke," she said. "Sorry."

He laughed but heard the strain in it. "Just because I *can* doesn't mean I *do*. Besides, it's a violation of FBI policy and state law." Not that there weren't ways around that, but he'd never felt comfortable using his job for that kind of thing. He knew others who did it, of course, but . . . not him. He liked his privacy and tried to respect others' right to the same.

"I wasn't serious, Holt. I know you wouldn't do that. You're an honorable man."

"I do my best." But one thing he would do would be a background check on Mike Bishop. Holt didn't feel one iota of guilt for that plan. The man had made a possible threat against Penny, and while Holt wasn't exactly happy with her at the moment, he couldn't simply dismiss Bishop's words. He needed to know what he was working with. All talk and no action—or something more sinister?

They arrived at the entrance to the locker rooms. Men's on the right, women's on the left. And a supply closet in the middle. She showed him where everything was, got him a pair of scrubs, and promised to meet him in fifteen minutes back in front of the closet.

Holt decided he'd never enjoyed a shower more, but he was anxious to check on his friends—and talk to Penny in depth. Not that anything would have changed since Julianna had texted him, but he'd feel better being there when Marty and Gus came out of surgery. He could write up his report while he waited.

As the steaming water beat down on his shoulders, he curled his fingers into fists and tried to block the flickering images from just a few hours ago. He'd thought his time had come. If it hadn't been for Penny . . .

His anger with her faded. She had her reasons for not telling him about her mother. He didn't like it because it meant she hadn't trusted him enough to share that with him and . . . it stung.

59

But Darius Rabor was dead. He could quit seeing the man in his head. And his nightmares. It was finally over.

He pressed his palms to his eyes and whispered a short but heartfelt prayer of thanks that he and Penny were alive and unhurt. Then said another prayer for his friends before turning off the water.

He had a report to write, a conversation to have with Penny. Then, depending on how that talk went, he could work on forgetting today ever happened.

CHAPTER
SIX

Penny and Holt stepped into the surgery waiting room. She noticed a group of agents in the far right corner huddled together and talking, others pacing from one end of the area to the other. Julianna, a bandage on her arm, sat in one of the chairs. Penny was sure they were all waiting to hear more about Marty and Gus.

To her left, she found Raina and Holly talking with a couple in their forties. Mr. and Mrs. Gentry, she'd be willing to guess. The woman was too thin, her makeup tear-streaked. Her raccoon eyes met Penny's and widened. "You're the pilot."

"I am."

A sob slipped from Mrs. Gentry's lips, and she stepped forward to enfold Penny in a tight hug. "I can't believe everything you went through to get my girl here alive."

Penny frowned and met Holt's gaze, hoping he could see the question in her eyes. *How does she know what I did?*

Holt gave a subtle nod toward the television hanging in the corner. The news. Of course.

When Mrs. Gentry stepped back, Penny patted her arm. "I'm so glad she made it to surgery. Is there any update on her prognosis?"

"They think she'll pull through," Mr. Gentry said. "It's been touch and go, but she's my girl and she's hanging tough." His voice choked on the last word and he blinked his red-rimmed eyes. "We'll never be able to thank you and the others enough for all you've done."

The waiting room attendant stood and motioned to the Gentrys. "I've got an update for you."

Claire's parents excused themselves and hurried over. Penny's gaze stayed on the television, reading the captions running across the bottom of the screen while she absently spun the watch on her wrist.

She recognized Mr. Benson, the friendly neighbor who'd given her the satellite phone. ". . . such a sweet lady. Very concerned for her patient and coworkers. The fact that she was willing to brave that terrible storm and possibly head into the path of a serial killer is just incredible. I only talked to her for less than five minutes, but it was enough to know she's an amazing person."

The screen switched to the woman whose home she'd broken into. "I couldn't believe it. I came home ready to lock up and get my gun in case that serial killer showed up and, instead, found a Life Flight helicopter pilot desperate to find a way to save her patient and coworkers. Truly incredible. It did my heart good to know there are still people like her in the world. And then to hear that she was attacked and fought back? And actually escaped him? Oh, my word. I simply couldn't believe it. But then again, she's hero material, so I don't know why I'd be surprised. I'm so glad she's okay and that killer is dead. And I had no idea that she was Geneva Queen's daughter. That's just wild."

Holt stood beside her and she looked up at him. "Are you kidding me?" she whispered.

"It's been running on a loop for the past thirty minutes," Raina said. "The interviews and the footage of you and Holt entering the hospital." She gave a disgusted grunt. "Can you believe those questions?" She twisted her lips into a frown. "Crazy."

"Great. Just great. This is all simply fabulous." How was this going to affect her job? Her *life*?

The screen flashed to the footage Raina had mentioned, and Penny gasped. "I look like a drowned rat." She glanced at Holt. "So do you."

"Thanks."

Holly giggled, then quickly straightened her face at Penny's scowl. "Sorry." She shrugged. "But you're right. You both look soggy and miserable."

"There's a reason for that."

Holt touched her shoulder. "I'm going over to that crowd to see if I can find out about Gus and Marty."

"Marty's was a flesh wound," Holly said. "Gus's is more serious. But they were both alive when we got here."

"Thank you." He glanced at the others. "I'll be back."

He left them and Penny turned her attention back to the television. Ugh. Unable to watch it anymore, she looked at Raina. "You and Holly deserve the spotlight, not me. You kept Claire alive. All I did was get wet."

"And fight off a serial killer," Raina said, her tone wry.

And the man was dead because of it. She still couldn't find it in her to be terribly grieved about it. The only thing she really felt bad about was that he wouldn't go back to prison and spend whatever remained of his life waiting to die.

Waiting to take that walk down death row to the execution chamber.

Waiting to feel the prick of the needle for the IV that would deliver the drugs that would still his evil heart forever.

Thinking about his decisions to take others' lives, regret his choices, make restitution.

Not that he could have ever done anything to make up for the grief and sorrow he'd caused or that she wouldn't have nightmares about the whole thing. But . . .

"You okay?" Holly asked.

"I'm . . . managing."

"Yeah."

"What about you? You guys were shot at too."

"Same as you. Managing."

Penny's phone buzzed and she glanced at the screen with a silent groan, then declined the call and shut the device off. Her mother would just keep calling until Penny answered, and she simply could *not* deal with her right now.

She spied Holt talking to Julianna. "I'm going to go tell her thank you," she said.

"Sure."

Penny made her way over to the group of agents and stepped in front of Julianna, then bent to hug her. "How are you?"

Julianna squeezed her tight. "I'm okay. A barely there graze. Like a bad scrape that didn't even need stitches. Stings like crazy, though. The doc's already cleared me to go back to work. I'll pick back up with the training class again on Monday. You?"

Penny grimaced. "I've been better, but I'm grateful you and the others arrived when you did. Things could have gone very differently."

"I'm thankful as well. You did amazing out there."

"Thank you. Any news on Marty and Gus?" She really didn't want to talk about herself.

"We had an update not too long ago. Marty's doing fine and being his ornery self." She paused for a sip of her coffee. "Gus is hanging in there. How's your patient?"

"Same as Gus, from what I understand. Holding on for now."

Julianna studied her. "I'm glad. I'm going to head back over to Raina and Holly, but I wanted to check on you."

Compassion shimmered in her friend's kind blue eyes. Julianna's eyes were one of the first things she'd noticed about her when they'd met ten years ago. "I'm fine," Penny said. "We'll get together soon. I've missed our chats."

"Promise?"

"Absolutely."

Penny walked back to find the Gentrys smiling and making

phone calls. Relief swamped her. It was easy to assume the doctor had given them a good report.

And now it was time for her to go have her cry and crash into sleep. And pray no nightmares came her way. Present ones or ones from the past.

■ ■ ■ ■

From the corner of his eye, Holt saw Penny leave. Her friends followed and he couldn't decide whether he should go after her or not. She kept him off balance—which was one of the things that intrigued him about her.

Usually, he had no problem reading people, but with Penny, he sometimes found himself unable to see past the face she presented to the world. Then every so often, she'd allowed him a few glimpses of the deeper Penny. Like today on the mountain. She'd been incredible, of course, and he'd found himself wanting to get to know her even more.

And then he'd discovered her mother was Geneva Queen. One of the most well-known, most sought-after actresses in Hollywood. He kept going back to the fact that Penny hadn't told him. Hadn't trusted him enough to let him in on that little fact after a year and a half of friendship.

Talk to her.

"Hey, guys," he said, "I'm going to take off and get that paperwork done." He squeezed Julianna's shoulder. "Text me updates, okay?"

"Sure thing."

Holt grabbed his bag containing his sodden uniform and hurried after Penny just in time to see Mike Bishop step around the corner toward them. Penny stopped, her body rigid. Mike pulled to a halt, his eyes narrowed and his nostrils flared. He brushed past her without a word and Penny whirled. "You're not supposed to be here."

He ignored her and Holt stepped in front of the man. "You were escorted from the hospital. What are you doing back?"

"Not that it's any of your business, but I left something in my locker. I came to get it."

"Since you don't have security personnel with you, I'm going to assume that you didn't let someone know you were here?"

"No, I didn't. I'm going to get it and leave. I don't have time to mess around because, thanks to you, I have to go job hunting." He snarled that last sentence at Penny, who simply crossed her arms and met the man glare for glare. "Just couldn't keep your mouth shut, could you?"

"No." She kept her tone even and Holt couldn't say how much he admired her restraint. "Not when it was putting people's lives in danger, I couldn't."

The calm tone seemed to infuriate Bishop further, but with one last glare at Holt, he stormed down the hall.

Penny sighed and pulled out her phone. "I'll call security and alert them that he's here."

"Good idea."

She did, then tucked her phone back into her pocket. "Where are you headed?"

"I said I'd see you home. I plan to do that." Maybe they'd talk on the way.

"I figured you'd want to stay here with Gus, Julianna, and Marty."

"I'll get updates from the others. My main priority is to make sure you get home."

"Only if you promise to stop at a drive-thru first."

It was hard to stay upset with her when he wasn't even sure if he should be—especially when she'd saved his life. Twice. He smiled. "My pleasure?"

"Yeah, that one."

This time he laughed. He definitely enjoyed her wit. They walked to his SUV, and once they were buckled in and on the way to the restaurant, he glanced at her. "I'm curious."

"About?"

"How long have we known each other?"

She frowned. "You know as well as I do it's been a little over a year and a half. Why?"

"And never once did you think you could trust me with who your family is or that you'd spent time in juvie?"

She swallowed and Holt turned his attention to driving. "It wasn't anything personal, Holt. It's—" She sighed and palmed her eyes. He almost felt sorry for asking, but . . . eighteen months and she couldn't talk to him? He couldn't allow his heart to get any more entangled with hers until he knew she'd be willing to share with him.

Like you've shared about Zoe with her?

He shut that voice down. That was different.

How?

He wasn't sure, but it was. It had to be. Somehow. "You don't have to tell me if you don't want to." If she didn't feel like she could trust him, his heart was going to be broken once more. His fingers tightened around the steering wheel.

"I was a very rebellious teen—for various reasons," she said, her voice low, "but mostly because I felt invisible to my parents, who had no clue what to do with me. In addition to that, I had some trauma in my childhood. Add that to my sister's death, and I had so much anger, I didn't know what to do. Long story short, I wound up in court and was sent to juvie."

"Is that how you know Julianna so well?"

She gaped at him. "You know about that?"

"Yeah, she's pretty open about her time there and why she was there, but she never mentioned you. I know you guys are from the same area, so it's not a far-fetched deduction that it was a possibility."

"Huh. Well, it's not a secret, but not something I advertise, either."

"Like being Geneva Queen's daughter?"

"No, like I told Dr. Kirkpatrick, that was definitely a secret."

"And you felt like you had to keep it from me?"

"Yes. No. I just—" A low groan. "It wasn't that I don't trust you. I simply don't like talking about my past."

"But that's what couples do, Penny. They talk. About their past, their present . . . and their future."

She went thoughtful while he ordered the food. Once they were en route again, she handed him a waffle fry and continued to study him.

"What?" he finally asked.

"Are we a couple? Because while we've gone out a few times and talked on the phone some, you've never indicated that I was more than a friend."

He hadn't? Quickly, he scanned his memory. "Sure, I have."

"When?"

"When we went out for dinners and—" Had he been so worried about scaring her off that he'd not made his intentions clear? "Do *you* want to be more than friends?"

She drew in a breath, then let it out slowly. "I don't know, Holt. I've thought about it because I always enjoy spending time with you, but we live in different states. We have crazy schedules. How would it work?"

"I don't know." And that thought depressed him. Which meant he had a lot to think about. "Can you finish your story about juvie and we'll worry later about how to make a relationship work if we decide that's what we both want?" If that's what *she* decided *she* wanted. He knew what *he* wanted—at least he thought he did, before tonight. But he wouldn't push her. Better to back off now and let her process everything. And find out what else he didn't know about her.

She gave a small laugh. "Yeah, sure. So . . . I was only there for eight months, but it was the worst eight months of my life. And the best."

"How does that work?"

"The worst is probably self-explanatory. The best is because that's where I met Mrs. Gibbs and the others."

"Mrs. Gibbs?"

"She was the psychiatrist on my block. She was about sixty years old and didn't take anything from anyone. She was also a Christian. The first genuine Christian I'd ever met. I hated her at first, but she eventually won me over."

"I have a hard time imagining you hating anyone."

"Ha. Well, I did. I was required to meet with her two hours a week, and she chipped and chiseled away at my attitude until all that was left was a hurting little girl who wept in her arms and finally decided to turn her life around."

"Are you willing to tell me more about that?"

"Maybe one day. When there's more time. But, yeah, it's also where Julianna, Grace, and I met. We formed a friendship that's lasted a decade so far."

"You're fortunate to have those friends."

"I'm blessed."

"Yeah," he said, reaching to give her fingers a squeeze. His annoyance, anger, or whatever it was he'd been feeling had faded with each word she spoke. "I know what you mean." His phone buzzed and Rachel's name flashed on the SUV's screen. He declined the call, his gut clenching. He needed to find time to call her back, but he didn't want to talk to her in front of Penny. His family was one subject he didn't talk much about either. At least not when it came to Zoe. *Hypocrite.* The annoying accusation rang in his mind. If he wanted Penny to trust him with her past, that meant trusting her with *his.*

And that would mean talking about Zoe. The thought made him slightly nauseous.

Five minutes later, armed with what was left of waffle fries, chicken nuggets, and milk shakes, he pulled into her drive. "The media aren't here," he said, surprised. "I expected them to be camped out on your doorstep."

"Let's enjoy it while we can. They'll figure it out eventually."

"Figure out what?"

"That I bought this house under a different name."

"Ah. Smart."

She led the way into her construction zone that was slowly turning into a home. Once inside the large Victorian, he spotted the light fixture she'd spent hours agonizing over. "You got the chandelier. Looks great."

"Thanks."

He shot her a sideways glance. "Let me guess. You hung it yourself."

"I did."

"And it works?"

"Ha ha." She flipped the switch and the multi-bulbed light popped to life. It truly was a spectacular piece. And he wasn't surprised one bit that it worked. Penny was talented in many areas. "It took me months to save up for that," she said. "I even took a few extra shifts on the ambulance, but it was worth it." Penny had trained as a paramedic and a pilot. Pilots had unusual schedules, so she had more leeway than some to serve in more than one area.

She led him through the foyer into the living room on the left. He'd been to her place only three times, but each time he was there, she'd finished something new. "Looks like you're in the homestretch now. No pun intended."

"Well, this beautiful old girl has brand-new electrical, new plumbing, and a refurbished exterior. And now, aside from painting the dining room, this floor is done. Just have to do the upstairs. I can do the labor like stripping wallpaper, but the other stuff is going to have to wait a bit while I reload the bank account."

He took a seat on the oversized sofa and set their food on the coffee table. He fit nicely into the corner and stretched his legs in front of him. She sank into the recliner facing the fireplace. A groan slipped from her and she sighed.

"You know," he said, "my dad and I built the house where he and my mom still live. I'd be happy to help you anytime."

She propped an eye open. "When you're not chasing serial killers through massive storms?"

"Yeah. And when you're not crashing helicopters on top of mountains."

The eye closed. "Too soon, Satterfield. Too soon."

"Sorry."

"And I didn't crash, thank you very much."

Thank God for that. "You did an amazing thing today, Penny. You should be proud of yourself."

Another sigh. "I'm just relieved, to be honest. And thankful. So very thankful."

"Me too." His eyes grew heavy and he glanced at the food. "Are you hungry?"

"I ate most of mine in the car. Sorry. I was starving."

Holt smiled. "I forgive you. You fed me waffle fries, so I'm all right." He pushed to his feet. "But it's time for me to go and let you get some rest. Are you going to be all right here by yourself?"

"Of course."

He raised a brow. "'Of course' nothing. That was a very scary thing that happened to you on the mountain. You're probably going to dream about it." *He* was probably going to dream about it.

"Maybe, but I'll be okay."

Still, he hesitated. "Do you want me to stay here with you?"

For a moment, he thought she might say yes, but she simply shook her head. "I know you want to go back to the hospital to wait for Marty and Gus to come out of surgery."

"I do, but I don't want to leave you if you need me to stay."

"Go," she said. "Check on them. I'll be fine."

Holt gave her a slow nod. "Once I know they're going to be okay, I'll go to the hotel for a bit of sleep. Then get back to it first thing in the morning. I'll check on you too. If you need me, you call me, understand? I'm not that far away."

"Sure. Thank you." She rose too. "Where are you staying?"

71

"A couple of miles from here. One of the chain hotels over on Tunnel Road."

"Are you going back out to look for Shondra Miller in the morning?"

"No, I'll be doing paperwork. Local law enforcement and other agents are doing the boots-on-the-ground stuff right now. If they find anything, I'll head out to the scene. I'll check in with you soon."

"I'll be fine. Thank you, Holt. For . . . everything. Including the talk."

She followed him to the door and then hugged him. Hard. He returned the embrace, kissed the top of her head, then slipped out the door. He had one more thing to do that he hadn't mentioned. He was going to have to assume that Mike Bishop's background check came back clean, since he'd been employed at the hospital, but it wouldn't hurt to put a bug in security's ear about the need to keep an eye out for the man. He glanced at his phone.

And then he'd call his sister.

CHAPTER
SEVEN

Once Holt was gone, Penny shivered in the sudden quiet of her home. She missed him. She wasn't sure if it was actually him she missed or just the presence of someone—anyone—in the house with her. No, it was definitely him. Which meant she had a *lot* to think about, but after her mountaintop experience, she wasn't sure she was okay with being alone. Who could she ask to come stay with her? Raina? Holly?

Both were still on shift. They always had longer shifts than she did. As a pilot she was limited to twelve hours on, twelve hours off, seven days on, seven days off. Today was day three of her seven days. She would return on Sunday and Monday to finish the shift, then have the next seven days off. Unless she took someone else's shift. Which she might—assuming one was available. At least she'd be sleeping in the same area with other people. An area where she never had nightmares. She only had those when she was home. Alone.

Another shiver sent goose bumps pebbling across her arms, and she went to the thermostat and bumped it up a degree.

Normally she didn't mind being by herself. Most of the time she relished it—except when she had to sleep—but tonight, her mind kept taking her back to the mountain. To the fight with a killer. To the overwhelming, mind-numbing fear. To the conversation about trust and relationships, her mother and her past. She was physically exhausted, but the emotional fatigue might be the thing that would do her in tonight.

Penny checked the locks and windows. All of them were new, but she hadn't had the alarm system she'd already picked out installed yet. She still needed to replace two of the windows upstairs. Then the house could be wired.

She might take care of that tomorrow.

For tonight, however, her big comfy couch and cozy blanket would be fine.

Since she'd showered at the hospital and changed into jogging pants and an oversized sweatshirt, all she had to do was crash onto the cushions.

Once she was stretched out, she grabbed the Sherpa blanket from the back of the sofa and pulled it over herself. She removed the watch from her wrist, thinking about the woman who'd given it to her. Her father's mother had loved her grandchildren and, when she was around them, made sure to make them feel special. Loved. Penny traced a finger around the face. It was a simple yet elegant watch. Solid gold and rimmed with tiny diamonds, it was the one piece of jewelry she always kept with her. A grown-up security blanket.

But when her grandmother hadn't been there . . . the nanny had been responsible for her sister and Penny. The nanny who'd—

No, don't think about her.

Penny sighed and pushed away the familiar ache of missing her grandmother, the memories of the abusive nanny, and plugged her phone into the lamp's USB port. She sent one text to her mother saying she was fine, at home, and going to sleep, then ignored the rest of the text messages and waiting voice mails. The woman knew Penny was alive and that would have to suffice for tonight. She'd call her tomorrow when she could think. And control her tongue.

She shut her eyes.

Only to pop them back open as remembered terror surged. She yanked the blanket over her head and considered the fact that she might need to get a pet in order not to feel so alone. But just thinking about her schedule made her discard the idea. What would she do with a dog while she was working seven straight days and living at the base? Even a cat needed company sometimes.

Go to sleep, Penny! The order helped. A little. Finally, she relaxed enough to keep her eyes shut. Her current world faded, only to morph into a dark, cold space. Hunger, thirst, and possible monsters pulled the sobs from her. She pounded on the door. "Let me out! Let me out!" The door flew open and Rabor's face leered down at her. He shook the satellite phone at her. "There's no one to call anyway, little girl. No one cares that you're scared."

A low creak from the second floor sent her upright, the blanket falling around her waist, the nightmare lingering at the edges of her consciousness. Her heart pounded and she sat frozen, trying to force the images from her mind.

When nothing else happened, she lay back down and waited for her pulse to slow. A quick glance at the mantel clock showed it was four in the morning. She'd slept a few restless hours and wanted more—just without the nightmares. She closed her eyes, only to pop them open once again when she thought she heard another sound from the upstairs. Penny sat up, pulse pounding once more. What in the world? Stupid house.

But . . . was it the house?

Of course it was. She settled back against the cushion and stared at the recently redone ceiling.

Maybe she should scratch the dog idea and get a gun. Then she wouldn't jump at every moan and groan the old house made. Then again, she'd probably wind up just shooting herself in the foot—or worse—so the dog idea might be the better route to go. If she could figure out how to make it work.

So, no dog and no gun. But maybe a taser.

A low whine reached her, and she flinched. She'd thought she was used to the different sounds the house made by this point, but these were new. Which sent more goose bumps popping out over her skin.

Should she get up and go investigate or hunker back down and try to ignore them?

The next soft screech of noise sent her upright once more. A thud that definitely could have been a footfall came from overhead. "Okay," she whispered. "That was not the house."

Penny shoved aside the blanket and snatched her cell phone from the end table. She tapped a text to Holt.

> I think someone's in my house.

Then she dialed 911.

"911. What's your emergency?"

"This is Penny Carlton." She gave her address. "I think someone's in my house."

"Can you get out?"

"Yes, but . . . ugh . . . I'm not completely sure someone's really here. I just wanted you on the other end of the line while I go check."

"That's not a good idea. Please leave and an officer will be there shortly."

"How shortly?" Penny walked to the base of the stairs and glanced up. Should she or not?

Definitely not.

"Five minutes out."

She placed her foot on the first step. The phrase "too stupid to live" briefly flickered across her mind. But surely she was just spooked from her run-in with a serial killer and the nightmares that followed. Who wouldn't be? And how would someone have gotten up on her second floor any—

Oh, wait. There was scaffolding on the side near what was going to be a guest room. So . . . possibly? *Very* possibly.

But the window had plywood over it.

Plywood that might squeak, creak, and groan if someone removed the nails? Her phone buzzed. A text from Holt.

On the way. Get out of the house.

Penny hesitated once more. "There's no one there," she whispered. She ignored the 911 operator trying to get her attention and tapped another text to Holt.

I think I'm just being paranoid. Obviously, today affected me more than I thought.

Then to the 911 operator, she said, "Never mind. It's probably nothing."

"The unit is about two minutes away."

A figure appeared at the top of the stairs and Penny let out a gasp and backpedaled. "There's someone here! What do you want?"

He held out a hand and started down. One slow step at a time.

"How did you get up there? Who are you?" Penny hated the sheer terror vibrating through her words as every murder mystery she'd ever watched or read flicked at warp speed through her mind. He didn't wear a ski mask but had a ball cap pulled low, disguising his features.

"Ma'am? Ma'am?" The squawk from the phone echoed around her.

His footsteps paused.

"I'm on the phone with 911," she told him. "Get out of my house!"

He took one step back up the stairs, his head swiveling toward the front door.

Penny spun and darted for her kitchen, pulse pounding in her ears. She shoved the phone in her pocket and grabbed the first weapon she came across. A golf club. A putter, but it would hurt if she could connect with something. Sirens reached her and she registered the operator's tinny voice coming through the phone once more, but could also hear the intruder's footsteps behind her. He must have decided not to leave the way he came in.

She whirled and swung the putter, taking satisfaction when it landed on the black-clad figure. He screamed and backtracked a few steps, which allowed Penny to dart toward the door. She twisted the knob and threw it open just in time to see blue lights heading up her drive. She raced out onto the veranda.

The cruiser pulled to a stop at the top of her circular drive about the same time she spotted a dark SUV turn in behind it.

Holt.

She turned to look back into her kitchen through the open door. Empty. Two officers climbed from their vehicle, hands on their weapons.

"He's still in there," she said, hating the breathless quality of her voice. "Unless he went out another door. The guy behind you is a friend and FBI. I texted him, then called 911."

"Great. Stay with him." The taller of the two officers climbed the steps and pulled his gun. "Marcie, check the perimeter."

"Got it." The woman mimicked her partner and palmed her weapon. She went around the corner while the other one—whom Penny dubbed Officer Tall—stepped inside the kitchen.

Holt joined her on the veranda and gripped her upper arms. "You okay?"

"Yeah, just . . . yeah. No. Actually, I'm not. There was someone in my house and he was . . . creepy. Super, super creepy and I don't think I'll ever be able to sleep again."

"Who was it?"

"No idea. I really thought it was all my imagination working overtime, thanks to all the fun we had on the mountain. And then Mike being so nasty. And nightmares." So many nightmares. "I heard creaking and noises coming from upstairs and thought it was just the house but decided I should probably check it out. I started to go up the stairs when he just . . . materialized . . . at the top. I ran and he chased me. Thankfully, you and the cops got here quick." She shuddered and clamped her lips on the rush of words. "I really thought I was overreacting."

Holt took the golf club from her. Penny hadn't realized she was still clutching it. "It's okay," he said. "You did the right thing."

Officer Tall came around the corner of the porch, his weapon holstered. "I'm Officer Martinez. Looks like he got away."

Marcie joined them from the other side and shook her head. "I thought I got a glimpse of him, but by the time I got to where he was, he'd disappeared."

"The French doors off your bedroom were open," Officer Martinez said. "I'm sure that's how he left."

Penny shuddered. "As long as he's gone."

Holt placed a hand on the small of her back and ushered her inside. The officers followed. "You want to look around and see if he disturbed anything upstairs?" Holt asked her.

"It's such a mess up there, I probably wouldn't know, but sure, I'll look." She rubbed her tired eyes. "I'm assuming he climbed the scaffolding to the second floor and got in through the window that had the plywood over it."

Marcie nodded. "Probably. There's a piece of plywood on the ground near the scaffolding."

Penny led the way up the stairs and Holt stayed close behind her. His presence soothed her battered spirit.

At the top of the stairs, the cold hit her and she paused. "To the left is the bedroom that had the plywood on the window. To the right are two more bedrooms. All of the floors have been replaced, so it's safe to walk on them."

"Lead on," Holt said.

She took them into the bedroom with the newly laid floors, peeling wallpaper, chipped ceiling, and one open window with a sheer white curtain billowing in the breeze.

"Any idea who could have done this?" Martinez asked.

Penny looked at Holt and wondered if he was thinking the same thing she was. "I have some thoughts, but I don't want to accuse anyone without knowing for sure."

"Give us the name and we'll look into it."

"Mike Bishop," Penny said.

Holt nodded. "He was my first guess."

Officer Martinez wrote the name down. "We'll check—"

His radio buzzed. "Shots fired." Dispatch reeled off the address. "All units in the area respond."

"That's only a couple of miles from here," Martinez told his partner. "Let's go." He looked at Holt and Penny as he backed out of the room. "We'll get on this as soon as possible." Then they were gone.

Penny sighed. "I hope no one's hurt, but my intruder just fell to the bottom of the priority pile."

"Yep."

"Then I need to go have a few words with Mike Bishop myself."

■ ■ ■ ■

"Hang on, what do you mean by that?"

Penny's jaw jutted and Holt's admiration climbed up a notch. She'd been through absolute purgatory and now she was in fight mode. "I mean," she said, heading for the stairs, "that after I put that plywood back over my window, I'd like to go get my car. Then I'm going over to Mike Bishop's and give him a taste of his own medicine."

Holt joined her at the bottom of the stairs, where she grabbed her car keys from the entry table near the front door. He caught her arm in a gentle grasp. "That's a really bad idea, Penny."

"Maybe so," she said, pulling out of his hold, "but if I don't go, who knows the story he'll be able to concoct, or the alibi he'll manage to arrange, before morning?"

She had a point. He sighed. "Fine, but I'm going with you."

"Can't you get in trouble for that? This isn't FBI jurisdiction."

"I'm not going as an agent. I'm going as your friend."

"Then good. I'd appreciate your company."

"I'll drive."

"Perfect." She paused. "I just need one favor."

"What's that?"

"No, two."

"Fine. What are they?"

"One, can you help me get that plywood back over the window, and two, can you use your connections and get Mike's address?"

He barked a short laugh. "Sure. To both."

It took him less than five minutes to get the address on Michael Alan Bishop and ten more to get the plywood back in place.

She climbed into the passenger seat of his car and her smile slipped into a frown. They were on the road and headed for Bishop's home when she let out a low sigh. "He scared me, Holt, and that infuriates me."

Her voice was soft. Hesitant. Almost as though she didn't want him to hear her. But he did, and his fingers flexed on the wheel. "I know."

"I don't like being afraid. I do everything in my power to *avoid* being afraid."

"And you fly choppers? Sure, that makes total sense."

She chuckled. "Choppers don't scare me. Landings like the one on the mountain do, but nothing like that's ever happened before." She shifted to face him. "You train for it, you know what to do should you have to do it, but you never actually expect to have to use the training."

"Yeah. There's a lot of similarities with being in law enforcement."

"I'm sure." She fell silent and he let her. The truth was, he wouldn't mind a little one-on-one time with Mr. Bishop. Make him see the error of his ways. He'd be professional and keep his cool, but he'd make sure he conveyed to Bishop that he needed to leave Penny alone and that he didn't want to run into Holt in a dark alley.

"Why do you do everything to avoid being afraid?" he asked.

She slid him a sideways glance, then looked down at her hands. "After Mom's first movie when I was six and my sister was nine, her fame skyrocketed. She was gone so much, Dad needed help, so they hired a nanny. She decided she liked Elise, but she didn't really care to keep up with me, so she would lock me in the closet, threatening to hurt Elise if I told anyone. My sister believed the lie that I was having play dates with friends. Until one day she figured it out and told my dad. He fired the nanny and found someone else. A good one that time."

"What?" The word exploded from his lips before he could stop it.

She lifted a shoulder in a small shrug. "I was terrified, of course, but I don't really think about it unless I'm in a small, dark space or have a really stressful day and dream about it."

"Penny, I don't know what to say. That's awful."

"Yeah, it was." She adjusted her ponytail, then looked at him. "Change of subject. Your turn. What made you choose law enforcement? During all of our chats, you told me about some of your closed cases, the people you work with, the things you enjoy doing, places you'd like to travel to and see, but I don't think you've said why you chose the FBI."

His fingers flexed on the wheel. "It's kind of a long, boring story."

"So, bore me. Hit me with all the details. Every last one."

Okay, here was his chance. He'd pushed her into being honest about her family. She'd shared one of her greatest fears from her childhood. Now, it was his turn to do the same. Right. "I've told you a little about my family."

"Very little. Your dad's in landscaping and your mom is a doctor. You have two sisters. Their names are Rachel and Zoe. Zoe has two daughters, ages twelve and eight. You have a brother named Joseph and he works with a school in some capacity." She squinted and tilted her head. "Yep, that's all I know and that's as vague as you can possibly be. Fill in the details, will you?"

He gave her a slow nod. "All right. So, like I've said before, my parents are awesome. My dad owns his own landscaping business and does pretty well. In the peak season anyway. He's an outdoors kind of guy—obviously—and always has his hands in the dirt. My mom is a pediatrician with a local doctor's office. She works the eight-to-five shift every day, then comes home and digs in the dirt with Dad."

"Okay, tell me about your siblings."

He didn't mind talking about two out of the three of them. "My brother, Joseph, is a former Army Ranger and now a principal at an inner-city high school in New Orleans."

"Well, that's a calling."

"For sure."

"Rachel is a forensic artist in Atlanta, Georgia."

"Your poor parents. Everyone is all spread out. What about your other sister?"

He pulled in a fortifying breath. Could he tell her? "She's an amazing cook and has her own bakery." One that his parents were running, believing her incarceration was a mistake and she'd be home to take it back over soon.

His phone buzzed and he didn't know whether to be relieved or frustrated. "That's Gerald, my SSA," he said. "I've got to take this."

"Sure."

He inserted his earpiece, then activated the Bluetooth. "Holt here."

"ERT's gone over the car Rabor and the girlfriend stole."

"And?"

"Looks like she changed clothes once they were on the road. The nurse's uniform was in the back seat."

"Anything else?"

"Some hair and other fibers, prints, and more. But we know who they are, so I'm not so concerned with all of that. I want to know where Shondra Miller is and I want to know that yesterday."

"Me too, Gerald, me too. Thanks for the update."

"I'll let you know if I hear anything else."

He hung up and spun the wheel into Bishop's neighborhood. The closer they got, the more he noticed Penny's jaw flexing. "I'll tell you more about Zoe later. You're sure you want to do this?"

"I'm sure."

"Then let me handle this, okay?"

"What's to handle? I'm simply going to ask him what he was doing in my house."

He groaned. "Penny, like you told the officers, we don't know it was him."

"Who else would it be?"

"I don't know that either. Just bear with me and let me do the talking. Please?"

She crossed her arms. "Fine, but since this isn't an official interrogation and you're not here *officially*, if I don't like his answers, I'm jumping in."

Holt refrained from smiling, but he must have failed at totally hiding his amusement since she narrowed her eyes at him. "What?"

"You're spunky. It's a good look for you."

That pulled a tight smile from her. "It's a trait I developed out of necessity. And, Holt?"

"Yes."

"Don't let me do anything stupid."

CHAPTER
EIGHT

Penny climbed out of the passenger seat as soon as he pulled the SUV to a stop. She sucked in a deep breath and hurried up the sidewalk leading to Mike's front door.

It didn't take long for Holt to catch up with her. She jabbed the doorbell and shoved her hands into the pockets of her sweats. Maybe if she was tempted to hit the man, the act of having to remove her fists before using them would give her some time to reconsider the wisdom of throwing a punch. "I'm not a violent person," she said.

"I never thought you were."

"But if that was Mike in my house, I'm going to have a hard time turning the other cheek."

"No one's asking you to do that."

"I know. I just want him to understand that I'm not afraid of him, and if he plans on harassing me, he needs to rethink those plans because I'll get the police involved." He cleared his throat and she shot him a sideways glance. "You're not the police. Harassment investigations aren't in your job description as an agent."

"It would be in my job description as a boyfriend."

"Are you applying?"

"Maybe. Are you hiring?"

"Maybe." She was quite proud of the evenness of her tone and the fact that she was only slightly breathless at the thought of being his girlfriend. But . . . he didn't know everything about her and might not want to be with her if she unpacked all of her baggage. The thought tightened her throat, and she distracted herself by ringing the bell again and pounding on the door. "Mike!" She looked through the side window. "I can see him on the couch and he's not moving."

"You think he's asleep?"

"I don't see how he'd sleep through all that racket. He could be hurt."

Holt stepped around her to take a look. "I think that's good enough for exigent circumstances."

He tried the knob. It turned and he pushed the door open to brush past Penny. For a moment she gaped, then hurried after him. He knelt next to the man and placed two fingers on his neck.

"Is he alive?" she asked.

"Yeah. He's alive. And he's not hurt. In fact, I'd say he's probably not feeling much of anything. You smell what I smell?"

"Booze. Lots of booze."

He nodded to the cans littering the floor next to the couch and on the coffee table.

"He's completely passed out."

Penny placed a hand on Mike's shoulder and shook him. "Mike, wake up."

She got a groan, but that was it.

Holt stood. "I'm going to see if I can find some coffee and a pot."

While Holt worked in the kitchen, Penny slipped down the hall to find a bathroom. The second door on the right opened into a recently remodeled, modern bath that had her a little green with envy—and mentally taking notes for the upstairs bath she still had to renovate.

Shaking off her bathroom envy, she grabbed a washcloth from the linen closet and soaked it in cold water. When she returned to the den, she slapped the cloth over Mike's face. He gasped and sputtered but still didn't open his eyes. She shook him. Then grabbed the cloth and slapped him with it again.

"Sh-top." He waved a hand in front of his face. "Stop. What?"

"Wake up, Mike."

Holt walked over and placed a cup of black coffee on the table and Mike blinked up at her. "Penny?" He swiped a hand down his face and grimaced. "Penny? Are you real or am I dreaming?"

"I'm real. You passed out."

"Oh yeah. I got fired."

"I'm aware."

"Because . . . because . . . why'd he fire me?" He paused and squinted at her. "Oh yeah, because of you."

"Actually, you brought that on yourself. But all that aside, were you at my house tonight?" She knew the answer but had to ask.

"What? No. I . . . um . . . I left the hospital, stopped at the ABC store, came home, and drank myself into a stupor because tomorrow I have to go job hunting."

"You threatened me. You said I hadn't heard the end of you getting fired. What did you mean by that?" She glanced at Holt and noted his attention was solely focused on them.

"I was mad. And Gerry broke up with me because of everything. She said—" A sob. "She said I was the worst mistake she'd ever made." Tears spilled over onto his cheeks and Penny sighed.

She tossed him the washcloth. "Dry up, Mike." She paused while he got himself together. "You said you weren't at my house earlier and I'm pretty sure I believe you, but I need you to prove it to me."

His frown deepened, although his tears had stopped. "How?"

"Let me see your arms."

"What?"

"I hit the guy who broke into my house. Take off your shirt, will you?"

He still blinked up at her, confusion written in his eyes, his poor alcohol-saturated brain unable to keep up. "What—?"

"She hit the guy who was in her house." Holt repeated her words, more slowly this time. "Do you mind if we see if you have any bruises?"

"Oh." Mike laughed and yanked his long-sleeved T-shirt over his head. Penny ran her gaze over the man's torso, then rubbed her eyes. "Thanks." She turned to Holt. "He's bruiseless."

"I noticed."

Penny stood and shook her head at Mike. "You might want to take a couple of ibuprofen before you go back to sleep."

"Yeah. I'll do that."

"Bye, Mike."

He flopped back onto the couch with a groan.

Penny followed Holt out of the house—locking the door behind her—and climbed into the passenger seat of his SUV once more.

After they were buckled in and heading back toward her home, she leaned her head against the cold window. She was sore all over and her temples had started a painful throb. She wished she'd snagged two of Mike's ibuprofens. "If it wasn't Mike in my house, who could it have been?" she asked.

"There's no telling. I'm actually surprised it wasn't him, but he's got a pretty solid alibi. He had to have been already passed out during the time you were calling for help."

"Right." A sigh slipped from her. "So, I'm a statistic and it was probably just some random thing."

"That's my guess."

She frowned and closed her eyes, uneasy and not sure why. The serial killer was dead, Mike had been all bluster and no action when it came to his threat, and the break-in had probably been some junkie looking for something he could sell.

So why did she have a really bad feeling in the pit of her stomach?

■　■　■　■

Holt followed Penny into her home once more, thinking again how he needed to tell her about Zoe. He'd had the chance to do it and blown it. Now, he'd have to make the chance. "Walk through the house with me."

She raised a brow. "Okay, why?"

"It would just make me feel better."

She shrugged and nodded for him to follow her. They'd come in the front door, and he noted the living room to the left. The stairs just past that led up to the second floor, and the kitchen and dining area were to the right.

"Everything look okay?" he asked.

"Yes."

She led him into her bedroom located beyond the living room, and he scanned the feminine, but not frilly, area. He could tell right away this was her haven. Her escape. Sturdy cherry furniture with a light-tan-and-blue comforter on the bed and matching curtains. Her French doors leading out to the patio were shut, but they'd been her intruder's way of escape.

No, wait. "Penny?"

"Yeah?"

"Your French doors are cracked open."

She frowned. "But I shut those before we left to go to Mike's." She shot him a wide-eyed look. "I don't believe this," she muttered. "He came back?"

He rubbed his chin. "In all the chaos, you may have shut them but left them unlocked. I have a print kit in my trunk. Let me grab it real quick and see if I can pull some prints. I'll send them to Martinez and he can have them run if he thinks it's important. I mean, it can't hurt, and we need to update him on the fact that we believe the intruder came back."

"Sure."

Holt hurried out to his vehicle, grabbed the kit from the back, and returned to Penny's bedroom to find her fastening her watch around her wrist. He went to the door. "It's going to be a bit messy, but I'll clean it for you real good when I'm done."

"It's fine."

He went to work and could feel her watching him.

"Well, the timing on this seals it," she said after a moment. "It definitely wasn't Mike."

"No, he's a dead end." Holt nodded to the watch. "I've noticed that before. It's a beautiful piece of jewelry." And he hadn't bothered to ask her about it until now. He hid his wince. If he wanted Penny to think seriously about a relationship with him, he needed to step up and do something that let her know without a shadow of a doubt that she was important to him. And what was important to her mattered.

"My grandmother gave it to me when I graduated flight school," she said. "She died three months later from pancreatic cancer."

He paused in his dusting and looked up. "I'm sorry."

"Me too. She was my dad's mother. She was an amazing woman and I loved her very much."

"What did she think about your mother and all the fame?"

Penny shrugged. "Part of her was proud. Another part was sad, I think. Sad to see what it did to my sister and me and my dad. My dad kind of just closed up after a few years. I'm actually surprised he and Mom didn't go their separate ways, but I guess their relationship works for them and that's all that matters."

"Still, I'm sure it took its toll."

"In many ways. In other ways, it was good. Or at least it wound up being good. Eventually. After he fired the . . . first nanny, and hired the second—and last—we traveled the world, saw lots of different cultures, learned to love various foods, met amazing people." She shot him a small smile. "Some parts of my childhood were really incredible. I just have to remind myself of that when the bad parts want to overwhelm me."

He stood. "I got a couple of prints, but I'm willing to bet they belong to you."

"I'm not surprised."

"It was worth a shot. I'll just clean everything up now. You can keep talking."

"About what?"

"Hmm . . . I know you had a sister and she died. Do you mind sharing what happened?"

Penny's smile faded and her eyes darkened.

"Never mind," he said. "You don't have to tell me." It's not like he wanted to tell her about Zoe or explain why his sister was in prison.

"No. You're right," Penny said, "talking to one another is good." She pulled in a deep breath. "When Elise was nineteen and I was sixteen, we went skiing in Colorado with our dad. By this time, we no longer had a nanny, of course, but Mom was busy making a movie somewhere and Dad wanted to do something fun. The second day we were there, he came down with a cold but told us to go on, that he didn't want to ruin the trip for us. We took off for the slope without checking the weather forecast."

"Ouch."

"It was dark and still and had a creepy feel, but being from California, we didn't put it together. Like dumb teenagers can do, we decided that the normal runs were too tame, so we went off the path into the 'Do Not Ski' area of the mountain. There was a storm coming, but we were invincible. Thought it would be cool to ski down the side of the mountain in a blizzard." Tears welled in her eyes but didn't fall. "Only we didn't count on how truly bad the storm was going to be or that the area where we were was known for avalanches."

"Oh no."

"Yeah. We got caught in it. We were skiing ahead of it and we

saw an overhang kind of area. I told her to aim for it. She agreed.
I whipped under it and she fell trying to do the same. The rush of
snow caught her and swept her down. She grabbed a tree and held
on for a long time. I thought it might be all right. Then another
wave of snow swept over her and she was . . . gone."

He stepped over to her and curled an arm around her shoulders.
"I'm so sorry."

Penny sighed and leaned her head against his chest. "Thanks. I
found her about thirty minutes later. She was over the side of the
mountain on a cliff. Much like Claire was. I had a cell phone and
was able to call for help, but because of the high winds, no chopper could—or would—fly. Paramedics finally made it up there,
but she died on the way to the hospital. She had a broken rib that
we later learned punctured a lung. If the chopper had been able
to get there, she might have lived."

He looked at her. "So that's why you do what you do."

"Yes."

"And why you flew into that storm?"

"Yes." She looked up at him. "I mean, I'm not stupid. I won't
take chances that would endanger my flight crew. But when we
left, the storm wasn't nearly as bad—trust me, I checked numerous
times—and I really thought we could get Claire to the hospital
before it got worse. But we were delayed at the accident site. They
had to get her stable before we could get her in the air and then
the winds shifted and—" She shook her head. "We almost made
it. If we'd left five to ten minutes earlier, we would have been okay.
At least I think so. Who really knows?"

"You're a hero, Penny, I hope you can see that."

"Aw, Holt, I was just doing my job. For real. If it makes me look
like a hero, then . . ." She shrugged. "I guess it makes me look like
a hero. The truth is, Raina and Holly are the real heroes. They
kept Claire alive."

"While you fought off a serial killer and saved my life. Again.
All three of you are heroes."

She snagged his hand and her fingers entwined with his. "Thank you, Holt."

His heart pounded out a faster rhythm, like it always did when he was with Penny. He'd been enjoying getting to know her, thought she was fun and interesting and amazing. And deep. Now, he just wanted to lean over and kiss her.

Penny cleared her throat. "Holt?"

He blinked. "Yeah?"

"Your phone is buzzing like a bee on speed."

"What?" The next time it went off, he sighed and snagged it from the clip on his belt. "Hello?" He didn't mean to sound quite so snappy, but he couldn't help it.

"Holt? This is Lexie." Lexie Anderson, one of the medical examiners for the city of Asheville. He'd worked with her before on several cases and was impressed with her professionalism and attention to detail. "I've got your dead escapee here and have just finished up his autopsy."

"Let me guess. Cause of death was a stake to the heart."

"Cute. No vampires here. The knife blade was all it took."

"Okay, well, thanks for letting me know." But he had a feeling she wasn't done.

"I have some information you might find interesting—and disturbing—about this guy."

Some days he hated being right. "What did you find out about Mr. Rabor that's disturbing?"

"That's just it. Mr. Rabor isn't Mr. Rabor."

CHAPTER
NINE

Holt blinked and Penny met his gaze. He looked a little shell-shocked. "What do you mean, Mr. Rabor isn't Mr. Rabor?" he said.

Penny gaped and Holt frowned. She stayed silent while he listened. A lot of "Uh-huhs" later, he hung up.

"What is it?" she asked.

"Let's go to the den. I need to sit down."

Returning to the living room, she pointed to the couch and he sank down onto it, then dropped his head in his hands. "Holt? Come on. You're scaring me. To repeat your question, what do you mean that Mr. Rabor isn't Mr. Rabor?"

"I can't discuss this with you. I'm sorry."

"Then I'll guess. The guy in the morgue is someone who looks like Darius Rabor but isn't him?"

He studied her and sighed. "I guess that wasn't too hard to figure out, was it?"

She gulped. "But . . . yes it is. It has to be. I've seen pictures of him on the news. I watched the documentary channel 7 did after he was arrested, and they had tons of pictures of him, his family, his church, everything. He talked about how he killed his wife because she disrespected him, but now that he thought about it, it really wasn't her fault because she'd never been trained and that—" Penny snapped her lips together to stop the outpouring. "That *was* Darius Rabor who fell on his knife and died."

"Well, since you figured it out . . . I thought it was him, too, but Lexie says no."

"Why? What was it about him that makes her say that? Can you tell me?"

"No." He held up a hand. "And not because of the case. She didn't say why, just that I needed to come to the morgue and she'd explain."

"Oh . . ."

Another sigh slipped from him. "I need to go." He stood, rubbed his neck, then dropped his arm to his side. "I also need to call Gerald and see how he wants to move forward from here."

Penny rose from her chair. "Okay. I understand."

Holt pulled her to him in a quick hug and kissed her cheek. "We'll talk later, okay?"

"Sure."

He paused. "What are you going to do today?"

"I have no idea. Work on the house, I guess."

"Are you going to be able to sleep here tonight?"

"No, but I'll survive."

He groaned and settled his forehead against hers. "I'm sorry, Pen."

"It's fine. Go." She gave him a slight shove toward the front door. "I'll pack a bag and go stay at the base at the hospital when I'm ready."

"Aw, Penny, I don't—"

"Holt. Go."

"I can't. Not without you. Go pack. I'll drive you there."

"But . . ." She frowned. Did she really want to work on the house? She'd be jumping at shadows and every noise the old house made. Yeah, not today.

Ten minutes later, on their way back to the hospital, Penny

glanced at an exhausted Holt. So much for taking the time off to rest. But the truth was, she wasn't a big fan of taking time off. She liked staying busy and she loved her job.

She also needed some peace. Some time to let her nerves calm down and some time to think. Not to mention, she liked a good night's sleep. If she stayed home, that wouldn't happen. They pulled into the parking lot near the base and he dropped her off at the entrance. She turned to wave at Holt and made her way inside.

Raina was sitting at the table, munching on an apple. Her eyes widened when Penny sat in the chair across from her. "What're you doing here?"

"Couldn't sleep."

"I guess not. Are the reporters all over your house right now?"

"Not at the moment. I expect them to show up at some point. They'll figure out I bought it under a different name eventually."

"Then what's going on?"

Penny told her about the break-in at the house and confronting Mike.

The more she talked, the wider Raina's eyes got. "Are you kidding me?"

"I wish."

"Well, you can share my bed if you need to, but you're not going back home."

"Thanks, but I'll just crash on the couch. I brought a pillow and a blanket, so I'll be fine."

The door opened and Byron stepped inside. He stopped when he spotted Penny. "What're you doing here?"

"That's the question of the day." She explained once more the reason for her presence. When she finished, she narrowed her eyes at the man. "Thank you for coming to the rescue earlier. You deserve the title of hero as well. I'm sorry everyone's so focused on me—and who my mother is."

He shrugged. "I almost told Mike to stuff it, that I wasn't flying, but I couldn't do that to you guys. And I'm a little starstruck at the fact that Geneva Queen is your mom, but I also know you, and you're . . . you. So, I'll get over it." He flashed her a dimpled smile, but she could see the sincerity behind it.

"Claire's alive because of you," she said. "Don't downplay it."

"She's alive because of all of us."

"Okay. True. We'll go with that." She yawned. "Anyway, I need to take a nap. I was up almost all night and I'm wiped out."

"Oh," Byron said, "some reporter stopped me in the hallway. Seems real interested in you."

Penny rolled her eyes. "No kidding."

"I told him to get lost, but he was pretty insistent. Just giving you a heads-up that he might turn up like a bad penny." He smirked. "See what I did there, *Penny*?"

She groaned. "Like I haven't heard that one before."

"Come on, I've been waiting to use that ever since I met you."

"You, and everyone else. Go away, Byron." She couldn't express her relief that he was treating her the same, even though he knew who her mother was now. But that was Byron. He was a good guy.

He laughed and went to the refrigerator, pulled two bottles of water from it, and tossed her one. "You did good out there, Pen."

"Thanks."

"Don't worry about all the extra. It'll die down soon enough."

"Yeah."

He disappeared into the game room, and soon she heard the dings and whistles of one of the video games that he liked.

Holly joined Penny and Raina at the table. "So . . . we need a vacation. Some time away. My parents have offered their condo at the lake. Do you think we could swing having a few overlapping days off?"

"Count me in," Penny said.

Raina nodded her agreement, then turned her attention to the television.

Penny groaned. "Seriously? Don't they have anything better to cover?"

"Geneva Queen's daughter faced down a serial killer," Holly said. "No, they probably don't have anything better to cover." She reached out to squeeze Penny's hand. "What was it like up there, knowing the guy was a serial killer?" Before Penny could try to form an answer, Holly went on, releasing Penny's hand and twisting her fingers together. "I saw him in the trees. His eyes locked on mine and he swung the gun right at me. Before he pulled the trigger, the chopper shifted and I was out of the line of fire. I think that's when he shot one of the agents." A shudder rippled through her. "How could you even think straight?"

This time it was Penny who reached across the table to grasp her friend's entwined hands. "It was terrifying. All I wanted to do was make sure Holt and I survived." And if it was that scary facing down the man on the mountain, how much worse would it have been if it were the real Darius Rabor?

■　■　■

Holt sat in the parking spot outside his hotel room. He'd spent the day chasing down dead-end leads and lunatic tips. But everything had to be checked out no matter how crazy it sounded. In lieu of beating his head against a wall, he made a few phone calls. Right now, he had his SSA, Gerald Long, on FaceTime. The man was in his office looking at him, his gaze steady but weary. "Gresham's funeral is next week. His family said they're doing a small private one but would have a graveside service for anyone who wanted to come. It's going to be in Texas, though."

"I'll see where we are on this case. I really hope we have Rabor in custody at that point."

"Amen to that. Marty texted me and said he was doing fine. Julianna too. Gus . . . not so much. I'm worried about him."

The words cut deep. The men and women he worked with were more than just coworkers, they were his friends, his brothers and sisters. Family. "I know. I am too."

"Well, nothing we can do but pray for them at this point. At least the guy who shot them is dead."

"Yeah."

"So Penny had a hand in saving your hide once again. How's she doing?"

"She's doing all right." He paused. "Truthfully, she's the reason we're both still alive." He explained in detail Penny's tackle that had kept the knife from doing him harm. "This was the second time she's saved my life." Nothing Gerald didn't know, since he'd been there the first time around.

"Brave woman. She interested in a career change?"

That pulled a laugh from Holt. "No, I don't think so."

"Hmm. That's too bad. What about Shondra Miller? The girlfriend who helped Rabor escape? Because the guy in the hospital was Rabor regardless of who was on the mountain."

"Nothing so far. It's like she dropped off the planet."

Gerald pinched the bridge of his nose, then looked back at the screen. "Okay, so let's go through what we already know."

"Well, Rabor has family on that mountain. We located them last time we hunted him. We sent officers all over, into good and really bad areas, and we watched and waited." Holt paused. "That profiler was right—Rabor did eventually show up where he felt most comfortable."

"One of the worst trailer parks up there."

"If it weren't for that kid calling us, we might not have caught him when we did." The boy lived across the road from the trailer Rabor had holed up in and was afraid the man would kill them next. "The whole thing was bad from start to finish. You know how it all went down."

"But you got him."

"We did."

"And you lived to do it again. Just try not to get stabbed this time."

Holt laughed. "That's my preference."

Gerald rubbed a hand across his balding head. He was one year from retirement and expressed his total dislike of the idea on a regular basis. "What's this nonsense Lexie's saying about the stiff on her slab not being Darius Rabor? Where'd he come from?"

Holt raised a brow. *Stiff?* "You've been watching old cop shows again, haven't you?"

The man shrugged. "Gotta do something to get my mind out of these files. Anyway, Lexie?"

"I know we've only worked with her a couple of times, but have you known her to talk nonsense?"

"No, and that scares me."

"She wouldn't give me anything more than it wasn't Rabor on her table. Said she was waiting on a couple of other test results but could meet with me in the morning as long as they came in. So I'll head to the morgue first thing tomorrow."

"Call me and let me listen in on how she concluded without DNA that the man isn't Rabor. I want a firsthand account of it."

"Sure thing. I'll FaceTime you so you can see what she's talking about."

"Good enough. We've got a lot of manpower searching for Rabor. You better get some sleep. You're going to need it."

"I'm headed in that direction now. You should do the same."

"Yeah, yeah. I'm going."

Holt climbed out of his vehicle and walked into his hotel suite. It had been a very long day of producing pretty much nothing. He'd had days like this before and tried not to let it discourage him. Tomorrow the case could break wide open. He just had to be patient and do his job. Easier said than done most of the time, but he was good at what he did. Unfortunately, so was Rabor. Holt just had to be better. Again.

He set his gun and badge on the counter and flipped on the television to the local news. The refrigerator held three bottles of water and a bag of Kit Kats. He pulled out a bottle, popped the frozen dinner he'd bought in the microwave, and chugged the water.

Then he checked on Marty and Gus and got the same information that Gerald had given him. For a moment, he bowed his head and prayed for his partner and friend. The microwave and his phone buzzed one second apart.

He removed the food while looking at the screen. His sister Rachel had texted.

Call me.

With a sigh, Holt tapped her name and put the phone on speaker. It rang once.

"Finally." Her voice vibrated with anger at him and Holt closed his eyes.

"I'm sorry. I'm working a case."

"You're always working a case, but for now, thank you for calling me back."

"Sure. Hope it's not too late."

"No, it's not."

"What's going on?"

"I need you to try to talk to Zoe. She's refusing to see me, Holt, and it's breaking my heart."

"Aw, Rachel, she'd talk to you before she'd talk to me."

"Well, she's not and it's making me crazy. I keep telling her I'm not going to let this go. She didn't just pick up the gun one day and decide to shoot Owen."

"She confessed, Rachel. Until she decides to change her story, there's nothing we can do."

"Yes, she confessed, but you and I both know sometimes things aren't what they seem. I don't understand why you won't give her the benefit of the doubt."

"She said she did it. What's to doubt?" But he'd admit to the fact that he really didn't want to believe it himself, regardless of his sister's claims of guilt.

"But why? It doesn't make sense! Argh! You're so hardheaded."

"It runs in the family." He pulled in a deep breath. "Look, Rach,

I went to see her. I talked to her before, during, and after the trial. I begged her to tell me what really happened and she refused. Told me to stay out of it. She said Owen's death was her fault and she deserved to be right where she was."

Rachel's harsh breathing came through the line. "Doesn't matter. I don't care what she said. There's something else going on."

"It's been two years, Rachel. Don't you think she would have said something by now?"

"No. Not if she's protecting someone."

"Who would she be protecting? No one else was there at the house. There's no one to protect."

His phone buzzed and he glanced at the screen to see a text from Penny. "Look, I don't like Zoe sitting behind bars either, but if she wants help, she's got to be willing to ask for it. Actually, she doesn't even have to ask for it. She just needs to not push away the people offering."

"Like I said, there's more to this than what's on the surface. Help me keep pushing for the truth."

Holt swallowed a groan. "Let me think about it. Tell the kids Uncle Holt loves them."

"I'll do that. They want to know when you're taking them fishing."

"As soon as this case is over. Love you, sis."

"You too." She hung up and he turned his attention to the text.

Penny
Are you awake?

He tapped his response.

I just got in my room, had a conversation with my sister, and am getting ready to eat a tasty microwave dinner. How are you?

He checked the food in the microwave and added some more time.

Sleepy, but can't seem to keep my eyes closed.

Because she kept replaying their fight with the killer?

And ew . . . Microwave dinner? You couldn't hit
a drive-thru? That's not great, but better than
radiation food.

He chuckled and ignored that text to respond to the previous
one.

Talk to God when you close your eyes.

The microwave dinged and he removed the plate and set it on
the table.

You really think he listens?

I do.

Holt paused, then sent,

You don't?

I used to. But life just makes me wonder
sometimes.

Who do you think got you and everyone else
off that mountain in one piece?

True. Okay, I'll give him that one. I prayed and
he answered. Maybe not exactly like I wanted,
but the end result was the same. We're home
and we're safe.

You do realize that he doesn't always answer
prayers exactly like we want him to?

A laughing emoji with tears flashed on his screen.

Fully aware of that.

> Okay, just checking. Doesn't mean he's not listening, though.

He took a bite of the food. Meh. But it would take the edge off his hunger.

Her response finally flashed.

> Yeah

He wasn't sure she believed him. Or agreed. Hmm . . .

> Talk later?

> Yes. Good night, Holt. Thanks for everything.

> Night, Penny.

He hesitated.

> I have to go to the morgue in the morning and talk to Lexie. Want to meet me for breakfast after?

> Sure. Where?

> At the cafe across the street from the morgue entrance? The Broken Biscuit? I've discovered they have good coffee.

> See you there.

He set his phone next to his gun and smiled. What was it about Penny that sent his heart thumping in anticipation of seeing her again?

Not exactly sure of the answer, he decided to ignore it and take it one day at a time. One conversation at a time.

Because he still had to tell her about Zoe—and the woman who'd walked away from him because of her.

CHAPTER
TEN

Penny woke when the duty alarm went off, signaling a call. She sat up and started to stumble from her place on the couch when she remembered she wasn't the pilot on call today.

Nope, she was having breakfast with Holt. After he talked to Lexie. She was dying to know what the woman had found but knew she wouldn't be able to tell Penny. And neither would Holt.

Now that the place was basically empty, she grabbed her bag and darted for the shower. Once she was dressed and ready to face the day, Penny texted her mother.

> I'm fine, Mom.

Her phone rang. Rats. She swiped the screen. "Hi, Mom."

"Penelope Jane Carlton, how dare you ignore my calls and texts. I have been worried sick."

"Mom, stop. I texted you that I was fine and that we'd talk later."

"I didn't want to talk later!"

"Will you please stop shouting?"

Penny heard the woman take a deep breath. "Fine. I'm sorry. You know I only shout when I'm upset."

Or happy. Or annoyed. Or mad. Or—

"How could you *think* of flying into that storm? And with a serial killer on the loose?"

"I didn't know he was there, Mom."

"But to land there in the same area?"

"Right. I'm sorry I didn't pick a better place to land. I was aiming for the hospital helipad, but the tail rotor—" She bit her lip and said a quick prayer for patience. "Never mind. I did the best I could. Trust me, landing in serial-killer-free zones is high on the priority list from now on."

"You're mocking me."

"No, I'm not, but you're a brilliant woman. Even you have to realize how silly you sound."

A sniffle. A slightly suppressed sob. Penny rolled her eyes. Her mother hadn't won several Oscars because she was a B-grade actress. Penny glanced at her watch, then twisted it around her wrist. She sighed and dropped her hand. If she had a "stress" tell, that was it. "Look, I've got to go. I want to check on some friends here in the hospital."

"How's the girl? The one you rescued? She was on the news. A senator's daughter, huh?"

"Yes. And she's fine, as far as I know. Last I heard, she should make a full recovery."

"But she would have died if you hadn't been there, right?"

"Well, it was a team effort, but yes. Most likely."

Another deep breath came through the line. "I'm glad she's going to be all right."

Penny's brow rose. "Thank you. I'm glad too."

"Still don't like you flying those monsters, but at least some good came from it."

Penny's fingers went back to the watch. She forced herself to drop her hand once more. "Yes, some good came from it." She paused. "So, where are you right now anyway?"

"I'm home. Just finished the movie that will be out in a few months."

"Good. I hope it went well."

"It did."

Penny grimaced. She hated stilted conversation, but definitely didn't want to talk about herself or her job.

"Well, hon," her mother said, "now that I've talked to you, I feel better. Please be careful and consider coming home. I'm sure I could get you a part in one of my movies."

Laughter spurted before she could stop it. "Um. That's very generous of you, but no thank you. I'm very happy here in North Carolina. Tell Dad hi for me."

"I will. And Penny . . ."

"Yes?"

"Oh, nothing. I'll talk to you later. I love you."

"Love you too, Mom." She really did love the woman, she just had no patience for her self-absorbed, manipulative behavior.

Penny hung up just as the door opened and a man who looked vaguely familiar stepped inside. She tucked her cell phone into her pocket. "Can I help you?"

"Hi, Penny. I'm Frankie Olander with the *Chronicle News* and I'd love an exclusive with you."

"Why?"

He laughed. "Why? Because you're . . . you."

"Who exactly am I, Frankie?" She crossed her arms and hoped her eyes adequately reflected the chill in her heart.

He frowned. "You're Geneva Queen's daughter and a pilot who made a stunning rescue, then helped take down a serial killer. People want to know more about you."

"But what if I don't want them to know more about me? What if I like my privacy? What if I don't want to be your next big story? My mother chose that life. I didn't." He blinked and she sighed. "Look, you're probably a very nice person, but I really want you to leave me alone so I can move past all of this. Now, will you please leave?"

Frankie scowled. "I'll leave, but can't you see that this is stuff movies are made out of? You have an amazing story just waiting to be written. Let me write it."

"I don't want it written!" The shout echoed through the room, then hung between them.

"Like you said, I'm basically a nice person," he said, "but this is my job and . . . I really need your story. I'll be honest. My boss has offered a big bonus to the reporter who gets it. I'd rather have your input and tell it your way, but I'm going to tell it with or without your help."

Her face heated and she narrowed her eyes. "Get out."

"I'm not going to be the only one coming after it, but I will be the only one who'll be fair and play nice."

"Get out!" Penny's fury had found a new level.

He dropped a business card onto the table and backed toward the door. "Think about it. Please?" Without waiting for an answer, he left.

Penny let out a low growl and punched the sofa cushion.

"My boss has offered a big bonus to the reporter who gets it. I'd rather have your input and tell it your way, but I'm going to tell it with or without your help."

Over her dead body.

■　■　■　■

Holt stood outside the entrance to the morgue and tapped a text in reply to Marty's plea to come get him from the hospital.

> You better take advantage of resting while you can. I have a feeling I'm going to have some news you're not going to like when I finish talking to Lexie.

> What news? You can't just drop that and walk away. Tell me what you're thinking.

> Let me get back to you in about thirty minutes.

I hate you.

Love you too, man.

He walked into the morgue. With her back to him, Lexie stood next to the body of the man who'd tried to kill him—and would have succeeded if not for Penny. Lexie was tapping the keys on the laptop that sat on a rolling tray, oblivious to his entry. Holt cleared his throat and she jumped, then spun.

"Holt. I didn't hear you come in."

"Obviously."

"Hold on one sec while I finish this." A few more taps and she pushed the computer away from her and approached the dead man. "I guess you'd like to hear more about John Doe?"

"I would. Hold on while I get my SSA on the line." He dialed Gerald's number and waited for the man's face to appear on the screen. "You ready?"

"Ready."

He nodded to Lexie. "All right. What makes you think this guy isn't Rabor?"

"Well, for one"—she swept the sheet back from the man to display his torso from the waist up—"do you see what I see?"

Holt held the phone so Gerald could see. He heard the man's disgusted sigh. "Yeah." Holt shook his head. "No gall bladder surgical scar."

"I got Rabor's records and they did the surgery laparoscopically. There should be three tiny incisions here, here, and here." She pointed to the three locations the scopes would have gone in. "Nada. Hence the simple deduction that this is not Mr. Rabor."

"Easy enough. Then who is he? The man's twin?"

"He doesn't have a twin," Gerald said.

Lexie wiggled her finger to indicate he should move closer. "Look at his hair line." Holt again held the phone over the area she pointed to. "I shaved this part for a better look. See those scars?"

"Plastic surgery?"

"Lots of it." More pointing. "And here. And here. Look at his eyes. The scars are super faint, and you really wouldn't notice them unless you were looking for them. I was looking after I found the ones at his hairline. In addition to his eyes, the brows have been raised a bit, his nose has been thinned, and his upper lip widened and made fuller."

Holt shook his head. "So, this guy isn't Rabor, but he sure wanted to look like him?"

"That's my guess. Unfortunately, we can't ask Mr. Doe here."

"No clue who he is, huh?"

"Nope. You could go through missing persons reports all day, but without a face to put to them . . ."

"All right. What about prints?"

"I sent the card to the lab. Haven't heard back yet."

"I'll make a call," Gerald said and Holt nodded. Gerald would have the Identification Unit hopping. An escaped serial killer took priority over just about everything else.

"I also sent a DNA sample to be tested," Lexie said. "Waiting on that too."

"I got that one covered too," Gerald said.

Holt raked a hand over his head. He needed to know who this man was. "You do understand that if you're right about this—"

"I am," she said.

"—then this means I still have a serial killer out there," he said, his voice low.

"I had kind of put two and two together on that one. That's why I called you on my way into that meeting yesterday. I figured you'd want to get back out searching for the real Darius Rabor ASAP."

"You figured right."

"I would have told you more, but I was leading the meeting."

"It was enough information at the time." He narrowed his eyes. "This isn't good."

"I know, but at least he's one you know. You're not starting from scratch to catch him."

Holt grunted. "Somehow that really doesn't make me feel that much better."

She shrugged. "Sorry. I tried."

Holt went back to Gerald. "So, Rabor and the girlfriend escaped from the hospital. But this guy . . . where does he fit in? Was he at the hospital too? Or did they call him on their way to the mountain? Did he meet them there? If so, there wasn't another vehicle that we came across, right?"

"Right," Gerald said, "no vehicle."

"Then was he staying with some of Rabor's relatives and he walked over to the mountain to join the fun? What was his role supposed to be? Decoy? Sacrificial lamb? Or just a part of a very weird and deadly trio?"

"All good questions," Gerald said. "Go get the answers."

"Yeah." But even while he was asking the questions, nothing really made sense. "We'll figure it out. Do you have any more questions for the doc?" he asked the man.

"No, I think you covered everything. Keep me updated."

"Will do." Holt signed off and he caught Lexie watching him from the corner of her eye.

"What?" he asked.

"You and Penny."

Okay, he hadn't expected that. "What about Penny and me?"

"I saw the news, of course."

"Who hasn't?"

"Exactly. Is she okay?"

"She's shaken, but she's strong and resilient. She'll be fine."

A half smile curved her lips and he narrowed his eyes. "What?"

"You like her."

"What gives you that idea?"

"How protective you were when y'all came off the chopper and the media was waiting on her. You looked like you wanted to murder the lot of them."

"Hmm."

111

"Well, that was vague. I get it. We're not close friends. But I know Penny pretty well. Not that you need my endorsement, but she's a great person."

"I think she is too."

"I'm just trying to decide if you're good enough for *her*."

He coughed. "Oh."

"I'm thinking you might be."

"Well . . . um . . . thanks." He nodded to the dead guy. "You'll let me know when you have something?"

"Of course." She paused. "I heard your partner got shot. How's he doing?"

"Better. I got a text from him this morning begging me to come spring him."

"And the other agent?"

Holt frowned. "Gus. He's not faring quite as well. Keep him in your prayers."

"Will do."

Holt left, bemused at the conversation with the ME and armed with the dreaded confirmation that Darius Rabor was most likely still alive and on the run. And his doppelgänger had bought him time to disappear somewhere to hole up and heal.

His phone buzzed. A text from Penny.

I think I've effectively dodged the reporters on the hospital doorstep and I'm on the way to The Broken Biscuit.

I'm going to stop by Marty's room to see him, then check on Gus. Give me about thirty minutes.

And when he got there, he'd tell her about Zoe.

See you there.

CHAPTER
ELEVEN

Penny claimed a booth in the back of the restaurant and shrugged out of her flight jacket. The breakfast crowd had thinned and there were only a few people scattered at the tables. She'd ordered two coffees in to-go cups, hers black with sugar and Holt's with cream and a pump of chocolate.

Right in the middle of her first sip, Holt stepped through the door. As always when in his presence, her pulse went haywire. She sucked in a breath and the liquid went down the wrong way. A coughing spasm took over and Holt hurried to her.

"You okay?"

She nodded and slipped into another round of coughing. He eyed her as though unsure if he should laugh or be concerned. That made her giggle, which sent her into another spasm. Finally, she caught her breath. "I'm fine." The words sounded strangled to her ears. "Really," she said. "I swallowed wrong."

"No kidding. I never would have guessed that one."

"Ha ha." Her next sip went down like it was supposed to and she set the cup on the napkin.

Holt snagged his drink and blew on it. "Did you get any sleep?"

"A little. I felt safe enough at the base and was comfortable on the sofa, so yeah. But I had an annoying visitor this morning." She told him about the reporter and Holt scowled.

"Do I need to have a chat with him?" he asked.

"No. I handled it." She hoped. "How are Marty and Gus?"

"Marty's chomping at the bit to get back to the investigation. Gus is still hanging in there." He leaned forward. "Listen, I need to tell you something about—" His phone buzzed and he frowned. "Hold on. I need to take this."

"Something about the investigation?"

"Yeah." He snapped the phone to his ear. "What's up?"

"ERT's gone over the car Rabor and his girlfriend abandoned at the base of the mountain." Penny could hear the voice on the other end of the line and looked away, trying not to listen. Holt must have realized she could hear and turned the volume down.

"And?" He listened for a few moments, then sighed. "Okay, I'm on the way."

"What is it?"

"I'm sorry. I wanted to stay longer and talk to you."

"Don't apologize. You know it's okay and that I understand. Be careful."

He paused. "Can I call you when I get a free moment? I'd love to take you to dinner—even if it's a drive-thru."

Penny's stomach did that weird somersault thing it had a tendency to do when he looked at her like he was doing now. At least she wasn't drinking anything to choke on at the moment. "Sure, that would be nice."

He nodded. "Thanks for the coffee. Sorry to run."

"Go."

He grabbed the cup and hurried from the café.

Penny's heart thudded and her smile spread. "Yes," she whispered. Then frowned. They'd thrown around the words "boyfriend" and "girlfriend" but hadn't come back to talk about that. They were both skittish, and Penny knew finding out about her mother had thrown him for a loop. But he was trying, and she was . . . what? What was she doing? Having a relationship with Holt Satterfield would be like . . . what?

Like . . .

She couldn't come up with an appropriate analogy, but it would be like *something*. Something she'd never experienced before. And while that was exciting, it was also scary as everything. She'd have to be vulnerable, let him see who she really was, and that would not come easy.

But when had she ever done anything the easy way?

She snagged her jacket and stood to slip it over her shoulders. It was only at that moment she noticed the man sitting three booths down. Frankie Olander. For a moment, she stood still while their eyes met. He raised a brow and she huffed a sigh, then grabbed her coffee and headed for the door. At least it was just one reporter and not a whole herd of them waiting to assault her with their nosy questions.

When she stepped outside the restaurant, she scanned the area, and seeing no one waiting to pounce, she hurried back to the hospital entrance and to the base.

She found Raina and Holly sitting at the table with a woman she hadn't seen in a while. "Grace! What are you doing here?" She rushed to get a hug and then stepped back. Grace Billingsley's dark skin, long wavy hair, and light brown eyes reminded her of the reality show actress Tayshia Adams.

"Came to see you, my friend."

"How'd you know to find me here?"

"She called me," Raina said, "to catch up. We talked about you."

"Of course you did. So, are you here because of Darius Rabor?"

"I am."

Grace was a brilliant former prison psychiatrist and current field agent on Holt's squad. She was also the Columbia Division's Behavioral Analysis Unit's coordinator—and a former juvie roommate. Thankfully, none of them had ended up in the juvenile delinquent center because of felonies. That would have made a law enforcement career difficult, if not impossible.

Penny had been a habitual underage drinker and occasional runaway. After her sister's death, she'd gone wild, the grief pushing her farther and farther over the edge. She nearly drove her parents crazy with all the negative media attention. Her mother especially. They finally had enough and allowed her to be sent to a juvenile facility.

She had never had the guts to ask them if they'd paid the judge to send her, but she suspected that was the case. Looking back, she couldn't really blame them. But at the time? She had been livid.

"Penny? Yoohoo. Anyone home?" Grace was waving her hand in front of Penny's face.

Penny blinked and laughed. "Sorry. I was reliving how we met."

"One of the best days of my life."

"Mine too. So, what can I do for you?"

"I wanted to talk to you about the man you and Holt fought with on the mountain."

"What do you want to know?" It didn't look like she'd be putting that incident behind her anytime soon. Maybe she shouldn't even try yet.

"Have you remembered anything else?" Grace asked. "Any detail that you may have forgotten or considered too minor to worry about."

Penny frowned. "I don't think so. Why?"

"Because it's my job." She laughed, a throaty chuckle that didn't hold much humor. "I'm working closely with Millicent Danvers back at BAU. She suggested I have a sit-down with you."

"Still have your eye on that profiler position with BAU, don't you?"

"Of course. Millicent wasn't the profiler on this case when Rabor was arrested a year and a half ago, but she's on it now. We've both read through all the previous reports, and I plan to view video footage at the prison. However, I wanted to speak with you because you had contact with him."

"Or whoever he was."

"So you know it wasn't Rabor?"

"I was with Holt when Lexie called. He didn't tell me exactly, but yeah, I know." She glanced at Raina and Holly. "Sorry. Should I have kept that to myself?"

"No, it won't be a secret in"—she checked her phone—"about ten minutes. We're releasing an official announcement that Rabor is still alive and the public needs to be aware. And to call in any sightings to the hotline."

"Good." Penny leaned forward. "So, who was he? Who'd I kill?"

"I thought we were clear on how that man died and that it wasn't your fault."

Penny jerked at Holt's voice and looked over Grace's shoulder. "Hey."

Grace turned. "Holt, good to see you."

"And you."

He walked over and took a seat at the table, then lasered Penny with a look. "Are we not clear?"

"The clarity fluctuates."

"Well, it shouldn't, but I won't harp on that for now. I have a question for you."

"Okay."

Raina stood and motioned to Holly with a slight jerk of her head. "We'll let you guys talk."

The ladies left and Holt turned back to her and Grace. "I know you say you don't remember what the man on the mountain whispered to you, but I need you to try. I think it could be important."

Reluctantly, she let her mind return to that moment in time. "I . . . don't know. He grabbed me. Held the gun to my head." She lifted a hand to her temple. "I remember it touching me . . ." A shudder rippled through her.

She narrowed her eyes and Holt stayed still, waiting.

"He *did* say something," she said, "and I know I heard him, but for the life of me, I can't remember."

Holt pursed his lips, then shrugged. "It's okay. Keep trying to think of it and maybe it'll come to you."

She frowned. "If I heard it, why can't I remember? That seems stupid."

"No, it's not," Grace said. "That was an incredibly high-stress moment. In fact, you had a few high-stress moments leading up to that one. Your mind was in survival mode."

Penny closed her eyes, remembered her panic, her terror, her desperate desire to save Holt, and the overwhelming will to live.

She also remembered the weapon pressing against her temple.

The feel of him behind her, trapping her.

Her mind scrambling for an escape.

His hot breath brushing her ear.

The words . . .

What were the words?

She opened her eyes. "I don't know, but . . ."

"But what?"

She rubbed her temple. "He was muttering, almost like he was talking to himself, but he wasn't . . . talking exactly, he was . . . mumbling or . . ." Penny pressed her palms to her eyes.

"Penny, stop," Grace said. "Don't push it. It'll come."

Penny stood. "If it's important, I need to remember. And it's like it's right there on the tip of my tongue." She planted her hands on her hips. "What do I need to do to remember? You keep saying don't push it. What if I want to push it? What will help?"

Grace pursed her lips and shook her head. Then sighed. "Nothing's a hundred percent, but . . ."

"But?" Penny asked.

"Maybe seeing the body would help."

■ ■ ■ ■

"No," Holt said, recoiling from the idea. "She definitely doesn't need to see the body."

Penny gaped. "I don't think that's your call to make."

He held up a hand. "I know. I know. But you're already having trouble sleeping. Do you think seeing him is going to help with that?"

"I have no idea. But it probably can't hurt. Either I don't sleep because I keep reliving the terror, or I don't sleep because I see him dead. What difference does it make?"

"It might actually help," Grace said. "Seeing him in the morgue and knowing he's not coming back . . ." She shrugged.

Penny nodded. "Fine. Let's go."

It was Holt's turn to blink. "What? Now?"

"Yep. He's in the morgue, which is downstairs. We don't even have to get in the car." She grabbed her phone, tucked it into her back pocket, and headed for the door.

Holt exchanged a look with Grace and they both hurried after her.

"Hold on, Penny, we'll get you in."

He caught up with her, letting Grace bring up the rear. Penny threw open the door and came to a stop. Holt barely managed to keep from slamming into the back of her.

"You're still here?" Penny demanded.

Holt looked around her to see who she was talking to and spotted a man who looked vaguely familiar. Holt sized him up in about three seconds. Early thirties, Asian features, intelligent dark eyes, and a physique that said he worked out on a regular basis. Holt put him around five feet nine inches.

"I thought I made myself clear," Penny said.

"You did. I think I did as well."

"Penny?" Holt asked.

"Holt, meet Frankie Olander, star reporter for the *Chronicle News*. He's working hard to get that big bonus his boss offered for a story on yours truly."

"Pleased to meet you, Special Agent Satterfield." The man held out his hand, and Holt narrowed his eyes, then shook it. Possibly squeezing a little harder than necessary.

Frankie never flinched. A smidge of respect reared its head, but Holt kept that to himself, as he didn't think Penny would appreciate it.

Frankie's gaze swept past Holt. "Special Agent Dr. Grace Billingsley. Nice to see you here as well, showing your support for your longtime friend. I'd love to get your input on what it was like to know Penny as a teenager while you two were in juvie together."

The respect faded. That was weird. Like one step away from the stalker factor.

"No comment," Grace said. "Come on, Penny." She took one side and Holt took the other.

"Bye, Frankie," Penny said. "Don't come back or I'll have to file a restraining order."

"For what? I was in the hallway."

She didn't answer, just shoved her fists into her flight jacket pockets and kept walking. They took the elevator down to the basement. When Penny stepped out, a visible shiver went through her, and Holt slid an arm across her shoulders. Grace shot him a sideways glance and a raised brow. He raised his brow right back.

She shrugged. "Yes, I was in juvie with Penny."

"So, is this some kind of reunion? You, Julianna, and Penny? You were in California, right? How did you all wind up on this side of the country?"

"Simple. We came out together."

"Oh." He let his arm fall away when they reached the door that would take them down the hallway to the autopsy room.

Penny looked up at him, then grabbed his hand. She gave it a squeeze, then let go and took a deep breath. Holt opened the door for her and followed her through, then held the door for Grace.

Lexie was the one working, and Holt was glad for Penny's sake.

The ME looked up from her laptop and adjusted her glasses over the bridge of her nose. "Penny?" Her gaze whipped to Holt's and she nodded. "Hi, guys."

"Hi," Penny said. "I need to see the man from the mountain."

Lexie frowned. "Why?"

"He said something to me while we were up there, and I need to remember what it was."

"And you think seeing him is going to help that?"

"I don't know, that's why I'm here."

Holt figured Penny's patience with all of them was about to run out. Lexie must have caught on too.

"Right this way." She walked to the steel locker that held the sheet-covered body, opened it, and slid the gurney out. "Ready?" Lexie looked over the top of her glasses at Penny.

"I guess."

Lexie pulled the sheet back and Penny stared. Holt held out a hand, thinking he might have to offer some kind of support, but she didn't move.

"Who is he?" she finally asked. "I need to know who he is."

Lexie flicked a glance at Holt and he nodded. "Still waiting on DNA results to come back," she said.

Penny pulled in a deep breath. "Okay. Thank you."

"You remember what he said?" Grace asked.

"No, but I do remember he wasn't talking, he was singing."

Holt let out a humorless chuckle. "I'm sorry, what? He was singing?"

"Yes."

"Singing what?" Grace asked.

Penny ran a hand down her face and shrugged. "I don't know. The tune was . . . familiar. Like I've heard it before, but it wasn't something I keep in my playlist."

"Would you recognize it if you heard it again?"

"It's just a feeling, but yeah." She nodded. "I think I would."

"Can you hum it?"

She hesitated like she was trying to pull the tune from her memory banks, then shook her head. "No."

"All right," Holt said, "you need any more time here?"

Penny shook her head and walked a few steps away while Lexie slid the dead man back into his temporary frozen quarters.

Grace and Lexie chatted, and Holt placed a hand on Penny's shoulder to guide her away from the two. "You okay?"

"I'm . . . I don't know what I am." She blew out a low breath. "But in some weird way, I think it did help to see him. Thank you."

"Want me to follow you home?"

"No, it's—" She stopped. "Yes, I'd like that. I can make sure those windows get put in today and get the alarm system put in."

"If you want the alarm system installed today, I know a guy."

"Of course you do." She nodded. "Home sounds good."

CHAPTER
TWELVE

Home *felt* good. In spite of the break-in. Holt stayed with her, talking on the phone in her den while she made arrangements to have someone come put the windows in. She could do it herself with a little help, but that would take time and she wanted it done now. Or at least as quickly as possible.

Holt stepped into the kitchen. "Benny said he could come install the alarm system around noon. You okay with that?"

"Sure. Thank you. The window installer is on the way. I told him what happened, and he was very sympathetic, and since it's only two windows, he said it wouldn't take him long." She frowned. "Don't you need to be out tracking down Rabor?"

"I want to be, but I don't have much to go on right now. The task force is busy. Someone's at the prison going through all of the footage to see if there's anything that might give us a hint of where he might go to hole up while he heals. We've got agents talking to relatives and friends and everyone else we can find."

"Sounds typical in this kind of investigation."

"It is. The thing that's going to take it to the next level is putting a name to the dead man."

She nodded. She really wanted to know that too. "Will you tell me who he is when you find out?"

"Yeah, it won't be a secret. It'll be all over the news."

She yawned and he motioned toward the couch. "You want to take a nap? I've got my laptop with me and can do some work while you sleep."

She hesitated. "If I was really tired, I'd take advantage of that, but for now, I think I'll work in the upstairs bathroom peeling that nasty green wallpaper off while I wait on the window guy."

"Want some help?"

"No, you need to work. I'll be fine. Just direct the window guys up there when they get here, will you?"

"Sure."

While he went to get the laptop from his car, Penny grabbed her supplies from the hall closet and climbed the stairs to the second floor. For a moment, she simply stood looking right, then left. A sense of pride filled her. She'd come a long way from the scared and grieving teen in juvie to present day.

She heard Holt return and smiled. She liked having him there. She liked him a lot and she knew he liked her too. The thought curved her smile south. Holt deserved someone without so much baggage. Not to mention the current trouble she was having with the media. She still couldn't believe they weren't camped out just beyond her property line.

But they weren't yet, and she'd take that as a win.

For the next forty-five minutes she worked, stripping the paper from the wall. Occasionally she'd hear Holt downstairs. Once, she heard him pacing while he spoke on the phone.

Then the doorbell rang. An hour later, she had two new windows installed. Three hours after that, she had a shiny new alarm system wired to the control panel just inside her kitchen door.

She studied it with Holt at her side. "You realize I'm going to set this thing off by accident, right?"

"You get a couple of freebies before they start charging you."

"Awesome."

"But you feel safer with it, right?"

"I do." She smiled up at him. "Thank you for making it happen so fast."

"Hey, what good are having connections if you can't put them to use every so often?" His phone buzzed and he glanced at the screen. "Excuse me."

"Of course."

While he took the call, Penny cleaned up the area under the windows, then went back to stripping the wallpaper in the bathroom. Just as she pulled the last strip off, she heard Holt's footsteps on the stairs.

"Hey," he said from the door. "DNA came back on the guy in the morgue. I'm heading back to the hospital to pick up Marty."

"Wow, that was fast."

"They rushed it due to the fact we have a serial killer on the loose, and the dead guy in the morgue is our only tangible lead at the moment. The more we know about him, the faster we're liable to catch Rabor. Are you going to be all right?"

"Yes. I'm just going to start prepping this wall for painting. Might as well take advantage of the extra time while I have it."

He shot her a smile. "I'll be back as soon as I can."

She met his gaze. "Will you tell me who the guy is as soon as you can?"

"Absolutely."

Penny waited until she heard him set the alarm, then finished prepping the walls while her mind replayed the incident on the mountain.

Please let them find out who that guy was.

■ ■ ■ ■

Holt drove to the hospital, berating his cowardice the entire way. He'd managed to blow it yet again. He'd had the perfect opportunity to tell Penny about Zoe and he wimped out. Not that he hadn't had business to take care of first and then things got a little crazy with the alarm installation. But he could have taken a few moments to fill her in.

He'd tell her next time he saw her. He found his partner sitting in a wheelchair, crutches across his knees and ready to go.

Marty scowled at him. "Took you long enough."

"Dude, I got here when you said to be ready."

"I know. I'm just itching to be gone from here."

"Then let's go."

They loaded Marty into the passenger seat of Holt's SUV, and Holt pulled away from the loading zone to head toward the hotel.

"How's Gus?" Marty asked. "No one's given me much of an update lately."

"Last I heard, he was doing better. Still in a medically induced coma, but there was talk of bringing him out of it in the next couple of days."

"Good. How's Penny?"

Holt filled him in. At the hotel, Marty maneuvered himself into the room and settled on the couch with the crutches at his feet.

"You handle those like a pro," Holt said. He set his laptop on the table and opened it.

"High school football injury. I told you about it. Was on crutches off and on for a year, thanks to surgeries."

"I thought you were making that up because you run so slow."

"Oh, please."

Marty rolled his eyes and emotion grabbed Holt by the throat in an unexpected move. He gave a light punch to his friend's arm. "I'm glad you're okay, man."

"Thanks. I am too."

Holt positioned the laptop for the virtual conference meeting and logged in using the secure link. His SSA's face filled the screen, and in smaller boxes, he noted several other members of the task force, including Richard Gaines, the RA for the Asheville office, as well as Lexie.

Her glasses sat on the tip of her nose, and she had her hair pulled up in a curly ponytail that looked like it had been shoved up in a hurry.

"All right, folks," Gerald said, "first things first. Marty, glad to see you doing so well."

"Thanks, Ger."

"Second, the K-9 team searching the mountain—using the scent from the nurse's uniform left in the car—found a blond wig. We assume this to be the one Rabor's girlfriend has been wearing all this time—even on her visits to the prison. Only we suspect that the girlfriend wasn't really a girlfriend. We suspect that the guy in the morgue has been using the female disguise in order to hide his look-alike features from cameras and the general public who know what Rabor looks like."

"So, Lexie," Holt said, "will you please fill us in on who the dead man in your morgue is?"

"Absolutely. His name is Joel Allen. He's thirty-eight years old and shares the same birthday with Darius Rabor. Hospital records show they were actually born four minutes apart. Albeit in different hospitals, but kinda creepy if you ask me." Sounds of agreement echoed through the speakers.

"Thanks, Lexie."

"You're very welcome. Let me know if you need anything else."

She signed off and Gerald cleared his throat. "Allen's DNA was in the system because of a prior arrest for shoplifting. He got off with a slap on the wrist and an order to behave himself."

"Did he?" Richard asked.

"Looks like it. Or he was never caught if he didn't. By all appearances, he's been squeaky clean ever since."

"Until a couple of days ago," Holt said, "when he assisted Darius Rabor's escape from the hospital and helped kill a few people in the process."

"Yeah." Marty's anguish came through loud and clear.

"So, our next move is to find out all we can on Joel Allen," Gerald said. "Track down his family, friends, church, cult, underground bunker. Whatever. I want to know everything God knows about this man."

"We're not that good," Holt said, "but we'll do everything possible and pray that God reveals what we need to know along the way."

"Or that." Gerald waved a hand. "Daria Nevsky is your analyst. Anything you need, send it her way. Holt, she's already got Allen's address pulled up and is sending it to you. I know you'll want to go talk to his wife."

"I will." *ASAP.*

"We're reviewing security footage and talking to the guards about Rabor's visitors and who he was in touch with on the outside. It's actually pretty unbelievable."

Holt frowned. "What are you talking about?"

"I'm getting there. His parents came once a month like clockwork. He has a brother who's never visited, and he had a bevy of thrill-seeking ladies who thought it would be exciting to 'date' a serial killer while he was behind bars. Rabor met with each and every one who was approved, which means he met with someone at least once or twice a week."

"At his level of security? How is that possible?" Higher security warranted less visitation opportunities—or at least it was supposed to.

"Apparently, the warden made a little deal with Rabor. The better he behaved, the more visits he got. And they kept it all secret from the other inmates."

Holt huffed an aggravated breath. "If the other inmates ever found out . . ."

"Talk about riots. I know." Gerald heaved a sigh and rubbed his eyes. "But so far, no one's said anything. Turns out the warden does this with a few of the other violent offenders as well. It's some kind of experimental program that he got approval for." He shrugged. "Gotta say, it seems to be working. Violent offenses in the prison have dropped by about fifty percent."

"Okay, thanks. Good to know."

"That's all I've got. Richard?"

"We're going strong on this end," Richard said. "Rabor's face will be back on the news tonight. We've got the hotline up and ready to take calls. We'll work together and find this guy, preferably before he kills anyone else."

Gerald leaned back in his chair. "All right, everyone, let's go."

Holt logged off and looked at Marty. "Sorry you have to sit this one out, partner."

"Me too."

The man scowled and Holt clapped him on the shoulder. "Your ride will be here soon."

"Yeah."

Holt gathered Marty's items for him. He'd be off duty until cleared by his doctor to return. Hopefully they'd have Rabor in custody long before that happened. In the meantime, Holt and Grace would be working together. A fact that suited him just fine. She wasn't Marty, but she was an excellent agent and he trusted her.

He checked his phone. His sister had called twice during the meeting. Once he was back in his SUV, he dialed Rachel's number.

"Thank you for calling me back."

"I was in a meeting. What's up?"

"I have Zoe's phone. I've been trying to get into it for two years and I did it." She gave a breathless laugh that morphed into a sob. "I finally figured out her password and I got in."

He frowned. "Okay."

"Holt, I found a video that very clearly shows Owen and Zoe arguing the night he was shot."

"What were they arguing about?"

"I'm not sure. The audio isn't very good, but I think they were arguing about their housekeeper, Yvette. Zoe wanted her to go and Owen didn't."

"What?" He'd never heard Zoe and Owen fight. Had never

once heard a cross word between the two of them. "And they were fighting over that?"

"It shook me, Holt. Seriously. I've never heard Owen sound like that before. Not in all the years he and Zoe were married. It's rocked everything for me. Everything I thought about them."

With dread curling in his gut, he swallowed. "Send it to me. I'll watch it as soon as I get a chance."

"And, there's more." Her voice hitched on a sob and he stiffened.

"What?"

"Ellie was there."

"What? I thought she was next door spending the night with her neighbor friend."

"I thought so, too, but you can see her reflection in the glass door that leads to the patio."

"Well, that changes things. What does Ellie say?"

"That she doesn't remember anything. She says she was never at the house, that she was at the sleepover."

"I'm confused."

"That makes two of us. We need to go see Zoe at the prison and find out if this will pry her tongue loose. Because she's hiding something. Big-time."

"Yeah. Okay. You've convinced me. I'll get back to you soon."

"I'll be working on the visit."

"Where's the housekeeper?"

"I don't know. I tried calling her, but her phone's disconnected and she's not at the address on her application."

"Give me her name and everything you know about her. I'll find her." Or the local investigator who'd handled the case would. Homicide detective Matt Nixon. He and Holt had become friends in spite of the investigation that found his sister guilty of murder. Holt didn't hold that against Matt. He hadn't shot Owen. Zoe had.

"Of course."

He hung up, his pulse pounding in confusion—and hope. If Ellie was there that night, it was possible, with help from a trained psychiatrist, she might be able to remember exactly what happened.

Then again, it might be more merciful to let her keep that night buried. But what about Zoe? What if she really didn't shoot Owen?

He'd wait for Rachel to get the video to him and then decide what to do about it.

With a conflicted heart, Holt aimed his vehicle toward the address Daria had texted him. He was very anxious to meet with Sally Allen, Joel's wife, because he desperately needed a lead on Rabor—and at the moment, she was their only hope.

CHAPTER
THIRTEEN

Penny jolted awake, heart racing, blood chilled, a tune playing in her head. *His tune.* Nausea swirled and she had to take several breaths before she could convince herself that she was safe.

She'd fallen asleep on the couch after showering off the dust and sweat left from her physical afternoon. She lay there for a moment, letting the tune run through her mind once more. She knew the song, so why couldn't she name the title?

"Argh." She threw the blanket off and stood. The lamp she'd left on was now off. Okay.

Penny grabbed her cell phone and darted into the kitchen to find the oven clock blank. No green numbers glowed the time.

"Power's off," she muttered. "Why?" A glance out the window revealed no storm, rain, or snow, so . . . what was the deal?

Her stomach twisted even as her eyes found the alarm keypad on the wall. The backup battery had kicked in and the system was still armed. Her pulse slowed slightly. No one was in her house this time, simply because there was no way in without setting off the ear-splitting screech.

Rubbing her chilled arms, she walked back into the den. "I'm getting a dog." She paused. "No, I'm going back to work. Anything's got to be better than this." She'd call Dr. Kirkpatrick in the morning and request to finish her shift.

Once she'd called the power company and was assured someone would look into her outage, she turned on the gas logs, fixed herself a cup of hot tea on the gas stove, and settled back onto the couch to watch the flames flicker and dance.

When her phone buzzed, she jumped, nearly spilling her tea. "Good grief. Get a grip, Pen." She set the cup and saucer on the end table and swiped the screen. "Hi, Holt."

"Penny, you okay? You sound a bit breathless."

"I'm fine." She wasn't going to cry on his shoulder. Again. "What's up?"

"I wanted to check on you."

"Well, my power's out, but other than that, I'm all right."

"Why's your power out?"

"No idea, but I'm safe inside with my new little alarm system, still nicely armed thanks to the backup battery, so I feel safe."

"Oookay." He drew the word out. "I'm not sure I like that."

"Well, it happens sometimes. Hopefully, it'll be back on shortly. Now, fill me in on what you can."

"We have the identity of the John Doe. We're going to pay a visit to his wife."

"Now?"

"Yeah, she lives about fifteen minutes up the mountain."

Penny hesitated, then sighed. "Do you think I could go with you? I feel like I should . . . apologize or something."

"Penny—"

"I know, I know. I have nothing to apologize for, but I just—" A knock on her door stilled her.

"Penny?"

"Someone's at my front door."

"Who?"

"I have no idea. But if it's that blasted reporter, I may have to hurt him."

"I'll stay on the phone with you while you check."

Penny didn't argue. She walked to the front. "Who's there?"

Silence.

Her heart rate kicked it up a notch.

"Penny? Talk to me."

She stood to the side of the window and peered out. "No one's there."

"This scenario does not make me happy."

"I can relate. Makes me wish I lived in a neighborhood right now." Okay, she was nervous. Her pulse pounded and her hands shook. No, she wasn't nervous, she was scared. Her jaw tightened. She hated being scared. Loathed the feeling. "What do I do, Holt?"

"Stay on the line. I'm headed that way."

"You can't keep coming to my rescue."

"Why not?"

"Because—"

"Yeah? I'm listening."

Penny moved into her kitchen. She heard his car door shut and the engine start. "Because you have a job to do."

"You're a part of that job right now, so I'm not seeing what the problem is."

She started to smile, then frowned. Was that movement in her backyard?

"So, have you gotten that dining room painted yet?" he asked. "I'm three minutes away."

"Not yet. It's on the list." Another flicker of motion in the backyard that was gone so fast she wasn't sure it was ever there. Her imagination? But someone had knocked on the door. For what? To get her outside?

"Penny?"

She appreciated what he was doing. Keeping her talking was keeping her calm.

At least it was until the alarm screeched its warning.

■ ■ ■ ■

When the alarm sounded, Holt flinched. "Penny?"

She didn't answer, but he wasn't sure if that was because something had happened to her or because she simply couldn't hear him over the wail of the racket. "Penny!"

He was only about a minute away from her and it felt like two hours. Finally, he pulled up to her house. The alarm was still sending out its piercing shrieks. Holt pulled his gun and aimed himself for the front door. "Penny!"

The alarm stopped and Holt froze at the sudden silence. Then the door swung open and Penny appeared, fingers wrapped around a baseball bat, face frozen in a mask of fear and fury.

She let out a low gasp when she saw him and lowered the bat. "Holt."

"Are you okay?" he asked. "What set off the alarm?"

"I don't know. Someone knocked. If he pulled on the door and jarred the sensor, it could have set the alarm off. Maybe trying to get me outside?"

"Possibly. Glad you didn't open the door."

She shot him a scowl. "I'm not that dumb. I thought I saw someone out there, so I let the thing ring until you got here. It took me a couple of tries to get it shut off."

"Did you recognize anyone?"

"I never saw an actual person, just some movement, but I'm guessing it was that snoopy reporter trying to get in. I was going to give him a piece of my mind." Her phone rang and she gave the password to let the alarm company know they could call off the cops.

Holt glanced around. "All right. Here's the deal. I need to follow up on a lead that just came in, but I'm not leaving you here alone."

"I'll be fine."

He shook his head. "Come with me." *Technically*, he should leave her there, but at the moment, she was a key witness and he

needed to protect her. Writing the FD-302 of the upcoming interview was going to be a load of fun, as he'd have to include Penny
in the list of those present—which could make her a defense witness. Potentially. The federal prosecutor would have a fit, but at
the moment, it couldn't be helped.

"Why?"

He hesitated. "We're going to see the man's wife. Maybe she'll
say something that will trigger your memory or she'll know what
song he was singing."

"You really think it's that important?"

He scraped a hand over his head. "I don't know, to be honest,
but I don't want to discount it and have it be something I should
have paid closer attention to."

Penny nodded, then shrugged. "All right, but don't you think
she'll recognize me from the news?"

He frowned. "Good point. Do you have a hat and some glasses?
And you can leave your hair down."

"I'll see what I can find."

While he waited, he scanned the area. Nothing seemed out of
the ordinary. Had someone been there and been scared off by the
alarm? Was it the reporter? Or . . . something else?

But what kind of *something else*?

He didn't know. "You're being paranoid," he muttered.

"Talking to yourself?" She stepped onto the porch and shut the
door behind her.

"Occupational hazard."

She laughed. "I do it too." She'd found a dark blue hat and a
pair of pink sunglasses that concealed her gray eyes. Her red-tinted
hair lay in soft waves around her shoulders and he blinked at the
transformation. "You look great."

"Thanks." She pulled the cap lower. "Think this will do the
trick?"

"Definitely."

Once she was buckled into the passenger seat, Holt climbed

behind the wheel and called Grace. "I'm on the way. Penny's coming with me."

"See you there."

He appreciated she didn't ask why he would bring Penny. He'd explain his reasoning later. She'd probably agree, might even have some suggestions on how to use the wife to jolt Penny's memory—assuming the wife didn't know the name of the song. And while Holt could have left Penny in a safe place, he felt better with her at his side where he could keep a close eye on her.

Twenty minutes later, he pulled to the curb of the small two-story home. It sat on approximately two acres and had two outbuildings in the back. A lawn mower sat rusting off to the side. A pink bike leaned against the front porch pillar, and a baseball glove had been tossed onto a hammock tied between two oak trees.

Penny hung back while Grace rapped on the door. Holt had already made sure the woman was home. She worked various shifts as a nurse for a local twenty-four-hour urgent care facility to supplement the income Joel had been bringing in. But today was Saturday and her day off.

Footsteps sounded from inside and the door opened. A young woman with a toddler on her hip looked up at them with wariness. "Yes?"

Holt and Grace identified themselves as agents and introduced Penny, simply using her first name. No one gave her a label and Mrs. Sally Allen didn't seem to care.

"FBI agents? What do you want?" she asked.

"We have some bad news," Holt said.

Dread filled her eyes and she swallowed. "What kind of news?"

"It's about your husband. Do you mind if we come in?"

She hesitated, then stepped back. "Sure."

Holt led the way inside to see a young girl sitting on the couch with a book in her lap. She looked up when they entered. "Hi."

"Hi." Holt walked over to her and knelt in front of her. "I'm Holt. Who are you?"

"I'm Mary and I'm seven. That's JoJo." She pointed to the little boy in his mother's arms. "He's two."

"I'm very happy to meet you. What are you reading?"

"*Charlotte's Web.*"

"Wow. That's pretty advanced for a seven-year-old, isn't it?"

Mary giggled. "That's because *I'm* advanced, right, Mama?"

"You sure are, kiddo," her mother said.

"This one's a library book," Mary said. "I left my book at my friend Dee's house, and Mama said there was no way she was buying me another copy."

The woman huffed. "Mary—"

"Well, you did."

Sally's face tightened, but her lips curved in a slight smile. "You're right, I did, but we don't have to tell everything we know."

"Dee said—"

"Mary, hush. We can talk about that later. Take your book and your brother into your room and play, okay, sweetie?" She set JoJo on the floor and he ran over to Mary to take her hand.

The little girl sighed. "Come on, JoJo. The big people want to talk and don't want us to hear."

Holt turned to Sally. "Smart kid you've got there."

"Too smart." She sighed and rubbed her forehead. "What about Joel?"

"Could we sit down?"

She gestured to the couch little Mary had just vacated. Once they were all seated, she looked at Holt. "You're scaring me. What is it?"

"I'm sorry to tell you that Joel . . . died the day before yesterday."

She blinked, then gaped. "What? Died? Joel's dead? Wha—How? Two days ago?"

"We've only learned his identity. As soon as we found out who he was, we came to tell you." Holt leaned forward and clasped his hands together between his knees. "Mrs. Allen, didn't you think it odd when Joel didn't come home for the last two nights?"

"No. Not at all." She stood and paced from one end of the room to the other. "We're in the process of separating. Sometimes he stays elsewhere. And before you ask, I don't know where he stays. I don't care, as long as it's not here." She hesitated. "But he's a good father—when he chooses to be—and I let him see the children whenever he asks to. Or I did."

Well, that explained a lot. Especially the lack of tears. But her shock at hearing of her husband's death had been real enough. "Ma'am, have you seen the news of the man killed on the mountain?"

"Yes, I believe I heard something about it." She gave a short laugh. "I don't watch a lot of television, and when it's on, it's usually on *PAW Patrol* or *Peppa Pig*."

"Understandable. I hate to say this, but the man who was killed on the mountain was your husband. He impersonated a nurse at the hospital and helped the serial killer, Darius Rabor, escape."

Her eyes widened, and for a moment she seemed to be at a loss for words. She sank back into her chair, then sucked in an audible breath. "But . . . but that's . . . that's . . . No, it can't be."

"I'm sorry."

She sat frozen for a moment, staring at him like she expected him to say "Just kidding" or something.

"Is there anyone we can call for you?" he finally asked.

Sally rubbed her eyes. "Um, no. I . . . no."

Holt caught Grace's eye, and she gave a slight shrug, then leaned forward. "Sally, do you mind if we ask you some questions?"

"I guess."

"Have you heard of a man by the name of Darius Rabor?"

"You just said he was a serial killer, but yes, I remember the news stories about him a couple of years ago, maybe a documentary or something one night." She paused. "Actually, I think Joel watched it a few times. But other than that . . ." She spread her hands, indicating that was all she knew.

Holt studied her. "Do you know what he looks like?"

She let out a low, humorless laugh. "No. I mean, I probably saw his face on the news, but if I ran into him at the grocery store, I wouldn't know him. Why?"

"Your husband had a lot of plastic surgery done. Do you know why?"

She let out a huff and shook her head. "That was one of our big issues. He wasn't happy with his appearance and was spending truckloads of money on the surgeries."

"Where did he get the money?"

Sally sighed. "He was left a lot by his grandfather. Instead of saving it, like we agreed when we found out he would be getting it, he spent it hand over fist on plastic surgery, of all things!" Her chest heaved with her agitated breaths. She closed her eyes. "I'm sorry, it just infuriates me that I was struggling to put food on the table for my children and he—" She waved a hand. "Never mind. I'm sure you get the idea."

"Yes, and I'm sorry."

"I told him to leave." A sob slipped out and she pressed her fingers to her lips. "I don't know what happened," she whispered. "He wasn't like this ten years ago. At least I didn't see it if he was, but in the last three or four years, he's become someone I don't know. Someone I don't like or even love anymore."

"It's always tragic when someone in a marriage changes," Grace said. "Not just himself, but his priorities. Especially if both agreed to a previous plan."

"Yes," Sally said, "exactly."

"One more question," Grace said. "Did your husband have a favorite song or something that you might hear him humming under his breath occasionally?"

"No. Not that I can remember. He liked oldies. Show tunes, television theme songs, that kind of thing, but I can't remember him saying he had a favorite."

Well, that was a bust. He glanced at Penny and she was staring at her hands, but she was listening, taking in every word. Her shoulders were stiff, her breathing slow and measured, tension in every line of her body.

Holt focused on Sally. "Do you know why he decided to do the plastic surgery?"

She shook her head. "He said he needed it to feel better about himself. To finally look like he was destined to look. Just a bunch of garbage that didn't make much sense to me. I thought it was all ridiculous and didn't hesitate to tell him so."

Holt held up his phone and turned it so she could see the screen that displayed two pictures. "The one on the right is your husband. The one on the left is Darius Rabor."

Sally gasped. Stared. Her eyes flicked from one photo to the other while the color drained from her cheeks. "What in the world? You're kidding me. He was turning himself into Rabor's twin? But . . . why?"

"That's what we're here to find out."

CHAPTER
FOURTEEN

Penny kept replaying the scene on the mountain in her head. Over and over. She'd tripped Rabor—or rather, Allen—he'd stumbled back and fallen, the knife plunging straight into his heart. She knew if she hadn't acted, Holt would have been seriously injured or killed.

She *knew* that.

And was completely grateful that Holt and she were alive and well. She just wished she hadn't been the one to precipitate Allen's death. That it hadn't had to end that way.

But . . . everyone had choices. Joel Allen had made his and died because of them. Period. She really needed to keep that at the forefront of her mind.

"Can you think of anything else that might help us figure out why Joel was so obsessed with Rabor?"

Grace's question snapped Penny from her thoughts.

Sally shook her head. "I can't. When he started doing the surgeries, at first it was, 'I don't like my nose. I'm going to have it fixed.' Then it was, 'My eyelids and brows need lifting. It will help me see.' And so on. I watched our money dwindle and confronted him. It enraged him. He screamed it was his money and to stay out of his business. I was so angry, but he was becoming more and more . . . scary. It frightened me to the point that I felt like I needed him to leave."

"What about the children?"

"He'd never hurt them." She rubbed her eyes. "He practically worshiped them. Thought they could do no wrong. Even when they were screaming their heads off, all he would say is, 'That's what children do.'"

"And yet, you were scared for yourself."

"I was . . . and I wasn't. I know that's confusing, but Joel's father killed his mother when he was young. It haunted him. He was very firm in his belief that children needed their mother. So, truthfully, I really didn't think he'd go so far as to kill me, but I found myself unable to sleep worrying about if he would snap. He might not plan in advance or deliberately cause my death, but what if, in his anger, he . . ."

"Did something he'd regret?"

She nodded. "And . . . I couldn't handle the stress he was putting on our finances." She swallowed and looked out the window for a moment. "The day I came home and realized we had no money to pay the power bill and no money for groceries and my children were hungry, I lost it. Screamed at him to get out. We fought and I could tell he didn't think I was serious. But when I started throwing things at him and tossing his clothes out the door, he figured it out pretty quick. I think it stunned him. He quit fighting and left. As soon as he was gone, I asked a neighbor to babysit, opened a checking account in my name only, and changed the locks on the house." She lifted her chin. "I let him see the kids because I had no way to legally keep him from them, but I never left him alone with them."

"How did he react to your desire to separate?"

"At first he was livid, declaring he'd sue me for custody of the children. I promised him he could see the children any time he wanted."

"And he believed you?"

She drew in a shuddering breath. "I don't think so. Not at first, but that night, he found another place to stay. He was gone for three days and I didn't hear a word from him. Then he showed up out of the blue, saying he wanted to see the kids. I knew he was testing me, so I didn't hesitate. I stepped back and told him to come in." A small smile curved her lips. "I think I actually managed to surprise him."

"How did that visit go?"

"It went fine." She shrugged. "He was almost like the man I'd married. Laughing and joking with the kids. Patient and kind with me."

"Did you rethink your decision to separate?" Holt asked.

"For a brief moment," Sally said. "When he left, I went and wrote down exactly why I was doing what I was doing and to remind myself who he'd become. And I checked the balance in our account. Still hovering around zero. So, that thought quickly passed."

Good for her.

"Mommy?" The little voice came from Mary, who stood at the door.

"What, baby?"

"I'm thirsty. JoJo fell asleep, but his diaper leaked again. I cleaned it up the best I could, but it still stinks."

She wrinkled her nose and Sally jumped to her feet. "Excuse me just a few minutes, please?"

"Of course."

She left and Penny met Holt's eyes. "Nothing's triggering anything for me, sorry."

"It's okay."

"There's a stack of old vinyl records over there," Grace said, pointing. "Why don't you go through them real quick and see if any of them strike a chord for you." She paused. "No pun intended."

A smile lifted Penny's lips. "Funny." But it was a good idea. She padded over to the stack and picked up the one on top. "Hoagy Carmichael's 'Georgia on My Mind.'" She moved to the next one. "Ben Selvin, 'When It's Springtime in the Rockies.' Every Elvis album imaginable."

"He listened to them each night after the kids were in bed," Sally said, returning to her spot on the couch. "Sometimes, we'd dance." She rubbed her eyes. "Is there anything else?"

While Penny continued to peruse the records, she still kept one ear open to the conversation.

"I wanted to ask," Holt said, "can you tell us where you think he might have been staying when he wasn't here?"

"I . . . can't say for sure, but I suspect he was parking his car out of sight somewhere and staying in one of the outbuildings."

Penny set the record down and turned in time to see Sally's gaze slide to the window. Penny let hers do the same and she could see the two buildings. One in each corner of the wooden back fence.

"What makes you say that?" Grace asked.

She shrugged. "Just a feeling."

"You didn't look?"

Her eyes widened and she shook her head. "About three months ago, I . . . started to go see what was out there. I wanted to know what he was doing when he would spend hours and hours out there. I went and knocked on the door and asked if I could come in. He grabbed my throat"—her hands went to the base of her neck and her eyes took on a faraway glaze—"and he squeezed so hard I almost lost consciousness. He finally stopped and made me promise never to invade his privacy, that he would consider it a gross betrayal. And"—she pulled in a deep breath—"and that he would know if I entered."

"Cameras?" Holt asked.

"Maybe. I don't know."

"Could be boobytrapped somehow," Grace muttered.

"Could you let us in the building?" Holt asked. "We're looking for any information your husband may have had on Rabor. Most specifically, a location idea."

"It has a padlock on it and I don't have the key."

"I have bolt cutters."

She hesitated. "You're absolutely sure it's him? That he's really dead?"

"That's what the DNA shows, so I'm comfortable saying it couldn't be anyone else."

Her shoulders lifted in a shrug. "I guess it doesn't matter now then, does it?"

Holt reached for his phone. "I'll get a K-9 team out here and we'll have them sniff around for any explosives before we enter."

"Good idea." Grace stood.

While Holt made the call, Sally stepped in front of Penny. "I did catch a brief snippet of the news this morning and I just recognized your face. You're the one they're saying is responsible for Joel's death."

"I . . . well . . . I guess. He had Holt on the ground and was about to stab him. I had to slam into Joel to knock him off of Holt. He . . . stumbled and fell onto his knife." She swallowed. "I'm sorry."

"I'm not. Thank you." She turned away. "I'm going to check on my children."

Well, okay then. Penny's guilt was fading fast.

Fifteen minutes later, a K-9 cruiser pulled to a stop behind Holt's vehicle. Kyra Knight climbed from the driver's seat and Penny waved. Kyra raised a brow as if to ask why Penny was there. They'd found themselves at several scenes over the past two years and had become friends. She'd probably text her later if they didn't get a chance to talk here.

From her spot next to Holt's Bucar, Penny watched Kyra and Happy do their thing. It didn't take long to cover the small buildings. "All clear," Kyra called. She played a quick game of tug-of-war with Happy, praising him for a job well done, before jogging over to Penny. "Surprised to see you here."

"Long story."

"I look forward to hearing it." She turned to Holt. "There aren't any explosives in there, but Happy was acting kinda weird."

"Weird how?"

"Like he smelled something he didn't like."

"But nothing that's going to blow us up."

"Nope. Nothing like that."

He nodded. "All right, then. Let's see what we've got."

■ ■ ■ ■

Holt clutched the bolt cutters and approached the door. Two large rings, one on the door below the knob and one on the side of the building, were used to hold the heavy-duty lock. He was almost afraid the cutter wouldn't be strong enough.

He had a bad feeling he knew what Happy had been acting skittish about. Unfortunately. Then again, just because his mind went straight to a dead body didn't necessarily mean that was the case. Maybe his line of work had jaded him.

He could only hope. He looked back to find Grace and Sally watching him. Penny leaned against his Bucar, arms crossed, eyes narrowed. Holt turned to Sally. "Are you sure you're okay with this?"

"As long as you're sure he's dead."

"I'm sure."

"Then have at it."

It took all of Holt's strength to cut through the lock, but he managed it. The metal fell to the small concrete porch and he kicked it aside. Grace stepped up beside him, her hand on her weapon.

With a nod to her, he stood opposite her, twisted the knob, and pushed the door open. Freezer-cold air hit him in the face and he paused to focus on the room. It was set up like an old-fashioned parlor with a table and chairs and tea service placed in the middle of the table. A woman sat at the table, her left hand curled around a teacup.

"Hello? Ma'am?"

She didn't move.

Holt pulled his weapon. "Ma'am?"

No response.

He looked closer and lowered his gun as realization hit him.

"Holt?" Grace's voice came from behind him to his right and her flashlight hit the body in the chair. "Is she—"

"Yeah. She's dead. Looks like she's frozen solid too."

The flashlight swept the room. "And so is she," Grace said, her voice soft. "And her."

"All frozen in time," Holt said, his heart aching for the victims and their families who'd soon be receiving the tragic news. He pulled his phone from his pocket, then paused. "Wait a minute," he said. "I know her."

"Who?" Grace asked.

"The one at the table. She was snatched from Virginia. Agents tracked her to a gas station in Raleigh, North Carolina, then lost track of her after that." He closed his eyes for a brief moment, picturing her face on the FBI's missing persons website. "I'll call this in and get the local officers involved along with the crime scene unit. We're going to need all the help we can get."

"Yeah. I'll start taping it off."

Holt made the call, then walked over to Penny, who stood with her arms wrapped around her waist. "Where's Sally?"

"She went to check on the kids."

"Stay right here, okay?" Now that he knew what was in the building, he didn't want to let the woman out of his sight. More officers were on the way, but until then . . .

"Grace just swept past me with crime scene tape. What'd you find?"

"I'll explain in a few. Don't go anywhere."

"All right." She frowned but leaned back against the Bucar and crossed her arms again. Holt jogged up the back steps and into the kitchen. He found Sally sitting at the table, her son in her arms and Mary in the chair beside her, reading her book.

"I saw the agent get the crime scene tape from the car," Sally said. "What did you find?"

"It's . . . there are . . . we found . . ." He didn't want to tell her.

She glanced at Mary, then back to him and mouthed, "A dead body?"

He nodded but didn't say anything about the body actually being plural. There were three that he saw. "You knew?"

"No, of course not." She gave a bitter laugh. "Just a guess. Now that I know about Joel's fascination with that serial killer, and his super secretive actions . . ." She shrugged. "It just seemed like that's the way this story was going to go." A pause. "Why didn't I . . . smell it?"

Holt ran a hand over his head. "He turned that whole building into a freezer. The temps in there are probably in the mid teens to low twenties."

She let out a low breath and shuddered. "How did I not see his evil? Or at least sense it? How could he do this and I not even—?" Her chin quivered and a tear rolled down her cheek. Then her dark eyes met his. "How?" The agony behind her words carried the weight of the world in them, and Holt's heart hurt for her.

"Mommy, are you okay?" Mary asked.

Sally nodded and patted the little girl's hand. "Yes, why don't you take JoJo into your room. He can play with his cars while you read."

"But—"

"Now, Mary." A hint of steel threaded her words and Mary obeyed without another word. She and JoJo left the kitchen and headed toward the back of the house.

"You can't blame yourself," Grace said, stepping into the room.

Holt flinched. He hadn't heard her come in. "She's right," he said. "This isn't on you."

"But I . . . I . . . should have . . ." Her eyes pleaded with them. "I should have noticed . . . *something*."

Grace shook her head. "You're a mother with two small children.

Your husband was having surgery to change his appearance without giving you a good reason for his desire to do so, while draining your financial resources. Your marriage was deteriorating. Just *one* of those situations is stressful, but all three? And maybe more that you haven't shared? I can't imagine the load of stress that would be. You were coping. Making it through one day, then the next, putting one foot in front of the other and just hanging on. Am I right?"

The shell-shocked expression on Sally's face confirmed Grace's words. Holt motioned he was going to head outside and Grace gave him a minuscule nod. She'd take care of Sally while he checked out the other building and talked to the crime scene unit, who'd just arrived on the scene.

Back outside, he glanced at the Bucar and scowled when he didn't see Penny. He let his gaze sweep the area and found her on the porch of the homemade freezer. She was staring at the interior. Far enough outside so she wouldn't contaminate the scene, but close enough to have a good view of exactly what was on the inside. "Penny?" She didn't move. He wasn't even sure she was breathing. He hurried to her and placed a hand on her upper arm. "Aw, Penny, I didn't want you to see that."

"He set it all up. Like he was having a tea party."

"Yes."

"It's . . . horrible."

"Agreed. Come on, let's go wait in the car." He tried to pull her away, but she resisted.

"How did they die?"

"I don't know. Lexie's on the way. We need to get out of the way and let the crime scene people do what they can before she gets here. And I need to take a look at the other building."

She pulled in a deep breath and shuddered. "Right."

He led her back to the Bucar. "I'm probably going to be here a while. Do you want to call someone to come get you?"

"No, not yet." A frown flickered and she had a faraway look in her eyes.

"What is it, Penny?"

"I know what the song was."

That stopped him. "What was it?"

"'Tea for Two.'"

CHAPTER
FIFTEEN

Penny hummed the tune while bile rose in the back of her throat. She stopped and swallowed. "He changed the words, though."

"Okay, do you remember any of them?"

"Yeah. They've been playing in the back of my subconscious, and I don't know if they're exactly right, but it was something like, 'Picture you at my table. A date for me and death for you . . .'" She paused. "I don't really remember any more. My grandmother liked the song and used to sing it—along with a bunch of other songs we call oldies. But that's why it was familiar, and yet I couldn't place it. When I saw the tea service . . ." She shrugged.

Holt scrubbed a hand down his cheek. "Well, at least we know what he was singing now."

"But why?"

Holt shrugged. "He was crazy?"

"Or it was part of his ritual?"

"Okay, yeah, but I wasn't going to say that."

She shot him a scowl. "I'm not stupid, Holt."

"Hey, I never thought you were."

"And I'm not some fragile, delicate little thing you have to protect from . . . whatever. I can handle hearing that kind of stuff. Mostly because I think of it anyway."

He studied her for a moment, then nodded. "All right."

"Thank you. I have another thought too."

"Sure."

"If that was the copycat's MO, does this mean that everything in that . . . that"—she waved a hand at the building—"*room* is also Rabor's MO?"

He stilled. "That is an excellent question."

"Of course it is," she muttered.

"In my dealings with Rabor, yes, those killings are very similar, but with a few differences."

"Such as?"

"Rabor never froze his victims."

"I see. So Joel Allen learned from Rabor and then added his own touch to things? So to speak."

"That's what it looks like."

"So, what now?"

"The crime scene unit gathers all of the evidence and we wait to see what they come up with. I'm going to go check out the other building and be back shortly."

"Fine. I'll wait and make some phone calls."

He headed for one of the crime scene investigators and Penny pulled her phone from her pocket. She dialed Raina's number and waited.

No answer.

She tried Holly.

No answer.

Great. They were probably out on a call. A call she'd be out on if she hadn't been recovering from fighting off a serial killer. Not that there was much more recovering to do. Except figure out how to deal with the nightmares. Past and present.

"Stop it," she whispered.

Lexie finally arrived. She waved at Penny but didn't stop to chat.

Penny watched her speak to several people before homing in on Holt. She said something and he nodded to the door they'd shut to keep the room at the correct temperature.

So the bodies wouldn't thaw out before Lexie was ready.

Penny grimaced and texted Raina.

Call me when you get a chance.

When Holt was finished going through the other building and talking to Lexie, he made his way back to Penny. "I've done all I can do here. Want me to take you home?"

She nodded to the smaller of the two outbuildings. "What was in there?"

"Looks like Sally was right. That's where Joel was staying when he didn't come home at night, and it appears he was staying there up until he helped Rabor escape. There's food in the refrigerator, along with some canned goods, several gallons of water, and more. He has a nice fifty-six-inch television on the wall, and with the windows facing the house blacked out, no one would see any lights. It's a very comfortable setup."

Penny frowned. "How could she not know?"

"Easy. He approached from the back, along the fence line, slipped through the gate and into the back of the building. He could come and go and no one would know. Even if she stood at the window looking at the place, she'd never see him approaching, with all of the trees."

"That's alarming." Truly creepy.

"Yeah. So, while I'm feeling fairly certain she had no clue what her husband was up to, we'll still look into her."

"If she knew what Allen was up to, she deserves a part in one of my mother's movies." She followed him around the side of the house and came to an abrupt halt. "Are you kidding me?" A channel 7 news van sat at the curb. A man with a camera on his shoulder aimed the lens in their direction.

"How'd they know to come here?" Holt muttered.

Penny eyed the individual leaning against the van. "There's that snoopy reporter, Frankie Olander."

"The one who threatened you?"

"It wasn't really a threat, as in he was going to do me bodily harm, but yeah."

"Close enough."

As soon as they came into sight, the reporters rushed forward. "Penny, can you tell us why you're here and what's going on?" The woman shoved the microphone at her, and Penny sighed, kept her head down, and aimed herself for Holt's car.

"Penny? You're spending an awful lot of time with the FBI. Are you helping them in some way?"

"Penny, what does your mother think about your latest adventures?"

For a brief moment, her eyes made contact with Frankie, and he gave her a small shrug as though to say if she talked to him, this could all be over. She kept her expression blank and continued her trek to the vehicle, doing her best to project that he was invisible to her.

Once she was in the passenger seat and buckled up, she pressed her fingers to her eyes, thinking. When she looked up, they were heading out of the subdivision. "Olander's following me."

Holt's jaw visibly tightened. "It's definitely a possibility."

"But how? I haven't seen anyone hanging around watching or anything."

"And we're in my vehicle."

"So, he's following you because he knows I'm with you?"

"He might have been watching the hospital and saw us leave together and simply trailed along. Or . . ." He scowled. "Your phone."

"You think he planted some kind of software on it?"

"We'll need to find out."

"Great."

"And just in case it's not your phone, I'll be more alert to watching behind us from now on."

They fell silent, with Penny thinking hard about the scene she'd just been privy to. "There are some sick people in this world," she whispered.

"True."

"I guess take me home. I'm trying to get permission to do the rest of my shift, but Dr. Kirkpatrick hasn't gotten back to me, and Raina and Holly aren't answering their phones either. They must be out on a pretty serious call if they haven't had a chance to check in."

He shot her a brief glance. "Why do you want to finish your shift?"

"What else am I supposed to do?"

"Work on your house?"

"Yeah, well, that can wait." It left her with far too much time to think. The exact opposite of what she was trying to do. Plus, she wanted to be around people she trusted.

"What's going on? You afraid of the nightmares?"

She closed her eyes and the images of Allen straddling Holt with the knife hovering over his face surfaced. He'd been . . . gleeful . . . about the fact that he was getting ready to take a life. Gloating. Her stomach lurched and she popped her eyes open. "That's part of it, I guess, but if I'm working, I'll be able to focus on that and think about other things less."

He reached over to squeeze her hand. "I'll stay with you if that'll help."

She sighed. "I can't ask you to do that. You have enough on your plate without worrying about me."

"I can handle my plate and you too. You've actually been very helpful."

"How so?"

"You mean other than the part where you saved my life a few times?" He shrugged. "The song is important, we just need to figure out how."

■ ■ ■ ■

156

Darius Rabor wanted to laugh, but laughing hurt, so he settled for a chuckle. And a grimace. He pressed a hand to his side and leaned back against the tree while he listened to the noises on the other side of the fence. He just needed a few more days to heal and then he could get back to his mission. He'd already tried to do too much, too soon. He just needed to be patient.

He'd heard Joel had died on the mountain, and while that was inconvenient for his long-range plans, because everyone thought it was him, it had benefited him in the short run. Being dead certainly had its advantages. With a knit cap on his head and a scarf over the lower portion of his face, no one had looked at him twice.

Hiding out in Joel's outbuilding might not have been the most brilliant plan—he'd known they would figure out Joel's identity eventually and come looking—but it had been the best he could do at the time. Joel had told him all about the place and offered it to him should he ever need it. Keeping an eye on Joel's pretty wife and cute kids was just a bonus. He had plans for them as well.

Rabor shoved his hand in his pocket and curled his fingers around the key, wishing the crime scene folks would hurry it up. He had things to do, plans to make . . .

. . . people to kill.

With a low grunt, he rolled over to peer through a rotted slat in the wood fence. Law enforcement milled and he smiled. He'd seen Joel's handiwork his first night there and been impressed.

His gaze lit on the lone figure leaning against the porch railing, studying the proceedings with massive interest.

Penny Carlton.

He recognized her from the news. Geneva Queen's daughter.

She'd been the one to send Joel to his fiery reward. Interesting. Okay, Joel had tripped, but she'd been fighting back when it happened, if he understood correctly.

And she was pretty too. Just like he preferred. But she was smart. Smarter than he was used to. Not to mention her law enforcement connections. Especially Holton Satterfield. The man stepped into view and Darius grinned. "Ah, Holt, my favorite agent." Darius had picked up on Holt's affection for the pretty pilot, but that wouldn't do.

Darius had plans for Penny and they didn't include Holt. The more he sat there, the more he learned. And the more he realized how much Joel Allen had taken on his persona, his habits, his . . . everything. Joel had pumped him endlessly during his visits, and Darius gladly told him every single detail he could think of, knowing somehow Joel's obsession with him would come in handy one day. He just hadn't expected it to be like this. Joel had copied Darius's killings down to the nth degree. And then taken it one step further. He'd frozen his victims.

Interesting. He'd have to try that next time.

His gaze found Penny once more.

All in good time. All in good time.

■ ■ ■ ■

Holt drove Penny home, and just as he pulled into her driveway, her phone rang.

"Stay here while I check the place out, all right?" he asked before she answered the call.

She nodded, then swiped her screen. "Hi, Raina."

Holt left her talking, paused, and went to the back of the Bucar. He popped the rear lift and grabbed a small mirror from his bag. Working slowly, he walked around the vehicle, searching. Nothing. He checked the license plate and behind the mirrors. Everywhere he could think of.

And still nothing.

When he glanced at Penny, she was still on the phone. He held up a finger for her to wait and she nodded.

He approached the house and punched in the code to unlock the deadbolt. It took him three seconds to disarm the alarm, then he let his gaze sweep the area. So far, so good. The fact that the alarm was armed comforted him somewhat, but he still wanted to walk through the entire house, just to be sure.

He checked the rest of the house and noted the progress she'd made on the upstairs bath. Her talented touch was everywhere in the home and he made a mental note to tell her she needed her own DIY television series.

Footsteps sounded behind him and he turned to find Penny grinning at him. "I go back to work first thing in the morning," she said. "One of the other pilots has the flu, so I'm up." She sobered. "Not that I'm glad someone is sick, but I'm relieved I can fill in. I'm going to spend the night at the base."

He nodded. "You want to grab anything from your house? I'll follow you to work, then check on Gus."

"Everything I need is at work."

His phone rang. "Then I'll take this while you lock up."

Once she was buckled in behind the wheel of her SUV, he let his eyes scan the area. Nothing looked out of place, but his nerves couldn't seem to stop humming.

He kept coming back to the song. "Tea for Two."

And the whole tea party setup Joel had created.

As soon as he made sure Penny arrived at the hospital safely, he'd find time to take a look at the crime scene notes from the other killings. The reason he'd even caught the case was because Rabor's first kill had been a federal employee—a single woman who'd just landed her dream job as a district court judge. She'd been engaged to a high-powered attorney who was devastated at her death. Holt still checked on the man occasionally, and he kept saying he'd rest when Rabor got the needle.

And now this.

Holt rubbed a hand over his cheek and realized he needed to shave. His five-o'clock shadow was quickly turning into a one-week beard.

He stayed right on Penny's bumper, his nerves tight, his head on a swivel as he analyzed every car they passed. He was almost surprised that they arrived at the hospital without an incident. But he hadn't seen the reporter or anyone else follow.

Not that he couldn't have missed someone, but . . .

Penny pulled into her assigned spot and Holt parked in the law enforcement space not too far from her.

He waited on her to catch up with him, then they both walked into the hospital. She kissed his cheek, then backed down the hall. "Thank you, Holt. For everything."

"Keep in touch with me. Promise?"

"I promise." She spun and darted toward the stairs that would take her to her second home.

He hesitated and raced after her, loath to let her out of his sight. He rounded the corner just as she swept through the door to her base. Holt stopped and waited. Watching.

For fifteen minutes, he stood there, watching. When nothing happened, it was almost anticlimactic.

He'd take it for the moment, because he had a feeling that moment wasn't going to last.

CHAPTER
SIXTEEN

At 7:30 Sunday morning, the alarm blared and Penny and the others scrambled to the chopper. Being in the cockpit always felt like coming home to Penny. All of her worries and stress faded into the background, and she focused on aiming the bird toward the interstate. "What's going on?" she asked.

"Attempted suicide," Holly said. "Someone jumped off a bridge and into the river."

"What else?"

"That's all we know at the moment."

Four minutes later, she hovered over the area. "Looks like they're ready for us."

Authorities had cleared the lanes in both directions, giving her the space she needed to land.

EMS was already on the scene.

An officer spotted her and hurried to direct her landing, and Penny set the chopper down with barely a bounce.

"Nice landing," Holly said.

Penny pulled her headset off and turned at Holly's low voice. She just now noticed her friend's tight features and shadowed eyes. "You okay?"

Holly nodded. "It's been hard climbing on board after the whole mountain scene, but it's getting easier—and I know God's in control. I just have to focus on the patient." She paused. "You're good?"

"Yes. Surprisingly. Discounting the nightmares of being chased by a serial killer."

Raina shuddered and grabbed the medical bag. "Enough of that kind of talk. I don't want to think about it." She jerked her head at the door. "Ready when y'all are."

They unloaded from the chopper and Penny scanned the scene. Multiple police cruisers with flashing lights, two ambulances, three fire trucks, and more. She followed Raina down the embankment to the edge of the water below the bridge, where the victim had been laid out on the grass. She was soaking wet, pale to the point of being white, with blue-tinged lips.

Penny recognized Eric Pollard as the lead paramedic. "She going to make it?"

Eric looked up. "Absolutely. Paddles!"

Penny stepped back and waited. If they needed any help, they'd let them know. Sometimes Raina and Holly worked on the patient, sometimes they let the first responders do their job. For now, her team waited. All Penny knew was that if she ever needed paramedics working on her, she wanted Eric.

"Come on, come on," he muttered. "You're not dying. Not while I'm here. Clear!" The victim jerked when he shocked her. His gaze went to the monitor. "Again!"

They worked over her for the next several minutes while Penny and the others watched. After the last shock, the sound of a beating heart reached her.

"She's back. Let's get her loaded in the chopper!" The paramedic nearest Penny rose to his feet and nodded to Raina and Holly.

"Guess it's our turn," Raina said.

They turned to climb back up the embankment. When Penny's

eyes scanned the bridge once more, they landed on one particular figure who stood to the side, looking down, watching the commotion.

A gasp slipped from her, and she blinked, sure that she was seeing things. But he was still there, and his eyes met hers for a solid two seconds. Then he smiled, turned, and disappeared into the crowd before she had time to draw in her next breath. Her fingers fumbled for her phone. The others carrying the stretcher passed her.

"Penny?"

Raina's voice snapped her out of her trance, and she hit Holt's speed dial number while searching for a cop. She raced over to the man. "Have you heard of Darius Rabor?"

"The serial killer. Of course."

"I just saw him on the bridge." She pointed even as Holt came on the line.

"Penny?" Holt sounded distracted. "What is it?"

"He's here. At the scene!"

The officer eyed her and she wasn't sure he believed her, but he got on his radio and Penny continued her climb toward the chopper.

"Who?" Holt's voice sharpened. "Rabor?"

"Yes! I told an officer, and now I have to get a patient to the hospital."

"I'll take care of it, but—"

"Penny! Let's go!" Holly's shout spurred her forward.

She made it to the top and darted for the cabin. She slid into the seat and snapped the headphones over her ears. "Holt? I have to fly. I'll talk to you later."

"Wait! I need details!"

"Those are the details! I'll call you when I can. Sorry!" She hung up and glanced back. "How's she doing?"

"She's stable at the moment," Raina said. "Broken leg, sprained arm, not sure what she hit, but she's got some internal bleeding.

The guy who saw her jump is an off-duty paramedic. She wasn't under super long before he had her on shore, but she was hysterical, screaming and fighting, and they had to put her under to treat her wounds. And then her heart stopped. That's the scene we arrived to see."

"Poor thing." Ten seconds later, Penny was in the air. She banked gently and headed for the hospital. Their ETA was five minutes.

When she touched down, Penny's mind was still spinning with visions of Darius Rabor and her desperate need to know if she'd really seen what she thought she saw. She itched to talk to Holt, but first things first. She cut the engine and Holly shoved the door open.

Once the patient was delivered to the medical team and she'd dodged the persistent reporters, Penny made her way to the base. She pushed through the doors only to come to an abrupt stop, with Raina and Holly nearly crashing into her.

Frankie Olander sat on their couch. They really needed to start locking the doors.

"You know," Penny said, "I'm not normally a rude person, but you're pushing it. You need to go away."

Raina and Holly stepped up beside her like protective bookends. "You heard her," Holly said. "She's not interested in being a feature story."

The man sighed and stood. "I get that. And honestly, if my boss wasn't pushing this so hard, I'd let it go, *Winston Hamilton, LLC.*"

Penny sucked in a sharp breath. "Get out." How had he gotten that name? That was the name she'd bought her house under, the name she did her banking under. Everything. It had been the only way to keep her mother's fame from touching her life.

"I'm going," he said, "but think about it. I can keep things secret when I have the right motivation. A story would do that for me."

"Get—" Penny stopped the shout and curled her fingers into tight fists. Resisting the temptation to land one on Frankie's chin, she instead planted them on her hips. Yelling at him to leave her alone and get out wasn't working. Time for a different approach. "Let me think about it."

Frankie's brows rose. "For how long?"

"Just"—she raked a hand over her ponytail—"give me forty-eight hours."

"What's to think about?"

"A lot. There's a lot to think about. And I need to talk to a few people who might be mentioned. So . . ." She waved her hand. "Go away and let me think. And talk."

He tilted his head and studied her. "All right." He looked at Raina. "I'm still working on you. It's interesting that you don't have a past that I can find any farther back than eight years ago."

Raina sucked in an audible breath and Holly pulled her phone from her pocket. "I'm calling security."

"No need," Frankie said, backing toward the exit. He nodded to Penny. "Forty-eight hours." He left and Penny let out a low growl and stomped her foot.

Then spun to face Raina. "He won't find anything."

Raina hurried past them and went straight to the refrigerator. "I'm starving. I'm making burgers and fries. Holly, can you grab the air fryer?"

"Sure." Holly studied Penny for a moment, then grabbed the air fryer from the pantry and set it on the counter for Raina. Penny figured Raina would talk if and when she was ready. For now, she would cook. And hopefully, de-stress. Raina had a past that very few were privy to, and cooking was how she dealt with it. Penny dialed Holt's number.

Once.

Voice mail.

Twice.

Voice mail.

When Holt didn't answer after three calls, Penny paced, ignoring all of the commotion going on behind her at the stove.

"Penny, you want your burger well done?" Raina called out.

"That's fine, thanks." She dialed Holt again. "Come on, answer."

But he didn't. She tossed the phone onto the table with a groan of frustration and slumped into the nearest chair.

"You okay?" Holly asked.

"No." Penny dropped her head into her hands to massage her pounding temples.

"You really saw that guy back at the scene? The serial killer?"

"Yes."

"What was he doing?"

"Just standing on the bridge, watching everyone work. Blending in with all of the other people up there." She paused. "But it was like he was waiting for me to look up, because when I did, he met my eyes and he stared. Just for a brief moment. Then he gave me this weird little smile, turned, and walked away."

"That's incredibly . . ."

"Disturbing?"

"To say the least."

"Or maybe I've just been thinking about him so much that I'm hallucinating."

Holly dropped into the chair next to her. "Or he was really there," she said, her voice soft. "I don't think you can discount that."

"But why?"

"Think about it, Pen, you've been all over the news. The media is reporting that you fought the guy who was supposed to be *him* and *that* guy died. Rabor has to have seen some footage or something. What if he's—"

"Watching me?"

"Yeah."

Penny shuddered. What a horrific thought. "But how would he even know I was there at the scene? How would he know about the call? That doesn't make sense."

"Yeah, true." Holly frowned. "I don't know."

"Unless he's got some kind of scanner?" Raina said, pausing in her kitchen activities. She sighed. "Maybe it's a crazy idea, but you know me. I'm always thinking about the worst-case scenario." She went back to the food. "Forget it. Ignore me." She walked over and set a plate in front of Penny with more force than necessary. "My specialty. Stop talking about scary and depressing subjects and eat."

Penny wanted to take her friends' advice, but what if they were right? "Now I'm never going to be able to stay by myself again. I'll hear every thump and creak and groan and moan that old house makes." She glared at Holly. "Thanks."

"I'm not saying that's the case, but . . ."

"Yeah."

"Eat!" Raina's shout echoed through the room and Penny flinched.

Holly rolled her eyes but shut her mouth.

Penny took a bite of the burger. She closed her eyes as her taste buds danced with delight. "Raina, not sure you made the right decision when you dropped out of cooking school to become a critical care paramedic."

Raina laughed, the sound more natural. "Don't get used to it. You're on cleanup duty, by the way."

"Fine." Penny wasn't wild about cooking, but she didn't mind cleaning up. She finished the burger and looked up to find Frankie Olander staring at her through the glass doors. "Oh, you're kidding me."

She stood and stomped across the floor to pull open the door. "I thought you were giving me forty-eight hours."

"I am. I just want to be close whenever you're ready."

She pulled the blinds, effectively blocking him from seeing into the base. Normally, because of the security in the hospital and the fact that someone was always in the base, they left everything open. Normally. Having a reporter as a stalker wasn't normal. She returned to the table and pressed her palms to her eyes.

"Pen?" Holly said.

"Yeah?" she said without looking up.

"It'll get better."

"I sure hope so." Having a reporter after her to provide him with a story was annoying to the point she was gritting her teeth, but the idea of having a serial killer know who she was—well, that was downright terrifying.

■　■　■　■

Back in his vehicle, Holt finally had a chance to glance at his phone to see who had been blowing it up. Rachel, Penny—a lot from Penny—Marty, Julianna, Grace, and his dad.

He called Penny first.

She answered mid first ring. "Did you catch him?"

"No, he was long gone by the time we got there, but we got some footage from the bridge cameras. He was there."

"So, I didn't imagine it," she whispered.

"No, you didn't." He paused. "Your buddy Frankie Olander was there too."

"What! I didn't see him." She frowned. "He was waiting on us when we got back to base. Sitting on the couch like he owned the place. How'd he get back here so fast?"

"I'm sure you had things to do once you landed and got the patient off the bird?"

"Yes, of course. We cleaned everything up and . . . yeah, okay. Frankie would have been able to get here and have a nap before we returned to base. Usually there's someone here. I guess everyone was out on a call or something." She sighed, and he wished he could wrap her in a hug.

"Penny, one of the witnesses said they didn't think the victim jumped. They think she was pushed."

"Pushed? By who?"

"They don't know, and the footage isn't clear, but I'm willing to bet it was Rabor."

"But . . . why?"

"I don't know, but I do know that he doesn't do anything without a reason."

"So, what now?"

"I'm coming by the hospital to talk to the woman. See if she remembers anything. I just got a call that she is awake."

"One of the paramedics said she was screaming something but not really making any sense. She was fighting them, and they had to sedate her in order to treat her."

"Did he say what she was saying?"

"No. Didn't any of the witnesses tell you?"

"None of them mentioned it. Maybe she'll be able to tell me. I'll come by and see you when I finish talking to her."

"I'll meet you there. I wouldn't mind checking on her."

"Penny, this is—"

"An investigation. I know. I'm not asking you to tell me anything. See you in a few."

She hung up and Holt let out a low huff under his breath. It would take him longer to get to the victim's room than it would take Penny.

Technically, there was nothing wrong—or even unusual—in her checking up on someone she'd just saved. She'd done so many times before. And it might not be a bad thing to have her there. The victim—Theresa Mabry—might be more comfortable with Penny's presence. That is, if she was aware of Penny's involvement in her rescue. Then again, if she really had jumped, she might be furious with Penny for helping save her.

He pressed the gas and made it to the hospital in record time. When he arrived at Theresa's room, he found Penny standing next to the woman's bed, talking softly.

"Penny?"

She turned. "Theresa's awake. Her mother was here but decided to take a break and let me hang out while she grabbed some coffee. I told Theresa I was just checking in with her to see how she was doing."

Theresa was in her midthirties with light brown curly hair cut short so that it rested just above her shoulders. Her blue eyes were foggy from pain medication, but they narrowed on him when he entered, then jumped back to Penny. "You really flew me here?"

"I really did."

"Thank you."

Holt breathed a slow breath of relief. She wasn't mad Penny had been a part of her rescue.

"Of course." Penny pointed to Holt. "That's Holt. He's a friend of mine. I'll just let you two chat a while."

"Hi, Theresa," Holt said, stepping forward.

Before he could officially introduce himself, she said, "You're a cop?"

"I'm with the FBI. I wanted to ask you about what happened out there on the bridge." He glanced at Penny. "You mind stepping out?"

"Sure." Penny headed for the door.

"No!" At Theresa's shout, Penny turned. "No," Theresa said, her voice softer, "let her stay. I want her to know the truth. I want everyone to know the truth."

Penny hesitated and looked at him. Holt nodded. Theresa could just tell her everything she told him later. He might as well spare the woman the effort and stress of telling the story twice. "What's the truth, Theresa?"

"I didn't jump," she said. "I didn't." Two tears tracked down her cheeks and Penny slipped a tissue into the woman's hand.

"So what happened?"

"I was leaning on the bridge, just watching the water, the families enjoying the sunny day. I was thinking about visiting my family next weekend. I don't know. Just having some downtime. And then—"

"Then?" Penny urged, and took her hand.

Theresa drew in a shuddering breath. "Then, I felt someone slam into me. The railing on that bridge isn't the highest. It only comes to your waist, depending on how tall you are. For me, it was a little higher than my belly button. I was leaning and then I was falling. Screaming . . ." She shut her eyes and swallowed. "I remember hitting the water and feeling massive pain. Struggling to stay above the surface, but hurting and sinking. Then someone was dragging me ashore."

"So, you passed out?"

"Yeah, I think so. I remember blackness. Then waking up and hearing the paramedics talking about me jumping. So I kept screaming, 'I didn't jump. I didn't jump.'" She rubbed a hand down her face. "But I was also crying and choking and trying to breathe." She frowned. "But I must have passed out again because I don't remember anything after that. The next thing I'm conscious of is waking up here."

"They had to sedate you to treat you," Penny said. "You were struggling so much, they couldn't get an IV in. And . . . your heart stopped."

"What?"

Penny frowned. "They didn't tell you this?"

"Um . . . maybe. I don't know." Confusion flickered in her eyes. "Why'd my heart stop?"

"You'll have to ask your doctor," Holt said. "Is there anything else you can remember? Did you get a look at who pushed you? A glimpse? Anything?"

"No. Sorry."

"It's okay." Holt removed a card from his wallet and passed it to Theresa. "If you think of anything else, call me, day or night, please?"

"Sure. Yeah." She blew out a low breath. "Maybe it was an accident."

"I think," Holt said, "if it had been an accident, someone would have been falling over themselves to apologize and make things right."

"Or they were horrified and scared of what they'd done and took off," Penny murmured.

"True." He turned his gaze back to Theresa. "I'll look into it and let you know if we manage to find anything—or anyone."

"Thank you." Her frown deepened. "Why are *you* here? I mean, not you specifically, but the FBI? They don't investigate this kind of thing."

"Not usually, but there are some extenuating circumstances that grabbed our interest."

"What kind of extenuating circumstances?"

"I'm sorry, I can't say, but I promise if I learn anything more about what happened out there on the bridge, or find the person responsible for you going over, I'll let you know."

They said their goodbyes and stepped out of the room. Penny looked up at him. "You believe her?"

He gave a slow nod. "Yeah, I do."

"You think she's Rabor's next target?"

"Obviously, I can't say yes or no to that, but I'd lean toward no. Rabor's MO is nothing like what happened today. And the truth is, serial killers don't like to deviate from their MO." He paused. "However, they're not above making things happen that will allow them to set up their next kill." A sigh slipped from him.

Penny bit her lip and her brows drew together.

"What are you thinking?" he asked.

"So, what's he doing? Pushing someone off a bridge? Maybe he didn't push her at all? Maybe it really was an accident and it was just coincidence that he was there when we showed up?"

"Possibly."

"But he definitely knew who I was. He . . . smiled. A weird smile. Like he'd been waiting for me to look up and notice him."

Holt didn't like that. At all.

Her phone rang and she glanced at the screen. When a groan slipped out, Holt raised a brow. "Let me guess. Your mother?"

"Got it in one."

"You can take the call. I need to check in with the rest of the task force and see what they've come up with on their end."

"Sure. I'm going to head back to base. I'll catch up with you later?"

"What about a late dinner?" he blurted. "I can pick something up and bring it to you. We'll eat in the base conference room?"

"Um . . . yeah. Sounds nice. Call me."

She swiped and lifted the phone to her ear while she walked back toward the base. Holt watched her go, his heart thudding a little faster, wondering at the minute hesitation before she'd agreed. Had he completely misread her interest?

He didn't think so, but . . . *"Um . . . yeah. Sounds nice. Call me."*

Why did that not sound promising?

CHAPTER
SEVENTEEN

Penny's gaze scoured the hallway. Frankie Olander was nowhere in sight, but that didn't mean he might not pop out at any given moment. Security had been on top of most of the reporters trying to get in to see her, but for some reason, Frankie seemed to slip past them with no trouble. He was gone when she'd stepped out of base to head to Theresa's room, and thankfully he'd stayed gone. She'd asked for forty-eight hours. Maybe he'd honor that.

Now, her rubber soles made little squeaking noises on the tile as she headed back toward base. Visitors passed her in the hallway. Doctors and nurses and other hospital personnel hurried to and fro, their footsteps echoing in the corridor.

Steps behind her came at an even faster clip and she moved to the side to allow the person to pass. Only she felt something hard—like the barrel of a gun—jam into her right kidney. She gave a gasp and stopped.

"No, no, my dear," a low voice breathed into her left ear. "Keep walking."

Panic flared and sent her pulse skyrocketing. "Rabor?"

"So, you know me."

"Of course I know you. Your face is in the news only slightly more than mine. What do you want with me?" Her gaze scanned the area, a scream building in her throat.

"Let's go somewhere private and talk. If you bring attention to us, I'll have to hurt you. Or someone else. You don't want that, do you?"

She didn't, but she wasn't going anywhere with him.

"Do you?" he asked again, this time more forcefully.

"No," she said, "I don't."

"Good. Now walk."

"Where?"

"To the stairwell."

The stairwell was just ahead. Penny didn't budge. "No."

A surprised chuckle slipped from him. "I'm sorry. What?"

"No. I won't scream and bring attention to you, but I'm also not going anywhere with you."

For a moment, he didn't speak. Like she'd rendered him speechless. Then he drew in a deep breath. "Then who shall be the first to die?"

"No one." *Please let me be right!* "You won't kill anyone right now. Surely you've noticed security is right there." She pointed to the second door on the left.

"No, actually, I hadn't noticed. Thank you for letting me in on that."

"So, what now?" She drew in a shaky breath, praying he couldn't feel the fear coursing through her veins. "I'm not going with you and you don't want to cause a scene. So what do you think about just walking away and forgetting this ever happened?"

More silence from the man behind her. Then he kissed her left cheek, and it was all she could do not to hurl.

"I think you intrigue me," he said, "and I really, really like that."

A shiver fluttered from the pit of her stomach to travel into the base of her neck. She stayed silent, praying she wasn't making a huge mistake and that he wouldn't realize she wasn't nearly as sure of herself as she sounded. She was terrified he'd turn the weapon on someone nearby—or her.

"Okay, Penny," he finally said, "I can see that we have a lot of work to do before we can enjoy our first date. When we get to that point, I'm sure I'll enjoy it. Almost as much as I enjoyed watching you work earlier today."

Another wave of terror and sickness pulsed through her. "So, you *were* there. Did you push that woman off the bridge?"

"How else would I get to see you in action? After hearing how you literally scaled a mountain to save young Claire Gentry, then fought off Joel to save FBI Special Agent Holt Satterfield, well, let's just say I had to meet you. And now, today? Your coolheadedness—is that a word?—is fascinating. Out of all of my girlfriends, I think you're the one that I've been looking for all this time. I can't wait for our time together. I know it will be challenging, but the end result will be so satisfying. You'll see."

Oh, Lord, help me . . .

It was all Penny could do not to wrench herself away from him and run screaming down the hall, but apparently whatever she was doing was the right thing. "You're—" She bit her tongue on the word *sick*. *Don't antagonize him. Keep your mouth shut and make him go away.* "—not going to get away with this."

"What a cliché. I would have thought you'd be more creative than that. But the truth is, I guess we'll find out, won't we? I'm leaving now, Penny," he said, "but only to go and make sure everything is ready for our first date. It's going to be absolutely perfect. I'll see you soon."

And then he was gone, the *whoosh* of the stairwell door behind him.

Penny raced to the security office and banged on the door.

Clark Haverty opened it, a frown on his face. "Penny?"

"Darius Rabor was just here. Assume he has a gun. He went down the stairwell. Is there anyone you can call to stop him at the bottom?"

"Who?"

"The serial killer!" Did he not watch the news?

His eyes widened as the name clicked. "Here? In the hospital?"

Without waiting for an answer, he got on his radio and ran toward the stairwell. She heard something about "locking the place down" and some other codes she didn't recognize. Probably a heads-up about a man with a gun in the building.

Penny stepped into the security office. Taylor Mills spun in her seat. "Penny? They're locking the hospital down. I just got the notice."

"I know." She locked the door behind her. "Can you pull up the cameras on the doors, and when I spot the guy, you can radio Clark and let him know which door?"

"Yeah, sure." The screens in front of the three-person workstation were live, and the huge monitors on the walls held sixty-four little squares. Each square depicted a part of the hospital. While Taylor pulled up all the exits, Penny scrubbed at her cheek, the feel of Rabor's lips still there and making her want to gag. Finally, with her face burning from her efforts, she dropped her hand and group-texted Raina, Holly, and Julianna the situation, then slid her phone into her pocket.

"You see him?" Taylor asked.

"No," Penny whispered. For the next few seconds she stood there, watching the people who managed to get out before the lockdown was announced—or completed. "Where are you, Rabor?" she muttered.

She yanked her phone from her pocket and dialed Holt's number. While it rang, her mind spun. Had he managed to get out that fast? Penny had been super quick to get in front of the monitors, but it was highly possible Rabor had slipped out before she had her view of the exits.

Holt didn't answer and she hung up to send him a text.

Rabor is here in the hospital. He came up behind me and stuck a gun in my back. I'm fine. He left after saying some unpleasant things. I'm in the security office. Officer Haverty went after him.

"What if he's still in the building?" Taylor asked. "What if he found a place to hole up and hide?"

That could be why she didn't see him leaving.

"He went down the stairs from this floor," Penny said. "Can you pull that footage from about three minutes ago?"

"Sure." She did. The door at the bottom of the stairs never opened. "He's either still in the hospital or he got out before we got to the cameras. He might have gotten off on another floor, or he's still in the stairwell."

Penny's phone rang.

Holt. "Hello?"

"Are you okay?"

"Yes. Yes, but I don't know where he went. He could still be in the hospital."

"Is it on lockdown?"

"Yes."

"We're wrapping up and on the way soon."

"Who's we?"

"Grace and me. Sit tight."

Penny hung up and continued to scan the monitors while she rubbed at the place on her cheek once more. "What's another way out of the hospital?" she asked Taylor. "An exit that doesn't have a camera? Anything?"

"No. This hospital is fortunate to have major donors who think very highly of security. Every exit has a camera—and they're all on the wall in front of you."

"Okay, I think it's safe to say that if he exited that stairwell, we should be able to see the footage."

"Yeah, let me just pull it up and rewind, then we can fast-forward to see who's coming out."

She did so and two people in lab coats exited during the time Rabor should have been in the stairwell. The third person to exit had long brown hair, a stylish hat, and a long overcoat, but had her head angled away from the camera. "Can you screenshot those two employees? Holt or someone will want to talk to them and see if they saw anything."

Taylor's fingers flew over the keyboard. "Done."

"Okay," Penny said, "if he's not still in the stairwell, then he got off on another floor and went down a different stairwell."

"But he still hasn't gone out any of the exits."

"That we've seen."

"Yes. That we've seen."

For the next hour, Penny kept in touch with Holt and continued to watch the screens. Thankfully, there were no calls requiring a chopper, and she was able to wait it out with Taylor. She sent Holt a detailed text message of what had transpired between her and Rabor, knowing he was going to ask her for a statement.

She also sent him details on the security footage, telling him to find out if there was any way out of the hospital that might not have been caught on camera. "He could have used some kind of disguise too. Maybe he actually did use one of the exits and we just didn't know it was him. Can we look at that footage once more of anyone coming out of the stairwell?"

"Of course." Taylor's radio crackled. "That's Clark," she murmured, then listened. "He said he's on the way back up. There's no sign of the guy."

Penny's phone dinged with a text from Holt.

Grace and I are on the way up.

When the knock came shortly after and Holt identified himself, Penny opened the door. He and Grace stepped inside, and Penny explained her thoughts about the possibility that the person who slipped out of the stairwell was actually Rabor in disguise. "If it was him," she said, "he was dressed like a woman. Maybe he got the idea from Joel and came prepared in case he had to make a quick exit."

Taylor played the footage for Holt and Grace. When the woman disappeared from the screen, Taylor picked her up at one of the side doors. "And there she—or Rabor—went. Across the street. Looks like she's heading for . . . the parking garage."

"Okay," Holt said, "let's get some footage from the garage. Depending on where he—or she—parked, we might be able to see this person's face. I want to see what car he gets into."

"The hospital takes pictures of every plate that comes through the entrance," Taylor said. "So, if we can find the car, I can find the plate."

"Would he really be so bold as to park in the garage?" Penny asked.

"If he thought no one would figure out that he'd managed to transform himself into someone who looked like a fashionable woman . . ." Holt shrugged. "Yeah, I can see that. He's brilliant, but arrogant. Thinks no one is smarter than he is."

"But you caught him once," Penny said.

"Yes, I did. Which is why he has a little more respect for me than the average agent or cop, but I guarantee you, he thinks he's learned from the mistake that allowed me to get him and is quite confident it won't happen again."

Grace nodded. "Yes, that's exactly how he would think."

"We'll just see about that," Penny muttered.

"Got it." Taylor's fingers had tapped the keys faster than Penny could follow, but now she saw the frozen image on the monitor to her right.

"That's him," Holt said.

"And that's not all." Taylor shot him a self-satisfied smile. "I've got a plate."

■　■　■

"God bless you," Holt said. "You're amazing. Thank you." He sent a text to Daria.

Can you run this plate for me, please? And put a BOLO out on it?

Less than a minute later, she texted back.

Belongs to a woman named Natasha Mitchell.

In her next text, an address came up, along with a photo.

Reported stolen?

How'd you guess? BOLO is out.

When did she report the car stolen?

Another pause.

Um . . . yesterday.

Thanks.

Holt studied the name and the face. "I know her," he said. Penny blinked up at him. "You do? How? Who is she?"

"The face is a little different and the last name is changed, but I'd swear this is Rabor's half sister."

"How common is the name Natasha?" Grace asked.

"Not very. And, if I remember correctly, when we talked to her about her brother, she had a guy with her she introduced as her boyfriend. I'd have to look at my notes, but I'm pretty confident I'm right. Could be they got married."

"Could be."

"We need to pay her a little visit."

Holt called her home and got no answer. He tried her cell—thank you, Daria—and got her voice mail. He sent another text to Daria.

Send me everything you have on Natasha Mitchell, please.

Okay, stay tuned.

His phone rang. Gerald. He answered and slapped the device up to his ear. "Hi, Ger, what's up?"

"I might have something for you."

"Lay it on me."

"One of our analysts was watching the videos of Rabor and his visitors. One of those, we now know, was Joel Allen, dressed up and masquerading as his girlfriend. If you listen to the conversations, Allen has a pretty high-pitched voice. Probably doing that on purpose, knowing he's being recorded."

"I would agree with that."

"Anyway, Yasmine is one smart analyst. She asked for daily footage of the areas Rabor liked to frequent. Turns out he was tight with an inmate by the name of . . ."

"Yeah?"

"It's Kip Jenkins, Holt."

Holt's entire body went cold. He froze. Then went hot. Grace, Penny, and the security officer were looking at him with expressions ranging from curiosity to concern.

"Holt?" Penny asked.

He cleared his throat. "I want to talk to him."

"I figured you'd say that. It's a good thing, because he said he'd only talk to you."

The thought of facing the man responsible for his former partner and best friend's death sent swirls of nausea through him. He wasn't sure he could be in the same room with the man and control himself. "He killed Max, Gerald."

"I know."

"You trust me to question him?"

A slight pause greeted the question. Then Gerald sighed. "I don't have a choice, but, Holt, you're a professional through and through. I tried to get him to agree to talk to someone else, but the guy was adamant that he had information but would only talk to you."

"He's wanted to talk to me before and I've refused. This is just him manipulating things to get what he wants."

"Well, you're going to have to give it to him. We need whatever information he might have on Rabor."

Holt pressed his fingers to his burning eyes. When was the last time he'd slept for a few consecutive hours? "Fine. I'll go see him ASAP."

"There's just one more thing."

"What?"

"He requested you bring someone with you. She's part of the deal if you want him to talk."

A bad feeling was growing in his gut. "Okay. Who?"

"Your friend Penny Carlton."

Holt closed his eyes. "How does he know about her? How does he know that I know her?"

"Most likely from the news. We're looking into that on this end, but asking him about it might be faster."

"I don't like this one bit."

"I don't either. Keep me updated."

"Of course."

Holt hung up and closed his eyes, picturing the day Kip Jenkins had killed Max. Max had been making a ransom drop and the shot came out of nowhere. His partner dropped, dead before he hit the ground. And Holt hadn't been able to do a thing about it.

"Holt?"

Penny's voice snapped him out of his trip down bad-memory lane. "Yeah?"

"What is it? Who's Max, and who killed him?"

Holt met Grace's compassionate gaze, then turned to Penny. "Max was my partner five years ago. We were working a kidnapping and Max was killed by the kidnapper. It's a long story. I can fill you in later. But the guy who killed Max is in the same prison as Rabor was and apparently has some connection to Rabor."

"I see. I'm so sorry."

Once again, Holt was struck by how little they'd actually talked—even when they were talking. In all the conversations they'd had, he'd never mentioned Max. Or the pain of losing him. They'd kept the conversations light, surface-level discussions. He wanted more than that.

He looked at Grace. "He said he'd only speak to me, so I guess I'm heading to Columbia to meet with him." He hesitated, not wanting to tell Penny that the guy knew who she was. For the life of him, he couldn't figure out why the man would have any reason to speak to her. "Penny, would you consider going with me? Like now?"

Grace raised a brow at him. Penny mirrored the look. "I mean, I would, but I'm working."

"But you don't have to, right? You have off until Monday. Is there someone that could cover the rest of your shift?"

"Well, yeah. I'd have to make sure I could arrange it, but . . ."

"What's going on, Holt?" Grace asked.

A flush crept up his neck. "I want to have a more in-depth conversation about Penny's run-in with Joel Allen on the mountain. And . . . I need to discuss something else with her as well." *Like Zoe? Yes, that too.*

Grace studied him for an embarrassingly long moment, then shrugged. "All right, if Penny's going with you, I'll hunt down Rabor's sister and see what she has to say about the car."

"Perfect." He turned to Penny. "Will that work for you?"

She blew out a breath. "I guess so. If you really think it'll help anything, I'll start arranging it. There's another pilot who was going to fill in for Byron, but I volunteered. It's possible I can un-volunteer and go with you. I can try, anyway."

"I'd appreciate it."

"Okay, then. I'll call right now." She pulled her phone from her pocket and stepped into the hallway.

"What are you doing, Holt?" Grace asked.

"I didn't want to say anything in front of Penny yet, but I'll tell her if she can arrange someone to cover her shift. Jenkins said he'd only talk to me if Penny was included."

Shock flashed across Grace's face.

"Yeah. Apparently, Penny and I are a package deal."

CHAPTER

EIGHTEEN

It had taken only one call to Benjamin Thomas and he promised to cover her shift. He and his wife had a baby on the way and he'd made it known that he wanted any and all hours he could get. She ran it by Dr. Kirkpatrick and he was fine with it. She really liked that man and hoped he found someone with a similar personality to take over Mike Bishop's job.

Penny slid into Holt's passenger seat and laid her head back against the headrest. It had been a long morning and she was starving, but wasn't sure she could eat without gagging, thanks to Rabor's kiss. She closed her eyes, wondering why Holt wanted her along on a three-hour trip that was going to be emotionally draining for him.

When the vehicle didn't move, she opened her eyes and looked over at him. He sat in the driver's seat, engine running, heater blasting. "What is it, Holt?"

"I had another reason for wanting you along, but I don't feel right pulling out of this parking lot without telling you."

"Okay, so tell me."

"This guy I'm going to see requested me, but he also said he wanted you there."

"*Me?* Why me? I have no idea who he even is. Do I?"

"His name is Kip Jenkins. Mean anything to you?"

"No. Nothing. How does he know me?"

"The only way he could know about you would be through the media, or—"

"Or Rabor told him about me somehow."

"Regardless of how he knows about you, I don't know why he requested your presence. Maybe he wants to meet Geneva Queen's daughter. Who knows? We can ask him when we see him."

"All of this is kind of wigging me out, Holt. I don't like this one bit."

"Join the club." They fell silent for the next several minutes before Holt said, "Okay, when we get there, I'm going to leave you with a friend of mine who's a guard. His name is Bill. I'm going to go in and see Jenkins, see if I can keep you out of this."

"And if he insists?"

"Then I'll have Bill bring you in."

She swallowed. "All right. And what do I do when I get in there?"

"Try not to let him see your fear. If you're nervous, do your best to hide it."

Try to hide her fear? Yeah, she could do that. She'd sure had enough practice. "Anything else?"

"If I interrupt you midsentence or something, I have a reason, okay? I'm not being intentionally rude."

"Sure." She paused. "Can you tell me how Max was killed?"

His jaw tightened and she wondered if he'd tell her. But then he breathed deep and let it out slowly through pursed lips. "Okay."

"You don't have to, but"—she shrugged—"I want to know. Maybe it'll take my mind off the fact that this guy who knows a serial killer also knows me. And it might help me understand you better. It occurred to me that while we've had phone conversations and a few dinners, we've never really talked about the deep stuff."

That seemed to get his attention. He quirked a quick smile at her. "I've thought about that too. I think you and I are deep people, but we're also super private. Talking about the deep stuff isn't easy for either of us."

"I'd agree with that."

"But I will say, I'm not that hard to understand. Basically, what you see is what you get." And yet, something flickered in his eyes.

"And I like what I see, so . . . ?"

"You really like what you see?" he asked, his voice low.

"Yeah, Holt, I really do." She paused. "And that's hard for me to admit because I feel like you're so . . . so . . ."

"So . . . what?"

Heat crept into her cheeks and she wanted to change the subject, but he also deserved her honesty. "So out of my league," she all but whispered.

"Out of your league?" He frowned. "What's that supposed to mean?"

She couldn't help the short laugh that escaped her. "I mean, you deserve a lot better than me."

"Penny! Why would you say that?"

"Come on. Surely you've noticed I have my issues. I have a crazy mother. I have a father whom I love dearly, but he has no idea what it means to *really* be a father. Which means I haven't had the best example of what marriage and parenting look like. I still haven't fully dealt with my sister's death and it's been over a decade since she died. And last but not least, I have somehow become the possible target of a serial killer." She reached up to scrub her cheek with her palm once again. She felt like she'd never be able to erase the feel of his lips on her skin and it made her want to hurl. "You don't want to saddle yourself with . . . that. With me."

He fell silent, then reached over to take her hand in his. "What are you doing? I noticed your cheek was super red. He didn't hit you, did he?"

"No. He . . ." She really didn't want to say. It would sound stupid.

"What?" He pulled the car off onto the next exit, then swung into a gas station.

"We need gas?"

He turned toward her. "No, we need to talk. What are you not telling me? Come on, Penny, we're going deeper, right?"

She sighed and groaned. "He kissed me, all right? He kissed my cheek and I can't get the feel of it off my skin and it makes me want to hurl."

"Aw, Penny. I'm so sorry."

The tears came from nowhere, but they spilled over her lashes and down her cheeks, burning a path to her chin. He brushed the tears away, released her seat belt, and pulled her against his solid chest.

"No. I'm sorry. You didn't ask me to come so I could cry on your shoulder." She sniffed and forced herself to get a grip on her emotions.

"You needed to."

"Why? Because I'm female?" She pulled back and scowled at him.

"No, because it's been a horrible week and sometimes you just need to cry. I've cried a few times in my career. The day Rabor stabbed me and I thought I was going to die, I cried. I cried at Max's funeral and . . . some days are just cry days."

Penny sighed. "I'm sorry, Holt, I'm just . . . scared. And when I get scared, sometimes I get mad and say things I shouldn't."

"We've all been there, but we'll get through this, okay? To-gether."

She nodded. "I don't know what I'd do without you right now. And I don't mind letting you know that."

He smiled. "The feeling's mutual." He sobered. "Try not to get mad if you wind up in the same room with Jenkins. The truth is, he'll probably try to push your buttons, get you to react. It's how he amuses himself."

Penny drew in a deep breath. "All right. I have no intention of being his entertainment. I'll be all right." She'd probably have to call on every coping mechanism she'd learned to deal with her fear, but so be it. "Let's get back on the road and get this done."

"Yeah." He continued to study her. "First things first, though."

"What?"

He reached out to cup her chin, then ran his thumb over the area on her cheek she'd practically scrubbed raw. He pulled her closer and gently planted his lips on her cheek.

Penny went still, relishing the moment even while her pulse kicked into all kinds of crazy rhythms.

"That okay?" he asked.

"Um . . . yeah. It's . . . nice."

A chuckle rumbled in his chest. "Nice? Wow. Thanks."

"No, I meant—"

His lips cut her off and she let go of the tight leash she'd been keeping on her emotions. When his mouth trailed from her lips back to her cheek once more, she realized what he was doing and almost wept again. He drew back and she clasped the hand that now covered her cheek.

"Thank you, Holt," she whispered.

"Forget about him."

"Forget who?" A slight smile curved her lips and gratitude filled her.

"Exactly." He kissed her cheek once more, then gave her a nod. "Just for the record, I like kissing you."

"Just for the same record, I like kissing you too."

"Good to know." He paused. "You kiss better than 'nice.'"

She let out a choked laugh. "You do too, Holt, you do too."

"Thank you." His eyes turned serious. "You really want to hear about Max?"

"I really do."

When they were back on the highway, he slid her a sideways glance. "There was a kidnapping."

"When?"

"About five years ago. The son of a high-powered attorney was snatched from his nanny in the park. She was shot and left for dead. She survived long enough to call 911 and give us a description of the kidnapper and which direction he went. However, he was long gone by the time the search was organized. A few hours later, he made contact with the family and demanded a two-million-dollar ransom. He said no cops, not realizing the nanny had already called 911. We did our best to keep it quiet that we were involved, let the father—his name is Sam—talk to the kidnapper, et cetera. Sam talked to no one. Not even his supposed best friend, Kip Jenkins, who kept calling and coming by to check on him." His fingers flexed around the wheel. "So, we know Jenkins had no clue that we were involved."

"Did you suspect him?"

"Not really. There wasn't anything about him that drew our attention."

"Then how'd you catch him?"

"He messed up."

"How?"

"Max was about the same build as Sam and volunteered to go in his place to make the money drop. Sam resisted at first, but Max convinced him that it was safer that way. For everyone. Only it wasn't safe for Max." He swallowed and cleared his throat. "Kip Jenkins was an excellent hunter. He sat on the building across the street, and when Max posing as Sam got out of the car, Jenkins shot him and then ran. Apparently he didn't really care about the money. Everything was just contrived to kill Sam and get away with it. But, after he shot Max, we caught him before he could exit the building. Once Jenkins was in custody—along with the weapon containing his prints, the bullets in his coat pocket matching the bullet that killed Max—he spilled everything. He had set up the kidnapping to cause as much pain and heartache as he could for Sam before he killed him. He had no idea it was Max posing as Sam."

"But . . . why?"

"Revenge. Sam and Jenkins's wife were having an affair and Jenkins found out about it. Instead of just asking her for a divorce, he took revenge on the people who'd betrayed him. It didn't hurt that with Sam gone, Jenkins would inherit his share of the partnership, giving him controlling interest and a lot of power."

"What happened to the kid?"

Holt grimaced and looked away. "He . . ."

"He killed the kid, didn't he?" She couldn't keep the agony from her words.

"Yeah."

"How awful. How old was he?"

"Nine."

"Some days I hate people."

"Yeah," he said, his voice soft, "the bad ones anyway. Although he did say Christopher's death was an accident, but no one cares how he died. He died as a direct result of Jenkins and his need for revenge."

Penny fell quiet, almost wishing she hadn't asked. She thought about his story and determined to do whatever it took to get all the information Kip Jenkins might have on Darius Rabor.

Finally, Holt turned into the gates of the prison, flashed his badge, signed the log, and parked. He looked at her. "You ready?"

"Why not?"

"Okay, first things first. Leave your purse in the car, but bring your ID. There's a first set of doors that will open and close behind us before the next set opens."

"Okay."

"I'll have to leave my weapon in a locker and then we can proceed. Got it?"

"Got it."

Holt led Penny through the prison security and introduced her to Bill Bolton. Bill motioned to the seat next to his as Holt exited and she let her eyes scan the monitors. They were set up much like the hospital system. He pointed to the screen. "That's Jenkins. Holt will be entering any minute."

Sure enough, the door opened about thirty seconds later and Holt stepped inside. "Can we hear what they're saying?"

"No, but if Holt needs you in there, he'll look at the camera and nod."

Penny leaned forward. The pictures on the monitor were actually pretty good. Lipreading had never been her forte, but she was going to give it a try.

Holt sat in the chair and placed his hands on the table. Penny noted the tension in his shoulders, but his face betrayed no emotion.

His mouth moved and she thought he said, "Jenkins."

A smile curled the prisoner's lips, and Penny shuddered, hating the wave of fear that swept over her. That wasn't a man she wanted to come face-to-face with. Not because she was afraid he could hurt her while she was in there, but because that was the face of a man who knew he had the upper hand.

And that terrified her.

■　■　■　■

Holt tamped down the waves of hate that wanted to rise up and crash over him. This man had killed his partner and a nine-year-old child. If he had a conscience, he didn't let it dictate his actions.

"Thank you for coming to see me, Agent Satterfield," Jenkins said. "I've been asking to see you for about a month now. It's about time."

"You're not looking well, Jenkins." In fact, Holt had thought for a moment he'd entered the wrong room. "Your color's not that good and it looks like you've lost a good bit of weight. Prison doesn't agree with you, huh?"

The man waved a hand. "I've adapted."

Whatever. "You had something you wanted to tell me about Rabor?"

The man leaned back and crossed his arms. "In due time."

Holt reined in his impatience. Jenkins wasn't going to be hurried. "Fine," Holt said. "What do you want from me?"

"I want to meet the woman you brought with you."

"Why?"

"I don't have to explain myself to you. If you want to know what I know, then you'll bring her in here." He coughed into a tissue, then drew in a deep breath, but the look on his face never wavered.

Holt wanted to get up, grab Penny, and walk out the front door. There was no way he wanted to expose Penny to this guy, but if he had anything that would help him stop Rabor . . . He lifted his eyes to the camera and nodded. "She'll be here in a few minutes."

"Excellent."

"Seriously, what does Penny have to do with any of this?"

"I saw the news. Geneva Queen's daughter." He shrugged. "I'm a fan. But this isn't about her. Penny intrigued me. Reminded me of my daughter."

A flicker of something flashed in the man's eyes. Sadness? Not likely. The guy was an excellent actor. "Your daughter doesn't want anything to do with you."

"I'm aware, thanks."

The door opened and Penny stepped into the room. For a moment she hesitated, then lifted her chin and walked to settle into the chair next to Holt. She mirrored Holt's posture and placed her linked hands on the table in front of her. Her eyes locked on Jenkins. "Why do you want me here?"

Not a smidge of shakiness was in her words. She kept her eyes steady and her face blank. Man, she'd missed her calling. There were so many qualities about her that would make her a great agent.

Jenkins blinked like she'd surprised him. "Hello, Penny."

"Well?"

"I see you've been coached in how to respond to me."

"Coached?" She shrugged. "Of course. But I didn't really need coaching. I can think for myself."

He leaned forward. "So, what are you really feeling and thinking? Knowing you're in the presence of a killer?"

For a moment she didn't answer and Holt tensed, trying to get his feet under him. He honestly had no idea how to handle this situation, and it had him unnerved.

"What am I feeling?" she finally asked. "There are a myriad of emotions. There's disgust, sure. But also sadness that you felt like you had to do what you did. Sorrow for the lost lives—including yours—and the potential that was snuffed out due to your choices. But also curiosity as to why you want me here. As to what I'm thinking? At the moment, I'm thinking this guy is pathetic if he has to pretend to have information on a serial killer in order to get the attention he craves from people who have no desire to be in the same room with him." She paused. "Is that what you want to hear?"

Jenkins held his poker face exceptionally well and Holt struggled to get a read. Finally, the man laughed, then coughed into the tissue again. "Well, the reason I wanted you here is quite simple. If you're here, I can use you."

Penny went still. "How?"

He sighed. "I've done some vile things in my life. I've willingly confessed that. I need to make amends, so to speak. And I think you can help me do that."

Holt frowned. "What kind of amends?"

"Like you said earlier, my daughter wants nothing to do with me. I, however, would like to see her at least one more time before I die. I write her letters and I'm told she burns them. I send emails, she deletes them unopened. This is the only way I know how to possibly get her to come see me."

"Go on."

The man's gaze turned back to Penny. "Darius Rabor and I became . . . friends. That's not really the word, but I'm not sure of the right one, so we'll just use that one for now."

"Sure. Why not?" She held herself stiff, but her hands stayed relaxed, unmoving.

"Where are you going with this, Jenkins?" Holt asked.

"I'm getting there. Learn some patience."

Holt held on to his tongue with effort.

"Rabor saved my life about a month after he was placed here," Jenkins said. "After that, I owed him, you know?"

"Right. And?"

"And, he milked that for all he could. The last thing I did for him was call his girlfriend to let her know he was on the way to the hospital for surgery."

Well, that answered how Allen had known what to do. "He was planning on escaping at some point, wasn't he?" Holt asked.

"Yes. He was obsessed with it. Had it all worked out. Only when he started hurting real bad and the doc here said he needed gall bladder surgery, he decided to fast-forward the timeline of his escape."

Holt was getting frustrated, but decided to let the guy keep talking.

"Rabor's visitor, the girlfriend," Jenkins said, "she wasn't really his girlfriend."

"We know."

Surprise raised his brows. "Huh. No kidding."

"We know exactly who was visiting. So, what do you think you have that we need?"

"Rabor communicated with me. He told me all kinds of interesting things."

"Like what?"

A slight lift of the prisoner's shoulder said he wasn't ready to reveal that yet. "Like why he kills, how he picks his victims, how it makes him feel . . . those kinds of things. And I know that he's been hiding out, healing and growing stronger with each passing day." He paused, then tapped the table with a finger. "And I know that he has his eyes on that one." He dipped his head at Penny.

Penny drew in a slow breath. "Why?"

"You impressed him." He clicked his tongue. "I can see why now."

"Enough," Holt said. "Do you know where he is?"

"No. I know you don't want to believe that, but it's true. I can tell you that his sister would do anything to help him. Not out of any special love for him, but she's scared to death not to. More scared of him than being arrested for aiding and abetting."

Understandable.

"Rabor's 'girlfriend' was a guy named Joel Allen," Jenkins said.

"Again, nothing we don't already know," Holt said.

"Wow, you guys are more efficient than I've given you credit for."

"You're here," Holt said. "I'd say we're efficient enough."

"Touché."

That weird little smile curved his lips once more. And once more, Holt wanted to wipe it from his face. He resisted. "Talk, man. If you're not going to help, quit wasting our time."

Jenkins narrowed his eyes and his nostrils flared slightly, but he nodded. "Fine. Here are my conditions. I will be totally open and honest with you and provide you everything I know about Rabor, but I want something in return."

This was the moment Holt had been waiting for. "What?"

"I want you—the two of you—to convince my daughter to come visit me."

Holt didn't say anything, he simply stared at the man.

"That's why you wanted me here," Penny said. "Because if I can say that I was in the same room with you and wasn't uncomfortable, then maybe your daughter would think she could come."

The killer's eyes turned to hers. "She's the same age as you are. Almost to the day."

Holt bristled. The man had been researching Penny?

"You're very smart, aren't you?" Jenkins asked Penny.

"Yes. I am."

He smiled again. This time it was simply a smile of amusement, and maybe even a flicker of hope that he'd come up with a plan that would garner him a visit with his only child. "I didn't kill that little boy on purpose," he said. "I was going to let him go home to his mother as soon as Sam was dead. I had nothing against the child or his mother. I actually felt sorry for her. She was as clueless as I was about our cheating spouses." His gaze locked on Holt's. "And . . . I had nothing against your partner. I thought he was Sam."

"The child's name was Christopher," Holt said, doing his best to keep his emotions in check. "His mother's name is Lillian. My partner's name was Max. All lives—and the lives of those who loved them—you traumatized because of your desire for revenge."

"Yes." Jenkins cleared his throat. "And I have my regrets—which is why I've asked to see you now."

An awkward silence fell between them and Holt let out a slow breath, ready to get out of there. "Your daughter has sworn never to visit you. Ever. I seriously doubt that Penny and I can talk her into it."

"Then I guess I'll carry my information to the grave. The doctor says I could have a few months, or it could be any day."

Holt frowned. "What are you talking about?"

"Pancreatic cancer," Penny murmured. Both men looked at her and she shrugged. "An educated guess. The jaundice, the saggy skin from what was probably recent and rapid weight loss, and I'm sure there are other symptoms that medication may be helping. But it's getting worse daily, isn't it?"

"Like I said, you're very smart."

Penny leaned forward. "You've been waiting for this moment for a while, haven't you?"

CHAPTER
NINETEEN

Holt swung his gaze to Penny. "What are you talking about?"

Penny kept her eyes on the man in front of her. Knowing his illness—and how weak he most likely was at the moment— removed a lot of her fear. But she still didn't want to underestimate him. "He's been trying to get his daughter to visit. If Rabor escaped, it was only a matter of time before it got back to you that the two of them were . . . friends. You'd come needing information and"—she spread her hands—"let the bargaining begin." She sat back and glanced at Holt. "The only question is, do we let him get away with it?" She narrowed her eyes. "I'm not sure I buy the whole needing to make amends thing. Does he really have anything worth bargaining with?"

The only change in Holt's expression was the slight widening of his eyes before his lashes lowered to cover his surprise.

For a moment, Jenkins's nostrils flared, then he laughed. "You remind me so much of Carol. It's almost like I've been blessed by a visit from her."

"Well, you haven't," Penny said. "And you won't be unless you give us something right now."

Penny's gut churned, but she refused to be the first one to look away. The staring contest went on for several moments before Jenkins let out a low sigh.

"Well, well . . ." He nodded. "All right, then. Rabor had a woman he was seeing on a regular basis—and I don't mean that idiot Allen who dressed up like a woman. Rabor had all kinds of female groupies. You guys wouldn't believe the letters he'd get." He studied Holt. "Well, yeah, I guess you would. But anyway, hundreds of letters a week from women begging him to let them visit. He'd add the ones who sounded interesting to his list of ten 'friends' and take off the ones he didn't want to see again. Then he'd replace them with the newbies. The man held court every chance he got with one woman or another. Even some men who wanted to come express their admiration for his . . . work."

Penny managed to keep the grimace from her face. Barely.

"But this one woman came once a month. Unlike Joel Allen, who came just about every time the door opened."

"Who was the woman?"

"I don't know, but she was different than the regular groupies. She kept her head down and didn't make eye contact with anyone. She also wore a wig and changed her appearance every so often, but I could tell it was the same person."

"But she had to show her ID," Holt said. "She had to be cleared to visit."

"And she had an ID to match each look, according to Rabor. I think she had three different identities. He admired her, said she was a *brilliant little mouse*." He paused. "Rabor never said much of anything else about her, but I think the three of them—Rabor, Allen, and the woman—were all working out an escape plan for him. He said my part was just to call the number he gave me when the time came."

"Joel Allen."

"Right. He said Allen was such an easy target and that grooming him was as easy as taking candy from a baby. Said Allen would do anything for Rabor."

"Including kill for him?"

Jenkins hesitated, then clicked his tongue. "Oh, yeah. The two of them were interesting to watch. Rabor told him exactly his process, explained what he did and how he did it. Each time he came to visit, he had 'homework,' and each time he returned, he had to give a detailed report to Rabor. And Rabor would give him a grade. Look at the footage, you'll see what I mean."

"Who was visiting you to give you the opportunity to sit there and watch Rabor?" Penny asked.

"My attorney." He chuckled. "And believe it or not, I had the occasional groupie, too, who I humored out of sheer boredom—and the desire to see who Rabor was entertaining that day."

Holt rubbed a hand over his chin. "Where is Rabor now? Where would he go?"

"Well, he and Allen and this chick, whoever she is, had all that worked out." He paused. "But I think I've given you enough. If you want to know where Rabor is, get Carol here to visit me. Once that's done, then I'll tell you where I think he could be."

■ ■ ■ ■

Holt rubbed a hand across his eyes. The whole drive to Columbia, he'd fought to find a way to bring up his sister Zoe and had fumbled the pass with each opportunity. Every time he pulled her name to his tongue, he froze.

Now, he and Penny sat in the fast-food parking lot, engine running, heater blasting, sandwiches in hand. Hers slowly disappeared, while his dripped ketchup on his fingers, his mind on Rabor, Allen, Jenkins, and Carol.

"She doesn't live far from here," Penny said.

"Uh-huh." Rabor was out there and he was convinced Jenkins knew where he was. It infuriated him that the man was pulling their strings.

"We could swing by and see if she's there."

"Uh-huh." There was no way he wanted to give in to the demands of—*okay, bargaining with*—a killer, but what choice did they have? They could talk to Jenkins's daughter, tell her what her old man wanted, and if she said no, she said no. If she said yes, then that would be a win, right? Jenkins was a walking dead man anyway. Maybe Carol would like the opportunity to settle some things with her father before he died.

A gentle punch on his arm jerked him from his thoughts. "Hey! What was that for?"

"Did you hear a word I said?"

Had he? He blinked. "Oh, the daughter." He took a bite. On a different day, he would have relished the explosion of flavors. For now, he just needed the energy the burger would give him. "I don't know, Penny. I don't want to give him that much power."

"I don't blame you, but if it will allow you to stop Rabor before he kills again, then . . ."

"It's a no-brainer. Yeah." He pulled his phone from his pocket and paused. "I think an in-person visit would be best."

"Absolutely."

"I'm going to run it by my supervisor first and . . ."

"And what?"

"We have to consider this may be an ambush set up by Rabor."

Her eyes widened. "Oh."

"But first, let's see if Carol is available."

He dialed the number and put it on speaker while he swallowed another bite.

"Hello?"

The soft alto voice held a gravelly edge that sounded like he'd just woken her up. "Carol?"

"Yes. Who's this?"

"I'm Holt Satterfield." Now, how much to tell her? Would she shut him down if he told her about his visit with her father?

"Should I know that na—" She went silent. "Wait a minute. I *do* know that name." All traces of sleep had fled. "My father killed your partner, Max Isaacs."

"Yes." And a little boy and his nanny, but he'd refrain from mentioning that for now.

A slight hesitation, then, "Why are you calling me?"

"I'd like to come visit you for a few minutes if it's convenient?"

More silence. "Or even if it's not?" she finally asked.

"Yeah, unfortunately."

"Why? He's not getting out, is he?"

"No, no. Nothing like that. But it is fairly urgent, and I'd rather discuss this face-to-face, and we drove down from Asheville."

"Um . . . sure. Okay. I assume you have my address?"

"I do. We're about ten minutes from you, but if you need more time, we can give it to you."

A sigh slipped through the line and Holt winced. "No, that's all right. I work third shift as a lab tech so I usually sleep during the day, but I'm off tomorrow, so I can rest up after I talk to you."

"Thanks, Carol. I really appreciate this."

"Sure."

He hung up and finished his burger and fries in less than a minute. Penny was eyeing him, her brows hidden beneath her bangs. "That was almost too easy."

"She doesn't know we're going to talk to her about her father."

"True."

"Now one more call."

He dialed Gerald's number and the man answered with a gruff "Yeah?"

"I need to fill you in." He explained the situation, and Gerald promised to arrange for local law enforcement to meet them at the house.

He programmed the GPS with Carol's address, then pulled out of the parking lot.

About ten minutes later, they arrived at Carol's home. A small house in a tiny neighborhood close to the private hospital where she worked. Holt climbed out of the car, waved to the officers on the curb, and walked over. "Everything look okay?"

"Yeah. We did some recon and she's alone. Ran her license and no outstanding warrants, no gun permits, or anything else. She's a lab tech who works third and has an outstanding record there, according to her boss. Looks legit."

"All right, thanks. Can you just hang out here until we're done?"

"Planned on it."

"Thanks."

He motioned to Penny and she followed him up the three steps to the front door. It opened before he had a chance to ring the bell. A young woman in her late twenties stood there dressed in sweats and a long-sleeved T-shirt. Her black curly hair streamed down her back, and her dark eyes glittered with a suppressed anger that Holt didn't think was directed at him. Not all of it anyway.

"Hi," he said. "I'm Holt and this is Penny." He showed her his badge.

She studied it for a long moment, then stepped back. "Come on in." Once he and Penny were seated on the love seat, Carol settled into the wingback chair in the corner opposite them. "What can I do for you?"

Holt blew out a low breath and said a silent prayer for the right words. "Okay, so I'm just going to come right out and tell you what's going on."

"Okay." That one word held all the wariness in the world.

"Penny and I went to see your father early this morning."

Carol's lips tightened and her eyes narrowed. "Why?"

"Because he asked us to come. Said he had some information on a case I'm working and promised to tell us what it was if we would visit him in person." *Blackmailed us* would be more accurate, but he didn't want to get off on the wrong foot with her.

"I see. What does that have to do with me?"

"He wants to see you."

"I know. I don't want to see him." She shrugged. "End of story."

"Not quite," Penny said, speaking for the first time. She shot a glance at Holt, as though asking for permission to continue, and he nodded. "Your father is very ill. I'm in the medical profession and I can tell you that he doesn't have much time left. He said he was told a few months, but I'd be skeptical of that."

Carol leaned forward, her face pale. "He's dying?"

"Yes."

The woman dropped her head and went silent for a moment. When she looked up, her expression held a frozen contempt that chilled Holt to the core. "Good," she said. "Then maybe I can finally be free of him and his tragic legacy."

Holt sighed and scrubbed a hand down his cheek. "I can understand how you'd feel that way, but there's more to this than just us delivering a message that your father is dying."

"I kind of thought so. Why don't you just spit it out?"

"I'm sure you've heard of Darius Rabor."

She frowned. "Who hasn't? The serial killer who escaped and—" She stilled. "Wait, let me guess. He has something on Rabor and he wants something in order to give you the info."

"Yeah." Holt nodded.

She stood. "No. Don't let him pull your strings."

"I wouldn't normally," Holt said, "but there's nothing normal about this situation."

"So, what does he want?"

Holt hesitated only a fraction of a second. "You to visit."

Her eyes flashed and her nostrils flared. "Yeah, that's kind of where I thought this was going. But . . . absolutely not. You can leave now." The finger that pointed at the door shook.

"Please," Penny said, her voice soft. "Won't you at least consider it? At first, being in the same room with him kind of creeped me out, but once I got a good look at him—he's not a threat to you or anyone else right now." She leaned closer. "He might have information leading to the apprehension of a killer. I'm not saying it'll be easy, but if you don't do this, someone else may die."

"Then you shouldn't have let him escape."

Holt raked a hand over his head. "You're right. He should have had better security. Something. But we can't go back and get a do-over. We have to stop him now."

"Then you'll have to do it without me. I'm not going to see him. Ever." She crossed her arms and clamped her jaw tight.

"What if it was someone you loved?" Penny asked. "Your mother, your sister, or your best friend? And you found out someone else could have stopped the killer and didn't? How would you feel?"

For a moment, Carol looked like Penny had reached out and smacked her across the face. Tears welled and she groaned, then dropped back onto the chair.

Penny pressed her palms against her temples. "I'm sorry. I shouldn't try to guilt you into it."

"No, you shouldn't, but . . . ugh!" Carol shook her head and looked at the ceiling. "Do you know what that man has cost me?"

"I can't imagine," Penny said.

"No, you can't." She swiped the tears on her cheeks. "Fine. I'll go see him."

Thank you, Lord. "Thank you," Holt said.

"When?"

Holt pursed his lips, then sighed. "Now."

Her eyes widened. "Now? But it's almost dark and visiting hours—"

"We have a serial killer to catch. Every minute he's out there could mean there's someone breathing her last. We have special permission to take you there."

Carol flinched and Holt felt bad about his direct shot, but . . . it was true.

"Wow," Carol muttered, "nothing like giving a girl a chance to prepare herself."

"I know. I'm sorry."

"Fine." She paused. "I'm not on the list of visitors."

"Actually, you are."

"Of course I am."

"Would you like to ride with us or—"

She waved a hand. "No. I'll drive myself. If you're from Asheville, then no sense in you having to come back this way."

Holt nodded. "Thank you."

She paused.

"Everything okay?"

"No, I'm just thinking . . . I'm going to call my best friend and ask her to go with me. I think after seeing my father, I'm going to need the support."

"Of course. I should have suggested it." As long as she didn't back out, he was okay with whatever she wanted to do.

"Let me just give her a call." Carol pulled her phone from her back pocket and stepped into the kitchen. "Hey, Jackie, you're not going to believe what's going on here . . . yeah . . . uh-huh . . . I need a favor . . ." She moved away and he wasn't able to hear the rest of the one-sided conversation but was again comforted that she seemed to be following through with everything.

Holt turned back to see Penny rubbing her temples. "Headache?"

"Yeah. Stress and still getting over being punched by Joel Allen, I guess."

He frowned. "You need to get checked out?"

"Nah, just need some Motrin."

Carol hung up. "My friend Jackie said she could go with me and just wait in the car. Why don't we just meet you there?"

Holt didn't like it, but it would give them a chance to grab some fuel and make sure everything was ready for Carol to visit. He nodded. "Text when you get close."

"I will."

Finally. They couldn't get this visit over with soon enough, as far as Holt was concerned. Because the longer it took them to find Rabor, the shorter someone's life was.

CHAPTER
TWENTY

Penny kept an eye on the mirrors, worried someone might have followed them, but so far, so good. A few minutes from the prison, Holt slowed. "Great."

"What is it?"

"A wreck, I think. They've got us detouring." He turned right. "I was trying to stay away from the back roads." He got his phone and called in their change of route.

"You think that's necessary?"

"Absolutely. Until Rabor is behind bars again, we're not taking any chances."

"You think the wreck was a setup? That it was done to get us off the main road?"

"No. Rabor's clever, but he had no idea we were going to see his prison buddy. I don't see how he had time to set that up."

"Unless his prison buddy called him after we left and told him what we were doing?"

Holt shot her a surprised look. "You sure you don't want to join the Bureau?"

"Why?"

"Because you think like an agent." His fingers flexed on the wheel and he took the next curve in a smooth motion. "But it wasn't Jenkins."

"How do you know?"

"Before I left, I made sure that Jenkins wouldn't have access to a telephone for the rest of the day. He'll be in solitary until we're done and back in Asheville."

"Oh. Good." She fell silent, then chuckled.

"What?"

"Not sure how good an agent I'd make since I thought about that much later than you."

He shot her a soft smile. "I've been doing this job for a while. You train, build your skills as much as possible, then learn from experience." His smile faded. "And you learn from your mistakes."

"You've made mistakes?"

He scoffed. "That's sarcasm, right?"

"Kind of. But not really."

"Oh, I've made my share of mistakes, Penny." His fingers clutched the wheel. "Like letting my partner walk into a situation that didn't have enough protection for him. He was too vulnerable and I—"

"Did you really have any say in the matter? Was it really you *letting* him do it?"

"Well, no, I guess I didn't let him do anything, but I keep going back to the fact that I never saw it coming. One minute he was making the drop, the next minute he was dead."

"Didn't he know the risks when he signed up for it?"

"Yeah."

"But it doesn't make it any easier."

"No."

A small pop sounded through the SUV and the vehicle jerked to the right. Holt yanked the wheel back. "What in the world?" He guided the car to the side of the road and cut the engine.

Holt stepped out of the vehicle. Penny pushed her door open.

"Everything okay?" she asked.

He popped the hood. "Getting ready to find out. Tires are fine, so it has to be something under here. This is a newer car. It's only got thirty thousand miles on it."

Even though it was a two-lane back road with open fields and pastureland on either side, traffic was still busy. Thankfully there'd been plenty of room to pull the vehicle over.

A car zipped past and Penny frowned. "They go fast on these little back roads, don't they?"

"Yeah. They do." He leaned over the engine.

An eighteen-wheeler approached. Yet another vehicle she thought should go much slower. "What'd you find?"

He looked up. "I'm not sure, but I think someone sabotaged the battery cable. There's some residue on the cable that wasn't there the last time I looked and I check under the hood often. There's no way this would have happened so fast."

Oh boy.

The semi whipped past, sending the vehicle rocking and Holt scowling. "Makes me wish for my state trooper days."

"State trooper? Really? How long did you do that?"

"About two years before I was accepted into the Bureau." His frown deepened. "Okay, I think we're set." He stepped back and put his hand on the hood.

"Uh-oh," Penny said.

"What is it?" He shut the hood as the roar of a motorcycle reached them.

Penny watched it from the corner of her eye. "Holt?"

"Yeah."

"He's got a gun."

■ ■ ■ ■

Holt grabbed Penny's arm and jerked her behind the cover of the Bucar. Bullets slammed into the side and Holt snagged his weapon from his holster. "Call it in!"

Penny was already dialing and he knew he could count on her to keep her cool. And her head down.

While she shouted their location at the dispatcher, Holt watched the shooter spin around and charge back his way, the bike roaring. This time no bullets came their way. Instead, an object flew through the air, bounced off the hood, and landed on the ground.

Sirens ripped through the air even as the rider gunned the bike and sped away.

Holt bolted after him, trying to see the plate but missed it. The whole thing took less than two minutes, and no other cars had been on the road at the time. Their attacker had chosen well.

Penny jogged up beside him. "What was that all about?"

"I have no idea."

"He threw something."

"Yeah, but at least it didn't blow up." Holt hurried to the vehicle's trunk and grabbed a pair of gloves. He slipped them over his hands just as the first cruiser pulled to a stop behind him in the emergency lane. Holt rushed to give the officer the direction the shooter had disappeared and the man took off. The next cruiser pulled up and Holt launched into a rapid-fire description of the situation. "It was all over incredibly fast." He'd have a better understanding now when a victim claimed everything was a blur. That's exactly what it was like. He stopped at the object the guy had thrown and noted the piece of paper wrapped around a rock. "How original," he muttered.

"A note?" Penny asked. "That's a lot of drama just to send a message."

Using gloved hands, Holt unwrapped the paper and dropped the rock into an evidence bag held by one of the officers. "Thanks."

"What's it say?"

"'I am discontented with the women I've killed, I keep searching for that perfect one. Creating a place in this lovely oasis, where no one can hear you scream. Far from the crowds and city lights, where pretty flowers float in the stream . . .'"

"What kind of nonsense is that?" the officer asked.

"It's not nonsense," Penny said, her voice tight. "Put the words to the song 'Tea for Two' and it kind of takes on new meaning."

"What are the words?" Holt asked.

She looked them up on her phone and handed the device to Holt. "Read them, then compare."

Holt did. And the more he read, the more his stomach dipped and churned. "Sicko." But he already knew that.

Rabor had been right there within twenty feet of him. Granted, he'd been shooting and flying past on a motorcycle, but still . . . "We'll get it to the lab and see if they can pull any prints, but I wouldn't hold my breath."

"Maybe they can find out the kind of paper or ink he used or something and trace it back to the store he bought it from," Penny said.

"It's a long shot, but I've seen stranger things."

She stared at the evidence bag that now held the rock and the note. "So, was that for me or you?"

Holt sighed. "Well, considering that the guy's victims are all female . . ."

"Right. Lovely."

"All right. We're going to have to leave this with the local cops and get to the prison. I don't want Carol showing up and us not being there."

It took ten more minutes to actually get on the road, but once they were away from the scene—with two officers following to ensure they got there with no more incidents—Penny looked over at him. "You're worried she won't show up?"

"A little, yeah."

"Yeah."

Penny fell silent, and soon he was pulling through the gate and back to the parking spot with no trouble. From there, he and Penny went through security once more and were led to the same private room they'd left not long ago.

Jenkins wasn't there yet, and Holt allowed himself to pace for the moment. The fact that Zoe was in this very prison haunted him. He should try to see her, but every time he did—on the rare occasions that she agreed to even meet him—his heart shattered all over again. And the anger . . . it was almost impossible to control the anger that blindsided him every single time. Not to mention the grief his anger caused her.

The last time he'd been there—about a month ago—she'd risen from her chair. *"Stop asking me to tell you something that I can't tell you. Go away, Holt. There's no reason for you to come back. You're a fixer and you can't fix this. So just go away and don't come back. For both our sakes."*

CHAPTER
TWENTY-ONE

"Holt?"

Penny had called his name three times and he'd continued to pace, his gaze on the floor. She didn't think he was ignoring her but was so deep in thought, she'd ceased to exist.

The door opened and Carol stepped inside. Only then did Holt look up. The relief on his handsome features said he'd been deep-down worried—more than he'd even admitted to her—that the woman would back out.

"Thanks for doing this, Carol," he said, pulling out the third visitor chair that had been added.

Carol nodded and slipped into the seat, then twisted her fingers together in her lap. "What do I say to him? How do I respond to get him to tell you what you need?"

Holt sat and faced her while Penny leaned against the wall. She was too antsy to sit yet.

"How do you want to react?" Holt asked.

"I want to continue to simply ignore his existence. But that probably won't get you the information you need."

"Right." Holt cleared his throat. "Well, you don't have to fall all over yourself or anything. Let him make the first move, then you can play it cool. He knows how you feel about him, and he knows that you wouldn't be here without our . . . *encouragement*. But if I read him right, he's also hoping for reconciliation before he dies."

The woman closed her eyes for a fraction of a second, then opened them and nodded. "I'm ready."

Holt walked to the door and knocked on it. The guard opened it. "Y'all ready for Mr. Jenkins?"

"We are."

"Be right back."

Less than a minute later, the door opened once more and Jenkins was led in, cuffs rattling, feet shuffling.

Carol didn't look up.

Jenkins settled at the table and the guard shackled him to the bolt on the table, then left.

Silence descended.

Penny's gaze stayed on the prisoner and Carol. Holt kept quiet as well.

Finally, Jenkins cleared his throat. "Thank you for coming, Carol."

She looked up and Penny caught her breath at the hate in the woman's eyes. "They made it hard to refuse."

Jenkins's eyes jumped to Holt's, then Penny's, then landed back on his daughter's. "Well, that was the deal."

"Yes. I heard. I'm here. Tell them what they want to know."

"Only if you promise not to bolt out the door. I have some things I need to say, and I can't do that if you're slamming the door behind you as soon as I finish giving them what they want."

"I won't bolt." She drew in a shuddering breath. "I'll let you say whatever it is you want to say before I leave."

He gave a slow nod, watching her, drinking her in. "Rabor has a sister on the mountain. Her name is Natasha."

"We know of her," Holt said.

"I heard Rabor talk about a little place on Fairfield Lake. He said Natasha's husband's family had a house there." He shrugged. "It's possible he might head there."

Penny could tell by Holt's sudden tension that this was news to him. He tapped the information into his phone while Penny studied the prisoner. She wasn't sure if she believed him or not. "What did Rabor think about Joel's desire to look exactly like him, do you know?" she asked.

The man didn't answer right away. Then he met her gaze. The lack of . . . anything . . . in his eyes sent a shudder through her. "He thought it was pathetic—and it made him feel like a very powerful god."

"He encouraged it."

"Of course. He said Allen worshiped him, and I had no reason to believe otherwise. It sure looked like it every time I saw them together at visitation."

"Did Rabor ever mention Joel's wife, Sally?" Penny asked.

"Only once to say he felt sorry for the woman, being stuck with a man like Joel."

Penny huffed. "I doubt he felt sorry for her. I doubt he feels much of anything except whatever drives his twisted behavior."

"Yeah, I'll admit, I don't understand that. I *do* understand the driving need for revenge and how it can overtake everything, but I can't understand killing just to . . . kill." At his daughter's audible indrawn breath, he looked at her. "I made my choices," he said. "Choices that I'd like to rethink if I had the chance."

"So, you regret everything that led up to my partner's death?" Holt asked.

For a moment, there was silence. "I regret the boy's— *Christopher's*—death. And the nanny's. And I regret that I killed the wrong man."

"But you'd do it all over again," Carol said, "if you thought you could kill the right one?" Again, she controlled her tone, her voice betraying nothing of what she might be feeling.

Penny was impressed, but maybe the woman had been practicing for a while.

Jenkins sighed and rubbed a shaking hand over his face. "I

figure now isn't the time to lie, so . . . while I want to say I'd make a different choice if I had it to do all over again, knowing I'd get the right guy . . . I don't know what to tell you. With the frame of mind I was in at the time, I don't know what I'd do."

"You're unbelievable," Carol said, her voice low. "Am I supposed to respect that or something? The fact that you're not lying?"

"No, Carol. I just . . . need to make peace. With you, with God, with myself. I can't do that if I add to the lies."

His daughter sat back and crossed her arms. Her throat worked and her hands trembled. She curled them into fists and continued to stare at her father. "Why should you get to have peace just because you're dying?"

Penny flinched. Not that she didn't want to agree in a "he deserves what he gets" kind of way, but the other part of her wanted him to find redemption. Forgiveness due to true repentance. She just couldn't decide if this was a charade and he was working toward some other agenda.

He looked away from Carol and down at his hands. "I want to be a different man. The kind of man you can love again. I want you to come see me because you want to, not because I have to manipulate it."

Carol gasped aloud and Penny placed a hand on the woman's shoulder. The muscles were knotted tighter than any fisherman's line. "Well, Dad," Carol said, "I don't know that that's going to happen. Now, before these people leave, do you have anything helpful to add that will send them in the right direction?"

He looked up. Met Penny's eyes, then slid his gaze over to Holt. "Darius Rabor is very good at getting whatever he wants. If he has his sights set on his next victim, then it won't be long before he acts. If you can figure out his next victim, you should be able to catch him when he goes for her."

"We know his next victim," Penny said.

Carol blinked and Jenkins raised a brow. "Who?"

"From all appearances . . . me."

■　■　■　■

Holt winced. Neither of them had come out and said she was Rabor's next victim, but after the attack in the hospital and then again on the road, it was obvious to him she was.

Apparently, it was obvious to her as well.

Jenkins coughed into the ever-present tissue and narrowed his eyes at Penny. "Well, now, little lady, I sure hope you've got some protection."

"She does," Holt said. "Anything else?"

The man rubbed a hand over his mouth and shook his head. "No. That's all. I promise. You held up your end of the bargain and I promised not to hold back. I know it's not what you were hoping for, but I would have said anything to get her here. She's here. If I had anything else, I'd tell you."

Holt stood. "I figured as much." He curled his fingers into fists and stared into the eyes he'd hated for so long. Eyes that had reflected nothing each time he saw them—or maybe that's what he expected to see and so did. But now, the same eyes were those of an old, sick man looking for forgiveness—whether he'd put that word on it or not, it was there. "I hope you find that peace," Holt said before he could stop the words from passing through his lips, but once he said them, he realized he meant them. He knew a pastor who visited those in prison on a weekly basis. He'd ask the man to stop in and see if Jenkins wanted to talk. He had to do it, because he wouldn't be able to live with himself if he didn't help the man find eternal answers he might be looking for.

Holt looked at Carol. "Do you need us to stay?"

"No. I'm going to let him have his say, then I'll head home. My friend drove, so I won't be alone."

"Good. Thank you again."

She nodded and Holt could tell she was hanging on to her emotions by a thread. He could only pray that whatever Jenkins said to her, it would give them both some peace and closure.

Penny said goodbye to Carol and followed Holt out of the room. In the hallway, she rubbed her eyes and blinked up at him. "Has Daria gotten back to you on the place at the lake?"

He raised a brow. She was always either right in step with him or one step ahead. Again, he found her incredibly intriguing. And attractive. "Yeah. They've sent some local officers out to take a look. Two agents from the nearest field office are meeting them. For me, it's just wait and see."

"I understand." She retrieved the belongings she'd been required to leave in a special area and checked her phone with a groan. "I have fourteen missed calls."

"From who?"

"Several from my mother, one from my dad, one from Raina, Holly, two from Grace, a bunch from someone with no name, but I have no doubt it belongs to the ace reporter Frankie Olander, and then a couple from Dr. Kirkpatrick, my boss."

"You can block the reporter."

"I blocked the first three numbers he used." She tapped the screen. "Let me just check the voice mails."

"Of course."

She listened while they walked. Holt checked his phone once he was in the driver's seat. Still nothing from Daria. He buckled up and headed toward Asheville. It was going to be close to midnight when they got back.

Penny hung up and sighed. "Well, nothing pressing there. That's a relief. I'm off tomorrow, too, so it looks like I have no excuse to put off painting my dining room."

"Want some company?"

"You? I thought you had a serial killer to find."

"I do. I'm thinking Julianna and Grace might be able to pitch in."

She laughed. "I love that you volunteer my friends for that. Sure, if they're free, that would be lovely, but don't they have to work?"

He shot her a glance. "They *would* be working."

"Oh. Right. I'll text them and see what they think." She sent the text and, within seconds, chuckled. "They both said they'd be waiting at my house when we got there."

"They're good friends."

Her expression warmed, then went pensive. "The three of us had a crazy childhood. I never would have pictured Grace working for the FBI and pulling Julianna in after her."

"How'd you escape?"

She shrugged. "I wanted to fly. Grace knew that."

"You could fly for the Bureau."

"True, but that's not where my heart is. I like the rescues. I like the daily possibility of being the reason someone is alive the next day."

He cleared his throat. "Um . . . well, yeah, I kinda get to do that, too, you know."

She wrinkled her nose at him. "I guess you do. You just get to go about it a bit differently. I'm not really interested in all of the investigative stuff."

"You'd be good at it. You have the mind for it."

"Well, thanks, I appreciate that, but I'll leave it to you and the others."

He reached over and squeezed her fingers, then let go. She yawned and leaned her head back against the seat. When her eyes fluttered shut, Holt turned his attention to the road and let his mind work through the case. From Joel Allen to Darius Rabor and Kip Jenkins.

And finally, to Zoe. And the fact that he hadn't told Penny about her. So much for being open and going deeper. He grimaced. He still hadn't looked at the video. He needed to find a moment to do so, but while Rachel was working diligently with Zoe and the new evidence, Holt would focus on the case and keeping Penny safe.

Three hours later, Holt pulled to a stop in her driveway and shook Penny awake. When she'd fallen asleep, he'd let her snooze. Now, she opened her eyes and stretched. "We're here already?"

"It helps to sleep away the miles."

"And no one shot at us or tried to run us off the road or anything?"

He huffed a short laugh. "No. We did have a state trooper in front of us and one in back, so if anyone was tempted to try anything, they resisted."

She smothered a yawn. "Great. Thanks. I think I can manage from here."

Holt watched her until the front door swung shut behind her. As he backed out of her drive, Grace pulled in. Followed by Julianna. They waved, and the tight knot of worry that had formed in his gut loosened a fraction. They'd promised to spend the night and help her paint tomorrow. She'd be all right with those two at her side.

Just as he headed for the intersection that would lead him toward his hotel, he caught sight of Frankie Olander sitting in his vehicle, with a very expensive camera aimed at Penny's home. Holt slammed the SUV in park, shoved out of the seat, and strode over to the reporter. "What kind of pictures do you think you're going to get in the dark?"

"You never know."

"What are you doing here, man?"

"Waiting."

"On what?"

"Her answer. When she tells me she's willing to give me the exclusive, I want to be right there before she has a chance to change her mind."

"What makes you think she's going to give you the exclusive?"

"Because she knows that this story is going to get told. And deep down she knows I'm not a bad guy. I've even managed to keep her home a secret from everyone else."

"How?"

"Mostly luck." He sighed. "Look, I'm the only one asking for her input, and she really needs to hurry. As soon as someone turns in a story, if the editor doesn't have anything else, he'll run it."

"Even if it's a bunch of lies?"

"Well, it won't be a bunch of lies, but it might not be the truth she'd prefer."

Holt sighed and shook his head. "Stay out of her way."

"I'm just sitting here."

Yes, he was just sitting there. Holt hoped he would get tired of "just sitting there" and move on, but he wasn't holding his breath. Then again, with the reporter watching the outside . . . Holt pulled a card from his wallet. "I can't believe I'm doing this, but if you see anything weird, will you give me a call?"

"Weird as in how?"

"You'll know it when you see it."

The man frowned but tucked the card above his visor. "Yeah, sure."

"Thanks."

Holt went back to his car to call Penny and let her know Frankie was watching her house. And to let him stay there.

For now.

CHAPTER
TWENTY-TWO

Monday morning, Penny rose early from a sound sleep thanks to Julianna and Grace's presence. She peered out the window, noting Frankie's Honda Accord parked across the street. Last night, Holt had said to leave the man alone and let him watch the house, that his presence might be a good thing in this instance.

Well, fine. But the man's persistence irritated her. However, she was willing to move past that since there were no other reporters on her doorstep. "Guess he's going to hold up his end of the bargain," she muttered. For the most part anyway. Apparently, he was going to give her the forty-eight hours, but he wasn't going to stop collecting whatever information he could during that time. And that meant watching her home. Whatever.

She sighed and Grace pulled her from the window. "Come on, girl. You got us here to paint and these walls aren't going to paint themselves."

"Right. Gimme a roller." Julianna slapped one in her hand and Penny frowned. "Are you sure you're up to painting? Your arm still has to be sore."

"The sore arm is my left one. I'm right-handed, so no more excuses. I've got the roller. You guys get the hard-to-reach places."

"Still as bossy as ever," Grace said. Julianna stuck her tongue out at her friend and Penny giggled.

"Thanks for this, guys, I needed it."

Normally, they'd crank the music up while they worked, but today no one suggested it. Loud music could mask an intruder. So, while they smiled and chatted, they also took turns looking out the window.

Each time Penny stole a look, Frankie was still sitting there, camera aimed at the house. She sighed. She was probably going to wind up letting him do the story. But she was going to make him wait the full forty-eight hours before she let him in on that.

Time passed and before she knew it, they'd finished the dining room, got the furniture moved in from the garage, and started on the bathroom upstairs. Just as Penny's stomach rumbled, her phone buzzed, and her heart fluttered an extra beat when she swiped the screen. "Hi, Holt."

"You guys hungry?"

"Starving."

Echoes of agreement came from Grace and Julianna.

"Pizza okay? Or is that too cliché?"

"Pizza is never cliché."

"I want just plain pepperoni," Grace called.

Julianna snickered. "I want a meat lovers with everything."

"I'll share with them," Penny said. "I like it all, and while Julianna will threaten to eat the whole thing, she'll spare me a couple of slices."

"I'll be there in thirty minutes."

"What about your visit with Natasha and the lake house? Did anyone get a chance to talk to her?"

"They came up empty-handed at the lake house and neither Natasha nor her husband are anywhere to be found."

Penny grimaced. "Another dead end?"

"For now. We're regrouping and going to come up with another plan. I have time for lunch, then have to get on a Zoom meeting with the others on the task force. Grace and Julianna will need to be on the call as well."

"I understand. We're ready for that pizza when you get here, then y'all can do your thing while I keep working."

"Sounds like a plan."

Holt arrived just as he'd promised, with pizza in hand. They sat around her dining room table that was now all moved in and set up. Normally, Penny would have opened the plantation shutters and let the light stream in from outside, but not today.

She caught Holt watching Julianna, then his gaze flicked to Grace. And finally landed on her. "Okay," she said, "what do you want to know?"

He shook his head. "You three have some major history together. How'd you go from meeting in juvie to . . . this?" He spread his hands to encompass them all.

"Lots of hard work and the prayers of a righteous woman," Julianna said.

Penny nodded. "Mrs. Gibbs."

"Tell me about her. You've mentioned her in passing but haven't really explained her role in everything."

"She was amazing," Grace said. "A godly woman who wanted to make a difference in the lives of the girls that came through her door."

"I was scared spitless when I got there," Penny said. "I tried not to show it, but I was."

Julianna laughed. "We could tell."

"I thought everyone was going to be mean and I was going to have to fight and defend myself. Not sure against what, but I'd heard horror stories about juvie. But"—she shook her head at the memory of that first day when she'd been delivered to the facility—"I walked in and there was Julianna, sitting on the couch reading Jane Austen. She looked up and said, 'Welcome to the crazy palace.'"

"I said that?"

"You did. Then you stood up and said, 'Come on. I'm pretty

normal. I'll show you around.' Then you introduced me to Grace and Mrs. Gibbs."

"Right." Julianna smiled. "I saw myself in you. I'd only been there for two weeks, and seeing you walk in with that look on your face, well, I knew exactly what you were feeling and I felt sorry for you."

Holt leaned back. "I'm just impressed you guys stayed in touch and remained friends all this time."

"It was easy. We promised each other we would."

"We all made the choice to do whatever it took to keep up with each other," Penny said.

"We all have choices, don't we?" Holt asked, his expression odd for just a few moments before it cleared. "Well, y'all, I've got to go get—"

The dining room window shattered. Glass flew and smoke filled the room. Penny yelled, the others pulled their weapons, and Holt raced for the door. "Call 911!"

Once again Penny watched Holt throw himself after the person trying to do her harm. She raced after him while Julianna and Grace pulled up the rear, with Grace pressing her phone to her ear.

Penny came to the open field where she thought she'd seen Holt disappear into, but now she couldn't spot him. "Holt!" She spun. "Which way did he go?"

Grace pointed. "That way. He used the post to leap the fence."

The three of them did the same. Cows roamed the pasture, making it hard to spot anyone at a distance, but Penny kept going, her heart pounding. If the person was Rabor, he'd thrown that smoking object through her window for a purpose.

Most likely to lure them out of the house.

And Holt was falling right into the man's plans.

■ ■ ■ ■

Holt clenched his fingers around the grip of his weapon and pressed on, dodging cows and never taking his eyes from the fleeing figure ahead. He knew the ladies were behind him, but this was it. This was his chance to take down Rabor, and he wasn't messing it up. The man was fast for someone who'd had surgery just a few days earlier.

But Holt was gaining on him.

Rabor turned, aimed, and fired all in one smooth motion that didn't give Holt a chance to stop or duck.

The sting of the shot burned along his upper arm. He stumbled, but kept going. Only, in seconds his legs wobbled, refused to work, and he went down. Rabor charged back to him and Holt fought to raise his weapon. Fear sliced through him as weakness invaded him. He blinked up at the man now standing over him.

"Hello, Agent Satterfield. So, we meet again."

Holt tried to speak. And found himself mute.

What was wrong with him?

"Don't worry, the paralysis is only temporary—before it kills you. Should I give it enough time." The man raised his gun and aimed it at Holt's forehead. Terror thumped a wild rhythm. He didn't want to die!

God, please!

"Goodbye, Agent Satterfield."

"Holt!"

Vaguely, he registered Penny's frantic cry.

A shot rang out and Rabor ducked. His finger pulled the trigger and his bullet landed in the ground near Holt's head. The man growled, turned his gun back on Holt, and yet another shot echoed around them. The bullet bounced off Rabor's gun. Rabor screamed and released the weapon. He scrambled backward, stumbling toward the wooded area behind them.

Penny dropped next to Holt, her hands cradling his face. "Holt, where are you hit?"

He could only stare at her.

And then realized he wasn't breathing. He couldn't drag in a breath. His muscles, his lungs, nothing would work. Panic hit him even as darkness closed in.

CHAPTER
TWENTY-THREE

"He's not breathing!" Penny immediately started mouth-to-mouth, watching his chest rise and fall. "Holt!"

Grace knelt next to them. "Julianna went after Rabor. Backup's on the way, as are paramedics."

"Check his pulse," Penny said between breaths. "He can't breathe on his own, but he's not shot. I don't know—"

"Pulse is good."

"I thought he was shot with a bullet, but this is something else. Maybe a drug?"

"What kind?"

"Not sure." She bent to breathe for Holt once more. What kind of drug would do this? Something used in surgery. She pulled in air. "Curare, maybe," she said, then bent to breathe again. And continued to do so for the next several minutes until she finally heard sirens. *Please, God, get them here fast.*

"He needs to be intubated," she gasped. She was starting to feel slightly light-headed but would breathe until she passed out if she had to.

"Let me take a turn," Grace said.

"No. I've got this. Just guide"—*breathe in*—"the ambulance

here." *Breathe for Holt.* His chest rose and fell, his eyes stayed shut. To all appearances, he looked unconscious. Or dead. But if it was the drug she was thinking of, he'd be aware of what was going on and unable to do a thing about his situation. "Hang on, Holt," she whispered. "I don't know what he got you with, but your heart is beating fine. As long as we can keep you breathing, you're going to be fine. Understand?"

No response.

"You have to be fine," she whispered.

Tears gathered and her throat tightened. She shoved aside the emotion and breathed for him once more.

Finally, after what seemed like an eternity, the ambulance arrived. And Raina was on it. When she caught Penny's eye, she shook her head. "I recognized the address and jumped on."

"Intubate him." Penny breathed for him again.

Raina didn't bother to ask questions. Instead, she positioned herself at the top of Holt's head and maneuvered the tube down his throat. Now it was up to the machine to keep him breathing.

"He got hit with some drug. I'm guessing curare, but not a hundred percent sure."

Raina and her partner moved Holt onto a stretcher and into the ambulance.

"I'm riding with him," Penny said.

"Hop in."

Penny turned back to look for Julianna, only to see her run up, breathing hard. "How is he?"

"Okay for now. Meet you at the hospital." There was no question as to whether or not the ladies would head straight there. At the last second, she remembered Frankie Olander and glanced in the direction she'd last seen his car. It was gone. Now she couldn't help wondering if he'd left before Rabor got there or if he was somehow involved.

All of which she'd have to think about later.

She climbed in next to Holt and the ambulance took off with

a scream of sirens. She snagged his hand. "Hang on, Holt. We're on the way to the hospital. You're going to be just fine when all this wears off in a few hours." She glanced at Raina. "Talk to him like he can hear. Just in case I'm right."

"Of course."

The ventilator breathed for him and Penny stroked his cheek, praying he could feel her touch.

■   ■   ■   ■

Holt kept telling himself there was no sense in panicking. He couldn't do anything for himself. Not even breathe. Or hear very well, thanks to the weapon's discharge near his ear. But Penny was right there with him. He could feel her hand on his cheek, and as long as she was touching him, reassuring him, he could keep from freaking out.

This was the third time she'd saved his life. And while he was beyond grateful for her ability to do so, he was livid that he'd allowed Rabor to get the drop on him once more.

Penny's words soothed something in his soul and he wanted to reach out, hug her . . . trust her.

God, please let me live. I still need to tell Penny about Zoe.

CHAPTER
TWENTY-FOUR

Penny sat next to Holt, watching him breathe on his own. That precious up-and-down movement of his chest that said he was really going to be all right. They'd removed the ventilator as soon as the drug was registered as being out of his system. His eyes finally opened and met hers.

She leaned in and kissed his forehead. "Hey, how do you feel?"

He cleared his throat and she grabbed the mug of water one of the nurses had brought in.

After a sip, he sighed. "Stupid."

"What?"

"I feel stupid. He got the best of me yet again, and I've gotta say, I'm getting real tired of it."

"You couldn't have known he had some device that could shoot curare at you."

"What's that?"

"A drug that paralyzes you but keeps you aware as long as someone's breathing for you. It's generally used in surgeries and obviously not supposed to be used without proper supervision."

"You breathed for me," he whispered.

"Yeah. Until the ambulance got there."

"I could hear you—even through my ringing ear." He lifted a hand to touch his left ear.

"How is it now?"

"Mostly gone, thankfully. The worst of it anyway." He shook his head. "I could make out most of what everyone was saying." He squeezed her hand. "You kept me sane."

She leaned over and lightly kissed him, then pulled back. "I was scared to death you were going to die on me."

"That makes two of us." He pulled in a deep breath. Then another. "That feels good. I'll never take breathing for granted again."

Penny shuddered. "What was he doing, Holt? If he was watching the house for any length of time, he'd know people were there. Your car was out there. Grace's and Julianna's cars were there. Even Frankie was there for a while. What was Rabor thinking, attacking a house full of people?"

Holt shook his head. "I don't know. Unless he was thinking I'd be the one to chase him and he could get rid of me fairly easily with his little cocktail. And . . ."

"And what?"

"And," he said, "that you would stay in the house and he could circle back to get you."

"But I don't understand. Why not just shoot you? Why use the drug?"

He shrugged. "I can't say for sure, but to him, that drug might have been a surefire way to make sure I died. A bullet is less of a guarantee unless you get a head shot or a vital organ. If I was wearing a vest, and he wasn't confident in his ability to get me in the head . . ." He grimaced. "But that drug would work no matter where he hit me."

Penny shuddered. "Whatever his reasoning, he's dangerous and we've got to find a way to take him down."

"There's no 'we' in that, remember? You don't like that side of things."

She scowled. "I know, but this is personal. I feel like I need to fight back. Like we need a plan."

He pulled her in for a hug and Penny rested her cheek on his chest, feeling his heartbeat through the hospital gown. Her phone rang and she groaned. "I'm going to have to take that."

"Yeah."

She sat up, snagged her phone from her pocket, and glanced at the screen. "Great."

"What is it?"

"Work. Raina's just letting me know that we could have a call at any moment."

"What? Are you serious?"

"Unfortunately. They're short a pilot. Byron's out with the flu now. David had a car wreck—minor, thank goodness, but he's got some bumps and bruises, so he's out for a day or two, and Benjamin has food poisoning or something."

"So it's just you?"

"It's just me."

"Does this happen often?"

"What? Having no pilots available due to illness or whatever?"

"Yes."

"No. It's never happened before that I can remember." She shrugged. "I guess there's a first time for everything." She stood and tucked the sheets around his shoulders. "I'll be back to check on you when I can. At least we're in the same building, if not the same floor."

Holt snagged her fingers. "Be careful," he said, his voice low. "Don't go anywhere alone, not even in the hospital. Keep someone with you at all times."

"Okay, I will. I promise."

"And stay away from Frankie Olander. I'm not entirely sure he wasn't in on everything that happened today."

Penny's brows rose. "You thought about that too."

"What? You too?"

"Yeah. He was gone when we were loading you in the ambulance. I didn't see him leave, so I have no idea how long he'd been gone."

"I'll get Grace or Julianna to see if there's any security footage on your system."

"Oh yeah! I forgot about that. Good idea."

He smiled. "I have those occasionally." His smile flipped. "I mean it, Penny. Please, please watch your back."

"I will. I promise."

She backed toward the door, not wanting to leave him. The look on his face said he felt the same.

Just before she reached the door, it opened. A woman stepped inside, and Holt sat up. "Rachel?"

"If you weren't lying in that bed, I'd punch you."

Penny frowned at the seething anger in the woman's voice and stepped in front of her. "I'm sorry, can I help you?"

She raised a brow. "You can step aside so I can kill my brother."

Ah, one of the sisters. "I'm afraid you'll have to get in line."

Rachel marched around Penny and stopped at Holt's side. "Have you even watched the video?"

Holt shot Penny a glance and sighed. "No. I'm sorry. I've been meaning to and—"

"She's in prison, Holt! This can get her out and you don't make the time to watch a simple video? Well, I need you to make time. Zoe needs you to make the time."

"Wait a minute," Penny said. "Zoe, your other sister, is in prison?" She walked over to Holt and planted her fists on her hips. "Your sister is in prison?"

"Yes, but—"

"You've got to be kidding me." She narrowed her eyes and fought the rising anger. And lost. "You pushed and pushed for me to tell you every little detail about my life, got mad at me because I kept the identity of my mother secret, said we had to go deeper in our conversations to have a relationship, and this is how I find

out about your sister? Wow, thanks a lot, Holt. Apparently relationships are a one-sided deal with you. The little woman has to
spill her guts while the big bad man hides his feelings? That's not
how it works. Not for me anyway."

"No, that's not true." He raked a hand through his hair. "Although I can see why it would look like that at the moment. I
wanted to tell you. Started to a few times and I just—"

"Just what? Just *didn't*, that's what. How many hours were we in
the car when we talked about everything. Including our *families!*"

"Oh boy," Rachel muttered under her breath. "Look, I'm sorry,
I didn't know about all . . . this"—she waved a Penny-and-Holt-
inclusive hand—"and truly, on any other day, I would be thrilled
to meet the woman who landed my elusive brother—and can tell
him off when he needs it—but I'm getting desperate."

Holt pressed his fingers to his eyes. "Rachel, can you step outside for just a minute?"

"Holt—"

"Please!"

With a half growl, Rachel turned and aimed herself at the door,
then paused and turned back to Holt. "Are you okay?"

"I will be."

She nodded and stepped outside.

Penny stared at the man in the bed, unsure if she wanted to stay
and talk or simply leave and lick her wounds.

"Don't leave," he said.

The plea in his husky voice stilled her. "Tell me."

"Zoe's in prison and has been for two years."

"I'm sorry. For what?"

"For killing her husband."

Penny gasped. "Okay, I did not see that coming."

He rubbed his forehead. "Neither did anyone else."

"Was it an accident?"

"No. It was definitely premeditated."

"I see." She looked out the hospital window. "He was abusive?"

"So she says. Her attorney argued self-defense at her trial, but the jury didn't buy it."

She whipped her gaze back to him, the agony on his features twisting like a knife in her heart. "You don't believe her."

He shrugged. "I want to."

"So, what's all this about? Why is Rachel tracking you down in the hospital, asking you to watch a video?"

"Rachel has always been very involved in Zoe's case. So much so, that if she took the bar, she'd probably pass. She's made it her mission to prove Zoe didn't kill Owen—or at least killed him in self-defense—but . . ."

"But you don't think so."

"She confessed."

"People have been known to confess to things they didn't do. For various reasons. Usually to protect someone they love."

"I get that. I'd even agree with the reasoning if there was someone to protect, but there's no one. It was just Zoe and Owen at home that night. The kids were next door at a sleepover. And the gun belonged to Owen."

"Huh. How old are the kids again?"

"Ellie is twelve and Krissy is eight." He picked up his phone and thumbed to a picture of two dark-haired, dark-eyed little girls, his face softening as he held the phone for her to see.

"So, they would have been ten and six when everything happened," Penny said.

"Yes."

She nodded. "Have you talked to them about what happened that night?"

"The girls?" He shrugged. "Not really. They weren't there. Nothing much to talk to them about."

"Surely they can give insight into their parents' marriage."

"They were asked and they've never said anything against either parent. That's what makes it so hard to believe anything abusive was going on."

"And yet their father is dead at the hand of their mother, for some reason."

"Yeah." He fell silent, emotions warring on his face.

"What did Owen do for a living?"

"He was a homicide detective."

"Oh my. And that's it?" she asked.

"Yeah."

"Why was that so hard to tell me? Seriously."

"Because the last woman I told I had bought a ring for, and when I went to her for support, she said she couldn't marry me because she couldn't take a chance I was like my sister."

Penny gaped. "And you thought I'd do the same?"

"Of course not. But every time I went to tell you, I . . . froze."

"I thought I'd lost you when Rabor shot you with the curare. I thought you were gone, and it nearly killed me." She swallowed. "I've got to go to work, but you think about what you really want. The ball's in your court. I want to see what we could become. I want that deeper, meaningful, life-changing relationship with you and I'm willing to say it. But it's your choice. You think about it and get back to me."

"Penny—"

She held up a hand. "Not now. Think about it. Make your choice and let me know when you're sure, without a doubt, what you want."

He opened his mouth once more, then snapped it shut and nodded.

Penny turned and walked out.

■　■　■

Five minutes after Penny left him to stew over everything going on in his life, from serial killer to falling in love to dealing with his family issues, Rachel pushed the door open and stepped inside, holding two cups of coffee. "Sorry, the line was long."

"Thanks. It was worth the wait."

"So . . . who was that?"

"A friend. I think." He hoped they were still friends.

"She sounded like more than a friend."

He sighed. "That was the plan, but I may have blown it."

"So, apologize."

"I did, but I still need to—" He waved a hand. "I can worry about that later. I still have a killer to catch."

Grace and Julianna, along with several local officers, were keeping an eye on Penny. She'd do her job and they'd stay close by in case there were any problems. He was good with that. If he could trust them with his life, he could trust them with Penny's.

But the fact was, Penny was Rabor's target. That meant other people might be in danger as well, if Holt's latest encounter with Rabor was anything to go by. Then again, the man *did* have it in for him and it might not have mattered what his proximity was to Penny. The fact that they were together could have had no bearing on the attack. Of course, Rabor had been at Penny's house, so . . .

"Hello?" Rachel waved a hand in front of his face and Holt forced himself to focus on her for the moment. "I know you're chomping at the bit to get out of here," she said, "but I need you to be present in the moment and *watch the video*."

"You told me what was on it—"

"I didn't tell you everything! I need an unbiased opinion. I need to know if you see what I think I saw!"

She was near tears, her frustration with him was so great. Shame, guilt, and every other self-castigating emotion swept over him. "Let me get dressed and I'll watch it right now."

"Thank you." She set his coffee on the table, then grabbed his clothes from the closet and laid them on the bed. She turned her back, and he climbed out of the bed to dress. He still felt a little weak, but not enough to stop him from doing what he needed to do.

"You've never been one to avoid dealing with things," she said. "Why this? When Zoe—and I—need you more than ever?"

He winced. "I'm assuming I have to tell the truth."

"Holt . . ."

"Fear, Rach," he said, scrubbing a hand down his face. He still needed to shave. "Just fear."

He sat down to put his shoes on and she turned to look at him. "Fear?"

"It's stupid and I'm not even sure it makes sense. When Zoe protested that she hadn't shot Owen, I believed her. Then a week later, she changed her story. Adamantly. At first, I was convinced she was lying. I figured she was just confused or afraid or protecting someone or something, but as time went on, and the evidence was presented in court—and it was *her* prints on *his* gun that was fired that night . . . *and* she said she did it . . . I guess, eventually, I came to believe she did."

"She often put his weapon in the safe for him, Holt. Of course her prints would be on it."

"I know, but she said she did it! And at the end of the last visit, she told me to leave and not come back."

"She didn't do it!" Rachel stopped and drew in a shuddering breath. "Just watch the video."

She tapped the screen of her phone and turned it so he could see. With each passing moment, Holt's stomach dropped lower and lower. When it finished, he looked up, feeling weak once again. "Ellie?"

"You see it too?"

He nodded. "It's kind of jerky, but that's what it looks like to me."

"I've watched it over and over and over," Rachel said, "and it's the only explanation I can find. The fact that you saw it too just confirms what it looks like. Ellie shot Owen."

"And Zoe took the blame." He pressed his palms to his eyes. "It all makes sense now. Where'd it come from?"

"It was security footage, just from a different camera that didn't turn up in any of the footage that was obtained by the police. How it got on Zoe's phone, I don't know. It was a saved file, so she obviously watched it and then changed her plea. Now, will you go to the prison with me? Zoe's agreed to meet us, and we need to leave immediately or we won't get there in time for the appointment that I set up."

"I'm calling Matt Nixon."

Rachel's eyes widened. "The detective who put Zoe in prison?"

"He did his job." Before she could protest, he held up a hand. "I know he's not your favorite person, but he's not the bad guy and he needs to be involved in this."

"But Ellie—"

"She's a minor. She was ten at the time. We'll make sure she gets the help she needs."

"You're sure?"

His gaze met hers. "Zoe won't help herself. We're going to have to do it."

"Right."

"Call Zoe's lawyer and tell him what's going on. Did you send the video to him?"

"No." She bit her lip. "I haven't sent it to anyone except you because it's . . . Ellie. She apparently has no memory of that night. She's never said one word in two years about being there, much less shooting her father. I want to protect her too. But Zoe shouldn't rot in jail for a murder she didn't commit." Her agonized eyes met his.

"I'll find us a flight. This is personal business so we can't use the Bureau's chopper, but I have a friend who flies helicopters. She may be able to help me out." He grabbed his wallet and shoved it into his back pocket. Then he got on the phone, praying Penny would answer his call.

She did. "What?"

"I need to get to Columbia ASAP on personal business. Do you have someone who can fly me and Rachel there?"

For a moment, she didn't answer. "Yes. Let me make a few calls."

"Thanks, Penny."

"Sure." She sounded so sad, the fissure in his heart widened a few more inches. But he pushed that aside to get on the phone with the detective as he followed Rachel out of the room and down the hallway while he explained the situation to Matt.

"Send me the video," Matt said. "I'll meet you at the prison."

Holt hung up just as his phone buzzed with a text from Penny.

> My friend will meet you at Gaston Airfield in twenty minutes.

Holt passed the information to Rachel, tapped the address in his GPS, then climbed into the passenger seat. While she drove, he sent the video from Rachel's phone to Matt, then punched in Gerald's speed-dial number. "We're going to get this settled with Zoe one way or another," he told his sister.

Rachel glanced at him, tears welling, then spilling over her lashes. "Thank you," she whispered and swiped the tears from her cheeks.

"What's going on, Holt?" Gerald asked.

Holt went through the explanation once more.

"You're on medical leave."

"I don't want to be on medical leave, but for now, I'll comply. I'm going to the prison as a family member, not an agent."

"Hmm."

"I have a friend of a friend flying me there, but I might need a chopper ready to bring me back here."

The man was silent a moment. "I'll have it on standby."

"Thanks."

Holt texted his thanks to Penny, finishing with one last plea. Please, please, be careful.

Then he shot a text to Julianna and Grace.

> Keep me updated on what's going on, will you? I'm headed to Columbia for a few hours. I need to know everything is okay with Penny.

Julianna
Everything's fine.

Grace
We've got her covered.

Their texts, only milliseconds apart, reassured him. Slightly.

■ ■ ■ ■

Rabor stood to the side of the road and watched the chaos he'd caused. A simple bullet to the windshield of the delivery van had done more damage than he'd envisioned.

He smiled. Surely someone in that pile would need a helicopter ride to the hospital. And he'd made sure the only pilot available to fly was Penny Carlton. It was time to get this show on the road.

Literally.

CHAPTER
TWENTY-FIVE

Penny paced in front of the base kitchen counter, her thoughts still on Holt and everything she'd learned. Two and a half very slow hours had passed since she'd stormed out of his hospital room, and she was still thinking. On the one hand, she could understand his reluctance to tell her about his sister after the experience he'd had with *that woman*, but still, his silence on the subject rankled. Made her wonder what else he wasn't saying.

At the same time, she couldn't think about the future without picturing Holt in it. Assuming she lived long enough to *have* a future.

Please, God, don't let me get killed.

A pot banged in the sink and Penny ducked before she realized it was just Raina scrubbing the dishes like she had a grudge against them. "Hey, are you all right?"

"No, I'm not." Raina didn't look up, just increased her efforts.

"Are you upset with me?" Nothing had seemed off when they'd been fighting to save Holt, but now the reporter and his veiled threats hung between them.

Raina dropped the scrubber into the sink and turned the water off. "No, Penny," she said, her voice soft. "Never you." She sighed. "I'm just afraid of what that reporter might dig up on me, that's all."

"He's not going to find a thing." She paused. "Have you talked to Grace? See if the reporter's said anything to her?"

"Not yet."

"You might do that before you panic."

Her friend nodded. "Yeah."

Raina had been in an abusive relationship and had run across the country, changing her name, her career, her . . . everything. The sacrifices she'd made to start over put Penny's own aggravation with the reporter to shame.

"I'll talk to Frankie," Penny said. "I'll keep the focus on me and off everyone else. I'll talk about my mother and what it was like growing up with her. I'll give him enough to satisfy his need for the story, and then he'll go away."

"No." Raina looked up, her eyes hard. "You don't have to do that. My mess shouldn't be yours."

Holly stepped into the kitchen. "Hi, guys." She set a puzzle on the table. "Have you seen the bathroom? It's so gross. Whose turn is it to clean it?"

"I'll do it," Raina said. She grabbed the mop and headed down the hall.

"Hey," Holly said, "I didn't mean for you to do it, I was just . . ." She trailed off when she realized Raina wasn't going to respond, then looked at Penny. "What's up with her?"

"You know Raina. When she's got something on her mind, she cooks or cleans. She's just dealing with some stuff, I guess." Penny pulled out a chair and sat down.

Holly grunted. "Aren't we all?"

"Yeah. We are."

"I'm sorry." Holly walked over and slid into the chair opposite Penny. "I don't mean to be a brat and make everything about me, it just comes natural sometimes."

"You're not a brat. Most of the time." Penny smiled to take the sting out of her words. Holly was in her early twenties and came from a privileged background. Sometimes that came through in her attitude, but she was an exceptional member of the team, so Penny and Raina let those rare moments slide. "I guess having four older brothers who spoiled you rotten from the day you were born can have an effect on a person."

Holly rolled her eyes. "Argh . . . don't get me started on them. I love them, but I'll admit they make me crazy sometimes."

Penny laughed even while part of her heart broke all over again. She'd give anything to have Elise back.

The alarm broke into her thoughts and she jumped up to grab her flight jacket and headed for the tarmac.

Grace joined her in the hallway. "I'm going with you."

"That's fine. You can go with, but I don't know about a return flight."

"That's okay. I'm just seeing you get there safely and back in the air. Someone will be here to meet you when you land with the patient."

Penny thought it might be a little bit of overkill, but she'd rather be safe than . . . not. "Let's go, then."

"Pileup on I-40 West." The dispatcher's voice came through Penny's headset loud and clear. "Reports are a six-car accident. Officers are on the scene and in control of the traffic. You'll be directed where to land when you get there."

Once Raina, Holly, and Grace were on board, Penny took off. The hospital fell away from her sight, and she aimed the chopper toward the location of the wreck.

Ten fast minutes later, Penny hovered over the accident scene, her stomach twisting into the familiar knot that always came with a call. A fine mist threatened to turn into rain, and she flipped the wipers on.

The officer below her directed her down onto the highway. Far enough away from the accident that her blades wouldn't cause a problem, but close enough to get the patient on board as quickly as possible. Fire trucks, police cars, ambulances, and every other vehicle with flashing lights lit up the highway. Law enforcement and health workers scurried like a well-oiled machine.

Raina and Holly were out of the cabin, racing to the scene while Penny stayed with the aircraft. Grace stood at the door, her gaze sweeping the area.

And a shot rang out.

Grace went down.

Screams echoed from those involved in the accident, and law enforcement pulled their weapons while ducking for cover.

"Grace!" Penny bolted for the woman, who lay on the ground gasping, her hand clutching at her chest.

"I'm fine. It got my vest."

Just as she reached the door to the chopper, a man dressed as a police officer rounded the corner and placed his weapon against her forehead. "Hello, Penny."

She swallowed. "Rabor."

"We meet again. Now, before anyone comes this way, we're going to take a little ride."

"I'm not going anywhere."

"I'm also not playing this game again. The first bullet got her in the vest. The next one will be a warning." He pointed the weapon at Grace's head and fired. Penny screamed, then realized the bullet had gouged the concrete. Grace held a hand to her ear while Rabor narrowed his gaze at Penny. "If you make me fire a third time, it goes in her head."

"Get in," Penny said. He wasn't kidding, and delaying the inevitable would only get someone hurt or killed.

He smiled. "Now that's more like it."

Still holding the gun on her, he grabbed Grace from the ground and dragged her into the cabin. Then he shut the door. "Get her in the seat," he told Penny. "Buckle her in."

Penny moved fast. Ignoring her terror and pounding heart, she grabbed Grace under her arms and did her best to heft her to the seat. But Grace wasn't a small woman and Penny could barely budge her. "Grace, breathe." She looked back at Rabor. "I'm going to give her some oxygen."

"And I want to get out of here." He motioned with his gun. "Get us in the air. I'll take care of her."

Penny glanced out the window and noted law enforcement approaching, weapons drawn and aimed at the chopper. What would he do if she refused to fly?

Easy. He'd kill Grace. Then probably her, and fly the chopper himself.

"Go!"

Penny settled into the pilot's seat and slapped her headset on. Without giving anyone any indication what she was doing, she powered up the bird, and within seconds they were in the air. Her hand fumbled with the phone in her flight jacket pocket.

"Throw me your phone," he yelled.

She glanced back over her shoulder to see Rabor strapping Grace into the seat. He caught her eye. "And don't even think about flying crazy and making me fall or anything. Your friend's life depends on your actions, at the moment. I shot her in the vest when I could have killed her. I've given her oxygen. She doesn't have any broken ribs or anything that needs immediate attention." He slipped into the cockpit and slid the extra headset over his head. Then he held out his hand. "Phone."

Penny shoved it into his hand with a low growl.

He inspected the panel to check everything. She wasn't worried. She'd done everything right. "Good job." He input a set of coordinates into the system and pointed. "That's where we're going."

"Why are you doing this?"

"Because I can."

"No, seriously, what is it that gives you so much pleasure? The chase? The catch? The kill? What?"

"All of the above, my dear." He reached out and stroked a

finger down her cheek, and Penny jerked away, shooting him a glare.

He laughed. "Soon you'll appreciate my touch. Welcome it."

"Not in this lifetime."

"No, maybe not, but no one said you had to be alive."

■　■　■　■

Holt didn't like being so far away from Penny but was comforted by the knowledge that he could be back in North Carolina in under half an hour on a Bureau chopper.

True to his word, Matt Nixon had met them at the door to the interview room. "I'm going to be behind the mirror. You're here as family, not an investigator, but she'll be more likely to talk if she doesn't know I'm here. We've got the video being processed by one of our best. He's trying to get any and all information from it."

Rachel glared at him and Holt nodded. He nudged Rachel and she turned her stare to him. "Stop lasering holes into the man," he whispered in her ear. "He's trying to help now."

"I can't help it," she muttered. "Zoe's in here because he didn't do his job."

He wasn't going to argue with her.

They followed Matt into the interview room—the very one he and Penny and Carol had used to talk to Jenkins. Rachel immediately started pacing, rubbing her hands together as though trying to keep them warm. She looked tired, but there was a fire in her eyes he recognized.

After Matt left, Holt pulled Rachel into a tight hug and kissed the top of her dark head. "I'm sorry, Rach. I should have listened to you. Been here for you. I should have believed in Zoe. I'm so . . . ashamed that I didn't. I'm truly sorry."

"It's okay," she muttered into his chest. "You're here now."

They settled themselves at the table and his phone dinged. He ignored it for the moment.

"If this video was from Yvette's phone, she had to know about it. Why didn't she come forward?"

"I don't know for sure, but I have my thoughts. Knowing Zoe, if she knows about the video—and I really think she does—she'd convince Yvette to keep her mouth shut to protect Ellie."

"I can see that."

The door opened and his eldest sister stepped inside, her hair limp. The sight of her in the cuffs and orange jumpsuit sent shards of glass slicing through his heart. He swallowed and hoped he managed to keep the pain from his features. Then again, it might be good for her to see it. To understand that her actions were affecting more people than her.

He forced a smile to his stiff lips. "Hey, ZoZo."

She blinked at his childhood nickname for her, and he thought he saw a crack in the armor she'd wrapped herself in. Then it was gone, and her hard eyes—the same green eyes he and Rachel shared—met his. "What is this? You weren't supposed to be here."

He flinched. He couldn't help it. "Why not?"

"Because I don't want you here. Every time you come, you try to get me to say things I don't want to say. So . . . leave."

"I won't say a word. I'll let you and Rachel talk, but don't make me leave, please." He couldn't help the husky timbre in his voice. He wanted to weep, to grab her and haul her out of the prison. To take her home to her children, who needed her.

"I have something I want to show you," Rachel said. "Then if you still want us to leave, we'll leave."

"Fine." Zoe dropped into the chair and clasped her fingers in front of her on the table. "What?"

Holt had gotten permission to have their phones in the room. Rachel pulled hers out, tapped the screen, and handed the device to Zoe. "Push play," Rachel said.

With a frown, Zoe did so. As the video played, her eyes widened a fraction and color leached from her cheeks, but that was all the expression Holt was able to find on her face. When the video ended, Zoe handed the phone back to Rachel. "What's the point in that?"

"What do you mean? It proves that y'all fought that night. Owen was yelling! He even shoved you, backed you up against the wall, and held you there while you yelled at him to stop. And Ellie—"

"Don't talk about Ellie!"

After her outburst, Zoe simply stared at her hands, but Holt knew that she was thinking, and thinking hard.

"That video was on your phone," he said.

"I finally managed to figure out the password," Rachel said. "Two years I've been trying and finally . . ." Tears slipped down her cheeks.

"We were arguing, it's true," Zoe said. "But I said some really awful things to him and he . . ."

"He put his hands on you," Holt said.

"But he didn't hurt me. I know what the video looks like. I saw it. But it looks a lot worse than it was. Owen was never violent. Not even on a bad day at work. But . . . we'd been having issues."

"What kind of issues?"

Zoe drew in a deep breath. "I thought he was cheating on me." Rachel gasped. "Owen?"

"He swore he wasn't, and I so wanted to believe him, but the evidence . . ." She buried her face in her hands. "The evidence really pointed that he was, and I was so angry, so hurt, so . . . broken at the thought, that—" Her voice broke and she shook her head. "And I still don't know. All I know is if I'd handled it differently that night, my husband might still be alive and I . . ." She shrugged and pressed her fingers to her eyes.

"Did Ellie shoot Owen?" he asked.

Zoe's face crumpled, and for a moment, Holt thought they might finally get the truth. Then the mask slipped back into place and her features hardened. "No." Even though her voice remained calm, Holt saw a new tension running through her. "She didn't. She wasn't even there."

Holt reached out a hand. "Zoe—"

"She was there!" Rachel cried.

Her outburst turned Zoe's attention to her. "I said don't do this."

"I don't understand." Rachel's desperate pleading nearly broke Holt's heart. "We could get you out of here! Find a way to protect Ellie—"

"I'm never getting out," Zoe said, her fingers clenching and unclenching, her breathing coming faster. "Just leave me alone!"

"Why are you doing this?" Holt asked.

"It's my choice. *This* is *my* choice and you don't get a say in whether it's right or wrong. It's right for me."

"You don't have to make this choice, ZoZo," Holt said, keeping his tone soft.

She looked at him, really looked at him, and he saw the intense agony she was trying so hard to hide. "Yes, I do," she whispered. "This is the hand I've been dealt, the choice I've had to make to protect my child." She snapped her lips shut as she realized what she'd just said. "End of discussion." She shot to her feet, turned, and rapped her knuckles on the door as Holt's phone buzzed.

He ignored it. "We can fix this, Zoe. We can get Ellie help."

She whipped around and glared. "Leave it alone! Leave me alone and don't come back. I won't agree to see you again."

The door opened and the guard led her out.

Rachel looked at Holt, her face pale, eyes wide. "Thought you were going to keep quiet."

"I failed."

"We both did."

He raked a hand over his head. "Matt will have someone pull every bit of information off of there, clean up the footage, get us a transcript of the argument, and find out exactly what happened."

"Finally," Rachel whispered.

They walked out together and Holt took a moment to check his phone.

A text from Julianna.

Grace and Penny are missing. Think Rabor got
to them in the chopper and forced Penny to fly.
Tracking them via the GPS on the chopper, but
need you here ASAP.

CHAPTER
TWENTY-SIX

Penny clutched the control stick and noted they were about five minutes out from his specified destination. "What are you going to do with Grace when we land?" Surely someone would be tracking them and would meet them at the location?

"I don't need her."

"Don't kill her and I'll go with you willingly."

"Why now? Why not in the hospital?"

She huffed a short, humorless laugh that did nothing to dispel the terror racing through her. "The hospital was a long shot for you. You were watching me and saw a chance to have a little fun. You obviously hadn't planned on snatching me, but probably thought you'd give it a try. My refusal to cooperate confused you. Surprised you. You weren't sure what to do, so you retreated to wait for another opportunity to strike. I guess this was it."

His cold stare lightened for a moment and a small smile curved his lips. "Well, well."

"What?"

"Nothing. You've just surprised me. You remind me of someone else that I admire."

"Is she dead or alive?"

He laughed. Actually laughed. Penny wanted to throw up.

"She's quite alive," he said. "But only because I like her that way. And I'll let you in on a little secret. This wasn't just an opportunity that happened. I created it."

Penny shot him a sideways glance. "You caused the pileup?"

"How else was I going to get you alone? You have more security than POTUS."

His irritation came through loud and clear.

"And you don't think they're tracking me at this very moment?"

"Of course they are."

The fact that he didn't sound a bit worried about that sent more darts of terror through her. What was he planning? "Where'd you get the curare drug?"

"Joel managed to procure that for me before his untimely death."

She hesitated. "He wanted to be you."

"Of course."

"Why?"

"It's a long story. And a boring one."

And one she desperately wanted to hear, but he didn't seem inclined to tell it. "You were never going to let him live very long after you got out of prison, were you?"

He raised a brow. "Why do you say that?"

"You're too smart not to use his obsession with you for your benefit. Were you going to kill him, then leave the country? I mean, by the time they figured out it wasn't you, you could've been gone without a trace."

He fell silent for a moment and Penny wondered if he'd answer. Part of her hoped he wouldn't. Then he looked at her, long and hard. "You're really very intelligent, aren't you?"

"So I've been told." She paused. "Well? That was the plan?"

"A lot of it. There are a few other things we had planned before all of that was to happen, but"—he shrugged—"guess it's not to be." He sighed. "It's a shame too. We all worked hard on that plan. Everything was going along perfectly until you killed Joel. We could have had a double date. But, alas, he'll just have to miss out on this one."

This one? Her. Another wave of nausea swept her and she breathed in through her nose. Out through her mouth. "I didn't kill him," she muttered. "He fell on his own knife."

"Yeah, that's something he'd be dumb enough to do." He paused, then gave another shrug. "Ah, well, it was fun while it lasted."

She stared at him a few seconds. "Who was the woman who came to the prison to meet with you?"

His eyes darkened, then shuttered. "I had a lot of women who came to visit. Not sure which one you're talking about."

"The one you admire," Penny said, her voice soft. "I'm sure she was there. Who was she to you?" Things were clicking in her brain, little pieces of information swimming around up there, but she had no idea how to put it all together.

"Shut up and land."

She wanted to question him further, but they'd arrived at their destination. She began the descent, her goal the freshly cleared plot of land. "A subdivision." With room for about a hundred houses. Several lots already had the foundation, but none were framed yet. And then there was one house that was already built. The sales office, no doubt.

"Well, it will be one day. For now, it's your landing pad."

A silver Buick sat in the drive. Hope sparked for a brief moment before reality intruded. Anyone in that house would be dead if they came out to see why a helicopter was landing in one of the yards.

Her stomach clenched and she looked back to see Grace unconscious. "What did you do to her?"

"I just gave her a little something to knock her out."

"Not the curare! She can't breathe with that!"

He rolled his eyes. "Naw, I only use that for the special ones. She just got a nice dose of ketamine."

She swallowed and had a bad feeling she ranked among those "special ones." Penny bit her lip on the question. She didn't want to hear him confirm it. "Why not just kill her?"

"Really?" he scoffed. "That's what you think of me? I don't just go around *killing* random people. There has to be a *reason* for it. She has nothing to do with this and can't tell anyone where we're going. Now, shut it down and let's go."

Penny cut the engine and left the keys behind. Someone might need the chopper once they found it. Not that there wasn't a spare—

What was she doing? *Think!* She needed to focus on finding a way to get away from Rabor, not worry about the chopper.

Her heart pounded and her hands shook.

He motioned her out the door. As she headed for the exit, she stopped for a brief second to check Grace's pulse.

"Go!"

She shot him a dark look. "I'm going."

"I told you she was fine. She'll wake up in about an hour none the worse for the wear." He jabbed her with the gun. "One thing you'll find out about me. I may be many things, but I don't lie."

"Unless it suits your purpose."

He laughed. "You are spunky, aren't you? Okay, yes, that's true, but I'm not lying now. Out." He gave her a shove toward the door and Penny stepped out of the chopper. She scanned the area, desperately searching for a way out, but the acres of wide-open land provided no place to hide.

None.

Even the subdivision home that served as a temporary sales office was most likely locked. Assuming she could outrun any bullets he sent her way, hiding behind the office would gain her three seconds of freedom. If that.

"To the car."

She'd noticed the lone vehicle but hadn't thought it was going to be *their* transportation. All hope of someone tracking and meeting them at the chopper faded. Flying was so much faster than driving, and they wouldn't know her exact landing spot until about right now. So, while they now had a destination, Rabor planned to be long gone before anyone arrived.

With the gun at her back, she walked toward the sedan. Her mind flashed to the outbuilding behind Joel and Sally Allen's home. To the bodies, frozen in time, never to draw another breath. That was going to be her if she didn't do something.

At the car, she stopped at the trunk, but he nudged her around to the side. "Open the door."

She did, then swung around and jammed her palm against his chin. His head snapped back, and with a shriek of pain, he stumbled backward. Penny kicked him in the side. Another cry ripped from him and he curled into a ball on the concrete drive. She darted for the house, only to feel the sting of something in her upper back.

She ignored it and kept going. Around to the side. Knowing she might not have much time, she dug a finger into some wet red dirt. The license plate. She'd memorized it. Her vision blurred and she was so tired. He'd drugged her. Frustration built, but she concentrated.

Penny dragged her finger over the siding, blinking and trying to see, fighting the darkness pressing in on her. She spun and stumbled away, aiming herself for the empty lot next door, not wanting him to find the plate number.

But her legs gave out and she sat down with a thud, the ground harder than she'd thought it would be.

Move! Go!

Her mind issued the order, but her body wouldn't work.

"Penny, Penny, you're not being a good sport at all." She looked up when Rabor stepped in front of her, legs spread, rubbing his chin and breathing hard. "You're going to pay for this. I'm not supposed to lift anything heavier than ten pounds and now I've got to carry you. Thanks a lot."

"What . . . did . . . you . . . drug . . . me . . . with?" She dragged in a breath, noting it came easy even while the darkness grabbed at her, snatching the light from around her.

"Don't worry, Penny, it's just ketamine. You'll have a nice nap and when you wake up, we'll have some fun—our first date."

Terror spiked, but her eyes shut and she heard him singing, "Tea for two . . . Nobody around to hear you scream, mm, mm. No friends, just corpses, mm, mm . . . mm, mm . . ."

"That's not the way the . . . song . . . goes . . . ," she slurred, then had to cave to the darkness.

■ ■ ■ ■

Holt's phone rang for the umpteenth time, and once again, he checked the screen and sent the caller to voice mail. He didn't recognize the number and didn't have time to deal with people he didn't know at the moment. He, Julianna, and local law enforcement had just arrived at the location where Penny had set the chopper down.

He'd left the prison as soon as he received word that Penny and Grace had been snatched and, with the help of the hospital, had followed the tracker to this spot. Rachel had called for a rental car drop-off and would be able to make her way home from the prison.

As soon as his Bureau chopper landed, he climbed out and raced to Penny's bird. He didn't expect to find her inside, but he was terribly afraid of what had happened to Grace.

He flung the door open and, to his right, found the cockpit empty.

To his left, Grace sat unmoving in one of the medical crew's seats, eyes closed. "Grace!"

He hurried to her and pressed his fingers against her neck, praying for a pulse. When he found it, he breathed a silent breath of relief, then turned to find a local officer peering inside.

"Paramedics are here if you need them," the woman said.

"I do. This is Grace Billingsley. She's an agent. Make sure they take care of her."

Within seconds, they had Grace out of the seat and on a gurney. Holt bolted to the front of the craft, scanning the area, praying Penny had left him some kind of clue as to where she'd been taken.

But nothing.

She'd left the keys, but there wasn't anything that told him where she might have gone.

"Come on, Penny, I know you left a clue somewhere." If she had the chance.

If she didn't . . .

Please, God, take care of her. This isn't the way it's supposed to end. Not for Penny. Not for us. I need her to be okay, God. Holt was more than aware that things didn't always work out the way he wanted or needed just because he asked God to do what he wanted, but it was always okay to pray for the safety of someone he loved.

Someone he loved. The thought didn't even faze him. He loved Penny. He'd probably loved her since he'd awakened midair, knife wound in his side and Penny's worried glances in the rearview mirror catching his eye. "You're going to be all right, Holton Satterfield, you hear me? Don't you dare die in my bird."

He'd wanted to laugh and reassure her he had no intention of dying. Now he wanted to rage and pound out his fury at the man who'd snatched her. Instead, he drew in a steadying breath and exited the chopper.

He stood there with his hands on his hips, thinking. Cops swarmed the area, and he was desperately afraid someone was going to trample evidence, but upon closer inspection he could see they were taking care, and he let that concern slide away. He had enough to worry about.

Julianna hurried to him. "Looks like she put up a struggle. There's some blood spatter on the drive. Not sure if it's hers or not. The light rain left the outline of a car, so there was one here not too long ago."

"He had a car waiting."

"Yeah." She nodded, brows pinched tight. "He had to. This area is in the middle of nowhere. Without a vehicle, they'd be on foot, and that doesn't make sense. I don't see him doing that. Especially if he drugged Penny."

"Which I feel sure he had to do. If she's awake, she'd be fighting."

Julianna pointed. "Hence the appearance of a struggle first, then he drugged her."

"So, let's go with the assumption that's the situation . . ." The idea sent chills through him. He'd seen what happened to Rabor's victims, and the thought of Penny in his hands made him physically ill. He swallowed hard. Getting sick wouldn't help anyone. "Someone had to be waiting with a car when Penny landed the chopper."

"Or he dropped the car before he went to the scene to snatch Penny and Grace."

"But how would he get there?" Holt gestured to the area.

"I don't know, unless he had a bicycle in the trunk."

"Or he hauled a motorcycle behind the car. The guy who attacked us on the back road was driving a bike." He rubbed a hand over his chin and shook his head. "No, if he did that, where's the trailer?"

"He hauled it off?"

"With what? How? That would require help. So, he either towed the motorcycle—and somehow got rid of the trailer that the motorcycle had to ride on—or he had help. Those are the two options. I'm going to go with he had help."

Julianna nodded. "Either scenario is plausible." She nodded to the corner of the office near the gutter. "There's a camera, and while I'm not going to hold out hope that there's anything on it, Daria's working on it."

"If anything's there, Daria will find it." He paused. "Okay, if Rabor had help pulling this off, who would it be?"

"I can think of quite a few possibilities."

"One of the many women who visited him in prison who would do anything for him?"

"That was my first guess. We're running them down, but so far nothing's sent up a red flag. Do you know there's over five hundred of them?"

He winced. "I'm not surprised. There's a lot of crazy out there." And one of those crazies had Penny.

His phone buzzed and this time he recognized Daria's number. He swiped the screen. "What do you have, Daria?"

"I got into the security feed. The whole thing was caught. It was like he wanted you to see what he did."

That stopped him for a second. "Okay, let me wrap my mind around that. If he's not trying to hide what he's doing, he's gloating about it."

"I'm sending it to you now. You've got to find her, Holt. She's in big-time danger."

No kidding. "We're doing our best."

"Hey! Over here!"

At the officer's shout, Holt told Daria to hold on, and he and Julianna hurried around to the side of the house. The officer pointed. "Looks like she used the mud to try to leave a message. At first I thought it was just dirt on the side, but that's clearly a *B* and an *A.*"

"4227," Holt said. "It's a license plate." He still had Daria on the phone. "Run this plate, will you?" He gave her the number.

"It's registered to . . . Joel Allen."

"Surprise, surprise," he muttered.

"And another car went past about ten seconds later. That one is registered to Frankie Olander."

CHAPTER
TWENTY-SEVEN

Penny blinked. Then blinked again. She was awake, fully and instantly aware that she was alone yet still in danger and that she'd been unconscious. She just didn't know how long, where she was, or if Rabor was nearby. She let her eyes adjust to the dim light of a single bulb while she swallowed faint waves of nausea.

Remnants of whatever he'd used to knock her out.

Ketamine. The same stuff he'd used on Grace.

Thankfully, it was a drug she'd had before and knew how her body reacted to it. She'd feel sick and weak for a bit, but then she'd be fine.

At least until Rabor returned to finish her off.

The chill of the cement floor pressed deep into her bones and a shiver wracked her. She tried to move her arms only to discover they were bound behind her back. Her legs were also tied together at the ankles. She had nothing covering her mouth, which meant he didn't care if she screamed.

So, she'd save her breath.

But she was *really* cold. Another tremor racked her and she realized her flight jacket was missing. And her shoes. She still had her thick socks on, but the ground was going to be wet and would soak right through to freeze her feet. Assuming she managed to get that far.

Lovely.

Whatever. Being cold was the least of her worries.

She maneuvered onto her left side, then wiggled her arms over her rear and under her legs. With her hands in front of her, she went to work on her ankle restraints. He'd used duct tape. A sliver of relief coursed through her. She could work with duct tape as long as she could control her shaking hands.

Her shaking, freezing, almost numb hands.

Pulling in a steadying breath, refusing to panic, she opened and closed her fingers several times until some feeling returned. "Come on, Penny," she whispered, "you can do this. Whether you live or die is up to you. Get busy." Ignoring the fact that her breath smoked out from her lips, she felt around the tape until her fingers brushed the rough edge. Using a fingernail, she worked it under the tape and lifted. Then snagged it with her thumb and forefinger and pulled.

The ripping sound echoed around her and her heart leapt with hope. She pulled the tape until it was off.

Penny dragged in a ragged breath, the panic hovering closer to the surface now that she was almost free.

Please God, please God, please God . . .

■ ■ ■

"Someone get Olander on the phone. I want to meet with him ASAP." If his phone buzzed one more time, he was going to throw it out the window. But he couldn't do that because he might need it for Penny. But seriously, what was up with all of the spam calls right now? He needed to keep the line open and didn't have time to deal with telemarketers.

He glanced at the screen.

Raina. Oops. He'd talk to her.

He swiped. "Hey, have you heard from Penny?"

"No, but I've heard from Frankie Olander, that reporter."

"Okay." If Raina was calling him, knowing Holt was frantically searching for Penny, then she had something important to tell him. "What is it?"

"He's trying to get ahold of you. Something about being able to find Penny, but he needs you to answer your phone."

He closed his eyes for a millisecond. That's why the number was slightly familiar. The reporter. "I'll call him right now. I have a few questions I'd like to ask him anyway." Like why had he been at the construction site and how had he known to be there? And where had Rabor taken Penny?

"Just dial the number that's been calling you over and over."

"On it."

"Keep me updated, please, Holt. I'm terrified for her."

"We all are. Stay tuned." He hung up and dialed the number that had irritated him so.

"About time," Frankie said halfway through the first ring.

"Where is she?"

"I want the exclusive."

"And I want to punch you in the teeth, but sometimes we don't get what we want. Where is she!" Holt knew he was losing control and dragged in a steadying breath. He was a professional.

So be one.

A sigh from the reporter grated on him. "Look," Frankie said, "I can help you. I can tell you exactly where he took Penny, but I want first rights. Someone's going to tell the story. It might as well be me."

"How? How do I know you're not involved and sending us on a wild-goose chase?"

"Ouch. Really? All I want is a story, the bonus my boss promised, and a possible promotion in the crime reporting arena. I have no desire to see Penny hurt."

"How do you know where she is when no one else has a clue? How did you know where she was going to be and were able to follow her after the chopper landed?"

Silence. Then, "How did you know I followed her?"

"Security footage on the sales office got the whole thing. Including your license plate shortly after Rabor left."

"I see."

"Well?"

Another sigh from the man filtered through the line. "That night someone broke into her house?"

"That was you?"

"Yeah. I couldn't find her address, so I went to the hospital base, waited until the place was empty—which doesn't happen very often—and found her flight jacket. I put a tracker in it. Fortunately, she wore it home and I simply showed up at her house when I figured she'd be asleep. Only getting inside was kind of a pain. I saw she was asleep on the couch, so going in the front door wasn't going to work."

"So you climbed up the scaffold and went through the upstairs window."

"Yeah. Only I guess I made too much noise and she woke up."

"Sending you running. But you came back later."

"I did. I put trackers in her two spare flight jackets and three pairs of shoes that looked like she wore often."

Holt bit his lip on a growl. He'd hold off on reprimanding the man if his actions wound up saving Penny's life. "If your information leads to Penny's rescue, I'll do my best to convince her to talk to you." Silence. "Come on, man! Where is she?"

"I'll text you the coordinates and you'd better hurry. I wanted to help her, I swear, but I didn't have a chance. I'm really sorry. I figured the best I could do was keep her in my sights and call you for help."

"You could have called 911 and gotten help there sooner!"

"They wouldn't have gotten here in time if I'd called, and if you'd answered your phone a little faster—"

"There's no time for this. Send me the coordinates."

"Right. Try not to ignore the new buzz on your phone."

Holt scowled. When he got his hands on the man—

However, if he managed to get to Penny in time, he might just hug the guy before he beat him to a pulp.

Please, God, keep her safe and I won't beat him up. I'll just be happy she's okay.

CHAPTER
TWENTY-EIGHT

Penny couldn't get the tape off her hands. The small building was more of a shed than anything. One with no insulation and completely empty of anything that she might have used as a weapon. Or anything that could have cut through the tape. She used her teeth on it while she inspected the door. She'd already tried the knob and it was locked, of course. She hadn't actually expected it to open, but . . .

The knob had twisted, but there must be some kind of bolt on the other side. Her mind went back to the days she'd been trapped in the closet. Terrified, feeling like all the air was being sucked from the tiny space and just wanting someone to come rescue her. Banging her fists on the door. *"Let me out! Let me out!"*

A sob gathered in her throat and she swallowed. "You're not a little girl anymore, Penny. You're a smart girl and can find a way out of this, so think."

Because as far as she knew, no one was coming to rescue her. Urgency pressed heavy on her chest and she dragged in a breath. She had to get out but needed her hands to do so. How long had she been unconscious? How long had she been in the car? Had he given her any more of the drug to keep her out longer? She didn't think so but couldn't swear by it. She glanced at her watch, but even though it said 8:15, she had no idea if she'd missed a day or not.

Penny stopped for a second. Was she hungry?

Yes, but not starving.

So maybe she'd been out only a couple of hours.

And Rabor would know how long the drug would last and would know approximately when she'd wake up.

Okay then.

He could be back at any moment and she really needed to not be here when he showed up.

Think, Penny.

She continued to work the tape with her teeth and finally got a small tear even as her gaze scanned the room once more.

Thin walls with exposed studs. No insulation. Cement floor. Two dirt-encrusted windows. She stopped tugging on the tape and pressed her hands against the nearest wall.

Wood and no drywall. Not brick. Hope sprouted and she went back to tugging on the tape. A sound at the door froze her for a brief moment.

"No," she whispered. "No, no, no." He couldn't be back yet.

She spun and kicked at the wall. The wood splintered, but stayed in one piece. Another kick sent her foot through the wood and she lost her balance, then went to the floor with a thud. A gasp of pain escaped before she could choke it down. She tugged her foot from the hole and scrambled to her feet.

Another loud sound at the door sent her heart thumping even faster. Then the door opened, revealing the silhouette of a man against the night.

Penny choked down a scream and backed toward the hole in the wall. She might be able to squeeze through it.

"Penny?" the man hissed. "Come on. We need to hurry."

Wait a minute . . . She stilled. "Frankie?"

"Yeah. Rabor just went into the main house, but I don't know how long he'll be in there. We need to go. Now. Hurry!"

Could she trust him? What if he was really working with Rabor? What if he wasn't and her hesitation wound up costing her? Did she have a choice?

"Do you have a knife?" She held out her hands even as she slipped out the door.

"Worry about your hands after we get away from this lunatic. I've called for help and they're on the way, so as long as you can run, we might just have a chance."

Good point. She hurried after him, going around the back of the building that had been her prison. Now that she could see it, thanks to a dim floodlight casting an eerie glow over the yard, it looked like it had been built by someone who had no idea what they were doing. Which had worked in her favor, and she'd take that for the win.

He stopped her. "Where are your shoes? And your jacket?"

"I don't know. They were gone when I woke up."

"Okay, that's not good," he muttered. "We may have a problem."

"What?"

"I don't have a signal and help might be going to the wrong location."

Penny jerked around to look at him. "Why?"

"Because I was following you, not paying attention to the fact that we were going somewhere different than where I told Holt to—" He pressed shaking fingers against his eyelids. "Never mind. It's a long story. If we get out of this, I'll explain it all to you." He glanced around the side at the house. "He's still inside, but I don't know about running across that yard. If he looks out a window, he'll see us."

Another good point. She held out her hands while she thought, and he pulled out a pocketknife to cut through the rest of the tape.

"Okay, let's think about this," she said. "Where are we?"

"About thirty miles from the subdivision where he grabbed you. I had to follow at a pretty good distance, and there were times I was sure he was going to catch me, but I guess he wasn't too concerned about being followed. He made one stop at a gas station and then continued on."

"What'd he do at the gas station?"

"I don't know. Got gas?"

Penny clenched her fingers into fists. "I meant, did he meet anyone, talk to anyone, do anything?"

"I don't know. I was parked pretty far away. I was trying to avoid being caught. Anyway, we're on a mountain, but not too far up. There are a few houses scattered along the route, but this one is definitely more isolated."

"Of course it is. He wouldn't want anyone around to witness his evil."

"Yeah."

"When did you notice you didn't have a signal?"

"When I parked."

"Okay, where's your car?" She shook her arms and grimaced as the blood flowed.

"On the other side of those woods over there. I pulled into someone's driveway so it would look like it belonged."

She groaned. He couldn't have picked a worse spot. "You don't think someone's going to notice and report it?"

"I don't care, if it brings help this way."

He was making quite a few valid points.

She raked a hand over her hair and narrowed her eyes. "Okay, I'm not crazy about running across that yard. What if we just go in the opposite direction?" She paused when he shook his head. "Don't shake your head. Why are you shaking your head?"

"This place is built practically on the side of the mountain. And like I said, while we're not too far up it, we definitely can't go down it, especially in the dark."

"He did that on purpose," she muttered. "One way in and one way out, right?"

"Appears that way."

She sighed. "I really don't want to go across that yard."

The door to the house opened and closed with a slam and Penny jerked. She peered around the edge of her "prison" and noted that Rabor was headed their way. He had a gun tucked into the waistband of his pants and the tune he whistled drifted toward her. Then he began to sing.

"Tea for two . . ."

Oh, God, please, help us . . .

"Okay," she whispered. "Hopefully he won't notice the hole in the side. When he gets to the door—"

"He's going to notice it's open. I didn't shut it."

She bit her lip. "That's okay. Our only hope is that once he's there, we take off running and get enough of a head start that we can get to your car before he can get to us."

He nodded. "I'm right behind you."

But Rabor's phone rang and he stopped to take the call. Penny's breath whooshed from her and her stomach knotted with so much tension she wanted to puke. "Wait. He has a signal."

Frankie checked his phone. "I don't. He must be using a satellite phone."

Duh. "Right."

So, she'd wait.

Freedom was so close she could taste it.

■　■　■　■

As soon as the SUV pulled to a stop at the gas station, Holt leapt out. The coordinates Frankie had sent converged in this spot.

A busy, run-of-the-mill convenience store.

A bad feeling settled in his gut.

Julianna stepped up beside him. "This doesn't feel right."

"No kidding." He curled his fingers in a fist and resisted the urge to hit something. "I'm an idiot," he said, his voice low. "He's got to be involved with Rabor. He spoon-fed me false information to lead us away from Rabor and I fell for it."

Julianna shook her head. "Great. Now what?"

Holt paced the length of the SUV, then back. "Let's search the place."

"What? Why?"

"Because I don't know what else to do and maybe he sent us here for a reason. If he wants to rub it in our faces, maybe he left us something to find."

Holt motioned to the others, and after briefing them, he walked inside to talk to the clerk. "Excuse me, I need to cut in line for just a moment," he told the waiting customer.

She didn't look happy but didn't argue.

The clerk raised a brow. "What's going on?"

"We're looking for someone." He showed his credentials, then held up his phone to display the picture of Rabor. "Have you seen him?"

She frowned. "That serial killer? Seen him on television, but not in here. Definitely not in here. I would have freaked out."

"He might not have come in the store. Could have gotten gas at the pump. He's driving a newer model silver Buick sedan." He showed her a picture of that as well.

She frowned. "You know, I think I did see a car like that pull up next to the dumpster. Didn't get any gas. I thought he'd pulled over to take a phone call or something."

"Thanks. That helps."

He turned and walked out of the store. Julianna looked up from the trash bin she'd been digging through. He had to hand it to the woman. He hadn't seen anything that made her squeamish. "Well?" she asked. She pulled her gloves off and dropped them into the can.

"We need to check that big dumpster over there to the side." He pointed. "I'll get Grace to pull the SUV around."

Julianna nodded and walked toward the bin while pulling on a clean pair of gloves.

Two other agents continued the gas pump trash cans search.

Holt didn't think they'd find anything in them, but they had to cover all their bases.

Once Grace had the SUV parked next to the dumpster, she and Julianna and Holt climbed on top to look down inside.

It was almost full, and Holt recognized Penny's shoes and flight jacket. With gloved hands, he grabbed them. "They were here."

"Yeah," Julianna said, "but where are they now?"

CHAPTER
TWENTY-NINE

Rabor's blood hummed as he finally hung up the phone. *She* was being obedient. Checking in with him as instructed. He'd asked her each new question and she'd answered appropriately. A thrill shot through him as he envisioned Penny doing the same. But first . . . the training. She was definitely the most stubborn woman he'd ever taken, and the anticipation was nearly killing him. He chuckled at the thought. Wouldn't that be ironic?

But Penny was the perfect one to work with next. Her training might be difficult at first, but in the end, she'd do as instructed. Just like—

He stopped when he thought of *her*. *She* proved his training could work. Which was why *she* was still alive. But every other one had failed. He couldn't wait to see how Penny would do. Her fire and defiance had immediately attracted him to her, and he knew she would be the true test of his skills.

She had been like that *before*. But had passed his test. Others had tried, of course, but he'd seen through their feeble attempts to placate him. There'd been no real desire to be better. To do the *right* thing. *She'd* been the only one.

He stared at the building—one very similar to Joel's—just . . .

warmer. If Penny passed his test, then she would live. If she didn't, she would die. The thought saddened him for some strange reason, and that made him angry.

Because, whether he wanted to admit it or not, he knew she'd fail the test. He shifted the gun and drew in a deep breath. "Let the training begin."

■ ■ ■ ■

Rabor's footsteps crunched closer while Penny's feet were turning into blocks of ice. She prayed she'd be able to run. A chill sent shivers through her. Rabor disappeared on the opposite side of the building.

"Go," she whispered.

She took off with Frankie right behind her.

A string of curses ripped through the air. He'd discovered she was missing.

She tried to run faster, but each step sent agonizing pain through her feet.

A shot rang out and Frankie gave a harsh cry. Penny stopped and spun to see the reporter hit the ground face-first. A dark stain blossomed on the back of his right shoulder. He rolled to his knees and Rabor took aim once more.

"No!" Penny darted to the man who'd risked his life to save her and put herself between him and the gun. Although, she had to admit she wasn't entirely sure Rabor wouldn't pull the trigger anyway.

Heart pounding, she waited for the shot.

Rabor stomped toward them, weapon held tight. "Move."

"Not until you promise not to shoot him."

He studied Frankie, who'd dropped back to the ground, silent, face pale, and breathing with shallow gasps. "Doesn't look like I'm going to have to shoot him again."

Penny yelled and rushed Rabor, catching him in the stomach and knocking him to the ground with a bone-jarring thud. She'd aimed at his recent surgery site, only to realize he was wearing a vest. He'd predicted she might fight back and had come prepared. His breath hissed from between his lips. The hard landing had to hurt in spite of the protection of the vest, but he rolled, hand still wrapped around the grip of the gun.

Penny scrambled to her feet as Rabor brought the weapon back around and aimed it at her.

"Don't . . . move." He sucked in a pained breath.

Penny froze, everything in her wanting to fight back, but something told her not to. Not yet.

For a moment, they stared at one another, her heart pounding, blood rushing. She noted Rabor's phone on the ground next to Frankie's hand. The reporter's fingers moved, then his palm covered the device. Penny sucked in a harsh breath, and Rabor flicked a glance at Frankie, who lay still, eyes closed.

"You killed him," she said. She didn't know if Rabor had, but it sure looked like it, and maybe if Rabor believed Frankie was dead, he'd leave him alone.

Rabor grabbed her arm and yanked her to him, jamming the gun against her temple. "To the house. It's time for our training session and first date."

She stumbled along beside him. She was strong and he'd had surgery a few short days before, but he was determined. His lack of reaction to the pain, even with the vest on, told her a lot. He was on something. Narcotics? Steroids? Whatever it was, his pain was minimal, and that was concerning.

"Can you please take the gun from my head?" she asked through gritted teeth.

He stopped his angry march and she skidded to a halt. He lowered the weapon. "Since you asked so politely."

What? Well, if that was all it took . . .

"If I asked politely for you to let me go, would that work?"

He laughed. "Not hardly, but at least I know you have some manners."

He liked manners. Politeness.

Interesting. Too bad he didn't have any.

"Go on," he said. "Inside."

She stopped at the front door. "Whose place is this?"

He gave her a hard shove, slamming her shoulder into the door. She winced.

"I said, inside! When I say something, you don't question me!"

She stared at him, the look in his eyes chilling her more than anything she could think of.

Please, God, help me . . .

The prayer whispered through her mind as she twisted the knob and stepped through the door. The first thing she registered was that it looked so . . . normal.

But the gun pressed into the small of her back was definitely *not* normal.

"This is Joel's mother's home," he said as though nothing had just happened. "It was hers before she married and she kept it in her maiden name."

In other words, untraceable. Nothing that would lead to Rabor.

Penny's mind spun. She could do this. There would be something inside she could use as a weapon.

"To the right," Rabor said, "through the den and into the kitchen, then down the stairs."

Penny walked slowly, one foot in front of the other, while she took in every detail. The den was homey, comfortable. A place where a family could hang out and spend time together. The blanket over the back of the couch, the book on the coffee table. She thought she recognized the back cover but couldn't place it.

He jabbed her. "Keep walking."

She stepped into the kitchen.

Car keys on the counter.

Teapot on the stove.

Teacups lined up on little hooks attached to the wall. Lots of teacups.

Table with four chairs.

Newspaper folded neatly on the table.

Dishrag draped over the faucet.

Absolutely nothing that could help her escape.

Desperation rose swift and hot.

Dear God, what was she supposed to do?

And poor Frankie . . . she couldn't let his death be in vain!

Help me, Lord!

"Walk faster," he said. "Down the stairs."

"What's the hurry?"

A hard grip on her hair snapped her head back and she gasped while gagging on a scream.

"One thing you need to get straight before you take another step," he said, his breath hot on her ear, "you don't question me. At all. The only way for the training to work and the dates to be successful is for you to do exactly what I say, without question. Do you understand?"

Penny swallowed while her terror rose. "I'm beginning to."

He released her hair and she lowered her chin. With her right hand, she massaged the throbbing in her head and walked to the first step, dreading the thought of going down into a tight space with Rabor.

Self-defense moves flipped through her head, but nothing would work at the moment. She turned the corner and relief flooded her. Four steps led to an area that had been separated from the rest of the house but didn't go all the way down to a basement. For some reason, that gave her hope.

At the bottom of the four stairs, she paused. And frowned. Confusion mingled with the ever-present fear. "It's a duplicate of your kitchen," she said. Right down to the newspaper, the teacups on the wall, the kettle on the gas stove. Just past it was the den with the exact furniture layout.

"These are the training rooms," he said, giving her a nudge with the barrel of the weapon.

"The training rooms." She took a deep breath and prayed her next words didn't set him off. "Is it all right if I ask you a couple of questions?"

"Sit over there at the table."

He hadn't answered her, but he hadn't done anything to hurt her either. She chose a chair that put the table between her and him, and sat.

He turned the stove on and placed the kettle of water over the flame. The whole time he worked, the weapon never moved from her. When he was finished, he nodded. "Since you asked so nicely, yes, you may ask me some questions."

"Why do you do this? Why do you need these training rooms? What are you training . . . me . . . for?" She had a lot more questions but stopped there, not wanting to chance angering him with too many questions at one time.

He studied her for a brief moment, then checked his watch. "I suppose it won't hurt to tell you. It might even help you."

Help her?

She waited.

"I was married to Brenda." His lips smiled, but his eyes remained chilled. "She was wonderful at first. Helpful, wanting to please, made sure I had everything I needed, but then . . ." He sighed.

"Then?"

"She changed." The hand not holding the weapon curled into a fist. "She started *questioning* me and my decisions. *Arguing* with me. It was truly absurd." His nostrils flared. "*I* was the head of the household. *I* was making the money, and she had a generous allowance. All I asked is that she keep the house clean and neat and cook edible meals."

"Sounds reasonable." She nearly choked on the words but forced them out. She'd say anything if it would keep him talking while she thought how to escape so she could help Frankie and alert Holt. Frankie had hidden the phone. She could only pray he was able to use it. Her gaze traveled the area and a plan began to form. She turned back to her captor.

"Exactly," he said, "although I'm a little surprised to hear you say that."

Careful, Pen. Choose your words carefully. Lord, give me the words.

"I'm not married," she said, all senses on alert to any changes in his body language, "but it seems to me that if two people come to an agreement of what they want out of the marriage, then that's okay for them. What works for one couple may not work for another."

He frowned. "That's what I'm saying. We had an agreement and she broke it."

"How?"

"She wanted to go back to work."

Okay, she could see how that might be a problem if they'd agreed that she wouldn't, but circumstances changed. *People changed.* "And you didn't want her to." And it wasn't something someone *killed* their spouse over. Except apparently, it was.

"We agreed she would stay home!" He slapped a hand on the table and Penny jumped, heart thundering.

"I can see how her changing her mind would be upsetting for you."

Her calm response seemed to take him by surprise. He backed away, still breathing hard from his surge of anger, but he was able to gain control and nod. "Exactly. And then at breakfast one morning, when she brought the subject up again, I forbade it. Told her she wasn't going back to work and not to mention it again. She grabbed the teakettle from the stove and dumped the contents over my head. Thankfully, the tea had cooled enough not to leave any serious burns, but I couldn't let her get away with that."

"So, you killed her."

"No, I trained her."

"How?" Did she really want to know?

279

"I'm getting ready to show you. You see, if my wife had gone through proper training before we were married, it wouldn't have been an issue. She would have known what to do and I wouldn't have had to take matters into my own hands."

"Can you please tell me what the training entails?"

"You fix me a cup of tea, we drink it, and we have conversation. I say something, you agree. If I think you're only agreeing just to escape punishment, then you're punished."

"How?"

"The training ends. And before you ask, I give you a nice dose of curare and then you're ready for the first perfect date."

"But I'll be—"

"Dead?" He smiled. "Yes, well, turns out those are the best dates ever."

Penny wanted out. Away from this lunatic and his narcissistic and murderous notions. But she had to know . . . "One more question, please?"

"Okay."

"Why are you training me? If you train me and I pass the training, what happens after that?"

He stared for a moment, clearly unsure how to answer her. "We'll cross that bridge if we come to it. The training begins now."

CHAPTER
THIRTY

Holt sat in the front of the SUV with Julianna beside him while they brainstormed a plan to find Penny. So far, neither of them liked anything they'd come up with.

Even though her expression gave away nothing of her internal angst, Julianna's hands shook as she ran them over her face. She closed her eyes and he figured she was praying. He added his own prayers, then tried to call Penny's phone again.

Straight to voice mail.

"Okay," he said, "it's a long shot, but let's try to think like Rabor."

"That's what I've been doing," Julianna muttered, "and it's scary." She held up a hand. "But I know what you mean." She paused. "He had an entire plan worked out. From finding the place to land the chopper, to being where Penny would be—"

"—and he set it up. I guarantee you he had something to do with no other pilots being available except for Penny."

"Probably caused the wreck on the highway too."

"I agree. Since this plan was one he didn't have a lot of time to put together, it probably means he's having to use what he has available to him. Especially a location where he can take and hide Penny."

"Officers searched the lake house Natasha's in-laws have," Julianna said, "and it was clean. No sign of him."

"And Joel Allen's place is still a crime scene. He wouldn't dare go there." Holt wanted to get out of the car and pace so he could think better.

"No," Julianna said, "definitely too many cops in that area."

"But there's got to be something . . ."

"What about a property in his wife's name?"

He grimaced. "Daria looked. Nothing."

"A fake name?"

"That would take a while to set up. He wouldn't have time." She groaned. "A friend? Some family we don't know about?"

Holt rubbed a hand down his face, then pinched the bridge of his nose. He didn't blame Grace for Rabor's success in snatching Penny. He blamed himself. He should have stayed with her.

His phone buzzed and he didn't recognize the number. Having learned his lesson with Frankie, he swiped the bar across the bottom. "Agent Holt Satterfield."

"121 . . . Higgenfield," the voice whispered.

"What?"

"Penny . . . needs . . ."

"Hello? What does Penny need? Who is this?"

Silence.

Holt memorized the number and sent it to Daria via text. "I need a trace on this number ASAP." Back to the person on the line. "Hello?"

More silence, and Holt's blood pressure went through the roof of the car.

His phone buzzed with a return text from Daria.

■ ■ ■ ■

Penny racked her brain, trying to decide on the best course of action. As soon as he'd stated it was time to begin the training—she shuddered to think what that might entail—the landline phone on the training-kitchen wall rang. He'd answered with a terse, "What?"

After listening for a moment, he walked away from her, backing toward the stove while the other person talked. He pulled two teacups from the wall. Finally, he spoke. "Don't call me again. I'll let you know when I'm ready to talk. For now, I'm conducting a training session. You have your instructions. Follow through with them." More listening. "That's a good girl." He hung up without another word, and Penny sucked in a breath and let it out slowly.

"May I speak?" she asked, keeping her voice low and her face free of the disgust and fear racing through her.

He raised a brow. "You're a quick learner, aren't you?"

"You said I was smart."

"Indeed I did. I'm glad you're seeing how this is to work." He eyed her. "You intrigue me. You're not like the others."

She desperately wanted to ask him about the woman he'd been talking to but figured not only would he not tell her, he might stop talking altogether.

"Can you explain the training to me?"

"I set up dates. We cook, have a little dinner, a little conversation. A little tea. You will do exactly as I say, obeying me in every instance. If you do well with the first date, we may have a second. But every date has to be perfect."

"May I ask another question?"

"Yes, of course."

He really did like the polite questions she was nearly gagging on as she spit them out of stiff lips. "Why does it have to be perfect?"

"Because that's the way it's supposed to be when two people love each other."

So, he was under the illusion that they were in love? "And, you're training me for . . . who?"

He scowled and she wanted to grab the question back. "What do you mean, for who? For me! For us!"

"Okay. Thank you for answering my questions."

His ire faded.

Penny sucked air into her lungs. "One more question, please?"

"What?"

"What if the date's not perfect?"

"Then I make it perfect."

She swallowed. Asking him how he managed to make it perfect wasn't necessary. The memory of the dead women posed at the table with the tea set intruded. "I'll cooperate. Please, tell me what makes the date perfect. In detail."

His brows lifted and he tilted his head to study her, his blue eyes dark. Empty. "Hmm. The perfect date. That's easy. One who doesn't talk too much about herself and one who doesn't decay too fast." He laughed, the sound sending chills pebbling her skin and nausea straight to the pit of her stomach.

"I see. All right, then. What should I do first?"

He slammed a fist onto the table and Penny jerked, her heart hammering. "Don't try to take control! This is my date! My training! Do you understand?"

The teakettle whistled, jerking Penny from her frozen state. "I understand." She took a steadying breath. "I'll wait for you to tell me what you want."

"You don't wait!" His scream echoed, bouncing off the walls. "You anticipate!"

Penny stood, and he narrowed his gaze. The teakettle continued its blaring whistle. She walked to the stove and turned off the flame. "Tea for two?" she asked.

His jaw dropped and his countenance changed. A smile bloomed, then a chuckle rippled from his throat. "Tea for me and you?"

She nodded and picked up one of the cups from the counter. "Please tell me where the tea bags are and I'll fix it."

He scowled. "You know where the tea bags are, Brenda."

Brenda? His wife's name. *Play along, Penny.* "Of course I do." She scanned the counter and noted the canister labeled "tea." She pulled out two bags and dropped them into the cups. Then poured the hot water over them.

He started toward her, hand outstretched as though to take his cup, and she tossed them both in his face.

His scream of rage echoed through his training rooms and she spun and bolted up the stairs while he grabbed at his scorched face and screeched his fury. Penny made it to the original kitchen, swiping the car keys from the counter, and raced for the front door. The Buick symbol on the black key told her escape might actually be possible.

"You're dead! That's not how the perfect date goes! You ruined it and now I'm going to kill you!" His footsteps pounded after her.

Penny hit the front door and threw herself out of the house and down the steps. His footfalls fell faster and closer.

The car. She had to get to the car.

She skidded to a stop. There was no car—and Frankie was gone from the yard. Hope sprouted that he was okay, but she had no time to look for him. Penny raced toward the nearest building. One that she'd noticed when Frankie had rescued her from her "prison."

She registered the fact that Rabor was still screaming at her and caught a few words. ". . . can't see, you stupid—"

Ignoring him and focusing on escape, she darted inside what she thought was a barn.

Only to come to a panicked halt. The moon cast a long sliver of light through the dirty window, but the odor of decaying bodies nearly sent her to her knees. She gagged, caught her breath, and tried to breathe in shallow pants through her mouth.

Penny pulled the collar of her shirt up over her nose and prayed. "Oh, dear Lord . . . ," she whispered. "Oh, God, help me." Where had the bodies come from? If Rabor had been in prison for two years—

Joel Allen. He'd been using this place too. Living out Rabor's fantasies. Making them his own in Rabor's backyard while the man plotted his evil in prison. Allen probably even reported back, fueling Rabor's sick fun. Unbelievable.

Rabor's shouts said he wasn't far behind, but Penny couldn't move. She stared at the dead bodies covered in plastic. She couldn't do it. No, no, no. No way. She took a step back. Her mind flashed to the closet. She'd pounded on that door until her hands bled. *"Let me out! Let me out!"* Then came Mrs. Gibbs's calm voice. *"You're stronger than you think, Penny, but where you're weak, the Lord is strong. Let him be your strength."*

I can't do it, God. I can't.

When she heard Rabor at the door, she had no choice unless she wanted to *be* one of the bodies.

With tears flowing down her cheeks, she moved to the middle of the "morgue," pulled up the edge of the plastic, and lay down in between two of the bodies. Moving fast, not stopping to think or she'd lose her sanity, she yanked the plastic over her and closed her eyes. *I want out, I want out! Let me out!*

The door squeaked open. "I know you came in here," Rabor said. His breathing echoed in the area. "It's the only place to hide around here. You don't think you're the first one to run here, do you? They *always* run here."

Penny held her breath, her lungs protesting. She breathed out, then in, then held it. If she survived this, she'd never get the sweet foul smell out of her nose, her mouth, her brain. *Please, God, help me!*

"Do you know how many women failed my training sessions? All of them." His voice was ridiculously close, and panic clamored even closer to the surface.

Don't scream, don't scream. Stay quiet. Let me out!

"Why do you think that is, Penny?" He sighed. "Because they all tried to run!"

The tarp flew from her and the scream erupted before she could stop it. His hand clamped around her left wrist and her eyes snapped open to meet his. The flesh on his face had already started to blister and his eyes were as dead as the bodies in the barn. "Do you think I don't know exactly how many women I have in here?" he asked, his voice low, lethal, and almost otherworldly. "Do you think I can't count? We're going back to the house and we're going to try this again. Maybe a little curare will help make you see things my way."

Penny realized she still held the car keys in her right hand. Working quickly, keeping her hand from his line of sight, she threaded individual keys between her fingers.

Panting, gagging, she let Rabor haul her to her feet, then swung her right fist at the left side of his face. The keys connected with flesh.

Once again, he let loose a bloodcurdling, pained shriek, and his grip loosened. Penny spun out of his grasp and fled toward the barn door.

He roared and charged after her.

Sobs gathered, stealing her breath, but the adrenaline racing through her veins gave her strength to run. Back out in the dark, she squinted and kept going.

And there was the car. Parked on the other side of the house. She aimed for it. Reached it and threw herself into the driver's seat. Penny slammed and locked the door just as Rabor reached her. He pounded on the window while she jammed the keys into the ignition with hands shaking so hard, she was shocked she actually succeeded in getting the key in the hole the first time. She twisted and . . .

Nothing.

"No," she whispered. "No, no, no." The sobs rose higher and one escaped. She choked the rest back and lowered her forehead to the steering wheel.

He'd won.

"Did you think I wouldn't notice the missing keys?" His shout reached her even through the glass. She turned her head to look at him, her hope gone.

He grinned, pulled out his gun, and aimed it at her.

A loud crack sounded, then another and another. Penny flinched, expecting to feel the burn of a bullet piercing her body. She kept her gaze on Rabor and saw his eyes go wide as he dropped to the ground.

Holt, Julianna, and a host of local officers hurried toward Penny.

She threw open the car door and jumped out. A hand grasped her ankle and yanked her to the ground.

Rabor lay there, his eyes open, gasping for air while his hand was like a vise, trapping her.

Penny snapped.

She drew back her free leg and slammed her foot into his burned, blistered, bleeding face. Her heel connected with his nose in a sickening crunch and his eyes closed. She kicked again and again and again. "Let. Me. Go!" Another kick. Another crunch. A pair of strong arms hauled her away and enfolded her into a tight embrace.

"You're okay, Penny," he said against her ear. Holt. "You did it. You hung on until help could get here. You're safe, I promise." A pause. "Get him out of here."

She let the sobs come for half a minute until she remembered. "Frankie!"

"We found him. He's still alive. He's also the reason we're here. Somehow, he got his hands on a satellite phone, remembered my number, and called. He gave me the street address before passing out and we traced him here."

She rubbed the tears from her cheeks. "Rabor had a sat phone. I tackled him when he shot Frankie. The phone fell out of his pocket and Frankie covered it with his hand."

"Well, it saved your life because we were still desperately searching for a way to find you when he called."

She looked for Rabor. They had him on a gurney, the sheet pulled over his face. "Is he really dead?"

"Yeah. One of the bullets caught him in the throat. Not a pleasant way to go."

She wasn't going to cry over that. "Rabor said the house belonged to Joel's mother."

"We would have found it eventually, but maybe not in time to save you. We owe Frankie big-time."

She groaned. "Like an exclusive?"

"Yeah."

She nodded, shivers of shock still running through her. She was safe. Holt had come. Rabor was dead. "I'm actually happy to do it. He's earned it." Penny sucked in a deep breath, the stench of the decomposition still lingering. "But for now, all I want is a shower. A hot, steaming, skin-scorching shower. As soon as possible." She told them about the bodies in the barn and Holt dispatched officers to secure the scene. "It's horrible, Holt. I can't even describe how awful it is. How absolutely abhorrent—"

He stopped her with a finger on her lips. "I don't even want to think about how scared you were, but, Penny, you're so amazingly courageous to have done what you did. I can't even—" He shuddered. "I'm so sorry it took us this long to find you."

"I'm just glad you did," she whispered.

He hugged her again, then stepped back. "Let's get you out of here. You can give your statement a little later."

"Thanks."

"I have a question for you."

"Sure."

"I know what I want."

She stilled and met his gaze. "That's not a question."

"I'm getting there. I want you, Penny. I want there to be an us. Will you go out on a date with me?"

"As long as it doesn't involve tea."

CHAPTER
THIRTY-ONE

The fact that she could joke after this latest trauma . . .

Holt smiled. "I think that can be arranged."

"And don't use the word 'date' around me for a while, if you don't mind. Let's just call it hanging out."

"That works for me."

"That being said, yes, I'd be more than happy to go to dinner and hang out with you. And drink coffee. Or hot chocolate."

"I get it. Anything but tea." He kissed her forehead. "That sounds awesome. Now let's get you into the car. I need to walk through the crime scene." He directed her toward the SUV that had replaced the bullet-riddled one, but Penny held back, her gaze on the house. "What is it?"

"There's someone else out there," she said. "Someone who's either a victim or involved with Rabor."

"Who?"

"I don't know, but she called him while we were in the room he called the training kitchen." She shuddered. "I'll go with you."

"No, Pen—" Her patient gaze cut him off. "Why?"

"So I can explain everything to you. Exactly what happened.

You can record it and have someone type it up and I'll sign it. That way I only have to go through it once."

"Okay, yeah, we can do that. But first . . . come here." She followed him to the car and he opened the glove compartment to grab a container of Vicks VapoRub. He opened it and held it out to her. "Slather it above your upper lip and in your nose if you want. You're not supposed to use it in your nose, but it does help get the smell out faster."

"I need to coat it on my brain." Once she was done, she took a deep breath and nodded. "That's a lot better. Thanks."

"Good."

She followed him back up the steps and into the house. He handed her a pair of gloves, and she pulled them on, then slipped on the little blue booties he'd grabbed when he'd gotten the Vicks. He placed a hand on her lower back and waited while her eyes roamed the room.

"Okay, where do I start?" she asked.

Holt hit the record app on his phone. "From the moment Rabor hijacked your helicopter."

"I landed. Raina and Holly got off and headed for the victims." She continued to the point where she said, "I was in that outbuilding, then Frankie showed up. He got me out and we hid behind the building until we had no choice but to run for it. Frankie had his cell phone on him but had no signal. Rabor had been on the satellite phone. When he hung up, he was on his way to get me when Frankie and I took off." She raked a gloved hand over her hair and shook herself.

"Rabor heard us, fired, and hit Frankie. I tackled Rabor and he got the better of me. I think Frankie played dead and it saved his life."

"And yours."

"Yes."

"The phone fell out of Rabor's pocket," she said. "Frankie took a chance on covering it with his hand." She breathed in, held it, then let the air out through her lips. She did it again and Holt recognized the calming exercise.

"I went through the den area." She walked over to it, her eyes scanning, then she turned and headed for the kitchen. "We came in this way. His keys were on the counter, and that was the only thing different than what was in the training kitchen."

Holt nodded. "Show me."

She walked toward the stairs and he noted her slight hesitation before walking down them. When he joined her, he paused at the sight that greeted him. "Whoa."

"Creepy, isn't it?"

"It shouldn't be. I mean it's just two rooms exactly like the ones we just came from, but . . . yeah. I guess knowing what they were used for makes it creepy." He frowned. "Why build two entirely separate rooms? Why not just use the ones you have?"

"I think he had to keep his . . . whatever you want to call it . . . serial killer deeds separate from his 'normal' life. If you know what I mean."

"Maybe. It's as good an explanation as any, I guess." He studied her, noting her pale features and tight brows. "You doing okay?"

"It's not fun, but he really didn't hurt me."

"You didn't give him time."

"Exactly." Another deep breath. "Look around. Do you see anything different from the other kitchen?"

He studied the area. "No." But he hadn't looked super close. "Do you?"

"No, that's my point. Not one detail is out of place." She walked to the table and touched the back of a chair. "I sat here. He stood over there. The phone on the wall rang . . ." She continued her recounting, and Holt let his gaze scan the area once more, looking for differences in the kitchen, and he couldn't find one.

"I saw the keys on the counter and realized there weren't any in here and figured those were his actual car keys. I thought if I could get them and get to his car, I'd be able to get away." She swallowed. "I threw the hot tea in his face and it stopped him for a minute, but only long enough for me to get out of the house."

"And you had to find a place to hide."

"Yeah. And he found me." Her gaze met his and the agony there seared him. "All those women," she whispered. "He knew exactly how many there were."

He gripped her fingers. "Penny, you did what you had to do. And because of that, no one else is going to die by his hand."

"I know." She shot him a trembling smile, then glanced at the training den. "I didn't go in there. I don't need to see it."

"Then let's get you out of here."

His sat phone buzzed with a call from Matt Nixon. "Let me catch this," he said. They stepped outside. "Hey, what have you got?"

"Your sister didn't kill her husband and neither did her daughter."

He stopped next to the car. "I'm sorry. What?"

"The video was edited, doctored—however you want to say it. In other words, it's fake. It's a very, very good fake, like professional-grade stuff, but our guy Pat, who's an audio and video forensics expert, was able to take it apart and figure out Ellie didn't pull the trigger. Ellie wasn't even there. She was dropped in, so to speak. I'll spare you the technical mumbo jumbo, but someone else was in the house and that person pulled the trigger."

"I think I need to sit down."

Penny looked at him, a frown on her face.

"Who?" he asked.

"Pat managed to pull a reflection from a picture on the opposite wall that goes into the kitchen. I'm sending you the image now."

His phone vibrated. He tapped the screen, and a blurry shot of his sister's housekeeper's face stared back at him.

He turned to Penny. "Matt has the evidence needed to get Zoe out of prison. He's going to the DA himself to ask that they re-open the case. I . . . I need to be there for her. I haven't been and I can never make that up to her, but I need to go after I finish getting everything done here." He needed to get Penny's prints and Rabor's—to make sure they had the right guy this time—and so much more. "You also need medical attention."

"I'll be fine."

Paramedics approached and he motioned for them to take her. He still had to contact the Identification Division to expedite getting the victims' prints and dental records for comparison with missing females in the NCIC database. So much to do when all he wanted to do was take care of his family. And Penny.

He called Gerald. "I'm calling to give you a status update."

"Hello to you, too, agent-who-is-supposed-to-be-on-medical-leave."

"Right. I promise to do that soon. But for now, this is the latest." He gave the man the condensed version of the latest incident, including Zoe's story, and had just finished when Penny stepped out of the ambulance.

"Holt?"

"Yes, Ger?"

"You have two weeks off starting tomorrow. I don't want to hear from you. Got it?"

"Got it." For the first time in his career, he was looking forward to his time off. He had important matters to attend to.

Penny reached him and he drank in her appearance, debating whether or not to tell her he loved her.

She held up a hand. "Don't you dare. The first time you say it will not have dead-body smell associated with it."

He laughed. He couldn't help it. That was so Penny. "Wait for me here?"

She nodded, and he went to finish wrapping up the details of his case. When he returned two hours later, he found her asleep in the passenger seat. For a moment, he stood there, watching her breathe, then sent up a silent prayer of thanks that she was safe. And whole. And breathing.

And hopefully, one day soon, his.

■ ■ ■ ■

Penny grabbed the robe from the hook on the wall and slipped into it. She ran the towel over her hair and decided the dead-body odor *had* to be gone after two days, even though she could still smell it.

She was supposed to meet Holt for lunch, now that he'd finished dealing with his sister's release from prison. He planned to fill her in on everything and she was looking forward to hearing about the happy ending. But, for some reason, she couldn't get Sally Allen out of her mind. While it was true the woman hadn't seemed terribly upset at becoming a widow, Penny needed to do *something* for her.

And the children.

She'd been a part of taking their father from them, and the desire to check on them and see that they were dealing with his death was something she just couldn't shake.

She dressed and texted Holt about her plan.

Once she was in the car, she headed for the nearest bookstore that also carried toys. Thirty minutes later, she still hadn't heard from Holt, but she was armed with several books for Mary and a couple of toys for JoJo. It had put a small dent in her checking account, but she was fine with that as long as it made the kids smile.

When she arrived at Sally Allen's home, she noted the van in the drive and breathed a sigh of relief that the woman was home. And alone with the children, by all appearances. Which was kind of weird now that she thought about it. The woman had just lost her husband. Where was the family's and friends' support? Her drive should be full of cars and her refrigerator overflowing with casseroles. She glanced at the bag on the seat. Maybe she should have brought food?

Her phone rang and she answered it so it came through the car's Bluetooth speakers. "Hey, Holt."

"Penny, you okay?"

"Yeah, fine. I'm just going to take this stuff to Sally's kids and check on her. I figured I'd do it on the way to meet you since she only lives about five minutes from the restaurant."

"Sounds good. I've just gotten into the office in spite of Gerald's objections, so I'm here going over the evidence collected at the crime scene, but I'll head to the restaurant in a few. I'm still trying to track down who called Rabor's landline. You don't have any idea who it could have been?"

"Gerald would be doing the same thing in your shoes. And no idea, but shouldn't that be fairly easy to find out?"

"Should be. But whoever called it blocked their number. We'll figure it out—it might just take the tech a little longer than usual."

"Okay. How's Zoe?"

"She's in shock, but overjoyed to be home. Ellie is a sleepwalker. Not every night, but some. All this time Zoe thought Ellie had walked out of the sleepover without anyone noticing. That she came home and heard them arguing, picked up Owen's gun from the coffee table—"

"Wait a minute, he left his gun on the coffee table with two small kids?"

"He'd walked in from work, knew the kids were next door, and left it on the coffee table with his badge. He would have put it away before the girls came home."

"Oh, okay."

"Anyway, Zoe thought Ellie had come in, heard them arguing, and when he put his hands on her, it scared Ellie, and she shot him. Zoe didn't want to believe it, of course, but with the video, she felt she had no choice but to sacrifice herself for her child. The crazy thing is, she said she didn't remember seeing Ellie there and just thought it was her brain reacting to the trauma. That after the gunshot and Owen dropped, Zoe was so busy trying to save him and call 911 that she never saw Ellie."

"Because she was never there."

"Yeah. Zoe just figured Ellie was so traumatized, she ran back to the sleepover and simply didn't remember anything."

"I can't even imagine."

"There's more, but I'll fill you in when I see you."

"Okay, I'll text when I leave here."

"See you soon."

Penny climbed out and grabbed her bag of goodies, then hurried up the steps to knock on the door.

Small feet pattered from the inside, the curtain to the right moved, and bright blue eyes looked up at Penny. "Mama! It's the lady from before!"

"Don't open the door, Mary."

"I'm not!"

Three seconds later, Sally swung the door open with JoJo on her hip. She'd been crying and her red, swollen eyes widened. "Hi."

"Hi, I'm sorry to come by unannounced. I can see you've been crying, so maybe this isn't the best time. I can come back later." The poor woman had been through the wringer. Even if she and Joel had been ready to go their separate ways, finding out the man was a serial killer had to be incredibly hard.

"No, it's okay. I think crying is going to be a part of my daily life at this point." She stepped back. "Do you want to come in?"

"Sure, thanks. Just for a few minutes, though. I don't want to keep you."

"What's in there?" Mary asked, her eyes on the bag.

Penny smiled. "Something for you and your brother."

Mary clapped and did a little dance. "Come in the den." She whirled and darted to hop up on the couch.

Penny followed and set the bag beside her. "Why don't you see what you can pull out of there. There's something for JoJo in there too."

Sally put JoJo down, and he walked to the couch and climbed up beside his sister. "Present?" He grabbed the bag and dumped it upside down. Everything hit the floor and JoJo laughed.

When Mary saw the books tumble out, she gasped. "Oh wow! Thank you!" She scrambled down to look at them and JoJo went after the toys.

Penny noted the boxes lined up against the far wall and glanced at Sally. "Are you moving?"

"Yes." She wrung her hands and pressed them to her eyes for a moment. "I can't stay here after . . . everything."

"I'm sure it's been hard."

"You have no idea." She swiped a hand over her cheeks.

Mary pulled on the hem of Penny's flight jacket. "I just finished *Charlotte's Web*, so I need a new book. Have you read these?"

Penny went still. What was it about *Charlotte's Web* that tickled something in her brain? "Yes," she said, "I have. You could start with *Stuart Little* or *The Trumpet of the Swan*. The author who wrote *Charlotte's Web* wrote them too."

"Oh, that's so cool, thank you!"

"I left my book at my friend Dee's house, and Mama said there was no way she was buying me another copy."

There'd been a book in the den of Rabor's home, but not in the training den. She could picture both rooms as well as if she were standing there looking at them. That book was the only difference.

Could Sally Allen's daughter have left her copy of *Charlotte's Web* at her *friend Dee's*—Darius's—*house?*

But how did that even make sense? She clenched her shaking hands.

She didn't know exactly how it all fit, but there was no doubt in her mind that Sally was the woman on the other end of the line when Penny had been captive in Rabor's training kitchen.

JoJo grabbed the toy car and took off for the hallway.

"I think I'll start with *Stuart Little*," Mary said. "I've heard it's a great story." She picked up the books and put them on the table.

Penny forced a smile. "I think that's the perfect choice." She flashed to the outbuilding Sally's husband had used because he needed a place to sleep. What if Rabor had stayed there and Sally knew it? Had hidden him all this time?

"Can I go to my room and read, Mama?"

"Sure, go on."

Mary skipped over to Penny and hugged her. "Thank you."

"You're very welcome, Mary."

The little girl headed to her room. JoJo zoomed his car down the hall one more time and Penny picked up the book on the end table. *Charlotte's Web.* She turned it over to look at the back cover and found it familiar.

She pulled her phone from her pocket and sent a quick text to Holt.

> What was the book in the den at Rabor's house?

She turned to Sally. "Well, I guess I'll leave you to have some time to yourself now that your children are occupied." Penny set the book back on the end table. "I really am sorry for my role in Joel's death."

Her phone buzzed.

> **Holt**
> Charlotte's Web. Why?

Penny sucked in a sharp breath and her gaze swung back to Sally, who had opened the drawer of the table next to the other end of the couch.

When the woman turned, she pointed a small gun at Penny. "How did you figure it out?"

CHAPTER
THIRTY-TWO

Holt checked his phone one more time and frowned. Tapped another message to Penny.

> I'm heading to the restaurant, but if you're not ready, I can run a quick errand. How much longer do you think you'll be?

He set the phone aside and went back to his laptop. He had the crime scene pictures up from Rabor's house, still looking for a clue that would tell him who the woman could have been who called Rabor while Penny was in his clutches.

The phone records had pulled up nothing, which meant the number had probably been hidden on purpose.

Naturally.

He glanced at his phone. Penny still hadn't answered him. If she didn't answer within the next few minutes, he'd just call her.

■ ■ ■ ■

Penny froze. Then swallowed while a slow-burning anger started to build. She was getting really tired of people aiming guns at her.

Her phone vibrated again and she glanced at the screen.

300

Penny?

"Ignore it," Sally said. "Throw the phone on the couch."

Penny obeyed without taking her eyes from Sally. "I don't know the details, but I'm guessing you had some kind of relationship with Rabor?"

"Darius. Yes." She lifted her chin. "I loved him. I would have done anything for him, because he was a real man."

"He was a killer."

"He wasn't afraid of anything. He knew what he wanted and did everything necessary to make sure he got it."

"And that included plotting with you and Joel to get him out of prison by creating a pattern of women," she said, her voice soft while her mind sorted through the information. "All of the women who wrote him letters and came to see him, those were all covering up your and Joel's visits, weren't they?"

Sally's eyes flicked to the hallway, where JoJo was still playing with his car. "Yes, it was clever, wasn't it?"

"So Joel dressed up as one of his girlfriends, helped break him out of the hospital, then you hid him from the cops when everything went wrong on the mountain?"

"Of course."

Penny's phone rang and Sally gave a low growl. "Seriously?" She jabbed the screen, and Penny could only assume she hung up on the person. Probably Holt.

"I have plans today, Sally. Holding me at gunpoint is just going to end in tragedy for someone."

"Shut up."

Penny fell silent, but she was thinking. Holt would be wondering why she'd dropped off the radar. He might even come looking for her at Sally's house if she didn't respond to his texts or calls soon.

Sally paced, worry dipping her brows down and crinkling her forehead.

"So," Penny finally said, "your whole story about the divorce and why Joel was doing the surgeries and even that he was staying in the outbuilding was the perfect cover for Rabor."

"I thought I did fairly well coming up with that on the spur of the moment," Sally said, stopping opposite Penny. "As soon as I realized I had the FBI on my doorstep, I figured they'd want to search the buildings." She glanced out the window. "I knew they'd find someone had been out there."

"How did Joel fit into your and Rabor's plans?"

"He was to play his part and then"—she shrugged—"he could die."

"How could you do that to your children's father?"

She scoffed. "Father? Some father. Wimp doesn't even begin to describe Joel. I have no idea how he walked upright, because he definitely had no spine."

"That doesn't fit with the man who attacked me, shot federal agents, and tried to kill another agent."

She lifted a brow. "Because I'd been training him."

Training him. Penny was so sick of that word. "Training him how?"

"How to act like a real man. Before he went to prison, Darius trained the women. I trained Joel." A small smile curved her lips as though she was replaying the training in her mind.

Penny suppressed a small shudder, and for the first time, a niggle of real fear crept up her spine.

"But Joel was going to Darius for advice on how to ensure that I wouldn't leave him. As a result, he learned everything there was to know about Darius."

"Including what had happened between Darius and Holt."

"Oh yes, Darius took great pleasure in describing their interactions—especially their last one—in detail to Joel. And Joel would come home and act it out. I told him it was a good start to becoming a real man. In the last month or so, if you'd placed them side by side, you would have had a hard time telling them apart." In essence, Joel had actually taken on Rabor's identity. By the time he died, he probably thought he *was* Rabor.

"How does a real man act?" Penny asked.

"In control. He can make decisions and choices without the effort sending him to bed to hide, trembling, under the covers. Or worse, to the local bar, to drink away his ineptness. He takes care of his family and loves them." She drew in a deep breath. "I had told Joel I wanted a divorce and he went into begging and pleading mode." Her lip curled. "I told him he had to change. To become a man. He said to give him an example to live up to. That night, the documentary on Darius Rabor came on. I told Joel that Darius was a real man. He killed his wife because she disrespected him. That was impressive to me."

Penny blinked. "You wanted your husband to kill you?"

She snorted. "Of course not. But I wanted him to stop being such a coward, to man up and take responsibility."

"So you told him to go to the prison to meet with Rabor?"

"No, surprisingly enough, he did that on his own, and that intrigued me enough to make me stay. I wanted to see where he was going with it."

"And that's when he started doing the surgeries?"

Sally nodded and Penny gasped.

"He wasn't doing them because he was obsessed with Rabor, he was doing them because he thought if he actually *became* Rabor, you wouldn't leave him."

"You're smart."

JoJo came into the den, carrying his car. Sally's gaze snapped to him. "Go stay with Mary, now."

Without hesitation, the little boy turned and ran down the hall, calling his sister's name. Apparently she'd been training JoJo too.

Penny's phone went off again and Sally snatched the device from the couch, the weapon never wavering from Penny. "Holt wants to know if you're all right and could you please answer him."

"If I don't text him back, he'll come looking for me."

Her eyes narrowed. "He knows you're here?"

"Yes."

Sally waved the gun toward the couch. "Sit."

Penny sat. "Now what?"

The woman tapped the screen and held it in front of Penny's face to open the device.

"What are you planning, Sally?"

The woman turned the phone back around and voice texted, "I'm leaving Sally's now, but she asked me to do a little grocery shopping for her so she doesn't have to get the kids out in the cold. I'm going to do that. Let's talk tomorrow, okay?"

Penny's stomach tightened. Would Holt fall for it? "So you're going to kill me?"

"I don't have a choice. I can't go to prison. I can't lose my children." She glanced in the direction of the bedrooms. "They'll be fine while we walk out to the building."

The building? The one where Joel had killed his victims? Nausea swirled and Penny swallowed. No way was she walking in that place. She had nightmares every night about the victims there and the bodies in the barn. She'd rather be shot than step foot in that building.

Sally motioned toward the kitchen door with the gun. "Let's go. I've got a job lined up with new identities and everything. It's time for me to get rid of you, leave this place, and start over."

Penny bit her lip. She wasn't sure Sally would actually have the guts to pull the trigger. But she wasn't sure she wouldn't, either. "You turned your husband into a killer. You're responsible for the death of every woman he killed."

"No. I finally turned him into a man."

"Put the gun down, Sally," Holt said from the kitchen doorway.

Sally gasped and Penny dove, catching the woman in the stomach. She went down and the weapon skittered across the floor to stop at Holt's foot. With a screech, the woman lashed out at Penny, her fingers curved into claws. Penny drew back a fist and swung, catching Sally on the side of her head.

She cried out once more and went limp.

Holt hurried over, flipped the woman on her stomach, and cuffed her as other officers swarmed the home. Penny sat on the floor, catching her breath.

Julianna met her gaze. "Glad I didn't have to use my skills."

"Me too." Penny pointed down the hallway. "The kids are in the back."

"I've got them," Julianna said.

She disappeared down the hall and Penny looked at Holt. "How'd you know?"

"The book. The one at Rabor's house on the table. All I could think of was Mary referring to her friend Dee."

"Glad we're on the same page." She glanced at the book on the end table. "So to speak."

"We're definitely on the same page." He looked at Sally, and Penny let her gaze follow his.

The woman lay on the floor, eyes shut, tears dripping onto the hardwood. An officer pulled Sally to her feet while another bagged the gun.

Penny stood.

And fell into Holt's arms. He hugged her close and kissed the top of her head. "I have a question for you," he murmured.

"Sure."

"Are you a secret football player? Because you have quite the righteous tackle."

She giggled. Then chuckled. "I have seven cousins. All male. If I wanted to have any fun during family holidays, I had to learn to play football. And I'm not talking about that wimpy flag football stuff."

"Well, I, for one, am glad you learned. It's saved my life on more than one occasion."

"Holt?"

"Yeah?"

"I want to go home."

"Let's go."

CHAPTER
THIRTY-THREE

A WEEK LATER

Holt pulled to a stop at Penny's home and climbed out of his SUV. He had another week of leave and had plans to put the time to good use.

By spending it with Penny.

And everyone else at her house, apparently.

He recognized Grace's and Julianna's cars, and Frankie's, but not the black Cadillac parked nearest the door. He glanced at the tag and noted it was a rental.

Okay then. Someone visiting?

Her mother. Had to be.

Oh boy. He knocked and the door swung open. Penny launched herself into his arms and kissed him. Not one to argue, Holt reciprocated.

When she stepped back, she laughed. "I'm happy to see you."

Her sheer joy sent his heart thumping. He could get used to coming home to that kind of greeting on a regular basis. He cleared his throat. "If you've got company, I can come back later."

"Not a chance. Get in here."

In her den, he found her mother entertaining Julianna, Grace, and Frankie with stories about her Hollywood life. Frankie had his recorder going, of course. When her mother saw Holt and Penny, she stood to glide over to them. "You must be Holt."

"Yes, ma'am, and you are?"

The room went silent, jaws dropped—and Penny giggled.

Penny's mother's eyes went wide, then she too dissolved into laughter. She threw her arms open and Holt leaned in for her hug. When she stepped back, she shook a finger at him. "You got me. Not many people manage that."

"It's a pleasure to meet you, Mrs. . . . uh . . . what do I call you?"

"Geneva is fine. It's actually my birth name."

"It's a pleasure to meet you, Geneva."

"Come have a seat. I was just telling this dear young man all about what Penny was like as a child."

Penny rolled her eyes at him. "Fascinating stuff."

She might disagree, but Holt wanted to hear those stories. He nodded to Frankie, Julianna, and Grace. "Good to see you all here. Penny said y'all helped her get the bathroom finished and one bedroom done. That was good of you."

"Her mom needed a place to sleep," Grace said, with a soft smile.

"I told her I'd be perfectly fine on the sofa," Geneva said, "or at a hotel."

"Absolutely not," Penny said. "If you were coming all this way to see me, you were staying here."

Holt leaned in. "So, about these childhood stories . . ."

Penny stood. "Uh, first, I need to have a short chat with Holt. We're just going to step out into the sunroom while you continue with . . . this." She waved a hand, then tilted her head at him. "Please?"

Curious, he stood. "Sure." He looked at the others. "No more Penny stories until I get back."

They laughed and he followed Penny through the French doors

and into her sunroom. She closed the doors behind them and shut the blinds. He smiled. "What are you doing?"

"I need a moment to breathe. We've been talking nonstop for three hours and I just . . . need a moment." Then she hugged him and settled her head just under his chin like it belonged there.

A sigh of contentment slipped from her and he silently echoed it. "Glad to see you and your mom are getting along."

"She's not a bad mother. She loves me. She's just . . . Geneva. And I have to learn to accept and love her as she is. I think I can do that."

He kissed the top of her head. "I think you can too."

"Not to be a downer, but how was your friend's funeral?"

"Sad. But he was honored for the hero he was, and that helped. I know I'll see him again one day—I'm just grieved at the way his life here on earth ended."

She lifted her head and looked him in the eye. "I'm sorry, Holt."

He kissed the tip of her nose. "Thank you."

"And Gus?"

"He'll probably go home from the hospital sometime next week. What else do you want to know?"

"How's Zoe? You haven't said much in our conversations."

"I know." He sighed. "She's managing. Yvette and her son were picked up in Georgia. He worked for a television station and was the one who edited the video Yvette sent to Zoe."

"What did they hope to gain from that? What was the purpose?"

"She finally confessed and that's partly what's been keeping me so busy. I've been in communication with Matt Nixon, the detective who had Zoe's case, and Zoe's lawyer, and so on. Between Yvette and Zoe and my nieces . . . anyway, the story is that with Zoe's job at the bakery, she worked some long hours, which left Owen with the girls quite a bit. But he was nothing but happy for Zoe's success and loved those girls so much. He didn't mind taking care of them."

LYNETTE EASON

"What about when he and Zoe were both working? I know a detective works some seriously long hours too."

"Yeah. That's where Yvette came in. She was part housekeeper, part nanny. Apparently, she was in love with Owen and started scheming to break him and Zoe up. She started planting things in the house for Zoe to find. A tube of lipstick that didn't belong to her. One of Owen's shirts with a different perfume, strands of brown hair on Zoe's pillow. You get the idea. She was also stealing from them. Little things. One place setting of the sterling silver. Some of Zoe's jewelry. The money from the kids' piggy banks. Stuff that would go unnoticed for a while. But Zoe figured it out and was going to fire Yvette. That was for the stealing, but she didn't know Yvette was the one planting the 'evidence' that Owen was cheating. The night they fought, Zoe had found a pair of women's underwear in one of Owen's uniform pants pockets. She always went through his pockets before taking his stuff to the cleaners and . . . there they were."

"And Yvette would know that."

"Exactly."

"That night, Yvette knew the kids would be next door. She waited in Krissy's closet for a long time, planning to pretend to be an intruder, kill Zoe, and run." He pressed fingers to his eyes and shivered. "But when she heard them fighting, she snuck downstairs to record it all. She had her own gun but saw Owen's on the coffee table, picked it up, and aimed it at Zoe, but just as she pulled the trigger, Owen gripped Zoe's upper arms and moved in close—he never shoved her, by the way. That was edited to look like it—and the bullet hit him."

"So, in the ensuing chaos, Yvette simply slipped out of the house with her video and, with the help of her son, hatched the scheme to send your sister to prison."

"Yes." He closed his eyes. "I don't know that I'll ever get over the shame of believing her guilty," he whispered.

Penny hugged him again. "You will. You're an agent, Holt. You

309

deal with criminals every day, and you had every reason to believe she was guilty. Like you keep telling me about Joel Allen's death, you can't blame yourself."

"Yeah. I know. Mentally."

They fell silent for a moment and she relished just being in his arms. Then she looked up. "I love you, Holt. Thank you for choosing me."

"We chose each other." He tightened his hold on her. "I love you too, Penny. I think I loved you the moment I opened my eyes in the chopper and saw you flying it."

"Really?" She laughed. "That was almost two years ago. I'll be honest. I was starting to wonder if you'd ever ask me out on an official date."

He laughed. "I was starting to wonder that too. I hate that it took a serial killer to bring us together, but I'm happy with the ending God orchestrated. Thank you for being patient and waiting for me to come to my senses."

He kissed her again, this time a lingering, sweet kiss that required a lot of restraint on his part but gave her a hint of the passion he was capable of. When he lifted his head, he was gratified to see her eyes a shade darker than they'd been a moment ago.

Then she smiled. "You were totally worth the wait."

Dear Beloved Readers,

Thank you so much for joining Holt and Penny on their tumultuous adventure to find a serial killer—and their love for each other. I hope you fell in love with the characters in this new series, and I do hope you'll be looking for the next installment of Extreme Measures. But until then, here's a treat for you. I want to encourage you to check out one of my favorite authors on the planet—not just because she is a fabulous person and a great friend, but because she is an amazing storyteller!

If you haven't "met" Lynn H. Blackburn, you're definitely missing out, because once again, she's crafted a brilliant story in Malicious Intent. Malicious Intent *is book 2 of her new series—a series that shows the Secret Service for the true heroes they are. Danger, suspense, and romance are jam-packed into this latest story. What more can a reader ask for?*

I always look forward to reading Lynn's stories, and you will too, because, trust me, once you start, you won't be able to stop. Enjoy the ride!

LOVE ROMANTIC SUSPENSE?

Turn the Page to Read the First Few Chapters
of Another Thrilling Story from R Revell

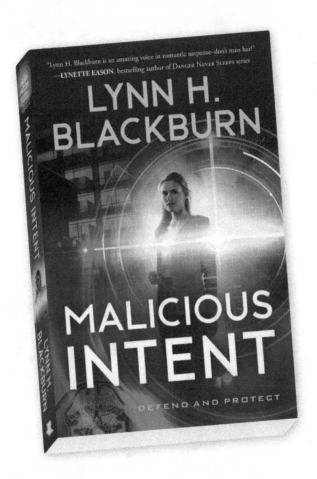

CHAPTER
ONE

The stack of cash on his desk was as close to genuine currency as squeeze cheese was to Brie.

US Secret Service Special Agent Gil Dixon turned one of the fraudulent twenties over and studied the back. There were a few similarities to the real thing, but not enough to confuse anyone paying attention.

"Free money?" Special Agent Zane Thacker asked as he passed Gil's cubicle for his own.

"Hardly enough to fool with." Gil glanced back at the file. Two hundred dollars in twenties. Even if the person who deposited it had been trying to do something illegal, no prosecutor would touch the case. It simply wasn't worth it.

"Where did it come from?" Zane asked the question, but his tone indicated he was making conversation to pass the time, not because he cared about the answer.

"Hedera, Inc."

Zane's head appeared over the top of the cubicle wall they shared. "You're kidding."

"Nope.

"Why would she have counterfeit bills?"

"No idea."

"When are you going to see her?"

"This afternoon. I thought I'd swing by her office first since the cash came from a business deposit."

"What's a company like Hedera doing depositing cash anyway?" Zane's question was the same one Gil had been pondering since the case hit his desk.

"Beats me." Hedera's accounts should have been almost entirely digital. The deposit had been for a little over two thousand dollars in cash, only two hundred of which were fake bills. "That's the reason I want to talk to Dr. Collins."

One reason, but not the only reason.

Everyone in the office knew that Hedera, Inc., was owned by Dr. Ivy Collins. But no one knew that Ivy Collins was *his* Ivy.

No. Not his anymore. And she hadn't been in a long time.

The Ivy from his memory had grown into a delicately boned woman with intense eyes that sparkled from the home page of Hedera, Inc., the company she'd founded four years earlier.

She'd been his best friend. They'd had their whole life planned. School, college, marriage. It was all so simple. Next to Emily, Gil's twin sister, Ivy was his favorite person in the world, so it only made sense that he would spend the rest of his life with her.

It never occurred to either of them that anything could tear them apart . . . until the day she said goodbye and climbed into her mom's sedan. He scampered up a tree and watched until the car disappeared from view, his nine-year-old heart broken.

When he saw her again, she was sixteen. He was seventeen. And that summer, she stole his heart.

And then . . . she was gone.

He'd thought before about confronting her, but he'd never followed through. What would he say if he ran into her? "Why did you cut me out of your life?" or "What is wrong with you?" or "I missed you." He had no idea what might fly out of his mouth. Their reunion was fifteen years overdue, but this certainly wasn't how he'd expected it to happen. Would she be surprised? Did she even know he was in town? Did she ever think of him?

Not that it mattered. Or it shouldn't matter.

Who was he kidding?

Ivy Collins was the girl who got away. The woman who had haunted him for years. The mystery he needed to solve.

It was time. He was going to get answers. Today.

■　■　■

Six hours later, Gil and Zane pulled into an empty Hedera parking lot. Zane waved a hand to indicate the empty spaces. "It's only four thirty. Why isn't anyone here?"

Gil parked in a visitor space and dialed the Hedera number. A recorded feminine voice with the barest hint of a Southern drawl told him Hedera's business hours were 7:00 a.m. to 4:00 p.m. and encouraged him to leave a message, assuring him he would be contacted during normal business hours.

"These people work seven to four? I wonder if they're hiring." Zane glanced at his watch. "What now?"

Gil wasn't ready to let this go. Not yet. "Do you have time to swing by her house?"

"What else do I have to do?" Zane laughed, but there was a bite to his words. Zane was usually a fun guy, but he'd grown somber and withdrawn over the last few months. Most people assumed it was because of the trauma they'd all been through in the spring. Zane had been shot, then he'd lost his car, his home, and almost everything he owned. And if that hadn't been bad enough, his transition to the protective detail had been delayed indefinitely. All solid reasons for a guy to be in a funk.

But Luke Powell, another fellow agent, was convinced it had more to do with Zane's tense relationship with the only female agent in the office, Tessa Reed, and Gil was increasingly sure he was right.

This wasn't the time to pry, but the time was coming. For now, he let it go. "She lives about five minutes from here. Let's see if she's home."

Gil slowed as he approached Ivy's house but didn't stop. The house was in an older part of Raleigh, where the lots were large and the subdivision delineations weren't clear. Two stories. Probably with a basement. Sitting on a wooded acre of land.

He drove past five more houses, turned around in a driveway, and came back. He pulled into Ivy's driveway and parked near the walkway to the front porch. Gil and Zane exited the car and walked to the front door.

Should he warn Zane about his history with Ivy? As far as Zane was concerned, there was no reason to think this would be anything other than a friendly chat.

If the roles were reversed, he would want to know. He paused on the step. "Zane—"

Zane reached around him and hit the doorbell. "What?"

He couldn't very well start this conversation now. "It'll keep." He hoped.

They waited, but there was no sound of footsteps. Gil stepped to the door and knocked. The door swung open as soon as his knuckles made contact.

Not normal.

Was it possible that Ivy had left her front door open? Sure. Was he going to assume that was the case? Absolutely not. Gil pulled his weapon from his hip.

Zane was already dialing for backup. Good. Better safe than sorry. He put his phone back in his pocket and gave Gil a quick nod.

Gil pushed the door all the way open. It swung silently. He concentrated all his senses on this new environment. The foyer was small, with a hexagon-shaped library/office to his left. To his right sat a formal dining room. Both were empty. Straight ahead was a living area with sofas, a large TV, and comfortable chairs. The room was tidy, and there were no apparent signs of a struggle.

But two distinct and wildly contrasting odors battered his senses. Cinnamon and charred flesh.

Zane lifted his chin in a quick up and to the left. Gil followed, and they cleared two bedrooms and a small bathroom. Then Gil took the lead, and they prowled through the living area. A door to the left was probably another bedroom. If the house plan made any sense at all, then the archway to the right would lead to the kitchen area, but he couldn't get a good sense of the space from where he stood. A door opened from somewhere at the back of the house and feet pounded down steps. But someone was moving in the space on the other side of that wall.

Was a drawer being opened?

After another quick glance at Zane, Gil swung into the next room. A breakfast nook was on his left with a door that he assumed led to the outside, and on his right was the kitchen.

Across the large island stood Ivy Collins.

His Ivy.

It was as if no time had passed. No years of silence. Something strong and true pulled him to her. His body tried to close the gap between them, but his mind resisted. Years of training forced Gil to scan the room.

"Hold here." Zane's voice vibrated with rage as his footsteps retreated. "I'll clear the bedroom."

Blood ran down her right temple and trickled from puffy lips. Her sweater was ripped and hung off one shoulder, revealing a nasty burn. Something was very wrong with her right hand, but Gil couldn't focus on that, because in her left hand, she held a gun.

Before he could tell her that he was there to help, she pulled the trigger.

CHAPTER
TWO

The man's body jerked backward. He crashed into the wall and slid down, landing hard.

His right hand reached toward his left shoulder, a reflexive action as he tried to stop the blood gushing from the gunshot wound. Self-preservation appeared to overrule all other instincts, including the one he should have called up—the instinct to flee.

Because if he thought he was in danger from her and her weapon, he clearly didn't have a clue how lethal the man who now stood in front of him was.

Ivy wasn't sure how she knew, but she knew. Gil could kill him. He might even want to. For that matter, she might want him to. She shouldn't, but in that moment, she couldn't dredge up any sympathy for the injured man.

Father, forgive me.

Gil kept his gaze focused on the bleeding man on the floor, but he didn't rush to offer aid *or* arrest him.

"Zane?" Gil spoke in a conversational tone, like he was going to ask if he could grab him a drink or something. "We're clear in here."

A man eased out of her den and into the kitchen area. "You okay?" The man Gil had called Zane did a top-to-toe scan of Gil, then repeated the process on her. His mouth tight, his eyes burning with fury as his gaze paused at her arm, her hand. "Get her. I'll get him."

Gil didn't turn his back on the man on the floor. He backed away. Every step brought him closer to her but kept him where he could rush to Zane's aid if it became necessary. Zane patted the man down, removed two guns—one from a shoulder holster, one from his ankle—then dashed to her hall bathroom. He returned seconds later with two bath towels. He tossed one to Gil. The other he tossed to the man on the floor.

Zane knelt before the bleeding man and applied pressure to the wound. When the man tried to jerk away, Zane's voice rumbled with disgust. "I'm trying to help you. I don't care one way or the other, but it's more paperwork for me if you die."

Ivy heard all this, but it couldn't hold her attention. She was keenly aware of Gil, moving in slow motion in her direction. Once Zane had the man fully under control, Gil didn't hesitate to come to her.

"Gil." His name came out rough. She tried to clear her throat, but her mouth was completely dry. What else could she say? Nothing would make this less awkward.

"Buttercup."

At the long-unheard nickname, spoken with unfathomable tenderness, Ivy forgot she hadn't spoken to Gil Dixon in fifteen years. Her feet moved. She tried to reach for him, but her arms refused to cooperate. She slammed into him, chest to chest, and his arms caught her. "Gil."

"I've got you, Buttercup."

He was so strong. Solid. And for the first time since her ordeal had begun an hour earlier, she felt safe.

■   ■   ■   ■

Five interminable hours later, Ivy stared at the clothing the nurse held out to her. "Where did that come from?"

Her nurse, Juliet, ignored the question. "You're cleared to leave. Would you like some help with the shirt?"

Ivy followed the nurse's gaze. Her right hand throbbed with every beat of her heart. Her ring finger and pinky were broken. The doctor said they should heal fine, with no loss of mobility.

Her right thumb sported two burns, courtesy of a cigarette. One on the tip, one at the base. The thumb contained numerous nerve endings. She knew that better than most. But she'd never experienced each and every one of them screaming in distress at the same time.

Neither the cut on her temple or her lip had required stitches, but that didn't mean her entire face didn't hurt. Her head throbbed. And then there was the nasty burn on her right shoulder. It had come not from a cigarette but from a very hot object that bore a disturbing resemblance to a curling iron but had never been used for anything so gentle. *Will I ever be able to curl my hair again?*

If they'd wanted to hurt her, those morons who tortured her would have threatened to shave her head. Facing that possibility, she might have at least considered giving them what they wanted. It was a small mercy, still having her hair. But in this moment, she would take it.

They weren't big on mirrors in this emergency department. Probably so people wouldn't freak out when they got a good look at themselves after a trauma. But she could imagine the state she was in. When they fried her shoulder, a few strands of her hair were singed. She couldn't see the damage, but the stench of burnt hair was unmistakable and inescapable. She caught a whiff every time she moved.

And there was no way she didn't have mascara and eyeliner tracks on her cheeks. She had tried hard not to cry. But when the big guy ripped her shirt, leaving her exposed and trembling, already aching from the broken fingers and burned thumb and two times he'd backhanded her, she expected the worst.

There'd been no time to mentally prepare herself to be toasted like a marshmallow. *Great. No more s'mores for me.*

Juliet tilted her head to one side. "Ma'am. Do you want some help getting dressed?"

"No. I can get it. But where did my clothes come from?" They were definitely her clothes. Black yoga pants and a butter-soft T-shirt. Socks. Tennis shoes. A light sweater. And . . . other things. Someone had brought these clothes to the hospital for her. Was it Gil? As much as she wanted to know where Gil was and why he had walked back into her life, today of all days, she couldn't stop the blush at the thought of Gil Dixon going through her underwear drawer.

Not because of the clothes—although that was cringeworthy—but because of the picture, framed and set in a place where she could see it every day. If he'd been in her room, there was no way he could've missed it.

"I don't know, hon. The unit secretary brought them to me." Juliet turned to the door. "I'll check on you in a few minutes, and we'll get you out of here."

Ivy waited for the door to close before she took the clothes into the tiny bathroom. She wouldn't risk changing in the main room, where any minute someone could walk in on her. She'd shown more than enough skin tonight.

She pulled the tie, curly from an untold number of washings, at the neck of the hospital gown, slipped off the gown, and reached for her clothing. She could figure out how to get her clothes on without the use of two fingers and a thumb. She was an engineer, for crying out loud. Thank goodness those idiots hadn't had the sense to look at her hands, pay attention to the calluses, and discern that she was a leftie.

Ten minutes later, she leaned against the doorframe, proud and exhausted. She'd done it. Now she faced a new dilemma. She'd arrived in an ambulance. An ambulance Gil insisted she ride in after she almost passed out in the kitchen moments after he arrived. The paramedics said it was due to a combination of shock and excruciating pain from the burns, but it was still embarrassing. After she swooned—unfortunately, there was no other word for it—Gil refused to let anyone ask more than the most basic questions.

"What did they want?" Access to her computer at work.

"Why?" No clue.

"Have you ever seen them before?" Never.

"How did they get into your house?" She didn't know. She'd been in the kitchen, removing her leftover pad Thai from last night's dinner with her ex-boyfriend (a fact she left out of her narrative) from the microwave. She turned, and they were there.

"You didn't hear them?" No. They could have rolled through her house in a tank, and she wouldn't have heard them. She had her AirPods in her ears. She skirted over the fact that she'd been singing and saw no reason to mention that she'd also been dancing or that she'd spun around and landed in the arms of the man who later tried to barbecue her shoulder.

At that point, Gil intervened. "Enough. She needs medical attention." He glared at the police officer questioning her. The police officer glared back.

Gil didn't flinch. His look was cold. Hard. Furious. "Dr. Collins is a prominent member of the community. Her home is here. Her business is here. She isn't going anywhere. She'll be available to answer questions later."

He wasn't wrong. But how did he know all this about her? And why was he here in the first place? Armed? With a partner? She had so many questions.

"Right now, she's going to the hospital." Gil spoke with a finality that brooked no argument.

The police officer backed down, but a few minutes later as the EMTs were strapping her onto the gurney, she overheard him on the phone. "No idea. Never been in a showdown with a Secret

Service agent before." A pause. "True." Another pause. "Yeah. She's gorgeous, but—" A longer pause. "Yeah. I'll find out."

Gil walked into the room, and the police officer walked away. Gil stared after him for a moment before turning to her. "Ivy." When he said her name, she could almost see the boy she'd known. Although that boy had grown into a man with jet-black hair, which was currently disheveled because he kept running his hand through it. He leaned close, and his sky-blue eyes captured hers. She couldn't look away. "I wish I could go with you, but I have to stay here. We'll have security for you at the hospital. I'll find you as soon as I can." He reached a hand toward her cheek and tucked her hair behind her ear, a move he'd perfected during their last summer together. Then the paramedics had whisked her away.

She probably should have called someone. But who?

She had employees. Coworkers. Business associates. She could pick up the phone and have a lunch date or coffee chat with any number of prominent Raleigh business leaders.

But she didn't have friends. She had colleagues.

And as of today, she had Gil. But she had no idea what he was.

If anyone had asked her this morning what would happen if she ever ran into Gil Dixon again, she would have offered up several scenarios. One possibility involved them making eye contact, after which she would turn and run away. Very mature, that one. Also, the most likely.

She'd also considered the possibility that she might burst into tears and immediately start babbling and asking for forgiveness. Or she might stand before him, mute and miserable, as he unloaded fifteen years of righteous anger. If he wanted to do that, she would have to let him. She deserved it all.

No matter how many times she'd considered the possible options, not once had she dared to hope that he would look at her the way he had tonight.

And never, not ever, had she expected him to call her Buttercup.

ACKNOWLEDGMENTS

Thank you to all who so freely spend your time helping get the job descriptions right in this story.

Dru, I can't thank you enough. I have no idea how many hours you spent making sure all my FBI "stuff" was correct, but it was more than I can ever repay.

Wayne Smith, the same goes for you! Thank you so much for fixing my mistakes and offering feedback to make the story "real."

I'm so blessed that God has put you two in my life and I thank him daily for you!

A huge thank-you to my cousin-in-law, Michael Wiggs, who is a flight nurse extraordinaire! THANK you for all the information you provided. I couldn't have written this without you.

I also need to say a special thanks to Scott Rhoades who describes himself as: Aerospace Nurse, Researcher, Explorer, Teacher, Author, Life Traveler, Christ-Follower, World Changer. I call him friend now. I can't thank you enough for your generous giving of your time and information. You've given me so much great material, I think I have enough for a whole new character! Thank you and may God richly bless you!

Thank you to my brainstorming buddies! Colleen Coble, Carrie Stuart Parks, Robin Carroll, Voni Harris, Pam Hillman, Dru

Wells, Lynn H. Blackburn, Edie Melson, Emme Gannon, Alycia Morales, Erynn Newman, Linda Gilden, Molly Jo Realy, Tammy Karasak, and Michelle Cox. Y'all are amazing and I love each and every one of you.

A shout-out to the Revell team who make the book shine! I can't say thank you enough to Andrea Doering, Barb Barnes, Karen Steele, Michele Misiak, and Laura Klynstra (and team) and EVERYONE! I love you all!

Thank you to Tamela Hancock Murray of the Steve Laube Agency. Thank you for your tireless dedication to helping me make the best decisions in my career and for always being on my side. Thank you, my friend, I love you bunches.

Lynette Eason is the bestselling author of the Danger Never Sleeps, Blue Justice, Women of Justice, Deadly Reunions, Hidden Identity, and Elite Guardians series. She is the winner of three ACFW Carol Awards, the Selah Award, and the Inspirational Reader's Choice Award, among others. She is a graduate of the University of South Carolina and has a master's degree in education from Converse College. Eason lives in South Carolina with her husband and two children. Learn more at www.lynetteeason.com.

WE WANT TO HEAR FROM YOU ON THIS EXCERPT
from Lynn H. Blackburn!

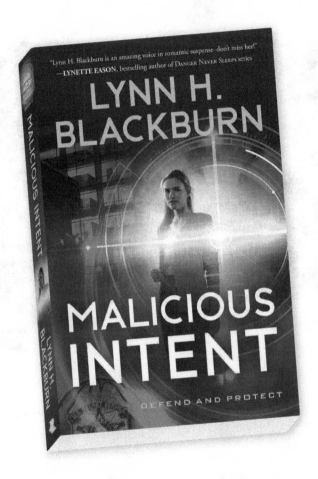

Visit **bit.ly/3hc9vdZ** to fill out a quick survey and be entered
to win free books and fun book swag!

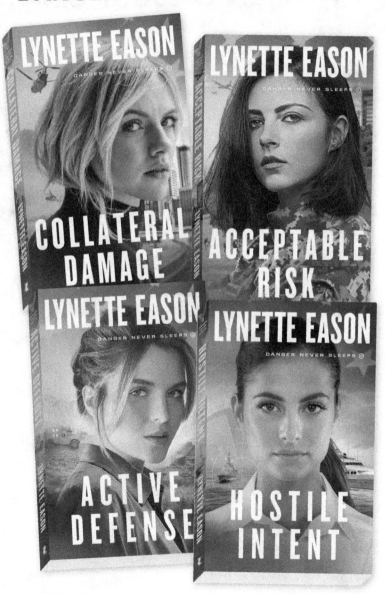

Also from Lynette Eason:
The **WOMEN OF JUSTICE** Series

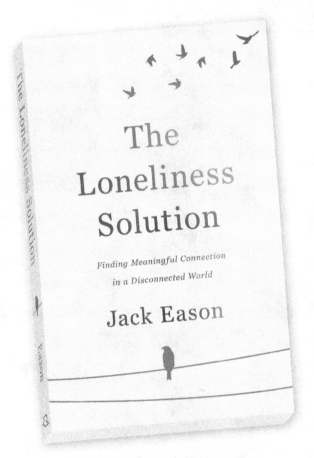

CPSIA information can be obtained
at www.ICGtesting.com
Printed in the USA
LVHW110122260522
719734LV00002B/128

9 780800 741068